Praise for *Unnatural Magic*

"The most unique, haunting, magical, treacherous, romantic, combative novel I've read in a long time. Action, betrayal, peoples at war, strange magic, and stranger love—a whole new take on fantasy!"

—#1 *New York Times* bestselling author Tamora Pierce

"Peopled with unforgettable characters whose changing relationships form the beating heart of this fast-paced, beautifully written story."

—Juliet Marillier, author of *The Harp of Kings*

"What a marvelous debut! I want to climb inside C. M. Waggoner's world of powerful trolls, cheeky wizards, and mathematical magic and make myself at home." —*New York Times* bestselling author Chloe Neill

"I didn't think you could fit so many things I loved into one book—tough-talking lady-trolls and cowardly captains, true love and found families, Holmesian hijinks and gender politics. . . . *Unnatural Magic* is a raucous, indulgent delight."

—Alix E. Harrow, Hugo Award–winning author of
The Ten Thousand Doors of January

"Complex and fascinating, Waggoner's debut offers fantasy readers a new viewpoint on magic, love, responsibility, and sacrifice."

—Vivian Shaw, author of the Dr. Greta Helsing series

"C. M. Waggoner's *Unnatural Magic* is a brilliant and terrifically fun book. There's adventure and magic and murder—oh, and did I mention how much fun you'll have reading this?"

—Kat Howard, Alex Award–winning author of
An Unkindness of Magicians

"I have never read another novel that gave me so much of what I wanted so soon, and then just kept delivering the goods, page after page after page. Love, lust, magic, murder. . . . This book has it all!"
—Lara Elena Donnelly, author of the Amberlough Dossier series

"Waggoner's delightfully playful debut offers a fresh take on traditional fantasy tropes to explore themes of love and sacrifice . . . the whimsy, mystery, and vibrant characters are sure to enchant readers."
—*Publishers Weekly*

TITLES BY C. M. WAGGONER

Unnatural Magic
The Ruthless Lady's Guide to Wizardry

THE
RUTHLESS LADY'S
GUIDE TO
WIZARDRY

C. M. WAGGONER

ACE
NEW YORK

ACE
Published by Berkley
An imprint of Penguin Random House LLC
penguinrandomhouse.com

Library of Congress Cataloging-in-Publication Data

Names: Waggoner, C. M., author.
Title: The ruthless lady's guide to wizardry / C. M. Waggoner.
Description: First edition. | New York: Ace, 2021.
Identifiers: LCCN 2020025679 (print) | LCCN 2020025680 (ebook) |
ISBN 9781984805867 (trade paperback) | ISBN 9781984805874 (ebook)
Subjects: GSAFD: Fantasy fiction. | Love stories.
Classification: LCC PS3623.A3533 R88 2021 (print) |
LCC PS3623.A3533 (ebook) | DDC 813/.6—dc23
LC record available at https://lccn.loc.gov/2020025679
LC ebook record available at https://lccn.loc.gov/2020025680

First Edition: January 2021

Printed in the United States of America
1   3   5   7   9   10   8   6   4   2

Cover art and design by Jess Cruickshank
Book design by Alison Cnockaert
Interior art: Vintage frame by Ozz Design/Shutterstock

For my mom,
the very best on earth.

1

Wherein Dellaria Hunts About for a Wayward
Relation, Is Not the Recipient of Maternal Warmth,
and Is Presented with an Opportunity for
Gainful Employment

Dellaria Wells had misplaced her mother.

That maybe wasn't so accurate, to be very fair to herself, which Delly preferred to be. To be very fair to Dellaria, she didn't have to do too much to misplace her mam. Her mam had a way of misplacing herself, like a cat who'd dart for freedom if you left the kitchen door open. But it'd been two weeks now, and even as gristly an old cat as Delly's mam ought to have gotten hungry and come home after a fortnight of roaming. Something had gone wrong, then, and as dreadful as her mam might be, it made Delly's stomach take disagreeable turns to think that she might be sleeping in a garbage pile somewhere. Delly, curse her eyes, was going to have to do something about it.

If you asked her mam, she'd probably say that her not having a place to stay was all her daughter's fault. That was the way it was when you paid someone's way: it went straight from you doing them a favor to them thinking you doling out cash was all part of nature's plan, like a bee making honey. But Dellaria hadn't yet discovered how to make a moneycomb, and at the moment she was so damn broke that she couldn't cover her own rent, let alone the rent of her dreadful brigand of a mother. She'd lost the steady work she'd had as a barmaid two weeks ago, when a regular got a little too insistent about trying to kiss her and she'd used her fire witchery to set his beard on fire. Now she was down a job and forced to live off of her wits alone. Her wits, as it turned out, made for very unsatisfying dining.

She was so presently impoverished, in fact, that she'd been avoiding her landlady for a week by only entering and exiting her room via the back alley. On this particular occasion, though, Mrs. Medlow was lying in wait for her by the kitchen door. "*Dellaria*," she said. "You know the rent's been due for a regular *span* now, dearie."

"Oh, might it so, ma'am, might it so," Delly said, thinking at her fingertips a bit. "I was just going to say when I saw you next, ma'am—and me having found it very right peculiar how I haven't seen you in some time, ma'am, right peculiar indeed—that I present you with ten sen of interest per day I've been late, ma'am, if that might be ensatisficating to your fine self?"

At that her landlady got a considering gleam in her eye, which she attempted to cover over with a delicate and motherly twitter. "That'll do very nicely, dearie," she said, "if you'll let me put another very wee hard promise on you."

Delly drew herself up a bit at that. Her landlady wasn't all that much of an expert wizard—just a gutterwitch, like Delly herself—but she could cast a hard promise with the best of them. Since the Lord-Mage of Hexos had invented the parameters for the damn things ten years ago, half of the ill-intended gutterwitches and debt collectors in Leiscourt had learned to cast a hard promise—there was nothing like them for extracting money out of the recalcitrant—but Mrs. Medlow's could have been used as examples in a course on the subject. Get your rent to her an hour late and you'd break out in throbbing pustules at best. "That ain't needful, Mrs. Medlow," she said. "I've always been as good as my word with the rent, you know that."

"You've always been as good as your word because I've put hard promises on you when you looked likely to run off to Monsatelle, dearie," Mrs. Medlow said, to which Delly was forced to concede a trifle. Let your landlady curse you once with an itchy rash on your haunches and you're unlikely to cross her a second time.

Delly narrowed her eyes at her. "Maybe I ought to take my custom elsewhere, then," she said. "To some kind personage less likely to set vile curses upon their paying guests."

"You might," said Mrs. Medlow, with wonderful placidity. "And pay eleven tocats a month for the privilege. That's the going rate these days, dearie, and here I am charging you six out of kindness, even in such hard times."

Delly sighed. Mrs. Medlow, though a dreadful old cat, had an air of plain honesty about her personage. Delly wasn't new enough to the copper-rubbing life to not know that any new room you moved into would inevitably be more expensive than whatever room you'd just been kicked out of for not being able to pay the rent. Enough of her memories had also survived her attempts to drown them in gin for her to understand that if by some thankful gift of the gods she managed to scrape together a bit of extra money this month, she wouldn't necessarily make the same the next. If she wanted to save herself from her own damn turnip-brained self, she knew very well what she should do: swallow her clever talk, keep the room, find some way to make some money, and pay as much rent as she could up front before she could waste her last sen on liquor and cards because she didn't have the self-control of a dog with a lamb chop. Which was what inspired her to open wide her gin-hole and say, "The hard promise, then. I get you your money in three weeks at latest, with interest compounding the whole while, or you hit me with what you like."

Mrs. Medlow twittered like a lark. "I would find that *very* agreeable, *dear* Miss Wells," she said, and grasped Delly's hand to force a hot bolt of magic through it.

Delly winced and shook her hand out. "What's my curse to be, then?"

"Pustules," Mrs. Medlow said, very cheerful-like. "The seeping kind. On the face, mostly."

Delly decided not to inquire as to where the type that *weren't* on the face would be. Instead she just gave Mrs. Medlow a resigned nod and headed out the door to search for her damn mother.

She knew better than to think that Mam might have managed to pay for another week's rent on her own. Still, she hoofed it down to Crane Street to check on the old bird's last known address—she wasn't there, no surprise—and then took a moment to buy a cup of coffee and a withered sandwich from a dingy coffee shop, sit on a bench in a park that was more a sanitarium for wan crabgrasses, and have a bit of a restful luncheon.

Thus refreshed (or close enough to it), she rose back up onto her trotters and started to look for her mam again. The real key with her mam, she thought, was to think of places where you could sleep for free without getting your head wet or having to listen to any sermons. Delly herself would much rather nod piously along to the sermon, soup, and predawn alarm if it kept her out from under bridges, but her mam had a way of advancing on people with her hand out, spouting off exactly the kind of thing that'd make even the most even-tempered hall officiant's ears go red, and then striking very radical and anti-establishmentary attitudes after they kicked her out of the meeting hall, by way of indicating that she hadn't wanted any of their damn soup in the first place.

Not that Delly really had any room to criticize the way her mam chose to live, when she herself had to get herself cursed with seeping mostly-on-the-face pustules before she could be trusted to pay her damn rent.

In any case, her mam did sometimes choose to appear more than once in the same location, which made her not completely impossible to track down. Delly went to a few choice bars on Six-Bend Island first. It took a bit of self-restraint to keep from bellying up and buying herself a drink. Her Elgarite refutation of fleshly wants was rewarded at the third bar, where the girl wiping the glasses said that ol' Marvie had been in a few times that week. Delly's dear old mam had been in the company of a fellow named Squint Jok, who had his bolt-for a few blocks away on Maiden Street. Delly could only think that it could be worse: Squint Jok could just as easily be Drunk Jok, or Fleabite Jok, or Worryingly Murderous in His Aspect Jok, any one of which wouldn't be the type of Jok you'd like to see in close association with your dear old mother.

She went to the house in question and gave it a good squint of her own. The door and windows at the front were all boarded over, which was a good sign in terms of the chance that her mam might be holed up inside. There was a side alley: she went down it and found a fence around what she supposed to be the back garden. At the bottom of the fence there was a hole large enough to admit a medium-sized dog. Delly gave a low groan, got down into the dirt, and endeavored to force her larger-than-medium-dog-sized carcass through the gap. She made it into the yard thoroughly besmeared with dirt and grass stains, with her dress ripped and her arms scratched and her good cheer considerably rumpled.

The house wasn't any more beguiling from the rear. Though she wouldn't hold that against it: the same could be said for Delly. Almost all of the windows back here were boarded over, too, except one that had had its boards pried off and the glass smashed out. There was also a trampled-down path in the weeds straight to the door. Delly followed it and tried the door handle. It worked, in that the handle didn't turn but the door swung open after she gave it a good shove.

Then she was in what had probably been a kitchen once. Delly tried not to look around herself too closely. Her mam had never been much for the domestic arts, but as the years had gone by she seemed to have made strides past simply ignoring the filth and toward actively cultivating it. If Delly's mam had been born with any gift of magic she would have made a fine necromancer of crumb-eating insects and pernicious creeping molds.

After the kitchen there was a hall, and then what she supposed must be a sitting room, as it had a number of people sitting in it. One of them gathered himself up and said, "Hey," by way of expressing either surprise or annoyance at discovering an intruder in their midst. Then, exhausted by his efforts, he slumped back against the wall again.

"Mam?" Delly said, giving the murky air about her a good slicing squint. "You in here? It's me, your daughter. Dellaria Wells," she added, thinking that her mam might need a bit of brain dusting when it came to clarifying the name and identity of the young fruit o' the maternal bough.

"Delly?" came a voice from the corner. Her mam rose up in a tide of shawls—she was always a devoted wearer of shawls, Delly's mother—and then came toddling toward her on the uncertain hooves of the recently indisposed. "That's you, then?"

"Might it so," Delly said. "Won't you come out into the air, Mam?"

Her mother followed her out into the backyard, where they gazed at each other for a moment through a thick fog of familial irritation. "Whaddya want, then, Dellaria?"

Mam's eyes looked strange. Like scuffed buttons. Delly's own eyes went grape-shaped. "You ain't just had a gargle then, Mam." She didn't *look* just drunk.

Her mam scowled. "What's it to you, Dellaria?"

"Well, I passed through you on my journey into this reliving, for what it's fucking well worth, Mam," Dellaria said. "What're you taking? I thought you hated drip." Drip was what most people were taking hereabouts to make themselves go button-eyed. Dellaria herself steered clear. Drip was like love, she figured: all good enough fun, but you'd better not let yourself get too used to it or it'd take you apart as sure as knives.

Dellaria's mam went all dreamy, like her new fella had a job with a steady wage. "But before I hadn't dripped the red, so."

Delly made a sound that expressed her feelings a mite. A squawk of sorts. Then she said, "The red's the killing kind, Mam."

"Might be you could call it that," Delly's mam said.

"It ain't about what I call it," Delly said. "It's what it is, so."

Delly's mam looked back at her with her button eyes. "You want something from me, Dellaria?"

It was a fool's game to want anything from Marvie Wells, but it was a game Delly had been playing since the day she was born. "Nah, Mam," she said, slipping further into the West Leiscourt alleychat they'd both grown up swimming in. "Only to get mirrors on thee, see if th'art still chewing air, so. If I manage to find the clink to pay for it, will you take a bolt-for I rent for thee, Mam?" Delly thought she'd get her into a boardinghouse for women this time, if she could scrape together the cash. It probably wouldn't keep whatever miserable drip-dealing Jok Mam was going around with these days away from her, but it might be some kind of start, at least.

"Might it so," Mam said, with a sly smile that made Delly want to slap her lips off.

She didn't do that, though. She just said, "Will I be able to find thee here, then, Mam?"

"Might it so," Mam said again. "Until the cops catch us or the place burns down." Delly expected that was the best she would get, so she took her leave of the mean old trout and let her inward currents pull her back toward her room, and the gin that lay below it.

Delly lived in a bare little room in a boardinghouse above a bar called the Hangman's Rest. She'd always figured that the name was meant to be a nod to the culmination of the career paths of some of the regulars, so in that way it suited her fine. It was a good little room. The floor didn't slant too badly, the ceiling only leaked a little bit in the one corner during heavy rain, and it was right above the bar's back room. She liked that. It gave her a comforted feeling to sleep above so much gin. If the floors gave out, at least she'd have a softish landing.

After a few drinks downstairs, she laid out all her money and trinkets on the bed—she'd never bothered to buy a table—and her gut straightaway started to lurch. As treasure troves went, a beetle might turn up its nose at it. She licked her lips and tried to do the math. She owed Mrs. Medlow six tocats on rent for this month, plus the interest she'd promised her, and the bartender downstairs two more. She had two tocats six sen tied up in the toe of an old stocking she had hidden under a loose floorboard, and about another tocat in scrap metal she'd stripped out of an abandoned house a few days earlier, assuming she'd be able to sell it for half what it was worth. That left her four tocats four sen short with no real time to make up the difference before she'd have to sleep under a bridge with seeping pustules all over her ass. To say nothing of her mam, who'd be dead of either exposure or the red drip at any moment, at this rate.

She was, to put it delicately, fucked up a tall tree without a ladder.

Delly, at this juncture, went to her basin to wash her face and have a ponder. The pondering went nowhere, but the face washing refreshed her to the point that she was emboldened to embark upon her armpits. Once those were taken care of, she sat back down on the bed to gather her courage a bit more. She needed to scrounge up some money, and sharpish. That meant she was going to have to run a game.

She wasn't looking forward to it.

A game was a delicate thing. Not all that hard to start with, but it'd complicate itself all on its own, like a cat made kittens even when you could've sworn it hadn't gone out the window in months. For one thing, you needed to trust yourself to lose enough money to reel in the marks before you started to earn it. For another, you needed the right marks. You might get five of them in three hours and be in gin and whelks for a week, or you might waste time, entertain the criticisms of the passersby, and then be chased off by the constabulary. For either outcome you needed nerve, and today Delly felt that she lacked it.

It was a sad fact, though, that Delly was too poor to lack nerve. Lacking nerve was a problem for women who had servants to fan their foreheads after they swooned on the chaise. Delly wasn't disinclined toward swooning on principle, but she didn't have a chaise to swoon on, to say nothing of the fanning servants. What she did have was a landlady, and it was Delly's mental portrait of her glaring face that got her back onto her feet and out the door.

She set herself up a few blocks away from her place, on a corner where she liked to work because bankers' and lawyers' clerks walked past it. A lawyer would ignore a youngish, plainish, plumpish lass running a game, but a clerk might sympathize or see a chance to flirt and throw her a few sen to play.

There was someone on her corner already when she arrived. Bessa, looking cool and fresh with her black curls peeping out from under her white bonnet. That was all right by Delly. Bessa was an Objectionist heretic, and she also sold meat pies. The heresy was refreshing, which helped wash down the pie. The pie, unfortunately, was stodgy as all of the releft.

Delly bought a pie, just to be neighborly, set herself up on the ground, and then asked for some heresy. "What's hell like, Bessa?" She assumed that Bessa, being a good businesswoman, would be unlikely to draw any direct comparisons to her pies, but you never really knew until you asked.

"Bright white," Bessa said right away. "A bright white plain covered in ice and snow. It's too bright to open your eyes, and the wind burns at your face and steals your breath, and every few steps you slip and fall, and your head pounds from the glare."

"Sakes," Delly said, impressed. "Sounds awful."

"Which is why you ought to change your ways, Dellaria Wells," Bessa said.

Delly nodded slowly. "Ought to indeed. Might be that I'm too short for it, though."

Bessa pursed her lips. "How does your height signify?"

"I reckon that sin, being denser than air, tends to settle close to the ground," Delly said. "That's why as a rule you'll find your drunks lying in gutters and your great thickets of pious young ladies up in choir lofts."

Bessa sighed. "You'll be going straight up to the white lands, Dellaria," she said, and then favored a young man who wanted to buy a pie with a smile.

Delly eyed up the other young fella standing around waiting for his friend to pay, then slipped him a wink. "Try your luck with a game while your fella eats his pie?"

"He's not *my* fella," the fella said straight off. "He's householded to a clanner."

Delly rumpled up her face, sympathetic-like. "I had a girl who did that. A lady who wore pearls took a liking to her, and she was householded before the year was out."

"Hard times," the fella said.

"Hard times," Delly agreed, though she reckoned that her girl up and leaving her had had more to do with Delly's own bad behavior than it did with the nation's economy. Then she said, "Interest you in a game?"

"Might be," the fella said, and threw down five sen.

Delly ran her game. She let him get pretty far: far enough that a crowd started to gather. Far enough that she started to sweat. If he was a clever fella, he'd walk now and take her for a few tocats. He wasn't, though, and he didn't, so she ended up a tocat ahead, with her heart pounding and three new marks lining up behind him. It looked like the day might be in Delly's favor after all.

Delly ran a few more games—let one pretty girl walk away with two tocats, for the sake of winning a smile as much as for the sake of keeping the game running—then took a break to stretch her legs, eat some whelks, and read the bulletins posted on the public board a street over. Sometimes the bulletins had something useful in them: she'd found work from one once before, helping a crew of workmen to strip pipe out of an old building. It'd paid well enough, and she'd fucked a nice burly workman from the northlands out behind the site privy, so it had all around been a bulletin to lift the spirits and incline the soul toward thankful contemplation.

There was nothing of too much interest in the first few ads she looked at. Lots of comfortable sorts looking for sober and upstanding young women to scrub out their underthings. Seeing as how Delly was often drunk, was never upstanding, and was barely prepared to scrub out her own underthings on any kind of regular schedule, most of these postings weren't of much interest to her. Then, one in particular caught her eye.

WANTED

Female Persons, of Martial or Magical ability, to guard a Lady of some Importance, prior to the celebration of her Marriage, during her period of Matrimonial Seclusion. Inquiries may be made at 332 Barrow Street, Elmsedge, Leiscourt, at the rear entrance. NO MEN to be considered for any positions.

Delly ate another whelk. This was one to engage the organs of ponderation, all right. Elmsedge, that was Clanner Hill, and only real steel-stayed traditionalists still practiced matrimonial seclusions. A good family, then, the type who had the one girl just to scrub out the underthings and another to dust the mantels and a third to make the cream cakes while a sober gent sat down in the cellar and tabulated the expenditures. But what the hell would a girl like that need a whole herd of *bodyguards* for? You had to be important to have people who wanted to murder you. Or rather, you had to either be important or be related to someone who owed someone else a hell of a lot of money, and if you owed someone that much cash, you'd probably be better off setting up a payment plan than you'd be hiring a bunch of lady pugilists to guard you. This, then, was something interesting, and Delly was a longstanding enthusiast of being interested.

She memorized the address, then headed back to her corner. The crowds had thinned out some, but there were still enough folks milling about for her to get a new game going, so that's what she did.

She was down a few sen and preparing to take a particularly prune-faced old geezer for a tocat or two when a matched set of cops lifted their boots in her direction. "Dellaria Wells?"

Delly looked about herself like she was looking forward to seeing some other silly old creature getting taken away in chains. The officer nearest her leaned in and grabbed her by the wrist. "Dellaria Wells," he said, "I am arresting you in the name of the First Headman."

Delly said, "Well, shit." Then she used a bit of magic and set her own skirt on fire.

The resulting conflagration was large enough to startle, amaze, and generally annoy the arresting officers, but not large enough to facilitate any escaptionary maneuvers. There was some shouting and hopping about, and then some helpful citizen of the fair republic tossed a glass of beer over Dellaria's person, which served very well to extinguish both the flames and Delly's hopes of sleeping in her own bed tonight. She gave the cops a smile. "Horribly sorry, fellas, only that just always happens to me when my nerves are on edge. Nervous flaming is what it is."

"Right," said the taller of the two fellows, and gave her a bit more of a shake than Delly thought was really needful before marching her off at a lockupwardly slant.

2

Wherein Dellaria Talks Herself Out of a Situation
That Was Really Entirely Her Own Fault in the First
Instance, and Establishes a Prospect

This entire day had really gone balls up at a canter. Delly was impressed with herself. In all of her history of turnip-headedness, she didn't know that she had ever fucked up so badly as to have gotten herself arrested before an early supper. Fortunately, what she did have was a whole sea of experience in talking herself right back out of the same shit she'd gotten herself into in the first place, and so she set herself to that task with all the energy she could muster.

"You've brought in the wrong woman, gents," she said. "How could I ever have melted a chandelier in a bank when I was being interviewed for a domestic position up on Elmsedge at the time the crime was being committed?"

"How could anyone who wasn't a damn thieving fire witch have melted the damn chandelier in the first place, you silly tit?" asked the warden, whom Dellaria suspected of harboring paternalistic feelings toward her person. He had, after all, practically raised her, considering all the time she'd spent in here before her age of majority. "And what the hell sort of domestic position could you be interviewing for? They want a girl around to drink them dry and make the house dirtier than it was to start with?"

"Those are hurtful words, sir," Delly said. "Very wounding indeed. And here my poor self had been thinking that I was practically a daughter to your honorable self, sir."

"Oh, shove it up your ass, Dellaria," the warden said, fatherly-like. Then he said, "And what was the position, then? Go on, I want to hear it."

"It was a *bodyguarding* position, sir," Delly said. "At 332 Barrow Street, to be exact about it."

The address, at least, caught the warden off his guard a little. Delly wasn't usually too keen on providing verifiable facts to her interlocutors. "What the hell would they want with *you* for a bodyguard?"

"They were looking for women of a wizardly persuasion," Delly said, with dignity. "To guard a lady in her matrimonial seclusion. And they're expecting to speak to me again tomorrow, so you might as well let me go now and get on with finding the *actual* criminal."

The warden dragged a skeptical eye up one side of her and then back down the other. Then he said, "We'll just see about that, Delly Wells," and removed himself from her presence.

Delly spent a few fruitful hours scowling at the ceiling, picking at her nails, and trying to teach herself to make miniature fireworks as she'd seen a fire witch doing once at a carnival. Maybe if she learned to do it well enough she'd be able to take up a life in the theater with her old pal Elo, which would provide her with a steady income and a reason to stay out of the fucking clink for once in her fucking life. Instead, she only succeeded in filling her cell with smoke, and she was pressing her face up to the bars to cough when a Lady appeared.

She was a very distinguished-looking Lady, thin and straight-backed, with a nose like an opinionated pelican and her white hair in a neat Hexian crop. "I've been told," said the Lady, in milk-souring tones, "that you have been bandying about the address of my employer in an attempt to extricate yourself from your current state of imprisonment."

Delly blinked. Then she said, in her most refined and least West Leiscourt accent, "There must be some kind of a misunderstanding, madam. I only meant to inform his honor the warden that I had the *intention* of presenting myself as a candidate for the position of bodyguard to your particularly honorable self's distinguished employer, madam."

They were both quiet for a spell, possibly stymied at having met another person with the same circumnavigatory habits of speech as themselves. Delly took a big breath of smoke, then gave a delicate hack.

The Lady frowned. "Did *you* produce all of this smoke?"

"Might it so," Delly said—she was still coughing—and then winced at herself and started again. "That I did, madam. In fruitless pursuit of the production of fireworks, madam." Then she added, by way of explanation, "I'm a fire witch, madam, which is why I wanted to present myself to yourself in search of a position guarding your employer, madam. I had intended on making my way to Elmsedge for the interview tomorrow morning, madam."

"My name is Magister Fentan," said the Lady. "You may address me as Magister. Why on earth would I be willing to interview a criminal for a position in my employer's household, Miss Wells?"

"If I might beg your pardon, Magister," Delly said, "I'm only a very *petty* criminal, but I'm a rare excellent fire witch, and we ain't so very thickly strewn upon the local thoroughfares, Magister. It might be that having useful and steady employment would deter me from the path of wickedness I set upon at an early age due to the dreadfully neglectful behaviors of my mother and father, Magister, who abandoned me in the coal scuttle of a public house when I was a mere infant, Magister. Also, if any brigand were to attempt to shoot or stab your employer, I would be able to melt the weapon before any harm could be done, which I imagine would be of a great comfort to her elevated self, Magister."

Magister Fentan looked at her consideringly. Then she pulled a pair of nail scissors from her pocket, handed them to Delly, and said, "Show me."

Delly put the scissors into her palm and concentrated a bit harder than she needed to, then watched as the scissors melted, puddled in her hand, then trickled through her fingers and fell in droplets upon the floor. It tickled a mite.

"Hm," said the Magister. Then she said, "I've already selected all of the women that I want to hire for the position."

"Oh," Delly said.

"I *had* been hoping to find a fire witch, though," said the Magister. Then she said, "I will be holding a meeting for all of my formal candidates for the group at eleven o'clock tomorrow morning at 332 Barrow Street. If you attend promptly, clean and sober, I might consider your application for employment."

"Fucking truly, then?" Delly asked, astonished.

The magister pickled up her face at her. "I'd also ask that you refrain from that sort of language when in the presence of my employer. You will be working for a woman of *quality*, not for the proprietor of a public house."

"Yes, Magister," Delly said. "Understood, Magister. But begging your honorable self's pardon, Magister, I'll have to be released from jail before I'll be able to attend a meeting, Magister."

Magister Fentan was already departing. "I will speak to the warden," she said, and within very short order an exceedingly irritated-looking warden reinflicted Dellaria Wells upon the populace.

Delly returned to her flat in a moderately discombobulated state and set at once to eating a bowl of porridge and laundering her least-tattered dress in a large tub in the pub's kitchen. Then she deposited her tired carcass into bed and slept like a sack of potatoes.

The next morning, Delly cleaned her teeth, combed her hair, and arrived at 332 Barrow Street at exactly the time the Magister had said, according to her goddamn dad's old pocket watch.

A servant let her in with a suspicious cast of his eye, which wasn't too much of a surprise; in her experience weasel-faced fellows in the butling profession had a sort of instinctive sense for her not belonging places. This gentleman looked like a terrier with a noseful of rat.

Another servant led her to a nice little sitting room, where there were already a few other people.

Magister Fentan directed her nose ceilingward and her eyes Delly-ward. "Miss Wells. You're late."

Delly made her own eyes into perfect circles, by way of expressing her extreme astonishment, and pulled the pocket watch out. "Politely begging the pardon of your honorable personage, Magister, but it's two to eleven by my pocket watch."

"It is, in fact, twelve after," the magister said. "Please, sit." She said it politely enough, but Delly thought she could see the crinkles of irritation starting to array themselves around the corners of her mouth. Delly arrayed herself in the nearest chair and had a look around the room.

There were all sorts of knickers on this washing line, all right. There was Delly herself: like a potato with freckles and brown hair in a bad plait. Nearby was an old lady with soft dark eyes, a broad nose, and a few white curls peeking out from under her bonnet. The old biddy was sitting next to a sea of blue-and-white frills into which someone had dropped a little whey-faced blonde girl. Delly figured if you directed a question to the girl, she might have to consult the frills before she answered. If she'd fought at all to prevent herself from being overcome by them, she'd lost the battle.

Next to the frills was a young lady who made Delly think of her auntie's cat. Not how she looked—she looked like a rare pretty girl, not like a cat—but the air about her. It was a fine cat Delly's auntie had: black and white and sleek and fat. It wasn't the mousing kind. It was the kind that sat and purred while an old lady brushed its fur and told it what a fine pretty puss it was.

This woman had an emerald on her finger the size of a grape, and thick black hair that gleamed in the sun against her powder-pale cheeks, and a silk dress that gleamed right back at it. She was plump and pretty and her nails were clean. Delly could almost hear the purring.

The lady beside her was something else altogether. Maybe not rich like the house cat, but beautiful, and *quality*. She had that look about her. The way she sat, maybe. How well her dress fit. She had a dark, cool brown complexion, long thin braids, and a contained, thoughtful sort of way of looking around her. She was so beautiful and so quality that it made Delly want to avoid looking at her too long or too directly, like someone might pop out of the floor and smack her for peeping at her betters, though the plain cotton of the woman's dress said that she was quality without the money to pay for folks to do her slapping for her.

The next up was an entirely different sort of creature again. Tall as anything, broad as a back gate, enormous hands, and a craggy, handsome, mirthful sort of face, all packed into a neatly cut and pressed black dress that she wore like she felt good in it. No slouch to her like you saw in some big women, no trying to look smaller: shoulders back, eyes interested in the room. Her face was young, but the long hair she wore piled up on her head was a bright silver, and her pale complexion had a distinctly gray-blue tint. Part troll if she was anything, which was interesting: Delly had a friend who'd slept with a troll, and she'd said that modern human-troll matches were all barren. Seemed like she didn't know the first thing she was talking about, which for one of Delly's friends wasn't too unusual. At least Delly wouldn't have to guess at whether this particular troll was a lady or a gentleman, as she'd heard was usually the way it went with trolls: if this one had answered that advertisement, then Delly could be safe in calling her *miss*.

"Now that we are all *finally* in attendance," the magister said, with a meaningful sort of glance toward Delly, "I would like to present you each to the group, so that you might start with learning each other's names. First, let us dispense with our latecomer. Please stand, Miss Wells."

Delly stood, suddenly struck with the horrible realization that she had no idea where she ordinarily held her hands and how her lips generally felt when she wasn't sneering hideously. "Miss Wells," the magister said, "is an accomplished fire witch. She may be of some interest to you, Miss Dok." The pretty black-haired cat arched an eyebrow. Delly bobbed an uncomfortable curtsy and then plummeted back into her chair.

The magister made a sound that sounded to Delly like a muffled sigh. "Thank you, Miss Wells. Now, allow me to present Miss Abstentia Dok and Miss Bawa Usad." The house cat and the high-quality woman both stood. "Miss Dok and Miss Usad are both senior students at Weltsir University." Delly tried not to wince at the mention of the Weltsir University of fucking Magic: she thought she did all right. No one seemed to notice her flinching, at least. "Miss Usad will act as my proxy for the duration of the seclusion, and Miss Dok will act as her second." The two ladies both curtsied at that—Miss Dok with a small smile that made her look more of a pleased pussycat than ever, and Miss Usad with a modest inclination of her excessively beautiful head—and then sat.

"Thank you, girls," the magister said. "Next, allow me to present Mrs. Corma Totham and her householded daughter, Miss Ermintrude Totham."

The old lady and the whey-faced blonde creature stood. The magister said, "Mrs. Totham is an accomplished body scientist, and Miss Totham is a cloved woman."

There was a sound like a strong wind blowing through from the women gasping or murmuring or shifting in their chairs. *Body scientist* was what polite water-drinking types called *necromancers*, and up till now Delly had been reasonably fucking certain that cloved women were just a goblin story for scaring kids with and not a type of person that actually existed in this particular and late period of human fucking endeavor.

"She ain't, *either*," said Delly, before she had time to tell herself to keep her damn herring-hole shut. Cloved women were supposed to be wild-eyed hillclanners who turned into feral pigs at will and ate men who came into their villages after dark, and this girl looked like she could be overcome by a largish pork sausage.

"Are you implying, Miss Wells, that I don't know my own business?" inquired the magister.

Delly shook her head, feeling her innards clamp up. She didn't know why she had to always go and *talk* when all she relefting well needed to do was *sit still* and *be quiet*. "No, Magister. I only meant to express my surprise, Magister, that a young lady of such daintitudinous aspect might be a cloved woman, Magister."

The magister looked at her cross-eyedwardly. "*Daintitudinous*," she said, "is not a *word*. And I have been made perfectly satisfied as to Miss Totham's abilities. As are the Bastennes, who have engaged the Tothams on more than one occasion for their services as bounty hunters."

The handsome trollish woman looked interested in that. "The Bastennes? My mother and father worked for them back when I was still the proverbial twinkle in dear Pop's eye. Jolly small world, eh?"

Delly blinked, not sure which way to squint at the expensive silver-coated plum-puddingness of *that* accent coming from *this* woman. The magister just looked resigned. "I suppose that I might as well introduce *you*, Miss Cynallum."

The big troll gull popped up to her feet. "Winnifer Cynallumwyn-surai, at your service and keen as razors," she said. "Winn Cynallum if you're short on time." Then she popped right back down again.

There was a bit of a pause from the throng before the magister gained the strength to continue. "Miss Cynallum," said the magister, "is a markswoman and illusionist." Then she stopped and looked constipated for a bit before she carried on. "As well as a practitioner of . . . *hand-to-hand combat*." Delly could see why she'd been looking like she found the words so indigestible now: had to be hard to make *that* sound nice and prim and ladylike.

Miss Cynallum didn't look like a woman who minded, though.

She looked comfortable as could be, like she thought she had every right in the world to be just where she was. Delly liked it. It was calming just to rest her eyes on. She seemed to notice where Delly's eyes were resting, too, because she looked right back at her and smiled. Delly felt her face heat up. "Wouldn't mind learning some of that" was what then came popping out of Delly's damn cursed pothole of a mouth.

"Oh, really? I'd be happy to teach you. Just pop around to my quarters once we're established at the job and we'll have a bit of a wrestle," Miss Cynallum said. Then *she* went red and looked as if she'd like to grab herself by the throat and squeeze.

The whole room sat in deep disquietude for a span. Delly offered up a prayer to her ancestors, wishing them eternal and painful relivings for having produced such a dunce of a descendant. Then Magister Fentan said, "On *that* note, I would like to inform you all of the work that you shall be required to perform and the standards of deportment I shall expect all of you to abide by during the duration of your employment."

Delly started to pay a mite less attention at this juncture. She thought she could guess at the main points. Essentially, she ought to do none of the things toward which she naturally inclined, and do all of the things she thought were a real pain in the tits. That seemed to be the thrust of it when she turned her ear toward listening: that they would be keeping an eye on the lady at her intended's fine house and during the journey to the place, and that they'd be expected not to make asses of themselves while they were doing it. Nothing that sounded too taxing to Delly, other than having to stay out of bars for a span.

It was when Magister Fentan got into the real meat of the matter that Delly endeavored to truly attend. The term of their employment was to start in five days—grand—and no advances would be given on payment—less grand—which would be fifty tocats for the two weeks—so grand that Delly gasped a bit at it. That was rent for more than half the year. No one else seemed near as impressed as she was, which just proved what a bunch of damned clanners the rest of them were. *Fifty in two weeks.* Sakes.

Delly gritted her teeth through the rest of the meeting, then got herself a signed note from Magister Fentan attesting to the terms of her gainful employment. As soon as that was in her hand, she was off like a frog on a hot rock. She first trotted by the jail in order to thrust the note before the disbelievingly narrowed eyes of the warden, who told her that she was a sly creature who, if actually employed, would soon give her employer every cause to regret a decision that was likely preceded by their indulging in strong spirits—a statement that Delly told him she found very injurious to her daughterly affection for him. Then she took herself off, whistling, to find her landlady.

Mrs. Medlow was pleased enough to know about Delly's impending employment but didn't see fit to lift the hard promise. Delly, defeated, retreated to the bar below her room for a drink or two and a few minutes of quiet ponderation.

It took about half a glass of gin to get Delly into an expansive frame of ponder. This job was a hell of a thing. Enough money to get her own rent settled, and enough to get her mam into a room, too. More than that, even. Enough to get her mam out to one of those nice places in the countryside where they sent rich clanner ladies with nervous conditions, which Delly always took to mean that they'd been on too much gin and drip and needed to be dried out. Maybe she could send her mam to dry out in a place like that where there were nice trees and flowers and clean beds with mattresses that got turned and aired every week. Maybe her mam would be the woman Delly remembered from a few weeks when she was eight years old, fresh out of a stint in jail, sober, and suddenly full of consternation over her daughter having raised herself like a wild animal up to this point without any civilized intervention. The woman who bought bread and butter and a new bar of soap and gave her daughter breakfast and bathed her and plaited her hair and took her to the Elgarite Hall to register her for the halton school. Maybe Delly would get to see that version of her mam again.

Or maybe Mam would take a vow of chastity and join a fucking halton tomorrow, while Delly was dreaming.

Delly ordered another gin. The first few sips pulled her back above the cold, killing waters of childhood memories, and a few more after that set her toward the contemplation of comely prospects for an evening's company. She started off thinking about a fella she knew who was a reliable way to waste a few hours, before her internal eddies pulled her toward someone else. That Cynallum gull from this afternoon.

She'd looked back. Delly knew that for sure. Delly had looked at her and Cynallum had looked right back. Babbled and looked embarrassed, even, which probably meant she liked what she saw.

A prospect.

Delly was used to having a prospect in her life. More than one, usually: she liked having options. None of them had been anything like the Cynallum girl, though. A girl like that was a prospect for more than just fucking. More of a long game. A girl like that—that accent, those expensive-looking clothes—could be a prospect for easy living for a lass's entire earthly amble, and a prospect like that was due more thoughtful consideration than a quick card game near Bessa's meat-pie stand.

And maybe Delly was getting a little fucking ahead of herself again, which she supposed might sometimes be the result that came from a day crowded with unusual incidents followed by a particularly invigorating glass or two of gin.

Delly had a few nervous gallops to get out, to put a delicate pin-end upon it, and she knew just the lad to go to when she was in want of a bit of nervous galloping: a usually unemployed actor named Elo, whom she'd been friends with since they were both crusty-kneed West Leiscourt kids together. So, with that thought in mind, she left some money on the bar and went to check for the lanky bastard at the places where he might be doing his part to keep a barstool from floating off into the firmament. She found him at the very first joint, his red curly head bent over his beer like he thought he might spy a better life at the bottom of the glass. He seemed glad enough to have a reason to abandon the fruitless search and head off for a heartless fumble instead.

After their gallop, she stayed in his room so they could have a bit of a chat and another glass of gin together. They got along a treat as old pals, though they both knew that he was always wishing that it was someone else he was galloping with, someone who might be interested in having a few dozen of his curly-headed children. Maybe someone who wasn't Wester trash like him, too: both of them had ambitions above their stations and were all the more miserable for it. She told him about her new real paying job, and her new plum-pudding prospect. He gave a slow nod.

"I'd go after it, Delly, if I was you. A slim prospect's a thicker prospect than I've gotten in years."

Delly tipped her glass at him. "To luck a-changing and opportunity arising, then," she said, and realized a moment later that it was the exact toast her mother had always given when the drink gave her a moment to forget her circumstances.

3

Wherein Dellaria Cozies Up to a Prospect and
Is Enormously Alarmed and Inconvenienced by
the Work She Chose to Engage In

Delly, as a loose rule of her tenure upon this, the World as Conceived by Mortal Man, did not leave the best of first impressions. She hadn't as a child, when she was ill-kempt and badly behaved through no fault of her own, and she still didn't as an adult, when she was ill-kempt and badly behaved through every fault of her own. The most dispiriting aspect of impressions, as she saw it, was that after the first one went bad she was better off avoiding any further impressions entirely, as any attempts on her part to fix the damage would generally end like the time when she'd drunkenly tried to cut her own hair with a pair of nail scissors. It was preferable, in Delly's view, to only ever meet any given person the one time: that meant that you only ruined one day out of however many they'd in the end be blessed with, rather than a whole packed trunk of someone's few precious remaining hours. On this occasion, however, she was stuck: only showing up for the interview would defeat the entire purpose of finding gainful employment. So on the day she was meant to start work she scrubbed herself from top to toe, put on a dress that she'd really and truly put through the mangle two days previous, and arrived with her carpetbag at the same room where the first meeting had been held more than an hour before she was meant to be there.

She wasn't alone, as it turned out. After a servant took her carpet-bag from her to bear it off to places unknown, Delly turned her attention to the two other figures from that first meeting who were there as well: the old lady and the victim of frills. Delly rummaged through her brain for their names and came up wanting. Her face froze into the sort of frantic position it usually got into when she saw the constabulary approaching. The old lady looked at her and smiled. "Oh, Miss Wells, how very nice to see you again! I was just commenting to my daughter Ermintrude on what a lovely specimen of Welkly's Fletchling that is perched just outside of the window. The Welkly is my householder Mr. Totham's *very* favorite type of Fletchling. Isn't it lovely when you can see the bright green on the male's breast at this time of the early spring! I always fancy that it's as if he loves the tender buds of the trees he perches on so much that his wife sewed him a waistcoat to match them. Are you very fond of birds, Miss Wells?"

"Ah," Delly said. At the moment she was only exceeding fond of *this* old bird, who Delly was sure as anything had just provided Delly with her and her daughter's names to save her from the awkwardness of having to ask them. She wasn't used to anyone going out of their way to keep her from being embarrassed. If her mam had ever spared her daughter's feelings in any way, it had probably been an accident. "Middling fond. I don't know as much about them as I should, Mrs. Totham. I'm a woefully underinformed creature, ma'am."

"Oh, no matter, no matter," Mrs. Totham said. She twittered like Mrs. Medlow, but she was a much pleasanter sort of canary. "I could teach you a few of the things that I know—though of course I don't know *nearly* as much as Mr. Totham. Gentlemen are so very clever with remembering all sorts of wonderful facts from books, aren't they? They're such lovely little creatures! Birds, I mean, not gentlemen. One never grows tired of birds."

Delly wondered, briefly, if she ought to take this to mean that

Mrs. Totham sometimes grew tired of gentlemen. Delly sure as shit did, especially the type that kept coming around her place to look for her after what she'd meant to be a one-off gallop, but she wasn't an elderly householded lady who figured her householder for a regular genius of birdology. Then Ermintrude, who'd been steadily sinking more deeply into her frills as her mother spoke, finally made her voice heard. "Really, Mama, she's just being polite. No one wants to hear about birds."

Delly spurred herself in pursuit of a change of subject. "How did the two of you come to be in this line of work?" she asked. "You seeming like you come from a very respectable family, if you pardon the assumption, ma'am."

"Oh, indeed, indeed," Mrs. Totham said. "It's been very difficult for poor dear Ermintrude and myself, I'm afraid. Mr. Totham fell ill several years ago, and we found ourselves in some difficulty. I had never worked before, he being my householder, and we had five younger girls at home to think of. Then my eldest daughters suggested that Ermintrude and I might be interested in joining them in their profession. I householded them when they were both adolescents, you see, and I'm afraid that they had both been stagecoach guards for several years by then. I had hoped to find them nice husbands or householders after I brought them in, but they've proven *very* stubborn about their independence. They are *very* good girls, though, and very dutiful daughters."

Delly raised her eyebrows. "*Eight* householded daughters, is it? Sounds—lovely." *Loud* is what she'd been thinking.

"Oh, it is," Mrs. Totham said, gently beaming. "When I was a young girl, I knew that I wouldn't be able to have children exactly as my school friends did, but I used to dream about growing up and being householded by a handsome man with a big mustache and living with all of our householded children in a house with lace curtains at the window. My own dear mother was the best woman on earth—God grant her easeful relivings!—and I wanted to be just like her. And now I have a wonderful husband, and eight *wonderful* daughters, so all of my dreams came to pass, almost exactly as I imagined them, until my poor Mr. Totham's trouble with his health."

"Oh," Delly said, trying and failing to prevent a sense of wistfulness from falling upon her. Just the thought of having a mam who'd wanted her there. She did her best to keep conversing, as that was the sort of thing she'd heard that nice respectable ladies did. "And did you become a nec—body scientist just for the sake of finding work?"

"Oh, no," Mrs. Totham said. "Gracious me. It's a craft that takes many years to develop any skill in. I began to study body science when I was still a young woman. My mother brought me to a local body scientist when I was a girl in order to address some delicate matters regarding my person, and I was so impressed by her abilities to explain the issues that had so troubled me and soothe my worries that I resolved to take up the study myself so that I could attend to such personal problems on my own in future. And then, of course, it was very useful to me when I became a mother and could easily address all of the usual bumps and bruises."

"Oh," Delly said again. That word seemed to be turning into the extent of her fucking conversational abilities. A mam who'd be able to really and actually kiss away the bumps and goddamn bruises of childhood. "You sound like the sort of mother any girl'd be lucky to have, Mrs. Totham." She snuck a peek at Ermintrude, just to see if the lass was as impressed by her own circumstances as Delly was, and caught the lass mid–eye roll, pupils cast boldly heavenward. Then Ermintrude caught Delly's glance, and the eye roll crystalized into a very distinct glare.

Delly slipped her a wink, which seemed to soften the lass's fury a mite, or at least confuse her enough to smooth the glare into a small smile. Delly decided right then that she ought to speak to this girl alone, later. Not as a *prospect*, for tit's sake—Delly had barely wanted anything to do with girls of seventeen when she was a girl of that age her own self—but by way of making sure she had allies in all corners for the next two weeks. If Delly had ever learned anything from a childhood of sleeping in whatever poorhouse would take her, it was that you'd best endeavor to make yourself agreeable to all and truly known to none, lest you have your belongings all stolen and your confidences broken before you made it to breakfast.

The topic of conversation turned to gossip then—turned out that Mrs. Totham was a keen observer of both interesting birds and the society papers—and they passed the time with that for a span until the pretty house cat and the high-quality woman with the braids walked in. Delly, of course, didn't remember a damn one of their names, so she spent a few minutes smiling politely and trying her best to listen in on their conversation to see if they might see fit to say their own names aloud. They didn't. Delly was resigning herself to never addressing either of them directly for the next two weeks when Miss Cynallum came breezing through the room in a crisp green riding habit and said, "Hello again, all! Would anyone mind dreadfully if I went around asking everyone's names again? I've got a mind like an absolute *sieve*."

No one expressed any objections out loud, at the very least, so Cynallum went around asking everyone's name again. The beautiful quality woman with the braided hair was Bawa Usad, and the pretty pussycat was Abstentia Dok. Then Miss Cynallum came around to Delly and favored her with a big bright grin. "You're Miss Wells," she said. "I remember you."

"And you're Miss Cynallum," Delly said, tilting her head up to look at her. "I remember you back."

"You may call me Winn," Miss Cynallum said. "If you'd like to, that is. I won't try to make you call me something that you wouldn't like to call me. Unless you'd like to call me something that wasn't my name, I suppose, which wouldn't really be regulation hammerball, what?" Then she stopped and looked pained.

Delly let her smile go wider. She was no kind of beauty, she knew, but she had good thick hair and a decent set of tits, and when presented to an audience generously inclined toward thickly behaired and generously betitted gulls, she'd been told that she could charm the fleas out of a mattress. Miss Winn here struck Delly as a more generous audience than most. Delly said, "Then I guess you can call me Delly, Winn."

Winn, to her credit, didn't stammer this time. She just smiled, and the two of them were spared from having their moment of flirtatious success running aground on the rocky shoals of continued conversation by the entrance of a stranger into the room.

She was tall and slender, but everything else about her was a mystery: she wore an enormous round hat with a thick white veil that obscured her face entirely. A seclusionary veil, that's what it was: Delly'd never seen one in the very cloth before. It all looked pretty bathtub brewed to Delly, but considering how often Delly herself had gone out into the world with great flapping holes in her dress, she thought that she probably didn't have much room for lobbing critiques. Especially critiques aimed at her betters, which Delly figured this girl must be. She figured that even harder when she saw Misses Usad and Dok dip into little curtsies as the stranger walked through the room. Delly nearly hit the ground trying to give a deeper one. A girl like Delly couldn't grovel too much around quality types, as a rule. Out of the corner of her eye she caught Winn contenting herself with a small inclination of her head, which astounded Delly into practically toppling over onto the floor. What the hell kind of a prospect *was* Winn? That accent said she had a clan name, sure, and being part troll probably meant she came from a family with money, but only giving a nod to a woman a bunch of high-quality women were curtsying to meant more than just a respectable clan. It meant something closer to the *headmanship*.

Fuck Delly's eyes straight out of her *head*, was this *ever* a prospect.

"They're all here now, Miss Wexin," Miss Dok said.

"Thank you, Abstentia," said Miss Wexin. Her voice, at least, sounded like the voice of a lady who might need a whole passel of ladies to protect her from brigands. A soft, high, butter-dipped sort of voice. A voice with cream and sugar in it. "And thank you, ladies. I will be brief. My family has hired you to protect me for the next two weeks because we have very good reason to believe that attempts may be made on my life by persons who, for reasons unknown, wish to prevent my marriage. Several such attempts have already been made, and I am afraid that my attackers may only grow more violent as the wedding date approaches. If any one of you is not prepared to face danger within the next two weeks, please speak now and you will be freed of your contractual obligations."

Delly, for a moment, seriously considered freeing herself from her contractual obligations. She'd been hoping for a couple of weeks of protecting some hothouse flower from imagined enemies, and she didn't particularly relish the thought of having to dodge actual bullets in the defense of some gull wearing a great white bucket on her head. Then she thought of her mam with her pinhole eyes, sleeping in that collapsing woodpile of a house, and reined herself in. Not that she'd be too eager to put herself between a bullet and her mam, either, but if things stayed as they were now, Delly'd be stuck scraping her out of gutters and dragging her to hospitals until Mam finally rejoined the unfortunates of the releft. That was to say nothing of the mostly-on-the-face pustules that would be Delly's unavoidable fate if she didn't keep this job, get her money, and pay her fatherprodding rent. That in mind, Delly kept her filthy biscuit-chewer clamped firmly shut.

Everyone else did, too. A few seconds ticked by in silence. Miss Wexin inclined her head. Either that or the bucket had just slipped a bit: it was hard to tell. "I thank you for your bravery," she said. Delly suppressed an indelicate snort. Miss Wexin said, "I am afraid that you will see very little of me over the next few days, as I will be spending most of my seclusion in prayer and meditation. I will be riding in my own carriage with Miss Usad and Miss Dok as my companions. I hope you will not think me churlish for not engaging with you further as I prepare for my marriage. Might I shake your hands?"

No one objected to this proposition, so Miss Wexin moved about the room to shake each of their hands. Then she left the room with

Miss Usad, while Miss Dok led the rest of them after her a moment later.

Delly lagged toward the rear of the pack and was pleased when Winn lagged right beside her. "Bit odd, what?" Winn murmured.

Delly cast her eyes a foot or so upward to look at her. "How'd you mean?"

"Well," Winn murmured, keeping her voice very low, "if that Miss Wexin is meant to be who I think she is, I've met her."

"Fuckin' truly?" Delly said, and then cleared her throat. "Pardon. What do you mean, who she's *meant* to be?"

"Just what I said," Winn said. "I met a girl named Mayelle Wexin when I was thirteen. I hadn't gotten so tall by then, and I was with my pop, so she probably hadn't taken much note of me." The corners of her mouth curled up then. "*Most* gulls don't take much note of me when I'm with my pop. But anyway, she would have been about sixteen then, which would make her about the age to get married now, and the Wexin clan is one of the only clans I know in the headmanship that still practices seclusions."

"So what's funny about it, then?" Delly asked. "Begging your pardon."

"Don't beg my pardon," Winn said. "My mother always says that it wastes time. And the *funny* thing is, when I met her, I remember thinking what a nice low voice Miss Wexin had for a human girl."

"And this girl had a voice like a field mouse," Delly said. They were both whispering now, and Delly had the fleeting thought that engaging in some intrigue could only serve to fan any romantic flames she might be producing with her prospect. "Sakes. You figure she's some kind of *imposter*?"

"I don't know," Winn said. "Maybe. Or maybe there's another daughter I've never heard of rattling about in the backs of the Wexin cupboards behind all of the stacks of reprobate younger sons. I've only heard of the one Wexin girl of the right age, but I haven't been in society much, these past few years. Any excuse to be out of it, really. You linger too long at the punch bowl at a society party and the next thing you know you're engaged to a fellow with a squint and a stamp collection." Then she gave Delly a big grin. "Soon we'll be examining the mud under the windows for footprints and questioning members of the underworld about their connection to the entire mysterious wheeze. Nice to have something interesting to engage the old mental whatsit while at work, isn't it?"

"I've got a *particularly* long-standing interest in being interested, myself," Delly allowed. Then, to her enormous alarm, the teakettle of her curiosity boiled over. "You're, ah, in *society*, you said?"

Winn gave a dismissive wave with one big hand. "Mother is head of clan Cynallum, and Pop works for the government," she said. "It's a very small clan, though. More of a biggish family, really. And in Hexos all you need to get a government posting is to be friends with the Lord-Mage, and Mother and Pop have known Uncle Loga for *ages*."

"*Sakes*," Delly breathed, still whispering even though they weren't talking secrets anymore and had emerged out onto the streets, where whispering suddenly seemed much more ridiculous than it had when they were in a dim and rich and atmospheric interior. She cleared her throat and said in a normal voice, "Greatest wizard I ever met was a fella who pulled beans out of folks' ears on the corner of Eagle and Wren Streets."

That got a laugh from Winn, who said, "And speaking of wizards, Miss Wexin isn't the only one about who's hiding her face. Miss Usad's got a bit of the old veil of wizarding illusion on her. Jolly nice little thing—I wouldn't have noticed it if I wasn't trained in illusions. I think she might be covering up that she wears spectacles."

"Sakes," Delly said again, admiringly. "High-quality ladies really are exceptional creatures, ain't they?" She was so absorbed in the consideration of the freaks of high-quality ladies—using up all that magic just so no one would see your specs!—and of the cleverness of Winn for having figured out the trick that it took her a moment before her eyes registered the horrible sight before her and her whole body gave a startled writhe backward, as if she were an eel being shown a plate of mashed potatoes and a bottle of vinegar. "Are those *horses*?"

They were, in fact, horses. Eight of them, if one demanded prissy exactitude about it: four attached to a coach that Misses Wexin, Usad, and Dok were climbing into, and four more just—standing about, being held by the leady leathery mouth bits by some likely-looking lads. *Plotting*, probably, was what they were doing. Delly didn't at all like the look of them. She'd watched a man be dragged almost to death by a horse once, when she was a small girl, and she'd never seen fit to enter into conversation with once since. Uncanny things, they were, with eyes on the sides of their heads.

"They *look* like horses," Winn said, in a slightly doubtful tone. "One never really blinking well knows, though, with wizards about. Why? Not a keen rider?"

"Never so much as touched one of the beasts," Delly said, keeping a wary eye trained on the nearest of the creatures.

"Oh," Winn said, looking suddenly much more concerned than she'd ever looked while they were discussing their employer's being a potential imposter. "Jolly bad luck, when we're heading off on a two-day ride."

Delly thought for a moment to ask where the hell *she'd* been when everyone else was learning about the two-day ride on horseback, then realized a moment later that the answer was likely *In the room, but not paying any attention to what was being said.* Instead, she gave a groan of desperation. "What in the releft am I supposed to do, then? The creature'll drag me to death after two minutes."

"Oh, none of that, you won't be *dragged to death*," Winn said briskly. "We'll sort it all out, what? Come along," she said, and went striding off toward the nearest of the horse-holding lads, likely to bend his ear over some equestrian topic about which Delly had absolutely no spirit of bright-eyed curiosity. She dragged herself after Winn and stood a few steps behind her, glowering at the air. Some sort of conversation was held amongst the lads that Mrs. Totham also suddenly, and without warning, intruded herself upon. A moment after that, the lads started leading off two of the horses. Delly blinked. "Am I being left behind, then?"

"Oh, no," said Mrs. Totham, stepping toward her. "I really must thank you, Miss Wells! A long ride on a big spirited animal like that would be very unsuitable for me, at *my* age, dear me. Fortunately, those nice young men say that they have just the thing for us to have a more comfortable journey. It really is true, what they say about how the headmanship can manage to hire such superior servants! My girl back home really is quite *impossible*. She breaks dishes as if a bit of crockery once caused one of her ancestors to stumble into sin and repeat his reliving. Why, just the other day—" Here she began to embark upon a very long and tedious story about poor hapless Mesteria doing something that Mrs. Totham found inexcusable to a batch of strawberry jam. Delly nodded and said, "Really! Shocking, that!" at what she thought might be the right intervals, until the two stable lads returned with two new great brown creatures. The closer of the two beasts eyed her. Delly eyed it right back, bold as she could manage. She figured that horses were probably more likely to attack if they sensed nerves. This one didn't attack, though: just flicked its long ears about and sighed.

"That's a funny-looking horse," she said after a moment.

"They're *donkeys*, my dear," said Mrs. Totham. "Nice, sensible creatures. *Very* unlikely to bolt."

Winn, nearby, was covering her mouth with her hand. Delly felt her cheeks heat. "I don't know how to ride *this* one, either," she said, rather more loudly than she had intended.

Winn pulled her hand away. She was still smiling, sure enough, but it didn't look to have any sharp edges in it. "That's perfectly all right," she said. "It's easy as can be. Come on," she said, and brought Delly over to the beast and tried to talk her through climbing onto it. When Delly still hadn't managed to get her ass up after a third try, Winn said, "I'll just give you a bit of a boost, that's the ticket," and Delly found herself perched atop a donkey and extremely astonished about it. The donkey itself betrayed nary a whiff of astonishment, and only carried on eating bits of grass from between the cobblestones as if it thought it'd been brought out from the stables for this express purpose. Winn, now on horseback herself—it hadn't taken *her* three tries—beamed. "There we are! We'll have you at the steeplechases, next!"

Delly craned her neck to try to see what her donkey was about, then felt off-balance and gripped hard at the saddle, then sat up straight again and looked about herself. Everyone was looking at her. Her face went hotter, and she looked toward Winn. "How do I make it go?"

"Oh, he'll go on his own," said one of the likely lads, and gave the donkey's rump a pat. Before Delly had much of a chance to wonder what the hell that meant the coachman called out to his horses, and Winn and her horse set forth as well, and Delly's little brown steed went ambling comfortably after Winn, as if he thought he'd figured out whom around here he ought to be taking his orders from.

"Got my eye on you, you long-eared bastard," Delly murmured to him, in what she hoped was a tone of convincingly firm warning.

The donkey didn't seem to take too much note of her, which, it turned out, was a sign of what was to come. Delly spent the first few minutes of the journey watching Winn, trying to figure out how it was that she got her horse to mind. There seemed to be some clicking of the mouth, and some pulling at the reins, and some other strange and subtle maneuvers. Delly attempted to imitate them, in a surreptitious way, but the results were disappointing: the donkey either ignored her entirely or stopped dead, gave her what Delly figured to be a reproachful look, and then started up with following Winn again.

Within about an hour, Delly was thoroughly fucking sick of being on the back of a big scheming animal, and within two, her back was screaming at her almost as loudly as her poor sore ass. Her rump, that was: not the untrustworthy beast she was seated upon. *That* ass, at least, was still following Winn closely enough to allow Delly to make conversation. Delly, Mrs. Totham, and Ermintrude were all riding sidesaddle, but Winn was scandalously astride: the skirt of her riding habit was split, and she had some sort of loose-fitting trousers on beneath it. "Is it more comfortable, then, riding like that?"

"Not a bit," Winn said cheerfully. "Murder on the unmentionable areas. It keeps you steadier on the horse, though, so if I need to gallop off abruptly to enter into combat with some brigand, I won't go toppling off the back end and land in a ditch, what?"

"Suppose that sounds right," Delly said, and then rode on in silence for a while. "Don't see why we couldn't have taken a damn train," she muttered eventually.

"I imagine because there would be no good way to secure the whole train," Winn said. "We'd end up in separate compartments, for one thing, so we wouldn't be able to see if anyone was getting close to Miss Wexin unless we stood up in the passage all night. That should also be why we're mounted and not in a carriage of our own: we've got to keep eyes on her, and you can't do that with walls in the way. Nothing to stop a murderer from disguising himself as a porter on a train, either. And she's not meant to be around men, in any case. Can't keep all of the men in Daeslund off of the rails just to maintain her seclusion, can we?"

"Suppose not," Delly said admiringly. Winn had a bit of decent enough thinkmeat between the ears. "How'd you learn all of this stuff?"

"From my mother, mostly," Winn said. "When I was a baby, she and Pop were still getting our household established, and her clan was short of money, so she picked up some bodyguarding work to help make ends meet."

"But," Delly said. "And—begging your pardon—and begging your pardon for having begged your pardon once again after you having said you'd rather I not, as well"—she paused here to take a breath—"but if you're—and this is only myself making bold assumptions—if you're a member of the headmanship, or thereabouts, then why would *you* have to take a job like this? Didn't seem too much to me like you looked too excited about the salary."

"Oh, I don't *have* to," Winn said. "It was this or go to university, and I can't stand just sitting in a dreary classroom all day, staring at dull old books. I'd rather be out in the fresh air having a bit of excitement while I decide what I think that I ought to do with myself for the rest of my life." Then she said, "Just so you know, it's not really regulation hammerball to ask society types anything about money. Bit ginny, really. The more they have of it, the more ticklish they get about it. You're better off dancing around it a bit and figuring out how much they've got by looking at their clothes."

"Oh," Delly said, her face going red, and launched into her usual patter for when she'd gone and put her foot into it. "I'm afraid I don't know much about behaving myself right, miss. My mother and father never had much to do with my raising, so I was forced to raise myself, with the regrettable results you see before you, miss." Delly said that sort of thing all the time, to all sorts of people: it was a fine way to embarrass someone into letting slip whatever bad behavior they'd caught her in. It'd been a long, long time, though, since she was the one finding herself embarrassed by it, by how much of it was just a plain honest truth of a life that most sensible people thought was awful and shocking.

"No need to apologize," Winn said firmly. "Or call me *miss*. I just thought I ought to pass on what I know to help you do well when you speak to the pretty misses up there in the coach, since we're all meant to be working together. My pop always tells Mother what she ought to do when she's in society, when she doesn't know, and it saves everyone all sorts of trouble when she doesn't go about telling Assemblors that she thinks their mothers ought to have treated them with a firmer hand when they were little boys. Casts a bit of a grim shadow over a party when your mother's gone and insulted the papas of half the young gentlemen who're meant to be filling out your dance card. Especially when I've already annoyed them by being taller than them and dancing with all of the prettiest girls in the room before they can manage it. Nothing worse than a party full of long-faced, short-legged gentlemen trying to kick your ankles while you ladle punch for the girls, what?"

Delly laughed. She couldn't help it. This Winn was some sort of a creature, all right. "Don't suppose you have your eye on any of those girls to household?" Winn struck her as the independent-minded type of gull who'd much rather be the householder, even if it meant she had to find paying employment in order to provide for her lady. Delly, for her part, would much rather be the householded and be provided for: her lifetime of experience with fending for herself had firmly convinced her that independence was a wildly overrated virtue.

Winn, interestingly, went pink. "No," she said. "'Fraid the gulls mostly just like to dance with me because I lead well and don't try any funny business."

"Oh, I don't think *that* can be right," Delly said, suddenly pleased to sense that she had finally gained the upper hand. "*I'd* dance with you, Winn, if I'd ever learned any steps."

Winn looked down at her, still pink, and smiled. "I could teach you a few of those, if you like."

"I *would* like that," Delly said, meeting her gaze. She let that settle itself for a second before she moved on. Best not to come on too eager too fast and give the game away. "What was that you said about looking at the clothes to tell how much money someone has? I've never been any good at that. Girl comes by with enough ribbons stuck on and I figure her for the Queen of Awa." This wasn't, strictly speaking, an entirely pure and honest statement: Delly had a good enough eye for judging the means of a mark. She wanted to keep Winn talking to her, though, and this seemed like a fine enough way to manage it.

It did the trick: Winn dove straight off into all sorts of details about colors and stitching and the thickness of the soles of a man's shoes, about half of which was new and potentially interesting information to Delly. She filed it all away in the cluttered hatbox of her brain and focused as much as she could on listening to what Winn was saying without sliding right off of her ass and onto her ass. Then, once this well of conversation went dry, she started to pay attention to what was all around her. They were well out of the city center now, out in the endless suburbs, where all of the houses came in straight, narrow identical rows. Delly'd been out in a place like this once, to visit the home of a lady who'd acted for a few weeks like she'd like to household Delly as her daughter before Delly had gone and fucked that up. She'd hated the look of the place then, and she hated this neighborhood now. There was unreality to it, like the cheap paper dolls the warden's wife had handed Delly when she was little and waiting for her ma outside of the jail, so flimsy that you couldn't get the dress to stay on the dolly without the whole thing wilting in your hand.

Eventually they left the suburbs and started moving through what looked to Delly a hell of a lot like countryside. "This what they call nature, then?" she asked, staring at something that she figured must be a bale of hay.

"Not how I see it," Winn said, and started talking about the troll side of her family's "summer village" and the bubbling streams and mountain air and wildflowers and all. That got them onto the topic of childhood, in general, and what games they had played with other children, specifically. This kept them occupied enough for an indeterminate span, until they came upon what Delly supposed must be what they called a *quaint old-fashioned village*, and Delly's ass came to an abrupt halt outside of someplace with a sign outside that said THE WOUNDED HART.

"What's this?" Delly asked.

"Looks like an early luncheon to me," Winn said, and hopped right off of her horse like it was easy as could be, and held out a hand for Delly to help her slide off of her ass without injuring any of the asses involved in the maneuver.

Once her two feet were firmly rooted upon the dirty ground, with which she was most comfortable and accustomed, Winn gave her a quick course in how to hand her donkey over to a stable boy, who would provide for its needs—the beast fixed her with a glare for her trouble that positively *bristled* with ill intent—before they footed their way into the inn. The Fine Misses had already gone through ahead of them and passed through a door at the back of the place, probably to some nice private room with lace tablecloths where the Finest Miss could lift her seclusionary veil to nibble at little cakes without the fear of a working person seeing her face. Delly proposed this charming scene to Winn, who gave a delicate snort.

"I don't know if it's quite as nose-up as all that. She's not supposed to be distracted by men in her seclusion, and there's a specimen or two of those hereabouts. Not the type that I'd think would be too tempting to the young lady inclined toward chaste and virtuous whatsit prior to her wedding day, though. If a gull was plagued by carnal thoughts at the sight of some poor fellow mopping the floors in a roadside inn, I'd think she might want to reconsider entering into the constricting bonds of matrimony in the first place, what?"

Ermintrude was trying to catch Delly's eye: wanting her to sit with her so she'd be spared having to eat alone with her mother. Delly made a quick mental calculation. She was focusing on her prospect, sure enough, but she'd been riding with Winn for hours, and it was always better to give a mark a second to breathe if you were in it for a long game. That being settled in her mind, she gave Winn her sweetest smile and wriggled her way into a seat next to young Ermintrude. "It looks to me as if you're quite the equestrian young lady, Miss Ermintrude."

Ermintrude looked pleased, then shrugged like it didn't matter. "My sisters taught me."

"Are those the ones that also work as stagecoach guards, then?" Delly asked, and then settled into asking Ermintrude polite questions about her family and her personal interests as plates of chicken and buttered turnips were delivered to each of them, presumably at the command of the Fine Misses. Winn, Delly was interested to note, took up speaking with Mrs. Totham about birds with every indication of genuine interest in the feathered subject. Her mam being distracted, Ermintrude leaned in closer toward Delly and whispered, "Do you like the theater?"

"Oh, sure," Delly said immediately. "Always like to go see a good music-hall act. I'm partial to a bit of juggling, myself. And contortionists. It's always nice to see a young lady exert herself in a bit of healthy contortion. It makes my poor aching back feel better just looking at it."

Ermintrude leaned in closer, as if preparing to share a confidence, and said, "I like the sen bloods. I've gone to loads and loads of them. Do you ever go?"

"Er, once in a while," said Delly, who didn't particularly see the point of the things. She didn't much enjoy getting jammed in with a great lot of drunken young boys jeering at the stage while a stout middle-aged lady from West Leiscourt pretended to be a sixteen-year-old virgin and some disreputable fellow with a mustache pretended to stab her to death. "Haven't been for years, really. Any good ones showing?"

Ermintrude developed a decidedly fanatical gleam in her eye and began to describe to Delly, in great detail, one play about a fairy headman who kept dispatching his human wives with an axe and burying them under the floorboards in his castle so that they would rise again as his ghostly mistresses, followed by another in which the story of two young lovers ended in one stabbing and several long and agonizing deaths by poison, and another in which a brave troll was shot, then stabbed, then shot again before summarily rending her enemy into pieces, an event that apparently in this production involved some model limbs and great gouts of blood spurting out from behind a conveniently located boulder.

Delly gave the remaining bits of chicken on her plate a mournful glance—she would have had the appetite to eat it, once, but that time was buried somewhere along with the ghost mistresses under the floorboards now—and said, "That all does sound as if it must have a very exciting influence upon the viewer, Miss Ermintrude."

"It *does*," Ermintrude said. Then she added, with a frown, "Except the one that I saw about a cloved woman. It wasn't at *all* realistic."

Delly was spared from having to formulate a reasonable response to that sudden twist in Ermintrude's standards of theater criticism by the Fine Misses sweeping back through the room to return to their carriage. The rest of their group trailed after them and scrambled back onto their respective horrible animals, and after a brief interlude of everyone trying to convincingly pretend that they were too ladylike to curse over encounters with bloody-minded beasts or newly formed blisters, they were off.

Delly and Winn were riding together at the back again, and they had a bit of a quiet jaw to recount their meals with Mother and Daughter Totham. It turned out that Winn knew a thing or two about the birds in the northern hill counties they were traveling toward, courtesy of her own mother, so she and Mrs. Totham had gotten along all right. Delly relayed the plots of Ermintrude's sen bloods, which made Winn laugh. They kept chatting off and on as they rode, sometimes coming up with topics to try to amuse each other, sometimes lapsing into a silence that was, if not altogether comfortable, also not particularly bothersome.

During the quiet interludes, Delly looked about herself, enjoying the change of scenery. Everything looked like the pastoral prints her landlady had hanging in the bar. Delly could practically taste the gin. She was staring at a cow and pondering whether the beast was likely to be more or less of a nasty-minded and deceitful personage than the average horse when she heard a startled screech from up ahead.

Winn, next to her, said, "What in the—*fiddle-faddle* is *that* blinkin' thing?" and pulled a pistol out of her riding habit before kicking her horse into a gallop and charging forward into the chaos. Delly thought she would like just as well to hang back and figure out what in the releft was going on before she plunged headlong into it, but it was no good: the donkey, true to its wretched nature, went stubbornly galloping after Winn. Delly clung desperately to the pommel of her saddle and felt fairly certain that she would at any moment be forced to encounter her no-doubt deeply disappointed ancestors among the releft. If she didn't die from being kicked off of this donkey, she would almost certainly be killed by the massive mechanical spider currently advancing upon her employer's carriage.

4

Wherein Dellaria Is Frightened, Injured,
and Astounded, and Intensifies Her Flirtatious
Efforts to Some Good Effect

The *thing* that was currently advancing upon Miss Wexin's carriage was among the worst things that Dellaria had ever been unfortunate enough to clap her eyes upon. It was something like a bucket if buckets were lobsters, and something like a lobster if lobsters were murderous. It creaked and clanked and groaned its way toward the carriage as if it had been constructed out of rusty scraps, but it advanced at such a horrible speed that it seemed certain that whatever wizard had called the vile thing into being was as rich in viciousness as they were poor in building material of any quality. It was, in short, *absolutely fucking awful,* a fact that did nothing to stop Delly's wretched steed from barreling straight toward it in pursuit of the equally wretched Winnifer, who as she drew closer had begun to fire at the thing with her pistol.

This all, Delly thought, was really not the fucking ticket. Then things only grew worse, as ahead of her Ermintrude leapt off of the back of her horse with far greater force than a young girl should ever be able to naturally achieve, and, in midair, began to transform. There was a great rending of fabric, a rain of frills, and a horrid twisting of flesh, and in the next instant, the great white tusked pig that stood at the center of the road gave a loud growl and charged.

At this, Delly's ass, which had previously been so determined to follow Winn to the very brink, decided to think better of its policy and dart in the opposite direction and away from whatever the fuck was happening before them. This, as far as Delly was concerned, wasn't on the damn afternoon's playbill: she couldn't be caught running away from the action like a coward before she'd had so much as a single free supper out of the venture. She hauled hard at the bridle, which, though it didn't stop the beast, seemed to slow it down for a moment, at which point she tried to emulate Ermintrude by leaping off of its back.

This went about as well as a reasonable person might imagine. Delly leapt, and her foot got caught in the stirrup. She went crashing into the ground, tearing up her hands and giving her nose a good wallop, and was like to be dragged to an inelegationary death when she remembered that she was a fire witch and melted through the stirrup the instant before the donkey bolted off in sheer terror.

Delly lay facedown in the dirt for a while in quiet consideration of the choices that had led her to this juncture. She imagined that most of them had been very grievous sins indeed. She lay there through the growlings and bangings and shoutings of the battle, until she heard a particularly loud shriek and the crunch of ripping and tearing wood, and reluctantly hoisted her weary corpse skyward to have a look around.

It wasn't looking as if things were going all that relefting well. Winn was reloading her pistol, and Ermintrude—or the pig that had previously been Ermintrude—was creating a terrible din by tearing at the spider's metal legs with her tusks, as the creature itself clambered into the coach through the splintered door and the coachman frantically endeavored to convince the panicked horses to drag the coach forward on a clearly broken wheel. Then there was an almighty boom, and a flash of light, and the spider-thing was blown through the air, landing about twenty feet from the coach and sending Ermintrude tumbling head over trotters. A moment later, Miss Wexin came stumbling out of the coach and sent another bolt of white light after the creature before she collapsed to the ground.

It was seeing this that finally spurred Delly into action. Battles with eldritch wizard-made abominations were all very well, but not when they threatened to kill the woman whom Delly was meant to be guarding before Delly had been paid. So she took off running toward the spider-thing, which was attempting to right itself by wriggling its great long wriggly legs about in a truly horrible manner. Delly ran up until she was close enough to grab ahold of one of the legs, focused her entire self upon the task, did her best to rattle off the right parameters to keep from setting her dress on fire, and *melted*.

She had melted largish metal things before, but nothing quite *this* large, and nothing at all that gave her such a nauseous, twisted-up feeling to touch. It was *wrong*, this thing, a bunch of healthy ordinary metal scraps infused with something that *shouldn't exist*, and after Delly finished melting all the way through the center of the thing where the evil was the most thick and clotted, its horrible legs finally stopped wriggling, and Delly stepped back and fell to her knees and was sick right on top of its wicked metal corpse.

Someone called out, "Couldn't you have done that a bit *sooner*, Wells?" Delly opened her mouth to object, but only croaked a bit.

"A little less of that, Dok," Winn said from close at hand. "Blinking bad form to criticize a gull when she's just saved your skirts from peril and then been sick." There was something cool and wet and refreshing at the back of Delly's neck for a moment, and then Winn was crouching down next to her and offering her a canteen of water and a wet handkerchief. "We all owe you our thanks," she said. "We'd all be in a dense thicket now without you."

Delly found herself blushing. She wasn't at all accustomed to having done the right thing at all, let alone to being so kindly tended to and complimented about it. She attempted to make herself less repulsive with the water and wet handkerchief, then allowed Winn to help her to her feet. She thought that despite her embarrassment over having just vomited all over a dead spider-thing she might take this opportunity for a bit of romantic squinting up into Winn's eyes. It was the sort of thing that seemed to work for gulls in bad plays, at least. It wasn't to be, though: Winn's attention was somewhere else.

Delly followed her gaze and saw what she was looking at. Miss Wexin, still unconscious, with her veil removed, was being cradled in the arms of Miss Usad, who looked . . . different. Not just bespectacled, which she was, but different altogether: younger and fresher, the cheeks a bit rounder and the eyes larger. Delly abruptly realized why her beauty had struck her as so uncomfortable: whatever glamor had been on her had been forcing observers to look away before anyone noticed anything unusual about her.

"But *you're* Mayelle Wexin!" Winn said suddenly to Miss Usad. "You look just like how I remember you. And she doesn't look like you a bit," she added, nodding toward the woman in Miss Usad's—Miss Wexin's—lap. This, at least, was obvious. The imposter was pale, redheaded, and very ordinary-looking: without the veil, a drunk bat would have been able to tell them apart. Winn looked a little cross. "Who in the blazes is *she*?"

"My householded younger sister," Miss Wexin said. Her voice was just as low as Winn had described it. She also looked a bit sheepish. "Her name is Ainette. She's the one who's the student at Weltsir. I'm afraid that I don't have a drop of magic in me."

"Only every *other* excellent quality," Miss Dok said stoutly. It seemed pretty clear that *she'd* been in on the secret, at least.

Miss Wexin gave her a brief smile, then continued. "She came up with the idea of switching places with me during the journey because as a wizard she'd be able to defend herself better than I could if we were to be attacked." Her expression slipped a bit then, from embarrassment to what looked like genuine worry. "I've never seen her *faint* from doing magic before. It couldn't be the *swoons*, could it?"

Mrs. Totham climbed down from her donkey—she'd kept sensibly out of the fray—and carefully knelt down at Miss Wexin's side to lay a hand on Ainette's forehead, then her chest. Ermintrude, who remained a pig, trotted quietly up to her mother's side. "It isn't the swoons," she said. "She's only exhausted herself. She'll come around in a moment, poor dear. *Miss Wells*, dear me, don't you look a sight. Come here at once, dearie!"

Dellaria, to her own bemusement, went there at once, and obediently held her torn-up hands out to be inspected. Just moving her fingers a bit hurt. Mrs. Totham seized her gently by the wrists, and there was . . . a change. Not that her hands were exactly as they'd been before she fell, but the pain stopped, and her palms went from looking raw and wet to looking more . . . crusted over. "And your poor nose," Mrs. Totham said, and touched Delly's face, and after a sharp jolt of pain, Delly could breathe properly again. "I'm afraid you'll still be a bit bruised, dear," she said.

Delly prodded gently at her working nose with one of her working fingers and beamed. "You're a blessing from God, Mrs. Totham," she said, meaning every bit of it. She was completely delighted, but there was also, for some reason, some illogical corner of her that wanted to cry. She couldn't make any sense of it, so she ignored it, which was by way of being her usual mode of doing things. Thinking too much about wanting to cry had never done her a damn bit of good, and actually crying had done her even less of it. Maybe crying was of use to the Fine Misses, but it'd only ever served to make Dellaria's sleeves damp.

Mrs. Totham beamed. "I'm very glad to be of any help that I can," she said. "It's lovely to be appreciated." Then she leaned forward and added, in a conspiratorial sort of way, "If only my own daughters appreciated my efforts so much!"

Ermintrude, at this, grunted and pushed at her mother with her snout. Mrs. Totham looked down at her and patted her head. "There's no use in your getting annoyed by my paying attention to other people, young lady. You always *do* get cross when I offer to help you with a cramp."

Delly eyed Ermintrude, who was presently rubbing her tusks in the dirt. "How long are you planning on staying like that, then?"

Ermintrude gave a scornful grunt.

Winn frowned. "I don't know if that's quite etiquette, what?"

Delly frowned back. "If *what's* quite etiquette?"

"Asking how long someone's going to be a pig," Winn said. "Seems a very personal question. Like asking a lady her age."

"I think it's a fu—very well *relevant* question," Delly said, indignant. "How're we going to get her back onto a horse if she's a pig?"

"We could strap her on, I suppose," Winn said, though she looked doubtful about it.

"Oh, there's no need for that, she'll run along on her own," Mrs. Totham said cheerfully. "She can achieve quite *remarkable* speeds on her own trotters." Then she added, "And she generally doesn't understand most questions that are posed to her while she's in this state, I'm afraid. She mainly responds to the *tone*."

"Oh," Delly said. Winn walked over to speak with the coachman then, and after a moment she lifted up the coach a bit, casual-like, so that he could finish getting the broken wheel fixed back in its place. Sakes. Not something Delly minded seeing, in a gull.

Miss Dok was giving Delly a speculative look. "Are you trained at all as a wizard? That was an impressive bit of work you did just now."

"Thank you," Delly said, her whole face gone hot. She gave a moment of consideration to the thought of lying, and then gave the thought up: she wanted these people to trust her, and any wizard paying close attention was likely to figure it out eventually, or at least a part of it. "I was one of that class of Lord Rett's students at Weltsir five years back."

It'd been a real sort of sensation, when it happened. In the papers and all. After it got out that the old Lord-Mage of Hexos had been some kind of street urchin, and his successor a clanless girl from Daeslund's North Country who'd gotten rejected from Weltsir—probably because she was a clanless girl from the relefted North Country—this prick named Lord Rett had gone all ingenious and decided he was going to prove that magical educations were best kept for the upper classes by getting his associates to pull a few magically inclined kids out of the sewer, bring them to Weltsir, and see whether or not they'd be able to learn to be wizards. He'd won all the bets he placed, sure enough. Most of the kids had left after a day or two: couldn't understand what in the world the lecturers were going on about. Delly'd hung on a year. A whole entire tit-sucking year she'd made it through, and then got kicked out after a senior student found her passed-out drunk in the library. One year. She'd learned some, sure. There was a reason she was the best fire witch in Leiscourt. She hadn't learned enough to keep herself in long enough to graduate, though. Just like that Lord Rett had figured. Blood told in the end.

Miss Dok's eyebrows were up near her hairline. "You're one of *those*," she said. "That makes sense."

Delly's whole body went hot. Then, suddenly, Winn was standing there. "Steady on, Dok," she said. "Not really the blinking sort of *thing*, is it? Not in line with Elgar's sacred whatsit of respect to your fellows, saying that someone's *one of those*."

Delly felt her innards unknot a bit. Miss Dok gave her pretty dark eyes a roll. "I only meant that I'd never heard of a fire witch who could direct heat like that, just onto one discrete target. She's obviously had some training in academic magic." She looked at Delly then. "What sort of parameters do you use for that?"

"Uh," Delly said. "Modified Reclid's channel. I had to write it up myself, a bit, since they don't got, uh, any kind of established parameters for fire witches. Once I'd used it a few times, it turned into a kind of—habit, I guess. I don't need to incant for it." That wouldn't make any sense to an academic wizard, but she'd accept it from a fire witch. They were supposed to be incorrigible gutterwitches, untrainable and instinct-driven, like alley cats. And dangerous, when they were as powerful as Delly was. Not that many people were.

"How clever," Miss Dok said. The way in which she said it made it hard to tell whether she was sincere about it. Probably not. Academic wizards were never impressed by gutterwitchery, no matter how clever and inventive it might be. "You must tell me about how you altered the Reclid's, sometime. I should be very interested to learn more about your . . . methodology." Then she gave a little smile and walked off a few steps to rejoin Miss Wexin. The imposter looked like she was waking up.

"Don't move about too much, Ainette," said the elder Wexin. Mayelle, who had previously been the beautiful Miss Usad and who was now revealed to be the equally beautiful Miss Mayelle Wexin, future Lady Crossick. Some people, Delly reckoned, must have to buy extra luggage for carrying all of their luck around with them. "You've just fainted."

The younger Wexin—Ainette, it was—cracked one eye open. It was a very bright blue. "What happened? Is it dead?"

"Miss Wells melted it," said Miss Mayelle. "We're all perfectly safe." Then, without looking up, "Boggs? Have you put the coach right?"

"Yes, miss," said the coachman in a very respectful tone. "As best as I could, miss. With the help of Miss Cynallum, miss."

Delly, for all that she ought to be used to it, was struck by how different the bowing and scraping looked from this new angle. From the vantage point of the *miss* instead of the *you, girl.* There was no time to stew in it, though. People were clambering back up into the carriage, and Winn was galloping off to retrieve Delly's ass from the field it was presently standing in, eating grass. They were, in short order, on the road again, with Delly's ass trailing after Winn just as if nothing at all had happened.

"You were right," Delly said after a while. "She *was* an imposter."

Winn gave her a quick smile. "I have a decent bit of space in the old brainpan for remembering people I met at parties as a mere slip of a six-foot-odd young girl," she said. "And it looks as if it all has a perfectly reasonable explanation to it, what?"

"It does look like that," Delly said. They went quiet then, for a while. Delly was developing an increasing awareness of every ache and pain in her body that hadn't been resolved by Mrs. Totham's quick work. She was thinking about that spider-thing and the horrible way she'd felt when she'd touched it. Wrong. It had been *wrong*.

"Are you all right, Delly?" Winn asked. "You're shaking."

"I ain't shaking," Delly said, and gripped harder at the pommel.

"All right," Winn said. "Well. If you *do* start shaking, let me know so that I can help. I wouldn't like to see you falling off again."

Delly didn't know what to feel about that. Maybe she was meant to feel grateful, but she didn't feel fucking grateful. She felt worn-out and aching and sick to her damned stomach, and sicker of having to mind herself around these rich high-class gulls. Sick to death of it, and it had barely been half a day since this entire venture had gotten started. She groaned under her breath, then tried to steady herself a little. It was just two weeks, that was all. Two weeks, and a big fat pile of cash, and she'd be living easy until the next time she managed to approach the smooth-running train of her life and herd a flock of sheep onto the tracks.

Delly stopped paying attention to the world around her for a while, finding herself trapped instead in the hot, crowded room of her body. Her hands ached, and her head pounded, and the afternoon sun heated the top of her head and the back of her neck until she imagined that if she dunked her head into a pond the water would hiss and sizzle. The atmosphere around her was enduring a process of ongoing endonkey-fication, until she began to imagine that even the rare cooling winds blowing in from the east smelled of hot barnyard. She kept thinking about how that thing had felt as she'd melted it. It was wrong. It was wrong. It *shouldn't exist*.

She didn't notice herself sliding off of the donkey's back until she found herself suspended, briefly, in midair, before Winn carefully planted her back into the saddle. "Not quite time for bed yet," Winn said with an alarming degree of jolliness. "Just another hour or so and then it's nothing but wine, song, and goose-down pillows, what?"

"If you say so," Delly said, rattled. "Thanks for keeping me out of the dirt." She'd never been a fainting sort of gull in her life, not even when she'd lived for days on nothing but gin fumes and spite. She pinched the inside of her elbow by way of delivering a stern warning to her own rebellious carcass, and kept pinching herself at intervals until they finally, finally came to a halt, just as the sun was starting to go down.

Winn had to help her down off of the donkey, Delly's stinking old corpse having gone rigid over the course of the past few hours. Then there was all of the bother of having to get the sinful-minded animal all fed and watered and bedded down for the night, until Delly was finally able to hobble her way into the dark, cramped little pub where they'd be spending the night.

There was food at least, once they were inside: a choice of kidney pie or an oxtail-and-vegetable stew. The Misses Wexin—the younger now deviled and ambulatory—gave their regrets and hurried off to their room to dine alone. Delly, for her part, settled down at a table in the dining room to have a big slice of kidney pie. She also ordered and received a beautifully frothing pint of beer to go with it, which she hoisted aloft in order to toast Miss Cynallum and the rest of the assembled ladies. "To our continued survival, then."

Miss Dok, who had deigned to dine with the inferior elements this evening, pursed her lips. Winn gave Delly a smile. "I'll have a swallow to that," she said, and ordered a bottle of hock and a siphon.

That was enough to set off the rest of them: Miss Dok consented to a glass of wine, and even the Tothams had a little nip of sherry each. Soon enough, though, they'd all packed themselves up into their rooms like heavy woolens put away for the summer. Then it was only Delly and Winn left, as cozy as could be in the nook they'd claimed for themselves in a corner, drinking and looking at each other. They'd be sharing a room tonight: hadn't even had to check with each other before they reached for the same key when Miss Dok handed them out. Maybe Winn had just figured that the Tothams would be with each other and Miss Dok would bunk with the Wexins. She hoped it was a bit more than just that, though.

"Don't your parents worry about your gallivanting?" Delly asked eventually. She hadn't any experience in having parents who'd fret over her gallops and gallivants, but she'd heard, at least, that it was something over which parents of young ladies might work themselves up into a real briny foam. "Not the sort of thing that young ladies do, is it, shooting horrible big metal spider-things with pistols," she said, and then immediately started trying to reel her words back down her gullet by adding, "That is what I imagine might be the opinion of many parents, I mean, and not the opinion of myself."

Winn's eyes had gone all crinkled up at her over the rim of her glass, which Delly couldn't help but interpret in a positive light. "I'm afraid that my mother would rather have me out gallivanting than safely at home learning all of the airs and graces she failed to teach me when I was a mere scrap. Pop does fret a little, though. He'd like me to be the mistress of a girls' school or go to work at his shipping company, something nice and reliable like that."

"Doesn't sound too bad to me," Delly said after another swallow of beer. "Why not?"

"Oh, itchy feet, I suppose," Winn said. "Troll blood and all that, born to wander, what? Pop always talks as if he went straight from school into a sober clerkship, the great blinking fraud. He was poor and saw the world and got into scrapes when he was young. Why shouldn't I?"

"Because it's fuckin' awful," Delly said. "With my many apologies for my language, but being poor and living in nasty dirty places where you don't have any choice *except* to meet a whole motley assortment of odd birds with peculiar habits isn't the first thing like going on a nice jolly wander off to Esiphe to see the ancient wonders and eat foods with new and interesting vegetables in 'em. Begging your pardon again." Her face felt a little warm.

"Well, that's true," Winn said after a moment. "This has all been good fun so far, but only because I know that if I wanted to I could send for Mother or Pop and have one of them come rescue me from the sloughs of fleabite and blinkin' indigestion."

"I think that those sloughs might be my mother's native land," Delly said. "She certainly seems comfortable enough in 'em."

Winn laughed, and Delly laughed, too, even though it hadn't really been a joke, at least not completely. Her whole body was gently throbbing. She said, "Aw, God's tits. I'm off to bed."

Winn gave her a nod and lifted her glass in a small salute. "I'll be up in three ticks," she said, and Delly was forced to hobble her way up the stairs on her own.

The room in the dumpy little inn would probably look like a real example of the slough to Winn, Delly thought. Which was a pretty unfortunate realization to have made, because, regrettably, it was a considerable span nicer than the room Delly lived in normally. Brighter, cleaner, and set more plumb, with a fireplace with a sturdy armchair beside for toasting your toes in the winter and a good new-looking washstand with a steaming pitcher set on it. Delly gave her hands, face, and particulars a scrub—no matter how bad things got, she never liked to let her particulars go unwashed—and then stripped down to her chemise and picked the less-comfortable-looking bed in the room to squeeze her weary bones into.

Winn was up not long after, and there were the usual rustlings and splashings of a gull getting ready for bed. Delly kept her eyes closed until she figured the danger had passed of her seeing her prospect pissing in a pot before they'd reached that wearied point in their acquaintanceship. When she dared to peep again, there Winn stood, resplendent and broad-shouldered in a frilly nightgown the likes of which Delly'd never seen outside of a fashion plate.

Delly laughed. She couldn't help it. She'd never seen such a thing in all her days. Never been with a gull who'd be able to afford such a trifle, and never thought to stretch a trifle like it over the frame of such a monumental gull, like an elephant in a pinafore. She regretted the laughter the instant it leaked out of her, fearing that Winn would be offended, but Winn only grinned back. "Jolly unnerving sort of thing, being laughed at this late in the evening." She sat down on the edge of her bed. "What's so funny?"

"Just," Winn began. "Nothing. Only all the ribbons and things."

"Oh, *those*," Winn said. "Ginny of you to laugh when I sewed them on myself. Part of the courses at Miss Belvin's School for Young Ladies, what? It was nightgowns or tablecloths, so I thought that I'd be better off equipping myself with something I'd be able to put to use."

"Sakes," Delly said. "You really made that yourself?"

"And a whole bushelful of others," Winn said. "My mother is always unconventional, to humans and to trolls both, but she's *very* strict when it comes to my knowing how to take care of myself, whether that's conventional or not. So I learned how to embroider a dress, catch a fish, bake a loaf of bread, and throw a punch, and I'm jolly glad for all of the education now, even though I always whined and sulked over the embroidery."

"Not over the fisticuffs, though?"

"Oh, no," Winn said, and got into bed. "I always thought that that part was fun. Good night, Delly."

"Good night, Winn," Dell said, and they put the lamps out.

They were woken up in the middle of the night by screaming.

They both went half jolting, half lurching out of their beds, but within about half a second Winn was already bolting out the door in the direction of the screams—the Wexins' room, just beside theirs—while Delly was still half-prone and all-hoping that this might turn out to have nothing to do with their traveling companions and she would be able to go back to sleep in a moment. Then, a moment later, she was up, too. The screams had only gotten louder, and she didn't figure anyone would want to pay a salary to a gull who lazed around in bed while her employer was being violently murdered in the next room over, to say nothing of the difficulty of paying anyone a salary when one had recently been the victim of said murder.

When she finally stumbled into the room, it took her a few moments to comprehend what was happening. Miss Mayelle was standing on a stool in the corner of the room, screaming, as Miss Dok and Winn fought off more creatures like the spider-thing that had attacked them earlier in the day. Miss Mayelle was bleeding from a cut to her neck. Her sister, the useless fucking trout, was unconscious on the floor.

These things seemed even more *wrong* than that horrible thing from before, though it took Delly a moment to realize what the matter was. It was as if they'd been made too hastily. They were much smaller than the other one, about the size of cats, but while the big one had looked very much like a spider, these things were like a child's drawing of the same: some with too many legs and some too few, some dragging one end along the ground as they advanced, some moving in odd jittery hops. It turned Delly's stomach to look at them.

Miss Dok successfully exploded one and gave a muffled shout that soon turned into a groan. The center of it was still rocking back and forth on the floor, still trying to get to Miss Mayelle, even though its legs were spread to the four fucking corners of the room and it couldn't go anywhere at all. The sight of that—the sheer fucking repulsiveness of it—was what finally sprang Delly into action. "Right, you lot get their legs off and I'll melt the bodies," she said, and set to work.

It was almost easy, once they had a plan. Miss Dok blasted the things with magic, Winn bashed them with a fireplace poker, and once they were incapacitated, Delly melted the little bastards. Then, just as they were nearing the end, Mrs. Totham came charging into the room. "Capture one!" she cried out. "Capture one, please! We need to examine it!"

"Bugger *that* up a tree," Delly said, and melted the thing in front of her.

"Right," Winn said, and bashed the last one with the poker to break its last working legs, grabbed it with her bare hand, and shoved it into a pillowcase she'd just snatched off of the nearest bed. Then she held it at arm's length, grimacing as it thrashed around. "And if you don't mind, Mrs. Totham, I think we'd all prefer it if you were a bit hasty with your examinations so that Delly can go ahead and melt it back to its first reliving."

"Oh, of course, of course," Mrs. Totham twittered, and took the writhing bundle from Winn.

Delly's eyes focused in on Winn's hand, which was dripping blood. "You're hurt," she said uselessly.

"Those things have mouths like razors," Miss Dok said. "If Mayelle hadn't woken up and jumped just in time . . ."

Miss Mayelle, who had just clambered down from her stool, was shaking. Mrs. Totham's voice, on the other hand, was steady as could be when she said, "Oh, dear. How very terrible."

"What?" Delly said. She never had much patience for anyone taking a long time to line up their dramatic statements before they took the shot.

"I must remind you that I am a *body scientist*," Mrs. Totham said. "And like most body scientists, I am strictly opposed to the abuse of the field in any way. With that said, this thing would seem—I am very afraid to say—to be the result of illegal necromancy."

"What does that mean?" Delly asked. She was starting to feel sick again.

"Well," Mrs. Totham said, "instead of the magic that has brought them to life coming from the wizard who created them, it has come from an outside source."

"Such as?" Winn asked. The room had gone very still.

"In this case, a cat," Mrs. Totham said, and closed her eyes. The wriggling lump in the blanket went abruptly still. Mrs. Totham shivered. "Oh, dear," she murmured. "The poor thing was so terribly afraid."

5

Wherein Suspicions Are Raised, Many Miles
Are Traveled, and Dellaria Is Disappointed by
the Moral Fiber of Her Betters

It was pretty damn uncomfortable trying to get to sleep after that.
Using more magic after such a long day of it left Delly feeling simultaneously sapped and jittering, as if she'd been drinking strong coffee
on an empty stomach. Her aches only got worse, too. She got back into
bed and just lay there awake, occasionally rolling from side to side like
a sausage being cooked. She felt as if she'd been cooked altogether too
well. Her brain was full of dead cats and metal spiders, and the growing light in the room didn't do a damn thing to diminish them, just
filled her with a greater dread that soon she'd have to be up and con-
fronting yet another wretched fucking day.

She might have dozed off for a while. When she woke up again, it
was still in the darkish hours of the morning when it was impossible
to do anything but worry. In the heart of the dimness sat Winn, very
upright and quiet in the chair in front of the cold fireplace.

"All right there, Winn?" Delly asked.

Winn jolted slightly. "Oh, fine," she said. There was a moment of
quiet. Then she said, "I miss my pop. Bit embarrassing, what? A big
girl like me. But I do miss him."

"That doesn't sound embarrassing to me," Delly said. "Just sounds nice. Having someone to miss, I mean."

"Maybe it is," Winn said after a moment. "It still feels blinking dreadful, though."

"I'm not too surprised to hear it," Delly said. "Most things are pretty dreadful, I'd say."

That was the end of their conversation that morning. They both got dressed and went downstairs, where they breakfasted on bread smeared with dripping and a bit of cress. Miss Dok came down before the Wexin girls, and Delly took the opportunity to put a question to her. "Who the fuck hates Mayelle Wexin so much that he'd want to kill her with a bunch of disgusting metal undead cat-spider-things?"

Miss Dok got a lemon-licking look to her. "You're speaking out of turn, Miss Wells."

"Then I am, too," Winn said. "None of us were told to expect anything like those things attacking us yesterday. If we're supposed to be defending Miss Wexin from her enemies, I think that we at least ought to be told who those enemies are, instead of being forced to fire bullets into the bleeding darkness. Rather brings down company morale to have to wage war against invisible necromancers for no real *reason*, what?"

Miss Dok pinched up her lips. Then she said, "It oughtn't make a difference to your carrying out your duties."

"And yet it does," Winn said right back. "And so I suppose that we've reached some sort of impasse. You could tell us and resolve our curiosity, or keep on withholding information that may turn out to be the difference between life and death for us and wait to see whether or not it will prevent us from protecting Miss Wexin to the best of our abilities."

Miss Dok gave her eyes a big roll. "For God's sake, it really oughtn't make a difference," she said. "But if you really must be difficult about it, I'll tell you now that we don't know. Mayelle received letters threatening her against the marriage, first, and then the attacks started. Mr. Crossick—Mayelle's fiancé—did have some trouble with a woman who misinterpreted his intentions toward her a year ago, but that's all long since over. Mayelle also has an uncle who's a bit fanatical about Old Land Elgarism and doesn't approve of the match, but that's hardly reason to engage in necromancy and attempted murder. It's really all such an annoying muddle," she added, as if she thought that attempted necromantic murder was something like trying to organize your notes the week before an exam.

"Does sound a little gin-faced," Delly allowed after a moment. "I'd bet on the misinterpreted woman." In her experience, a man who allowed that sort of *misinterpretation* to come about deserved all of the attempted murders that he got, though she'd never understood why the victim of the misinterpretation would take out her understandable ire on the new gull and not the two-faced barnfucker responsible for the problem in the first place.

"I'd bet on the uncle," Winn said. "I never trust fanatical types, m'self. Find them generally likely to give you alarming pamphlets and set public buildings alight."

"There's no need for anyone to bet on anything," Miss Dok said briskly. "We'll be arriving at Crossick Manor this evening, and once we're there, we'll only have to wait until the wedding. The manor wards prevent any magic worked from the outside from entering without the permission of the master of the house, so as long as we can keep anyone from climbing in through the windows at night we'll be quite safe, and the wedding will be held, and we'll all be able to get back to our normal occupations."

"Those of us who have one of those, at least," Delly muttered.

Winn piped up again then. "I don't know that I agree," she said.

Miss Dok raised her eyebrows. "You don't know that you agree about what?"

"That it will all resolve so simply," Winn said. "It seems to me that anyone who's willing to engage in necromancy in order to kill a young girl two weeks before her wedding isn't all that likely to be put off by the prospect of a bit of cat burglary, what?"

Delly cast her an admiring glance for her perceptiveness, but any more conversation on this count was cut off by the arrival of the rest of the women. For the first time, Delly found herself seated beside Ainette Wexin, who was being fussed over by the company on the subject of her fainting spells.

"I'm sure that it must be the wizard swoons," her sister said. "You really must stop using magic. It can't possibly be good for you."

"It's not the swoons, Mayelle," Ainette said, with a smile at her sister. "That's contracted in childhood, for one thing. I think that I'm just a bit run-down. The country air will do me good."

"I could examine you," said Mrs. Totham. "It might be something more pernicious that you haven't yet considered."

"Oh, no, no, thank you," Ainette said in a firm tone. "You needn't bother, Mrs. Totham. I'll be much better once we're off the road and I can rest."

That seemed to serve as the group's cue, as everyone stood at the same time and filed out. Then there was the usual fuss with the donkey—at a certain point Winn was forced to intercede and coax the beast out of its stall—and eventually they were off again, Delly trying not to allow her groans of discomfort to grow too loud and distracting. She didn't want Winn to come away with a poor impression of what Delly's moans could sound like when she was at her best.

They rode for several hours without major incident, then stopped for lunch at a little place without so much as a single other customer in it, just one sleepy-looking man to serve the beer and an equally sleepy-looking little orange cat walking to and from the kitchen. Once they'd eaten, they got back up into the saddle again, and Delly's braying reprobate of a donkey decided to go ambling around to the back of the inn instead of the front, where Delly saw the crumpled figure of the little orange cat on the ground, its fur matted with blood.

Delly swallowed. Then she whispered, "C'mon, fella, time to follow Winn again," and managed, despite herself, to urge the donkey back to rejoin the rest of the group.

She and Winn ended up near the rear of the assemblage again, and she leaned in to murmur to her. "Did you notice who all went back to the privy just now?"

Winn raised her eyebrows. "I'd have to suspect that practically everyone used the privy, after all that beer, though that's a bit of a delicate question to ask about a lady, what? Why do you ask?"

Delly explained, as quietly as she could, about the dead cat. Winn went very still for a moment. Then she said, "I suppose that I owe an apology to the blinkin' fanatical uncle." She paused. "Who do you think we ought to worry about?"

"Dok and the sister," Delly said. "They both know her. Or the Tothams could be hired on by someone. And Mrs. Totham's a necromancer, so she'd be the likeliest to know how to extract the spirit from a cat." Then she added, "Or I could be the one."

"Or I," Winn said. "But I don't think that you're a murderer."

"Pretty generous of you," Delly said. "I won't say that I *wouldn't* attempt a murder, if enough money was offered."

"And that's why I don't think that you're a murderer," Winn said. "I imagine that any personage who wanted to murder someone would be unlikely to put themselves forward as a suspect just out of a sense of fair play, what?"

"I don't have the sense of fair play that God gave weasels," Delly said. She was blushing, which she found somewhat confounding. "So what do we do now?"

"Watch and wait, I think," Winn said. "And have your melting hand ready."

They watched and waited and rode in silence for a while. This time, when the attack came, the others barely had time to react before Delly and Winn had set upon the creature. It was, partly, simply easier this time; this thing was more hastily constructed than any that had come before: it was clearly and evidently a rough assemblage of buckets and horseshoes and other spare parts barely held together with magic and the fury of the poor dead animal. Winn smashed it apart a bit with a poker—Delly had a brief amused moment of imagining where she'd stolen it from and how she'd smuggled it out—and Delly melted it, and then everything went quiet.

"It was another cat," said Mrs. Totham.

"Yeah," Delly said. "We had a suspicion of the same." Then she looked about herself a bit. Everyone was present and accounted for except for the Wexins and Miss Dok, who a moment later popped her head out of the carriage. "Could you please come here, Mrs. Totham? Ainette has fainted again."

Winn and Delly exchanged a glance and then whispered to each other. "Funny how she's started fainting without having used any magic at all, what?" Winn said.

"Convenient," Delly murmured back. "How she's always unconscious just when we might need a bit of assistance preventing her sister from being killed by a murderous spider bucket."

"Or it could just be a coincidence," Winn said. "Maybe she faints when she's nervous."

"Nervous flaming," Delly muttered. "Fucking likely." Then she added, "We ought to keep an eye on her when we get to that manor."

"I'll agree to that," Winn said. "I didn't take on this job just to be an unwitting assistant to a sororicide, what?"

"I'll agree to that," Delly said, and they exchanged a quick handshake before they rode on.

By the time they were in sight of the manor it was getting dark, which made it a little difficult to get a good clear look at the place. Delly had imagined some sort of foreboding old ruinous place, probably because she read too many cheap horror novels. From what she could see it was pretty and well kept up enough, broad and white and thickly speckled and coiffed with windows and chimneys, with a wide, sweeping lawn in front like they had in the kinds of novels that Delly usually got bored of halfway through because she couldn't keep all of the lords and ladies straight.

They rode up the broad driveway toward the house, and before they'd reached it they were waylaid by a gangly fellow—a footman, Delly thought, that seemed about the thing, or maybe a butler—with a grim look to his face, who quickly set to attempting to split them up between the quality ladies and the dirt-common girls. Delly was sorted with the Tothams and was in the process of being steered toward the servants' entrance when Winn put her foot down. "I'll just be going with them, then, if we're going to be split up. Not good for company morale to have half of our comrades drinking gruel in the cellar and the rest eating Esiphian cakes in the blinkin' drawing room, what?"

For a moment Delly was the appreciative audience to a tableau: Quality Young Ladies Feeling Wretchedly Uncomfortable on Manor Lawn. Then Miss Mayelle said, "I'm afraid that Lady Crossick has only expected four guests for dinner, and an added three might put her out considerably. Perhaps all of us could retire to the small parlor together after we've dined?"

"Not the drawing room, then," Winn said, whatever in the releft *that* meant.

"Oh, please, Cynallum, you're only making yourself difficult," Dok said. "If you drag Wells into the dining room and put out Mayelle's mother-in-law, you'll accomplish nothing to advance your Adaptivist politics and everything to make Lady Crossick hostile, which will ruin all of our digestions for the evening and probably embarrass Wells exceedingly. She won't even be able to dress for it, for God's sake. Let us bear the personality of Mayelle's future mother-in-law while you enjoy a pleasant meal downstairs, and then we can all gather in the small parlor for sherry and gossip while free of unpleasant relations, like civilized people."

Winn looked a bit pink in the cheeks, which Delly found fairly fucking endearing. No one had ever tried to fight a high-quality gull to defend Delly's honor before. It was a pleasant sort of feeling, even if it had been a misguided attempt: Delly'd been trotted out before rich old ladies before and hated every second of it. How the hell could anyone's guts work right with some superior creature in silk wincing over their table manners while they tried to eat a nice slice of ham?

"Sounds all right to me," Delly said, in a nice loud, booming voice. That was enough to rattle the quality ladies free of their stalemate and allow the gangly fellow to continue his herding. Winn, the stubborn beast, went along with the common-as-dirt gulls as they walked around to the back of the house. Her presence earned her a glare from the Herding Gangle, who leaned in to whisper to Delly, "Don't see how we're meant to sit and eat with a clanner at the table." He had a nice lilting Gally accent that made her think of misty shores and fresh fish. Not that she'd ever been to the Gallen Islands, but she'd seen a play set there once, and it sounded like it might be a nice place for a holiday, if you were the sort of person who had those.

"Just pretend she ain't a clanner," Delly whispered back. "It'll be good for her. She's not a bad sort of gull."

"Oh, no," murmured the Gangle. "She's one of those nice Adaptivists. Probably brings food baskets to the poor sometimes and tells her friends about how we're all equal in the eyes of God and doesn't know how to manage a staff properly." Then he gave Delly a nod. "Jok Fairnbrook."

"Delly Wells," Delly told him. She didn't mind a tall, dark-eyed ironical fellow, not a bit. She had to remind herself that she was pursuing a prospect and keep her eyes up at the face level.

"Welcome to the lion's den, Miss Wells," Fairnbrook said, and gave her a little wink. Then he said, "You don't seem like you're in service."

"Not a day in my life," Delly said. "And not a respectable bone in my carcass. What makes the ladies and gentlemen lions, then?"

"That's what I like to hear," Fairnbrook said. "And they're all at each other's throats. Half of 'em think that this Wexin girl's not good enough for 'em. Going to be a bunch of miserable old prunes at that wedding, sure enough. Lady Crossick's pleased, though. The Wexin girl's father just died and left her a fortune, and this place leaks cash like a rusty bucket."

Delly rolled that round in her head like dice in her palm. "So, once she's married the money would be the Crossicks', then."

"That's right. Husband or householder gets the property."

"Mm," Delly said. Then she said, "What if she never married? Who would inherit then?"

"Closest living relative, I expect," Fairnbrook said. "Parents are both dead, so I suppose it'd be the sister. Not that the sister's got much hope of inheriting a fortune. Miss Wexin doesn't look too likely to get carried away by a fever the week before her wedding."

"No," Delly said after a moment. "Fever doesn't seem likely."

Delly practically squirmed herself into a fit during dinner, wanting to tell Winn about what she'd learned. She managed to hang on all through the bread and butter and pea soup, and then through the rice pudding and tea, until the people of the house began to rush out to serve the grander meal to the people abovestairs, and finally Delly had a moment to catch Winn alone. She relayed all of the information she'd gathered in one long rush. Winn looked grim. "Dok must know about Ainette being set to inherit before her sister marries. Why wouldn't she have said something about it sooner? She and Mayelle are thick as thieves."

"Might be in on it," Delly said. "She's chummy with both sisters."

"Or she won't believe it of Ainette, because she's chummy with both sisters," Winn said, and bit her lip. "They'll be dining with everyone else upstairs now, so she's safe for the moment, I suppose. And then we'll all be with her in the parlor."

"So it'll be later tonight, then," Delly said. "If Miss Ainette tries something else."

"*If* it's her, and if she won't wait for some time when she can get her sister alone when she's meant to be somewhere else, so no one will suspect her. You can't blinkin' well inherit a fortune if you're in Stretworth jail waiting to be hanged for murder."

"True enough," Delly said. "Nasty piece of business. Her own *sister*. Should we tell Dok?"

"I'd keep it close to our knickers, myself," Winn said. Delly tried not to look shocked at such language out of a *young lady*. Not that she didn't say worse six dozen times a day herself, but she'd always been under the impression that *young ladies* weren't supposed to know what knickers *were*, even while they were putting them on in the morning. "Just in case we're wrong, and one of the others is involved."

"Makes sense," Delly allowed. "Bleeding f—fiddle-faddle, it's enough to put you off your oats. Her *sister*."

"We don't know that for sure," Winn said. She looked pretty grave about it, though. Then she sighed, glanced about herself, and produced a pack of cigarettes from somewhere on her person. "Do you . . . ?"

"All right," Delly said, and they slipped out to smoke.

It calmed Delly's nerves a bit. At least she felt like it did, though that might have been her imagination. She nodded at Winn. "Your parents know you smoke these things?"

"You're very worried about my parents, aren't you?" Winn asked. "And whether or not I'm quite the blinkin' young lady I ought to be." Then she said, "They know. Pop smokes. I only do when I'm nervous."

"And you're nervous now?"

"Oh, no. I'm never nervous when I'm about to mingle with a murderer in a third headman's small parlor, what?"

And here Delly hadn't thought Winn had it in her to be ironical.

They stayed out there for a while. Long enough that the people upstairs had finished with their dinner and one of the parlormaids popped her head out to tell them, in tones that indicated how little she thought of them, that they were kindly invited to join the ladies in the small parlor. Delly couldn't stop herself from shaking her head. "Think it'd be a hanging offense if I said I had a headache?" she asked. "Don't think I can face that crowd at the moment."

Winn looked at her. Her expression was soft. "You look ready to drop," she said. "How about I post myself close to Mayelle for the next few hours, and I wake you up in the wee hours to take over, after you've gotten in a bit of an amble in the gardens of peaceful dreams and all of that?"

"That'd be kind of you," Delly said. "Very kind. Though I don't know if I'll drop off straightaway, after the day we've had." That cat. That damned pitiful dead cat.

"Take these, then," Winn said, and handed Delly her cigarette case. "They'll kill the time, at least." Then she said, "I'm off to strap on the old battle garments," and strode off.

"Thanks," Delly said to her back. Her throat felt tight.

She stayed right where she was, growing roots to the spot and smoking for want of something to do with her hands. Then the gangly form of Mr. Fairnbrook appeared through the kitchen door.

"All right, Miss Wells? It's getting a bit nippy out here."

"Yeah, I'm all right," Delly said. Acting concerned about her. All sorts of people making tender worried faces at her today. She didn't know why it was making her stomach clench. She offered him a cigarette. He took one, and they smoked silently together in the dark. Maybe it was just the smoking making her a bit sick.

It felt inevitable when he ground out his cigarette and gave her a sidelong look. "Don't suppose you'd be up for a bit of fun, Miss Wells?"

He did suppose, obviously. He wouldn't have asked the question of a gull he didn't suppose all sorts of things about. She couldn't bother to get all rain-drownable about it, though. He wasn't wrong. She said, "Might it so, if you got a privy bolt-for," just in case he was worried he'd been wrong about her being Wester trash up for an easy gallop.

"I know a spot," Fairnbrook said.

Delly dropped her cigarette and ground it out with her heel. "All right, then."

She'd expected a spot behind a stable or in a muddy ditch. Instead it was a house. A real little house, far finer than any place she'd ever lived, down a little path about ten minutes' walk from the manor. "The game-keeper's cottage," Fairnbrook said. "He was fired a month ago, but before he left he told me where he hid the spare key." Under a rock, it turned out. Then he let her inside and shut the door and started to kiss her.

He was a fine kisser, she thought. Nothing to set her skirt ablaze, but she'd plenty of that this week already. He kissed *kindly*, like he was saying, *I think you're worth the bother*, and she kissed back to say, *Thanks very much, and I think that you are as well.* God knew that a man in service and a piece of disrepute like Delly were used to little enough of that.

There was a bed in the house still covered by a worn quilt. He fucked her very courteously on it: took his time and knew how to use his fingers, and realized that he didn't actually know how to use his fingers when she told him so and made the needed adjustments. He was kind. She felt something big and hurt rattling out of her. She thought she could feel something like it in him, too.

They passed a cigarette back and forth after they were done. She asked, "Who're you sweet on, then?"

"Elgar, is it that easy to tell?" His accent was even broader now. Nice Gallen boy here living in a stranger's house, shining a stranger's shoes.

"A bit, yeah," Delly said. Poor thing.

Fairnbrook was quiet for a while. "Young Mr. Crossick," he said after moment.

"The one who's marrying Miss Wexin, so?" Delly asked, astonished. "Has he been—encouraging you?" She'd read about that sort of thing in novels, at least. Nice young people in service being ruined by wicked gents in grand houses. Not that fellas were ruined as easy as girls, as a rule, but the idea bothered her in any case. It occurred to Delly that Winn would be offended by it, too. Not regulation hammerball, that sort of thing. Winn cared about doing things the way that gentlepeople were *supposed* to do them, as if the rules really did apply to them, too. At least, she *acted* like she cared about doing things the right way. That was easy enough, when you weren't the one backed up to the wall by your circumstances.

"Yeah," Fairnbrook said, and cuddled up closer to her. "Well—never made any promises, did he? Not like I could give him anything that he needs." Money, kids, a higher-ranked headmanship, someone he could take out to parties who'd impress all his clanner friends. Delly knew the rules of the game all right. She petted his hair. It seemed like a thing to do. He asked, "You're going after that clanner girl? The troll?"

"Elgar, is it that obvious?" she asked. She was imitating his accent, trying to make him laugh. She wasn't sure why she was bothering, exactly. She usually didn't spend much time tending to anyone's feelings, after a gallop. But she felt something sort of tender and gentle right now, in this house, in this bed, looking at this long fellow all knotted up from the meanness of everything. She almost liked how she could see the hurt in him. Maybe she'd been like him once, a whole full barrel that someone had just stuck a tap in to drain dry. Then she figured she had to answer his question and said, "Yeah, I am. Best prospect I've ever had. Not that I've had many. Figure she'll be good for some expensive jewelry and a hearty handshake, at least, if I play it right."

"Me neither," Jok said. "I'll wish you luck, then. If you think she's all right."

"She's all right," Delly said. "It's me that's the problem." Out here galloping with strange men and talking about expensive jewelry while her big, strapping good-hearted prospect went to guard a lady from peril. What in the releft did that say about Delly's virtuous qualities? Nothing good, from what she could see.

"Only," Jok said, "won't you stay a while, maybe? Play a game of cards?"

"Might it so," Delly said, and watched as he got up and dressed, marveling a bit over this deeper trough of strangeness in a long, strange night.

Jok caught her glance then and smiled. He looked tired. "You can leave if someone will miss you," he said. "Only I thought we might try to have a laugh while we have the chance."

"No one will miss me," Delly said. She could always say *that* with confidence, at least. "And you're right. Might as well have a cackle while we can." You always took your chances when you could, she figured. Never knew when they'd decide to run out.

She played a few rounds with Jok, then stood and kissed his cheek, giving him her sweetest West Leiscourt now. She couldn't give him whatever farmer's cottage he'd grown up in, but she could give him a rented room where a poor Gally boy wouldn't be a scrap less than anyone around him. "I'm having to scramble now, pup. It'll be my turn to watch Miss Wexin. Can't just lie about kissing thee, so."

"All right," Jok said, and then went a bit pink. "Think you might consider another round, this week?"

"Might it so," Delly said. "As long as you don't get any romantic ideas." That was a joke. Poor Jok's fella was getting married in two weeks: she didn't figure he'd be looking to fall in love with someone like Delly in the meantime. Just wanted someone to hold while he tried not to cry, that was all.

He smiled. "Just so long as you don't."

Jok insisted on escorting her back up to the house, which Delly thought was all right of him. She gave his hand a squeeze and said, "Keep your chin up," for want of anything better to say, then found her way up to her room.

It was a room for guests, not for servants, and was probably one of the nicest rooms Delly'd ever set foot in, let alone been inside of while taking her clothes off. She got herself all cleaned up and ready for bed, and put her shoes out into the hallway—she'd seen other pairs out there and figured she might as well give it a whirl just to find out if someone would put chocolates in them overnight—and then fell into bed and immediately fell asleep.

She was shaken awake by Winn at some incomprehensibly early hour of the morning. It took her a while to focus her eyes. Then she said, "Huh?"

"Your turn to keep watch," Winn said. "Turn right when you leave our room, head down the hall, past the staircase, second-to-last room on that end of the hall. I'm dead on my stumps," she added, and fled to bed.

Delly grunted, still half-unconscious, and went through the motions of dressing herself and heading out the door before she realized, to her befuddlement, that her shoes had vanished. Well, hell. Maybe they put out the ones that they wanted thrown away. Nothing to be done about it now, though: she trudged her way down the hall in her stocking feet and settled herself outside the door, passing a few very stern and intimidating axe-wielding suits of armor as she went. There she waited, with perhaps less anxiety than the situation might have warranted, for someone to attempt a vicious murder.

6

Wherein Things Go to Hell and Come to Light

There were, unfortunately, no attempted murders in the night. Instead there was only a very contemptuous-looking lady's maid sweeping past Delly and into the room with a tray of tea and toast, and a bleary Dellaria unpeeling herself from her position like cheap wallpaper and stumbling back toward her own room, wondering vaguely whether or not there might be tea and toast for the working classes. When she got back to her room, she blinked: her shoes had been returned to her, looking cleaner than they'd been the day she bought them. "Sakes," she murmured, and picked them up to carry them inside.

Winn was already there, sitting at the desk in the corner of Delly's room in a dressing gown, writing a letter. There was a steaming pot on the table and the smell of coffee in the air, good and strong enough to make Delly ready to weep. Winn looked up when Delly walked in. "No exciting developments, then?"

"None other than my shoes being cleaner than I've ever seen 'em," Delly said, and let herself thump down onto the edge of the bed with a sigh.

"Well, that's something, at least," said Winn, with a kind of teeth-baring good cheer. "Boosts the spirits to have tidy-looking shoes, what? Suppose we'll just have to be on our toes, waiting for grisly death for the duration! Might as well be looking our best! Coffee?"

Delly eyed her. "Didn't get much sleep, then?" she asked, in what she hoped was a delicate fashion. She started inching sidelong toward the coffeepot, with the general thought that if things began to plummet downward she could always snatch up the coffeepot and canter off. "Just a small cup, if you don't mind."

Winn poured until the cup was filled to the very brim, sloshed a bit onto her hand, said, "*Blinking relent!*"—there was, Delly thought, something a bit lamentable about polite replacements for a bit of good strong, healthy bad language—and then mopped everything up with a handkerchief, handed the coffee over, and said, "Awfully sorry, old thing. I'm afraid that all of this has been working on the nerves a bit. You'd think that a murderer from the upper classes would have the decency to get their murdering done on some sort of appropriate schedule, what?"

"Well," Delly said after a moment. "That sort of old-fashioned adherence to schedule is something we *would* like to think that we could expect from our better class of murderers, but you know how standards are, these days."

"In the blinkin' privy," Winn said gloomily, and they sipped their coffee in silence for a while, the room cloaked generously in despond. "I suppose we might as well go down for breakfast, then."

"Oh, is there breakfast?" Delly said, enormously relieved. "I thought that perhaps it was just toast and tea and self-denial, for the gentler classes." It would explain a lot about the publicly displayed attitudes of members of the assemblage, if they were making laws and generally jerking about the nation under the influence of starvation-induced headache.

Winn, as it turned out, had the right idea. There was all manner of breakfast, a whole vast sideboard covered in enough food for an army regiment. Delly started out pleased about it, and filled up her plate, and ate her fill, and then was so struck by the *excess* of it—all of that food that no one would eat, that would probably be fed to the dogs—that she pushed her plate away, disgusted, and turned to Winn. "What's our schedule, then?"

It wasn't the worst schedule that Delly had ever been induced to follow—though, to be evenhanded about it, the last time she'd been on a schedule she'd been living in a charitable house for wayward girls. Their schedule at the manor included considerably less scrubbing and praying, and considerably more cards and teas and reading books and long, aimless walks on the manor grounds. Delly marveled at it: at the long, easy laxness of the days, at the almost wizardly effortlessness that came with money. There was food before you realized that you were hungry, clean clothes when you'd barely dirtied them, hot water, endless gaslight. Even breathing was effortless when someone else had already carried away anything that might make a stink. Stink was left to places like the ones that Delly had grown up in. Her childhood memories all seemed much worse now, and people who'd grown up with something better seemed like something other than ordinary people. Like trees, maybe, or tigers, or creatures that lived at the bottom of the sea. The sort of creature that wouldn't have any reason to know how human beings went about their long, stupid, grasping little days.

Winn noticed Delly's sour mood a bit but chalked it up to nerves over what might happen next. The murderer had been quiet. There hadn't been any attempts since they'd arrived at the manor. It did, Delly had to admit, wear on one. There was something distinctly unnatural about sitting about in a nice parlor, or walking through a garden, or eating a lovely dinner, and all the while thinking, *Will it be now? What about now? Is this when another one of those creatures will leap at us from the dark?*

It might have been the lack of sleep that was starting to wear on her. She kept going to see Jok to gallop the nerves out, and then she'd get to her bed at midnight and snatch three hours of sleep out of the jaws of nervous jitters before returning to her post at Miss Wexin's door. After the second night like this it occurred to her that her very presence might, in fact, be preventing the thing that she was worrying about. It would take a bold murderer indeed to sail past the disgruntled fire witch standing at a fine lady's doorway, murder the lady in question in complete silence, and then sail back out again while remaining entirely undetected by said fire witch. A canny murderer would be much more likely, she thought, to see said fire witch and head back to her own warm bed, probably whilst shaking her fist toward the ceiling and vowing eventual vengeance against her sworn enemy, Dellaria mostly-on-the-face Wells.

Delly had hauled herself through five full days of this unending and relentless ass-up-headery when, at breakfast, the Miss Wexins announced a treat. "An excursion," Miss Mayelle said, "to a renowned local beauty spot overlooking a gorge." Whatever the fuck *that* meant.

Winn, who had been eating toast and sausages with infuriating serenity, looked only mildly interested in this announcement but pulled Delly aside as soon as the meal was over and the young ladies had retreated to change into their walking clothes. "If you were a murderer," she said, "what d'ye think you'd make of an opportunity to take an excursion to a renowned local beauty whatsit overlooking a blinkin' gorge with your intended victim?"

"I'd figure I had a real prime opportunity to shove a well-bred young lady into a gorge, that's what I'd make of it," Delly said.

Winn tapped her finger against her temple in a very knowing way. "We'd best keep her in our sights, I'd say."

"Heard and affirminated," Delly said, with a feint toward briskness, and went off to pretend that she had clothes to change into that were any more well-suited for walking than the ones she was currently wearing.

This useless exercise continued for half an hour or so, after which all of the young ladies and lady-adjacent personages trundled down to the drive and clambered into one big open carriage and two contrivances that Winn and the Miss Wexins referred to as *dogcarts*, despite

the fact that the carts were pulled by horses and entirely unendogi-
nated. Winn, to Delly's great astonishment, positioned herself in the
driver's seat of one and gestured for Delly to sit beside her. "So you're
a coachman now as well, then?" Delly asked, once she'd managed to
clamber atop the thing.

"I can drive a bit," Winn said, as serene as ever. "Bit of a bother to
always have to wait for a man and a chaperone before you can harness
up the horses and have a bit of a jaunt, what?"

"Suppose so," Delly said. "I generally jaunt under my own power,
without any animals or chaperones coming into it."

Winn laughed at that and performed whatever odd noises and arm-
flapping maneuvers were necessary to encourage the horse into forward
motion, and they were off.

Delly found that she was, with extreme reluctance, enjoying herself. Riding in a little cart through shady country lanes with cushions
under her particulars was a whole relefting span better than bumbling
along a dusty highway on donkeyback. There were cool breezes and
babbling brooks, chirping birds and all of the other expected Joys of
Country Living furbelows. "It's not half-bad out here," she said after a
while.

"Glad to hear that you think so," Winn said. "Despite the close
proximity to a possibly villainous horse, what?"

"Steady on, Cynallum," Delly said, because that was the sort of
thing that Winn generally said when she thought that someone was
coming on a bit stiff, and she wanted to make Winn laugh.

It worked. Then Winn said, "Who've you been flitting off to meet
when you're meant to be getting the old nine-odd reclining hours?"

Delly felt her mouth go dry. Shit. *Shit.* Wasn't *this* a development.
The very-high-quality prospect she had every intent of slowly and deliberately cultivating over the next week had caught her out *fucking a
footman.* She didn't reply immediately, as she was too preoccupied with
thrashing about in search of a response that would ring more pleasantly than *I've been getting up to no good with the Gallen footman in the*

gamekeeper's cottage. Winn, fortunately, spoke again before Delly's hand was forced. "Awfully sorry, Wells. None of my blinkin' business, is it? Not a sporting sort of question to ask a gull, what?"

Delly's tongue, at this juncture, unglued itself from the roof of her mouth and devoted itself to making ill-considered statements. "I could stop," she said, "if you'd like me to."

The ensuing pause weighed more than the dogcart.

"There's no need for that," Winn said. "No use in you altering your habits because you're worried about the sensibilities of us—*clanners,* when it's no business of ours what you do in your own free hours."

"It wouldn't be because you're a clanner that I'd give it up," Delly said quickly. There was something very unnatural about a clanner calling herself a clanner. If Delly was in the assemblage she'd work to have the practice outlawed. "It's because of you, particularly. I won't flit off to meet anyone if you'd rather I didn't." There. She'd played her hand, and earlier than she would have liked to. She hadn't had time to work up as much of a bond as she'd have liked. That was important, in a long game: you had to get them to trust you first before you really went in for the take. But it was too late for thinking too much now: part of running games was knowing that a mark wasn't always going to do exactly what you expected. Winn had moved first, and now Delly would just have to try to keep up. She turned so she could try to look at her face, and pitched her voice soft and trembling. "You angry at me?"

She didn't look angry. She was blushing, which struck Delly as auspicious. "I wouldn't like to—tell you how you ought to comport yourself, Delly."

A *Delly,* even. Sakes. "I almost wish you would," Delly said. A vile lie. "Ain't you worried about my ruination?" A little extra dirt-common color, since Winn seemed to like it when she acted like the trash she was. Thought it was romantic to be gutter-raised, probably. Delly's mam might be offended by that, but Delly sure as shit wasn't. Better a prospect who liked her being trash than a prospect who treated her like it.

Winn's eyes went wide. They weren't very exceptional, Winn's eyes.

Just brown and medium-sized and occupying the usual positions in the head. Nothing that a gull might find herself accidentally lost in. Just as well. "I'd never call you *ruined*," she said. "My mother's a *troll*. She didn't raise me to think that a gull ought to be tossed out with the bathwater for a bit of, ah. *High spirits*. And you needn't worry about me gossiping. I shan't breathe a word of it. Jolly bad form to go chattering away about indiscretions that you were too dull to get up to yourself. Only—bit jealous, I suppose."

Delly's rusty old heart gave a clang. She was going to be rich. She was going to be householded into the headmanship. She was going to be the heroine of the sort of novel that nice young ladies like Winn didn't read. "Jealous?" she asked, like she was a great dizzified dolt and didn't know what Winn could possibly mean by the word.

"Dreadfully sorry," Winn said quickly. "Demmed forward of me. Forget that I said it."

"I'd rather not," Delly said, doing her best to look coyly at her from the corners of her eyes. "Forget, I mean. I'm—*ever* so flattered, Winn." She was immediately disgusticated with herself. Who the fuck said *ever so flattered* when they weren't running a game?

Winn didn't seem to have noticed. "Really?" she asked, and went pinker. "Well—I'm wretchedly blinkin' glad to hear it." She cleared her throat. "I don't know if—I know what the proper way to declare my intention to court you would be if, ah. If we'd been at school together. Might have to consult the old etiquette manuals, though, when it comes to you." The dogcart had come to a stop: the horse was having a bit of a graze on the path in front of it. Winn shook herself and beseeched it to move by means of more arm shaking and odd noises. Once they were in motion again, she said, "I do chatter on dreadfully, don't I? Like a runaway train. Oughtn't be thinking about any of this until our posting here's over, what? Got to stay the course and defend the lady from brigands before we can set ourselves to—the lighter side of life." She looked pained. "Blinkin' fates, won't you say something and spare me from myself, old thing?"

Delly laughed, and that suddenly broke the spell a bit, snapped the tension that had been winding tighter between her shoulder blades. It was just Winn, that was all. No reason to act like she was talking her way out of the gallows. She had her mark well and truly netted already, but besides that, she *liked* Winn. She generally tried not to let herself get fond of a mark—defeated the whole purpose, really, if you liked them too much to cheat them out of a few sen—but this was, after all, different from taking a mark for the cost of a casual bet on a card game. It occurred to Delly all at once that this was a game that, if she played it right, could last the rest of her mortal span, which was a fair span longer than she could keep up a grateful simper. If she *liked* Winn, that was only an excellent development, and one that might increase her chances of success.

"I think you're right," she said finally. "It's nothing we should worry about right now. And I figure I've got the fortitude to wait a week before the—lighter topics."

"Oh, well. Jolly good, then," Winn said, and then cleared her throat again and urged the horse forward.

They chatted a bit about nothing in particular—about nothing in par-theater, specifically: Winn had seen a few plays on opening night that Delly had seen two years after, in the washout-actor productions they held in Dogbite Alley. They praised the good ones—Delly could tell when the writing was good, even if the actors were slurring their ways through the production—and mocked the bad ones, and generally acted like two people who weren't locked in an agonizing spasm of discomfiture until they reached the point of their jaunt where they were meant to leave the dogcart and walk.

This, fortunately, meant that they could mingle amongst the other ladies and were no longer forced to painfully associate exclusively with the object of their filthy un-Elgarite intentions while perched atop an irritatingly romantical dogcart. Winn walked with her equals, Miss Dok and the Miss Wexins, while Delly went with the Tothams. After a few moments, Delly could only feel pity for the quality ladies:

Mrs. Totham was in absolute raptures over all of the birds evident in the surrounding foliage, and her joy in observing and commenting upon them was irresistible. Delly did her best to contribute to the dear old thing's delight and peppered her with asinine questions on the various birds, and their plumage, and their individual habits, just for the pleasure of witnessing Mrs. Totham's uncomplicated happiness over responding.

After what struck Delly as an inordinately long walk—she had worried that the enormous breakfasts of the better classes might have endowed them with legs powerful enough to withstand endless miles of casual jaunting—they arrived at the Renowned Local Beauty Spot. It was, it turned out, less a spot than a stripe: a whole long, winding path along the edge of a horrible drop above a deep, rocky gorge lined at the bottom by a blue-and-white ribbon of river.

Delly and Winn exchanged a glance when they saw it and maneuvered themselves into a position where they followed after the Tothams as they walked ahead. Delly, for her own part, wasn't remotely interested in allowing someone to be shoved into a gorge because she was lollygagging about and enjoying the view. Ainette Wexin certainly didn't seem as if she was particularly inclined toward lollygaggery, either. She was hurrying her sister along, making vague protestations about how there was some particularly attractive bit of scenery up ahead, but Delly saw Ainette glance over her shoulder at Delly and Winn behind her and felt her stomach clench. There was calculation in that glance. It wasn't the look of someone who simply wanted to see who was walking behind her. She wanted to know how far back they were for a reason. Maybe it was only because she wanted to gossip with her sister out of the reach of prying ears. The thought didn't do anything to dejangle Delly's nerves.

There was a turn in the path up ahead. Delly tried to quicken her steps without drawing undue attention to herself. The sisters disappeared around the turn. Winn launched herself forward in a silent sprint and went around the turn, too. Then Delly rounded the corner herself to see several things happen in one instant. Ainette, her back to Winn, gave her sister a hard shove. Mayelle screamed and began to fall. And Winn, the great brave miracle that she was, dove forward and caught her with one strong arm, yanked her away from the precipice, then turned and punched Ainette in the face.

Ainette hit the ground like a sack of wet clothes. For a long moment the only sound was a bird nearby taking off with a chittering cry, then silence.

"Oh, dash it all, I hope I haven't killed her," Winn said.

Mayelle burst into tears.

There was, unsurprisingly, not very much pleasant chitchat over the course of the journey back to the manor, which commenced the instant that Miss Dok came running up demanding to know why Winn had violently assaulted Miss Ainette. Miss Mayelle was far too hysterical to properly explain the situation (reasonably enough, Delly thought, for someone whose sister had just attempted to murder her in broad daylight), which resulted in Delly being forced to act as the supposedly neutral party who was meant to confirm Winn's account and soothe everyone's anxieties and help Winn to frog-march Miss Ainette (Mrs. Totham had looked her over and apparently patched her up enough to be transportable) back toward the coach and dogcarts. She was refusing to answer any of their questions, which was what finally convinced Miss Dok of her guilt. *That* was something, at least: having to figure out what in the releft was going on, with Miss Dok still firmly convinced that Winn and Delly had plotted together to frame the blessed Ainette for the wicked deed, would have very sorely tried Delly's already highly strained nerves.

They finally arrived back at the manor after what felt to Delly like a journey of about twelve hours. Mayelle, now very calm and very sad, sat in a chair in the small parlor and asked to have her sister brought before her. "I don't *understand*, Ainette," she said. "It wasn't *money*, surely? You know that I've promised to provide for you always. What possible need could you have for money that would merit this? Have I—offended you, somehow? You must know that I could *never* mean to hurt you. You're my—my own little sister." Her voice wavered. "Won't you *speak*?"

Ainette stared ahead of herself like a woman in the dock, which Delly supposed she was now, or was shortly to be. If someone had tried to shove *Delly* off of a cliff, the constabulary would probably toss her assailant into the cells for a night to sober up, give him a paternal talking-to in the morning, and then send him on his way, but Delly was fairly sure that attempting to murder a young lady of the second headmanship was a hanging offense. It would be if Mayelle wanted it to be, certainly, though Delly suspected Mayelle of being inclined toward begging for lenience on her *own little sister's* behalf. In this moment, Delly found herself rather admiring both of the Wexin ladies: Mayelle, for her calm and compassion, and Ainette, for her stoic silence, her refusal to simper and plead and offer flimsy explanations as Delly would if she were in her place.

It caused a bit of a ginny feeling, to compare oneself to someone who'd just made a failed attempt at sororicide and find oneself distinctly lacking.

They locked Ainette up in what had been Mayelle's room—they moved Mayelle in with Miss Dok, just in case—in that hall with the grim rows of suits of armor lining the walls. They posted the furious Miss Dok and a particularly strapping footman to watch the door. Then the low-class girls sat down for a late luncheon.

It wasn't a very cheery luncheon, but as they hadn't had their planned picnic lunch at the Renowned Local Beauty Spot, it seemed the thing to do, Delly supposed. The sandwiches were very nice. After the sandwiches, the Tothams relieved Miss Dok at the door, and the rest of them went up to Ainette's room to look through her things, thinking that maybe there'd be a bit more of a clue in them as to what in the releft she'd been thinking.

Ainette didn't seem to own as many things as Delly would have expected, for a clanner. Maybe it was because she'd been traveling, though Miss Mayelle certainly didn't lack for trunks. Delly expressed her surprise aloud to Winn, and Miss Dok snapped out, "Ainette is a householded second daughter who was brought into the family as a favor to a friend of Lady Wexin who got herself into trouble. She's never had the luxury of demanding more than her lot."

They looked through what had been her lot. It wasn't an array to lift the spirits. A few dresses and overcoats. Some books—nice, improving magical theory and history books, nothing interesting. Hats and shoes and jewelry that looked fine enough to Delly. Then, finally, at the bottom of a chest with a lock that Winn smashed open with the heel of one of those nice shoes, a pretty little wooden box. That one had a lock on it, too. Winn looked to still be in a frame of mind for smashing things, but Delly waved her off. "Let me," she said, and did her usual work with the lock: just enough of a melt of the inside to jiggle it open without warping it. Not that there was any reason for her to want to avoid anyone seeing that the lock had been disturbed in this instance, but she wanted to show off for Winn. Winn made gratifyingly impressed noises when the lock popped open—undoing mechanical locks with magic was one of those feats that deeply irritated mediocre academic wizards by being far harder than they really thought it ought to be—and Delly suppressed a smug grin and opened the box with a very restrained flourish.

It was nothing but papers in the box—looked like correspondence—which would have been very disappointing to Delly in the ancient many days ago of her more disreputable past. At the moment, however, she was rather intrigued: maybe they would be scandalous letters between Ainette and some ill-intended rake of a lover who goaded her into murdering her sister for their mutual profit. "Shall we read them, then?" she asked, with perhaps a shade too much good cheer.

Miss Dok gave her a fairly withering look, as if she was disgusted by the very notion. Then she started handing out the letters. "It will go more quickly if we divide them up," she said. Then she stopped. "What's that?"

It was a little bottle, filled halfway with a dark reddish brown liquid. They all leaned in to peer at it.

"It looks like blood," Winn said.

"It looks like some sort of chemical," Miss Dok said.

"It's drip," Delly said. "Red drip. I'd put five on it, at least. What the f—*fruitcake* does she have *that* for?"

Miss Dok was scowling at her. "I beg your pardon, Miss Wells. What is it?"

"Drip," Delly said. "They call it manufactured laudanum, but that seems a hair polite to me. You wouldn't take this stuff for a headache. Easy way to be sure of what it is, though." She uncorked the bottle, moistened her fingertip with the barest bit of the red—even a small drop would be enough to knock her off her feet, if it was the expensive stuff—and licked her finger. There was a faint unpleasant taste of sour sweat. Her face went numb. A few downy moments drifted by. Winn nudged her. "Delly?"

"Yeah," Delly said, after a pause. "That's the stuff."

"But—why on earth would Ainette be carrying about a bottle of that stuff?" Miss Dok asked, sounding genuinely puzzled by the idea.

"Well," Delly said, "not to be rude, miss, and begging your pardon if I drive my cart before the horse to the slender end of a limb, miss, but I expect that she brought it along because she uses it."

Miss Dok's expression went a bit stormy. Then she gave a quick nod and handed Delly the last bundle of letters. "Maybe these will help to clarify the situation a bit," she said, as if she thought that the letters were likely to contain information that would absolve Ainette entirely of being a drip-sick murderess.

Delly herself was less optimistic on that score, but she began to read the first letter in her stack at once in any case. She was rather disappointed by the contents. It was a light, chatty letter from a friend of Ainette's, full of nothing on the whole crowded first page but gossip about various parties where she'd encountered mutual friends and acquaintances. Then, on the second page, something that Delly thought a bit more telling:

As to the matter of the loan, I'm afraid that it's entirely
impossible, my sweet. You know that I would gladly move
mountains for you, but moving my father to loan money to you,
me, or any other living being that doesn't guarantee his interest
on the loan would be a greater feat of persuasion than any you
could see at a traveling Hesendi mind-healing show. I know that
you'll understand, darling, and won't think me too mean for not
being able to help you. I do so look forward to seeing you again
when we all go back to Leiscourt . . .

"She was hard up," Delly said aloud. "Asking her friends for money and getting turned down."

"Not everyone turned her down," Miss Dok said, with a little wave of her own letter. "She owed one of our old school friends thirty tocats." Miss Dok looked pale. "But what on earth could she have needed such an awful amount of money for? Surely not—that *stuff.*"

"Could be," Delly said. "Miss Dok, you're the one who knows her. Has she been acting strangely at all, recently?"

Miss Dok hesitated for a moment before she responded. "I'd put it down to her anxieties over her sister's betrothal," she said eventually. "As I've said, she's dependent on Mayelle for her allowance and a place to stay, and she wouldn't be the first person to lose everything because their elder sibling was married or householded to someone who took a disliking to them. She hasn't met her soon-to-be brother-in-law yet, so I thought that it must only be nerves. We did have an argument a few weeks ago when I told her that she had been uncivil to Mayelle's other guests at a dinner party. She's been much moodier than usual, and prone to slipping off and sulking alone in her room, which isn't like her at all. It seemed the sort of thing that one ought to make allowances for, though, considering the circumstances, so I didn't think much of it."

She was a tough thing, Miss Dok. Tough but good to her friends, at least, which Delly thought spoke well of her. Not that it was Delly's place to be having opinions about a woman like Miss Dok, especially when she clearly didn't have much use for Delly.

"Look at this," Winn said suddenly, and handed over the letter that she was holding.

It was a nasty old letter, that was for certain. There was a bit of blathering at the beginning and end, but the real crux of the thing was this:

> *I gave you your goods on advans becoss I thought you was a respectibal lady but now I see you are a sly bitch like the rest of them you get me my money by the end of this formonth or there will be all of the releft for you you mark my words.*

Delly raised her eyebrows and handed the thing over to Miss Dok, who hissed at it like a cat. "How *dare* the creature! And what goods could she possibly be—" She cut herself off, looking like she'd managed to put bones and peas together to make a soup. "Ah."

"I suppose that solves the mystery, then," Winn said cheerfully. "She got into that red stuff, she got into debt, and some nasty blighters threatened her until she lost her head a bit. Understandable, given that I expect that the red stuff might make the processes of the logical organ go a bit fruity, when the old thing was already under a strain. Saw her sister on the ledge and decided in the moment to give her a shove. Let her sober up downstairs and explain to her sister about her needing a bit of cash and she'll be right as brown toast in time for the wedding."

Delly tried and failed not to grimace. "That would be a lovely thing to think," she said, "if it weren't for those spider-things."

Winn looked a bit defeated at that. "Oh," she said. "Right."

"And," Delly said, "using drip doesn't turn you into a murderer if you weren't murderously inclined from the start." Her mam had never murdered a person in her life, to Delly's knowledge, unless she'd actually succeeded at some point in annoying someone to death. Then she added swiftly, "Not that I'd know, uh, as to *myself.* But I know a few drippers, and none of 'em have ever murdered anyone. Done things they wouldn't otherwise do, sure, but not *murder.*"

"She killed a dog," Miss Dok said suddenly.

Delly frowned. "Huh?"

"About a week before we left," Miss Dok said. "Mayelle was worried over one of her father's dogs having gone missing. It was a bit of a doddering old thing, not the sort to run off on a spree. She must have killed it and used it to make that first horrible spider."

Winn looked uncomfortable. "Hurting dogs is really a bit past the mark, isn't it? But one doesn't like to think it of a gull one *knows,* dash it."

"Well," Delly said. "*Someone* knows everyone who's ever murdered anybody. Might as well be us."

"I suppose," Winn said. Then she sighed and squared her shoulders. "What now, then? Bit of—interrogation of the suspect?"

"I believe that the police will take charge of that," Miss Dok said. "The family has sent word that they're needed. There isn't a real detective in Crosward Village, though, so I imagine that they'll arrive in the morning, at the earliest."

Delly tried not to wince. The cops weren't coming here after *her,* Dellaria Wells. Not this time, at least. "Isn't there a jail in the village that we could put her in?"

"I don't believe so," Miss Dok said. "Not that I've ever had occasion to inquire, but there isn't in most of these country places. They generally keep prisoners at the constable's house. She'd probably have a far greater chance of escape there than she would here, when the house here is packed full of wizards."

"And fire witches," Delly added, unnecessarily.

"We ought to knock together a schedule for watching her door," Winn said. "Including everyone, I mean."

Miss Dok raised her eyebrows. "Including everyone? Why *shouldn't* everyone be included? I'm sure that we're all prepared to do our part."

"Ah," Winn said. "Well. Miss Wells and I had been watching Miss Mayelle's door on our own over the past few evenings. We'd rather suspected that Miss Ainette might have been the guilty party, which would make Miss Mayelle wretchedly vulnerable in her bed at night, what? Servants wouldn't think twice about seeing Miss Ainette in the hall in the evening." Then she explained about Delly having found the dead cat.

"Good God," Miss Dok said. "And it didn't occur to either of you to inform Mayelle or myself? I could have stayed in her room with her at night."

Winn and Delly exchanged a guilty glance. "We were worried that you might have balked a bit at a pair of strange gulls accusing your friend of being a murderess," Winn said.

"Or suspecting that you were in on it," Delly said. Winn gave her a quelling look.

"Oh, for—" Miss Dok began, and then quelled herself. "I was not *in on it*, thank you," she said. "Is there any other information that you've concealed that I ought to be made aware of? If not, we might as well work out that schedule."

They worked out the schedule, then went downstairs to inform the Tothams. They'd decided to leave Mrs. Totham out of it out of deference to her age, and because her healing capabilities would be of little use should Miss Ainette make a bolt for freedom.

"Oh, dear," Mrs. Totham said with a soft sigh. "I do feel so dreadfully foolish. I ought to have compared the magical signature I found in that spider construct to those of all of our company. It simply didn't occur to me that it could possibly be the work of one of you lovely young ladies."

"None of us would blame you for a minute, Mrs. Totham," Winn said, at her very heartiest. "Would we, gulls?"

The assembled gulls murmured their agreement. Then it was Delly's turn to guard the door, and the rest of them dispersed, leaving Delly to enjoy the company of her own thoughts, such as they were.

The time dragged like a brick at the end of a leash until Winn appeared with a novel and a tray of tea and cakes for them to share. Having such a nice afternoon tea on the floor in a hallway was unusual enough to have a bit of entertainment value, at least, and Winn did her best to make Delly laugh the whole time. Then she left—off for a walk to clear her head before her own shift at the door, she said—and Delly rolled the time along pretty well with the novel and the rest of the tea until Winn arrived to relieve her.

Her instinct was to go look for Jok. She didn't, though. She'd made a promise to Winn, and he was busy working at this hour, anyway. Instead, she took herself out on her own walk, striding across the lawn and up the hill until she finally reached the folly that she'd been wondering about for days. It had looked like a real authentic old ruin, from the house, and she'd embarrassed herself by asking Winn what she thought it might be. Then Winn had explained about follies, and Delly had gotten it into her head that she'd like to see it for herself.

So now, after a long, damp slog up the hill, she was here. It was a rather cozy little spot, she thought, with a hidden room in it with seats and all to rest on. Narrow windows and a faded rug on the floor. It was a good feeling to be inside of it and see the sweep of the whole grounds before her. A thought plinked into Delly's head like a raindrop into a puddle: that it would be nice, one day, to have a nook like this of her own to live in, with a view onto something pleasant. She had that thought and then was astounded with herself for having had it. "Not like you at all, Delly Wells," she said aloud. Not at all like her to daydream about things she could never have. Still, it stuck with her as she made her way back down to the manor. A little nook with a view onto something pleasant. It was likely Winn's fault, she thought. Spend too much time with a clanner and a girl was likely to get ideas above her station. *A few clean windows, a comfortable chair, a rug on the floor. Why not?*

It was time for supper when she got back, which suited her fine: all of this marching about to scenic viewpoints and witnessing attempted murder did wonders for the appetite. Miss Dok had relieved Winn at her post, so Delly sat next to Winn for the meal and did her best to chatter with charming effect while they had their soup and sliced ham. Delly was yawning before the layer cake had even reached the table. Winn smiled at her. "Might as well take a shift at the dream workshop before your shift as a jailer, old thing. You look ready to make that cake a pillow."

"A bit," Delly admitted. "Been a long day."

"So go to bed, then," Winn said. "Someone will wake you when it's your turn."

Delly obeyed, rather giddy over having had a Quality Young Lady gently boss her about for her own good, not because she was spending her spare time providing Aid to the Poor, but because she liked Delly personally and didn't want her to feel badly. That was a refreshing sort of feeling, all right. She, Delly Wells, the sort of person that a Quality Young Lady might feel moved to gently boss. This must be, she thought, how people who lived in nice houses in the suburbs felt all the time: pleasantly encased in the silky glove of their own superiority.

She fell asleep almost the instant her face found a spot to settle on and didn't wake up again until something jolted her from sleep some few hours later. Odd. It wasn't someone knocking on the door that had woken her. It was something else. A sort of strange thickness in the air.

She got up and dressed and headed down the hall to the stairs. The air got heavier as she walked. She didn't like how her throat was tightening. She didn't like how her skin was prickling. She didn't like how no one had come to wake her up.

She turned the corner and was confronted by something strange. One of the suits of armor in the hall had left its proper place. Instead of standing with its back against the wall it was at the center of the hall, facing Delly. Delly thought, for a moment, of how odd that was: she had thought that the suits of armor must be attached to the wall somehow to keep them from falling over onto particularly heavy-footed types as they walked down the hall. She was still gawping at the thing and thinking these unhelpful thoughts when the suit of armor began advancing toward her.

Her first, strange response was to feel delighted: it was as if all of her childhood imaginings about her beloved doll coming to life to play with her had come true. In the next moment these rosy-hued thoughts of dancing with Miss Pansy in fields of daffodils in sugarplum-land were rudely destroyed, as the suit of armor came a step closer and raised its axe to swing at her.

Delly barely had the time to think, let alone formulate a plan of action. All she could do was follow her first instinct, which was to push all of the power in her body into her right hand and catch the blade of the axe with it.

It wasn't exactly like a knife through hot butter. More like hot butter through a knife, which was a very peculiar thing to witness. The axe was reduced in a moment to a pole with a misshapen hunk of metal stuck at the end, which, though less dangerous than a sharp axe, still struck Delly as an object with which she'd much rather not be clobbered. She was dizzy from having used too much magic at once, but she couldn't stop for a rest now: the suit of armor was turning its empty head toward her, trying to orient itself to take another swing. So she swung first and managed to push her hot knife of a hand through the center of the thing's breastplate.

It kept moving, of course. It was a fucking empty suit of armor animated with the life force of an innocent creature: it couldn't be killed that easily. The next few moments were one long, agonized scrap, the suit of armor managing to land stinging blows of the axe handle on Delly's back as Delly pushed her hand over and over into the metal of the thing, trying to get it to fall, trying to ignore the sickening feeling that coursed through her every time she touched it. Eventually she managed to melt enough of one of its legs for it to list sharply to the side, then clatter onto the floor. After that it was a moment's work to gather up the last of her strength, aim for its head, and melt the rest of it into a pile of writhing scrap.

She stood there for a while, watching the fingers of the armor twitch. She kept watching it because it was better than looking at the other thing in the hall, just beyond that suit of armor that had been left to guard it. A pig. A dead pig. A pig that had been hacked open and bled and died on the floor.

Ermintrude.

Delly moved closer. There was a stink in the air like nothing she'd ever smelled before. She reminded herself, *This is Ermintrude*, but her mind skidded off of that and rolled away. It couldn't be. Ermintrude was a live person, and this was a dead animal. She stepped in closer. Closer. The floor was sticky. She kept her eyes up and kept moving until she made it to the door, which was standing open.

Inside the room everything looked ordinary. A bed, a trunk, a pretty little dressing table, a vase of flowers. A thick rug with a dead mouse on it.

That makes sense, Delly thought distantly, as if the thought belonged to someone standing in the other room. The mouse had wandered into the room, or Ainette had lured it out. There had probably been enough power in that little body to bring the suit of armor to life just in time to cut down Ermintrude. After that it would be nothing to open the door, nothing to escape, nothing to leave in the night with a suit of armor left to guard the hall and slow down anyone who might pursue her.

It must have been fast, at least. Otherwise the pig would have squealed the house down.

The pig. The girl. The young girl. Ermintrude.

She looked down at the corpse and finally saw it. It wasn't a pig, not entirely. She had been killed in the exact moment of the change. A pig's body, with the shreds of a frilly dress around it. A few wisps of blonde hair. A horrible, half-human, terrified face.

Delly wasn't really sure when exactly she started to scream.

7

Wherein Revenge Is Sworn, Plans Are Laid,
and Dellaria Is Confronted by Elevated Opinions
About Her Person

Something strange happened to Delly after her scream. Time
stopped working in the usual way. It writhed around as witlessly
as an eel in a barrel, and Delly watched it and herself with amazement
at how little sense it made.

At some point, days, weeks, or seconds later, other people began
running up to her in the hall. They didn't see the body because there
was a blanket over it. Delly had thrown a blanket over it before the
others arrived, something that she didn't remember doing. She just
remembered screaming and then thinking that Mrs. Totham shouldn't
see her daughter like this. Then there was a blanket over the body.
Then there was another blanket over Delly's shoulders, and Winn's
hands on her shoulders, and the sound of Winn praying.

Mrs. Totham came up then, in her nightdress and white cap. She
knelt by her daughter's body and laid her hands on where a human
chest should have been, and the body under the blanket moved and
twisted and shrank down to the size of a dead young girl. Mrs. Totham
turned the blanket down to expose Ermintrude's pale face. She pushed
back her pale hair.

"My poor girl," she whispered. "My poor, sweet girl. It's all right, darling. I'm here now. You're safe now, sweet baby." She kissed Ermintrude's forehead. She was crying without making any sound. There were just tears.

"I'll have revenge for you, sweet girl," Mrs. Totham said. There was a strange hum of magic in the air. "Don't worry, love. I'll see that bitch ruined for you, darling. Don't worry. I'm here."

There was movement in the corner of Delly's eye. The mouse on the rug in the empty room. It was moving. It was standing. It skittered its way to Mrs. Totham's side. Its head was still twisted around wrong.

"Ah," Mrs. Totham murmured, looking down at the dead-living mouse. "How very silly of me not to have noticed you. *You're* not meant to be alive at all, are you?"

She held out her hand. The mouse climbed into it. She twisted its head back around the right way, then stroked it with one finger between its soft round ears. "You may come to be useful, though," Mrs. Totham said to the living-dead mouse. "Yes, indeed. I think that I'll keep you this way, for now."

"Come on," Winn murmured into Delly's ear. Delly jumped. Winn steadied her. "Come on, Delly. You ought to sit down."

Time skipped. The night wore out. Delly came back to herself as the sun came up. The things she had seen before seemed less real, and the things before her now solidified at the edges. She was in the small parlor, which was crowded with people trying to figure out where Ainette might have gone to. They all seemed very interested in that, though Delly was struggling to understand why. Everyone else seemed very interested when Miss Dok sat back in her chair, her forehead glistening with sweat, and said, "She's gone."

Jok, standing nearby, made a disrespectful gesture just outside of Miss Dok's range of vision. He and his fellow footmen had searched the grounds on foot from just past midnight to just before dawn and come to the exact same conclusion, but Miss Dok had insisted on enlisting Winn into helping her to temporarily lower the magical walls of the manor in order to search for Ainette's presence on the grounds with the use of some set of parameters recently published by the Lord-Mage of Hexos. It was more magic than a couple of young ladies really ought to be performing unsupervised, and it had wrung both of them out like wet mops. Delly, for her part, was exempted from any exertion for the morning. It was a bit embarrassing, really. They'd all seen her in the night, when the text of reality had bled like wet newsprint.

Mrs. Totham was in the room now. She was sitting, like Delly, with a blanket around her shoulders and a cup of hot tea in her hands. The dead-alive mouse was on her knee. A strange atmosphere hung around the thing. No one seemed quite able to look directly at it, or, by extension, at Mrs. Totham. Their eyes skipped right over her and straight to anything else.

It seemed unfair, Delly thought, when Mrs. Totham was mourning. A bit cruel. So she moved her chair a little closer, cleared her throat, and asked, "How are you, Mrs. Totham?"

"Oh," Mrs. Totham said in her softest twitter. "How kind of you to ask, Miss Wells, how very kind of you. I'm as well as can be expected. I believe that word has been sent to my family?" She was stroking the alive-dead mouse with her fingertip.

"I'm sure that it has been," Delly said, though she wasn't sure at all. "I'm sure someone will be coming here to collect you and bring you home any day now."

"Oh, no," Mrs. Totham said, in a tone of the very mildest and powder-scented surprise. "I won't be going home with anyone. I'll be going after that Wexin bitch."

Delly coughed tea all over her lap. Then she cleared her throat, wiped her mouth, and said, "Pardon me, Mrs. Totham, but how exactly are you planning on doing that?"

"That doesn't concern me, at the moment," Mrs. Totham said. "My first responsibility will be to find people to accompany me in the endeavor."

She had a very suggestive look on her face. Delly frowned and started casting around for an excuse. *I think I'm coming down with a head cold* probably wouldn't fit the occasion. "I wish that I could help," she said, "but I promised my own dear mother that I would take the money I made at this job and use it to help her find a more salutary place for her to stay and resolve some difficulties in which she has unfortunately and recently found herself." There. That sounded good—like her nice, genteel mam had just been the mark of a man selling imaginary tracts of vineyard in Mendosa and lost all of her money in the scheme—and was a respectable reason to not want to go off on a revenge-driven quest to kill or capture a magically accomplished murderess.

"Ah, yes, your dear mother," Mrs. Totham said. "She's also a user of the drug that brought the Wexin girl to this point, isn't she?"

Delly's face went hot and her hands went fishbelly. "Who the fuck is telling you things like that about my mam?"

Mrs. Totham gazed placidly back at her. "Of course, I could never allow my daughter to be in the presence of so many strangers without looking into their backgrounds first. Certainly *not*, goodness me. I ought to have found out about the Wexin girl's habits, but no one had heard about her in my circles. They'd heard about Dellaria Wells and her mother, though."

Delly could slap her, the miserable old cow. Putting on her sweet face, and all the while she was digging into Delly's secrets. Finding things out about her mother. Delly could spit. "What are you talking about my mother for?"

"Oh, dear me, I certainly didn't mean any insult," Mrs. Totham said, and suddenly her round brown eyes went bright with tears. "I do hope that you aren't angry at me, Miss Wells, when you've been so very kind to me, so *very* kind. I only meant that the same wicked drug that turned the Wexin girl to hurt my dear Ermintrude has seized your mother as well. I do hope that you might feel some pity for a poor mother who has lost her own sweet girl, and find it in your heart to help avenge her?"

Delly stared at her. She was talking a bunch of nonsense, of course.

Temporarily moon-addled with grief. She'd get over this revenge business once she'd had a night or two to sleep on it. She'd come to her senses and realize that the wicked and well-connected only got their just deserts in improving books for children, and that she'd be better off going home to her village and finding solace in her surviving daughters than she'd be trying to find justice for the dead one.

"I'll think about it," she said, and took a sip of her tea. It had gone cold. She wasn't really sure how long it had been in her cup for. "I think I ought to go to bed," she said. Her eyes ached.

She took herself to bed. Took her clothes off and got under the blankets. She kept thinking of the agonized half-pig face and the mouse standing up with its head on backward. They were there when she closed her eyes, but there when her eyes were open, too. Dug into the back of her skull, maybe. Caked under her fingernails. Pumping through her body along with her heartbeat.

She wanted to sleep. She needed to sleep. She told herself to sleep.

She just drifted, instead. She floated until the leaky little ship of her mind struck against something horrible, and that woke her until she settled, and drifted, and it happened all over again. She was almost grateful when Winn shook her awake, even though she screamed and tried to leap away in the moment.

Winn winced and squatted down next to the bed to make herself smaller. "Sorry, old thing," she murmured. "Didn't mean to startle you." She reached out like she wanted to touch Delly, then dropped her hand again before she did it. "Miss Mayelle is asking for us to all gather round for a meeting. If you're feeling as if you're quite up for having a venture downstairs, that is."

"Suppose I ought to be," Delly said. "Can't just lie in bed all day, can I?" She climbed out of bed in an illustrative fashion.

"You can, I think," Winn said. "It's not every day that a gull finds a dead body." She was watching Delly drag her dress back on. "You really ought to rest, Delly," she said. "I can tell you whatever she says down there. Probably nothing important, anyway."

"Can't rest," Delly said shortly. "Keep on seeing horrid things every time I try to close my eyes. Might as well do something useful instead of lying around like I'm already a corpse myself." She regretted that last part as soon as it left her mouth. It was awful. She shivered. Ermintrude. Had she chosen to wear those frills, or were they her mother's doing? Too late to ask now.

"All right," Winn said after a moment. "But then after the meeting you ought to have something to eat and then try to lie down again."

"Will you sit with me?" Delly blurted out. Then her face went red. "Sorry. I don't know what got into me. Must be the effect of unanticipated corpse sightings."

Winn gave her a look. "Of course I'll sit with you. You shouldn't have to be alone, after what you've been through."

"I haven't been through anything," Delly snapped. "*Ermintrude* went through something, which is probably what this fucking meeting is about. Maybe Miss Wexin wants to take up a collection for her funeral expenses. Now, let's go, before we're late."

"All right," Winn said softly. "All right, Delly." She was speaking in the voice people used when they thought you'd lost the plot. Delly hadn't, though. She was holding on to every last sentence of the plot with all of the strength in her body.

They went down to the small parlor. It was nice and sunny in there, on a fine afternoon. The windows were open and a breeze was blowing in. There were vases of flowers on the tables. Miss Mayelle was sitting on a little velvet settee, looking fresh and lovely in a pretty light-green frock. That was a funny thing, Delly thought. How someone might be a beautiful young woman, about to be a bride, with the whole world lying at her feet, both before and after someone had been murdered in her own house. One would think she might have the consideration to look a bit uglier until Ermintrude was under the ground, at least.

The world didn't operate like that, though. Delly'd known that all her life. The trains never stopped running in the name of some poor nameless bastard's suffering.

"I've asked you all to come here," Mayelle said in her low, soft voice, "to beg a favor of you. I don't like to ask it of *you*, of course, Mrs. Totham. Please, won't you go and rest? I'll have my lady's maid look after you."

"How very kind of you," Mrs. Totham said, in almost her ordinary twitter. "How very kind. But I think that I would like to remain here and listen, thank you."

Miss Mayelle looked as if she'd like to object, and then as if she thought it wouldn't be seemly. So she just gave an uncertain little nod and then said, "I pray that you won't be too offended, then, by what I'm about to ask of your colleagues." She took a breath. "As you know," she began, "my sister—" Her voice cracked. She started again. "My apologies. My sister—has done a very terrible thing. But she's still a Wexin, and now that—our parents are gone, I am—responsible for her." She was clearly having trouble getting the words out. Miss Dok looked pinched. Winn leaned forward and handed her a big white handkerchief.

"It's all right," Winn said. "Perfectly reasonable to be a bit choked up when your only sister's done something so blinkin' rotten. I'm half in tears m'self, and I'm not even a relation. Just take your time, what?"

Miss Mayelle dabbed at her eyes with the handkerchief. "Thank you, Miss Cynallum," she said. "You're very kind." She took another deep breath. "The police have been informed of what's happened, of course. I imagine that there will be men looking for Ainette all over Daeslund soon. And I want very badly for her to be brought to justice. She doesn't deserve another moment of freedom after what she did to poor Miss Totham. But—I'm so terribly sorry, Mrs. Totham. But she's still my, my only dear little sister, and I don't want her to be—set upon by bounty hunters. If all of this has come about because of that—filthy red stuff, then the place for her ought to be in some sort of *sanitarium*, not—" She stopped and squared her shoulders. "I don't want to see her hanged. I couldn't bear it."

"That's very understandable, Miss Mayelle," Mrs. Totham said, and lifted her gaze to look straight at her. "I, too, would do anything at all for the sake of my family."

Miss Mayelle met her gaze, and they looked at each other in silence for a moment. Miss Mayelle lifted her chin. "I am prepared to offer," she said, her voice firm and clear, "one thousand tocats to whoever captures my sister alive and returns her, in good health, to my custody."

Delly's heart started to pound. One thousand tocats. *One thousand fucking tocats.* Enough money to—she didn't even know. She didn't even know what people *did* with that much fucking money.

"I'll do it," said Mrs. Totham.

Everyone turned at once to look at her. "Mrs. Totham," Miss Mayelle said after a moment, "I don't know if it would be appropriate for me to ask you to—"

"I think that it would be *highly* appropriate," Mrs. Totham said, "for you to allow a grieving mother to express her grief in the way that feels the most natural to her. In my case, that will be for me to track down and bring to justice the woman who murdered her."

"I'm in, too," Delly said, before she could stop her own damn bread-and-butter-hatch from falling open. Words just dribbled out of her. "Ermintrude deserves better than our letting the woman who killed her go running all over fuckin' creation as she likes. Begging your pardon for my language, miss."

"Oh, dash it all, then I'm in, too," Winn said, and blushed.

Miss Dok raised one of her very elegant—*and daintitudinous,* Delly thought rebelliously, whatever that parched-looking old magister had said about that not being a word—eyebrows at that, and looked slowly and deliberately between Winn and Delly. Then she said, "You know that I'll help, Mayelle. And that I won't take a sen of your money." Delly tried not to smile at that. She'd been doing the math on what one thousand tocats looked like after you'd divided it up amongst any number of irritatingly helpful women, and she hadn't liked the look of how her sums were coming out.

"Oh," Miss Mayelle said faintly, as if she hadn't quite expected such an overwhelming response to her request. Then she sat up straight and proud again. "Thank you," she said. "And God bless you all." Then she stood, said, "Please excuse me," and left the room so suddenly that Delly suspected her of a ladylike flurry of tears.

"Right, all of you, don't go anywhere," Delly said, as the others looked like they had the mind to follow her. "We need to start making some kind of plan."

The rest of them looked around like they were expecting some responsible person to drop down from the ceiling and start issuing orders. Delly plowed on. "We ought to go through her correspondence again," she said. "See if those letters from her faucet—her drip dealer, I mean—say anything about where he's writing from. It's almost certainly going to be Leiscourt, so we can head there to start tracking her down."

"And why," Miss Dok asked, in her silky way, "do you assume that it must be Leiscourt?"

"Red drip's a Leiscourt drug," Delly said. "It might have made its way to Monsatelle by now, but it'll be harder to find and more expensive farther away from the source, and no dripper's going to make getting the red harder on themselves than it has to be. Once we confirm it's Leiscourt, my mam will be able to point us toward people who sell the red. We can start looking from there. Ainette won't go too far from whoever gets her her stuff."

"That seems a very bold assumption," Miss Dok said. "If I was Ainette, I'd know that my usual haunts would be the first place that anyone would look for me, and head immediately for the nearest port to sail for Sango."

"*Really?*" Delly said after a beat. She was getting a little fucking aggravated with smug know-it-all clanners. "If you were a dripper, and going without your stuff for a few hours would give you the galloping shits, you'd get on a two-week-long journey to Sango, knowing that they probably don't even have the red drip there to sell you for ready money?"

Miss Dok's face bloomed red. Then she said, abruptly, "Are we meant to be competing with each other?"

Winn frowned. "What do you mean by that?"

"I mean," Miss Dok said, "if any one of us in this room is primarily interested in that one thousand tocats, then that person might be inclined toward sabotaging the group in order to have a better chance of catching Ainette on her own."

Now Delly was the one whose face was going red. "You got something to say to me you can spit it out," she said.

"Then I shall," Miss Dok shot back. "I think that you should be the captain of this venture. You're the only one of us who has any experience with the class of persons that Ainette has gotten herself mixed up in, so we'll need you, but you're obviously only interested in the reward money."

"*Steady* on," Winn said.

Miss Dok ignored her. "Mrs. Totham and I both have personal interests in catching Ainette. I, for one, am willing to pledge all of my portion of the reward if you will swear to work with me in good faith in pursuit of our shared goal. That will leave you with five hundred tocats to do with as you wish. I am willing to do as you instruct in pursuit of Ainette for as long as I believe that you're acting in good faith. If you cross me, my offer of my portion of the reward money will be withdrawn, and I'll let Mayelle know that you're not to be paid a solitary sen. Do we have an agreement?"

Delly stared at her. "So what you're saying is, you think I'm such a nasty bit of work that I'll stab all of you in the back to try and get that whole reward for myself, but you're willing to give me your part of the money in exchange for me being in charge of the whole operation, because I'm the only person you've ever met who knows how to talk to Leiscourt trash? And you're willing to do what I say because you want to catch Ainette that badly?"

Miss Dok lifted her chin. "Precisely."

Delly wasn't sure whether she wanted to laugh or slap her. She settled on shrugging. "All right. You've got yourself a deal, Dok. Shake on it?"

"If the others agree," Miss Dok said.

"Goodness me," Mrs. Totham said. "I don't know if I care for your tone, Miss Dok. But I think that I should be glad to have the benefit of Miss Wells's expertise in this matter and would be happy to contribute some part of my family's portion of the reward money to her to thank her for her efforts."

"I'm blinkin' well *certain* that I don't care for her tone," Winn said. "And you can have half of my bit as well, Delly. Blinkin' *nice* of you, Dok, to go turning up your nose at Delly when she's the one who kept melting those spider-things, *and* that suit of armor, while you've been sitting around keeping your skirts tidy. Without Delly we'd all be up the proverbial river, what? You ought to be thanking her."

Delly half wanted to laugh. These nice ladies defending her from the one woman in the room who saw her exactly as she was. Poor old Dok. She didn't say that. She only said, "Thank you, Miss Cynallum. Mrs. Totham, what did you mean by *your family's* portion?" It would be just their collective luck if Mrs. Totham was currently factoring the help of her dead daughter into their venture.

"I've sent word to my two eldest daughters to join us," she said. "Mura and Vitna will, of course, be very eager to help."

This, to Delly's ears, sounded ominous. "They're the stagecoach guards, aren't they?"

"Yes," Mrs. Totham said. "They should be arriving within the next two days. They're *very* good with knives."

"Oh," Delly said, immediately deciding that it would be her first decision as leader to let Mura and Vitna do absolutely whatever they wanted for the duration. "Good. I'm sure that they'll be very . . . helpful, Mrs. Totham."

"So, Miss Wells," Miss Dok said, in a tone that could take the tarnish off a fork. "What should we spend the next two days doing while we wait for the other Misses Totham to arrive? We all await your instructions."

Delly gnawed on that for a moment. Then she said, "We're all good at different things, which all is very nice and reflects the grand mosaic of God's creation and all of that, but I think we'd all be better off if we weren't like chess pieces that can only move three spaces sideways, or whatever it is. Not that we could learn all that much from each other in two days, but trying will pass the time better than just sitting around and feeling nervous. I could teach everyone to pick a lock, say."

Miss Dok frowned. "Can you *teach* fire witchery? I thought that it was one of the forms of magic that defies traditional parametric systems."

"Ah," Delly said. "I think you can teach a bit of it. But I didn't mean with magic. I meant with a hairpin, more." She cleared her throat and hastily tried to change the subject. "Anyone else got something they wouldn't mind teaching?"

There was a moment of silence. "I could teach anyone who hasn't received any formal magical education some simple parameters," Miss Dok said. "What do you think might be useful, Wells?"

Delly couldn't tell whether Dok wanted to trip her up or she really wanted to know Delly's opinion. She decided to treat it like a real question. "Can you do one of those forget-my-face things? Or one like the one Miss Mayelle was using before, to make her look different? That might come in handy, if we don't want people wondering why they keep seeing the same strange women snooping around."

"Of course," Miss Dok said. "Though I might need the assistance of Miss Cynallum, who I believe is a more accomplished illusionist than myself."

"Oh, not me," Winn said. "I'm a dabbler, that's all. Had a good mentor for illusionary pursuits. I'm happy to assist you, though." Then she looked toward Delly. "D'you suppose everyone might benefit from learning to shoot a bit, Delly?"

"Probably ought to," Delly said. "I reckon that firing a gun's the sort of thing that we might want to know how to manage, considering that we'll be circulating ourselves with all manner of unsavorationary personages for the next—however long it takes us to dig her up." She paused. "She have any living people of her own, Miss Dok? She's a householded daughter to the Wexins, ain't she? Don't suppose she has any spare relations lying about that she might pop off to visit in a moment of crisis?"

"Not that I've ever heard her mention," Miss Dok said. "Though she'd never mentioned that she was using that drip stuff, either, so I suppose that what I know about the woman isn't worth so very much." She looked even more vinegar-dosed than usual when she said that. Delly supposed that made enough sense: finding out something like that about a friend wasn't the sort of thing that you brushed off a few hours after breakfast.

"How long have you known her for?" Delly asked, by way of applying a bit of bridge-building, fence-patching, and generally constructive effort toward their thus far less than entirely smooth and easy relationship.

"I've apparently never known her at all," Miss Dok said crisply, which rather put an end to that line of conversation. Delly tried not to wince.

"Would anyone care to learn a bit about dressing wounds and otherwise aiding the injured?" Mrs. Totham asked. "I couldn't teach any *real* aspect of body science in such a few days, of course, but it might be of some benefit to us if we all know what to do the next time—the next time that one of our number is—" She stopped then, her eyes welling up. "I'm terribly sorry," she said, and wiped at her eyes.

"No need to apologize," Delly said hurriedly, hoping desperately that she'd be able to avoid a storm of tears from the grieving mother. She could already sense a bit of an ache in the space behind her own eyeballs. Exhaustion, maybe, but there was more to it as well. That dead face again. The way that Mrs. Totham had knelt beside the body.

"Right, then," Winn said. "It sounds as if our captain here has put together a fine plan for all of our self-improvements. I'd like to propose that we pack it up for the day and have a rest. All opposed to the motion, say nay." No one said nay, probably because no one knew what Winn was babbling on about. Winn beamed. "Topping! Come on, Delly." And with that, she took hold of Delly's elbow and began steering her out of the room.

"What in the releft are you doing, Winn?" Delly asked, once they were out of earshot of the rest of them.

"Serving as your personal secretary, I suppose," Winn said. "You need *rest*, not to go running about organizing enriching educational courses for ladies. I'm sure we'll all maintain our ignorance for long enough for you to have a bit of a snooze, what?"

"I hadn't thought that personal secretaries made an especial point of dragging their employers out of meetings by their elbows," Delly said.

"Well, that just shows how jolly little about the subject you know," Winn said. Her aggressive good cheer had reached a pinnacle by now: a veritable summer storm of jollitude. "My dear old pop sometimes acts as the personal secretary to the former Lord-Mage of Hexos, and he probably drags Loga out of meetings by his elbow once a fortnight."

"Your father—shit," Delly said. "Do *all* clanners know each other?" Then she said, "Sorry, Winn. Don't know why I'm being such a miserable trout today."

"Oh, I don't know," Winn said. "Do you suppose it might be because you used up half the magic in your body melting a marauding blinkin' animated suit of armor, and then found a dead body and saw a blinkin' mouse walking around with its head on the wrong way?"

She'd steered Delly all the way to the kitchen by then, and sat and watched as Delly ate a substantial butter-and-ham sandwich. Then she herded Delly from the kitchen to Delly's bedroom. "Right," she said, and sat down in the chair beside the bed as Delly started getting her shoes off. "Would you like me to read?"

"Huh?" Delly said, in just the kind of articulate manner you'd expect from a gull who was being courted by a high-quality lady.

"You asked me to sit with you," Winn said. "Should I read aloud?"

"Oh," Delly said. Her face went hot. She didn't know how she ought to be responding to this peculiar question. She'd never been read to in her life, unless you counted the Hall Officiant reading from *Elgar's Letters* when she was in the home for wayward girls, which she for one very certainly didn't. That had been less a matter of being read to and more one of being read *at*, which was another thing entirely. She felt herself fidgeting. Then she said, finally, "If you like."

"I do, thanks," Winn said, and smiled at her, then gave her own thighs a satisfied smack before standing up and ambling toward the bookshelf in the room. "What sort of a book? Adventure? Romance? Moral improvement?"

"Not that last one," Delly said. "I'm of the belief that too much moral improvement causes looseness of the joints and pernicious fatigue."

"Is that so?" Winn said. She sounded like she thought that Delly was pretty funny. "Well, in that case, we'd better have an adventure story." She pulled one off of the shelf then, and sat by Delly's bed and started to read. It was a jolly enough story, with lots of sword fights straightaway, and galloping around on horseback—which led Delly, considering her new experiences of riding, to worry about the state of the gentlemen's particulars—but Delly was having trouble paying close attention to it. She drifted in and out of the story, mostly just pulled along by the sound of Winn's voice, which was soft and low and as familiar as anything else in Delly's life. It was nice. It was a very nice thing.

Delly woke up to the sound of someone crying.

She did her best to sit up, still groggy even as her heartbeat sped to a trot. Her first thought was, *Someone else has gotten themselves killed.* Then she looked to her left and saw Winn still sitting there in her chair, her head in her hands, emitting moist, inelegant sobs.

"Fuckin' *sakes*," Delly slurred out, astonished. "Winn—don't—" She stopped, stymied. What in the fucking releft did you do with a crying gull next to your bed?

"Awfully sorry, old thing," Winn said, and sat up to sniff and wipe at her eyes with her handkerchief. "Don't mind me, just—go back to sleep, eh?"

"I don't know if I can now," Delly said. "What's wrong with you?" It occurred to her, belatedly, that this was a rude thing to say, and definitely not the kind of thing that a person was supposed to say to a crying young lady. Crying young ladies were meant to be dealt with *kindly* and *sensitively*. Delly attempted to dig up some words to throw over the words that had already come out of her mouth, like covering up a mess she'd made on the floor of a bar with some sawdust. "I mean, won't you tell me what's wrong, Winn?" Maybe Winn was too occupied with her crying to have noticed the less than delicate quality of her first two comments.

Winn didn't seem outraged, at least. She dabbed at her eyes some more. "Oh, it's nothing," she said. "I was just—thinking about poor Miss Totham."

"Oh," Delly said, and immediately started thinking about her herself. The dead, twisted face. She shivered.

"She was so *young*," Winn was saying, and Delly felt like a real flea. If she was a decent sort of person she would be concerned about poor Ermintrude and not her own wretched self. "And her poor *mother*," Winn added, which made it even worse. Poor Mrs. Totham.

"Poor old bird," Delly murmured, and immediately knew that that certainly wasn't the right thing to say, either.

"She's a dear old thing, isn't she?" Winn said, having apparently once again not noticed that she was conversing with a moral cockroach. "And she loved poor Ermintrude so much. And I was just thinking about that, and then that made me think of my own pop, and that set me off into the blinkin' musical fountain show."

"That's all right," Delly said. "Anyone would cry in your place." Then, on impulse, she said, "Lie down for a bit and tell me about your pop a little?"

Winn's shoulders hitched up a bit. "Well—hm! I, ah—"

"No funny business," Delly said hastily. Truth be told, she hadn't the merest of interest in a gallop at the moment. It hadn't really been the sort of day that whetted the carnal appetites. That dead body. That dead face. "I lived in a home for wayward girls for a few years. We slept two to a bed. I always thought it was cozier than having to be alone, on a bad night."

"Well," Winn said again, "all right." Then she kicked her slippers off and clambered into bed. "I always used to climb into my parents' bed at night when I was little," she said, her nice low voice gone soft. "Do you have any siblings, Delly?"

"Nope," Delly said. "Not so much as a snot-nosed little crust of a brother. You?"

"No," Winn said. "I always wanted one, though. I even imagined myself a sister to play with, but no joy on that count. I think that Pop would have liked more children, but more never appeared."

Delly listened to all of this and felt rather perplexed, as well as a bit consternated. The perplexity was inspired by Winn's desire for a sister, which Delly was forced to chalk up to a harmless mental peculiarity brought on by being a clanner who'd never had to worry about the last bit of bread being snatched away by some grubby little creature who was new to the home for wayward girls and didn't know better than to try to take food that Delly was reaching for. The consternation was aroused by the fact that Winn had climbed into bed with Delly and immediately started talking about how she'd always wanted a sister, which seemed a bad few tea leaves indeed if Delly was looking for signs of romantic interest in her prospect. Winn had seemed keen enough on the idea when they were riding out for that God-hated Noted Local Beauty Spot, but a dead young girl with half a pig's face and an unliving house mouse had both cropped up in the interim. Delly couldn't really blame anyone involved for noticing a dampening of their amorous fires after seeing what they'd all seen over the past few hours.

She tried to make conversation, anyway. "He likes having kids running around, then? Your pop?"

"Well," Winn said after a moment. "He liked *me*. I don't know how much he liked other people's children. But he's like that about most people, really. He only likes the people who he likes, and everyone else can go chew on sand."

Delly raised her eyebrows. "But he likes *you*. That is, ah, not that he *shouldn't*." It was a funny thing to think, was the thing: a man, a *father*, who disliked other people but liked one's own horrible scabby-kneed, waxy-eared self. It was a fascinating idea, really.

"I should blinkin' well *hope* so," Winn said. Then she said, "He does. We're good pals, Pop and I. He was always there with me when Mother wasn't. And he always—looks after me, and worries about me, and tells me that he's proud of me." Her voice, to Delly's horror, was quaking a bit. "And I was just thinking—that Mrs. Totham must love her girls the way that Pop loves me, and how—cut up he would be if something ever happened to me, or how I would feel if something happened to *him*, and I just—" She was, dreadfully, welling up again. "It's so horribly *sad*."

"You're right," Delly said, for want of anything better to say. It *was* sad, she supposed. She wondered what Winn's pop looked like, and imagined a big stout fellow with a mustache and a bald head who enjoyed a nice hot meal as much as Winn did.

"That's why I want to—help find Ainette," Winn said, her words sliced up a bit by her tears. "Mrs. Totham deserves to know that she's not—running around out there free. And I'd feel responsible if—we'd seen what Ainette was capable of, and *not* stopped her, and she went on to hurt some other parent's child just out of the want of money for her drip."

Astounding was what it was. Like a light so bright it forced you to look at the shape of your own ragged shadow. Those tears for the thought of some other parent's child. "Not just the drip," Delly said automatically. "Just the drip couldn't make a person murder. Something inside of her, too." Then she said, "You're a good person, Winn. Just—you're just perplexingly good."

"So are you, Delly," Winn said. "You're better than I am."

Delly turned her head to look at her, astounded to a peak. "How the fuck do you figure?"

"Just now," Winn said. "When you reminded me that just using the drip wouldn't make someone a murderer. That was a very good thing to do. I'll have to keep that in mind, if we'll be around other people who use it while we look for Ainette. I shouldn't be going about thinking that half the people I speak to are all vicious murderers. That'd be blinkin' unfair to the poor souls, eh?"

Delly just stared at her for a moment, this generous interpretation of her words a bit hard for her to fit through her ears. "I didn't . . ." she started, and then stopped. There was no good in her trying to convince her valuable prospect that she was a dreadful beast of a thing who didn't give half a pinched shit whether or not some dripper she didn't know from Elgar had been misjudged. She'd been thinking about her mam, that was all. She was better off having Winn think she was good, though, so she decided to let her go on thinking it. "Thanks."

"You're welcome," Winn said, and sighed. "Suppose we might as well try and get some sleep. Neither of us will be any good to anybody if we go stumbling around like Mrs. Totham's mouse all day tomorrow."

"Mm," Delly said. Then she decided to seize her chance and said, in her butteriest tones, "Do you think you might kiss me, Winn?"

There was a long pause.

"Well, no," Winn said. "I only got into the bed because we'd promised no funny business. Not really regulation hammerball to try and further a courtship when we're both exhausted and in the extreme throes of blinkin' emotion, eh? What sort of a householder would that make me, if I went after gulls without consideration of the circumstances like that?"

"Oh, right, yes, you're right," Delly said, wondering if anyone had ever accidentally lit a bed on fire through the sheer force of their regret of their own decisions. "Sorry."

"No need to apologize," Winn said. "We're both not really driving with all of our axels greased, are we? Things should look brighter in the morning. G'night, Delly. Or good afternoon, I suppose."

"G'night, Winn," Delly said back, grateful at least that Winn had seen fit to smother the conversation before it was weaned. Winn went quiet, and Delly listened to her breathing and waited to be swept away by terror. If she'd been awake to consider it, she would have been astounded when sleep caught her first.

8

Wherein Dellaria and the Others Are Educated,
Meet Two Interesting Personages New to Most of
Their Company, and Set Out on a Journey

When Delly woke up she was still in the same world that she'd been in when she fell asleep. She had thought, somehow, that it would be different, that she would open her eyes and it would all feel as if it'd been a particularly gin-sodden dream. It didn't feel like that, though. She woke up with her heart pounding and Ermintrude's dead face still firmly printed behind her eyelids. If she sat with herself for longer than a moment or so all of the thoughts and memories that she was the very least interested in contemplating turned themselves into a thick, awful stew, and she herself became the spoon being dragged through it.

Busyness was the only thing that did much to distract her, so Delly made herself busy. It was easy enough. There was plenty to be busy with. She put together a schedule for the lot of them to teach each other everything they said they'd attempt to teach, and planned to go around herding everyone into place so that they'd be educated whether they wanted to be or not. It was a surprise to her when they all showed up to their first lesson—it was going to be Delly teaching them how to pick a basic cheap lock—and acted as if they were glad to learn what she'd be teaching. Maybe the rest of them were just as in need of distraction as Delly was.

In any case, they got along all right with their lessons. Delly found herself pretty taken with Winn's pistols, and the shooting of them. Not that she was any good at it. She missed her target more often than not. But there was something that she liked about the act of shooting, the aiming and the slow, steady breaths and the ringing in her ears, and Winn's hands on her adjusting the way she stood. It shut the rest of the world out. She liked watching Winn line up bottles on a stone wall and then take them out, one by one.

"Who taught *you* to shoot like that?" she asked one day. "I figure it isn't on the curriculum of many schools for young ladies."

Winn laughed. "It isn't," she said. "My pop taught me to shoot, and my mother taught me to fight."

Delly raised her eyebrows. "Did they expect you to be attacked all that often?"

"Oh, no," Winn said. "I think I told you that my pop wanted me to work at a girls' school, or something like that. They just wanted me to be ready for anything that might happen so I wouldn't have to be afraid."

"Huh," Delly said, and just chewed on that thought for a while. Must be a real kick of a thing, to love someone enough to want to plan for them to not be afraid.

There were other lessons, too, in addition to the shifts they all took in pairs to keep an eye on Miss Mayelle and make sure that no one else decided to take their shot at her before she was well and truly wed. There were the lessons that Delly taught in lockpicking, at which Miss Dok proved herself to be suspiciously adept. There were Mrs. Totham's simple little lessons in dressing wounds. There were the parameters that Miss Dok impatiently attempted to shove into Delly's skull. Miss Dok set them up in the parlor for that as if they were in a real classroom, and prowled around the room to make disparaging comments at her pupils' attempts to copy down her parameters. It made Delly's neck sweat, even though she managed to get everything down correctly and fire the spell without any particular mishaps. Miss Dok gave her a look that a person might give to a dog wearing a bonnet. *I suppose that you look very nice*, the look said, *but I don't know how you put that on with only your own rude paws.*

On the fourth day after Ermintrude's death, Mrs. Totham's two eldest daughters arrived.

When Delly first saw them they were seated in the small parlor—it had been at this point completely abandoned by the family of the house and taken over by their own company—perched in little velvet chairs that seemed as perplexed by the people sitting in them as the sitters looked discomforted by their current environment. The sisters looked both very like and entirely unlike each other: both tall, with similar thick eyebrows and soup-ladle ears, but one—Mura—had a strong nose, thick black hair, and a tan complexion, while the other—Vitna—was aggressively pale and violently redheaded, with freckles covering most of her face. Neither was what Delly would be moved to call *pretty*, but when they stood and met her eyes and shook her hand, there was a good, straightforward, healthy sort of air around them that Delly couldn't object to very strongly.

"We came as soon as we got Mother's letter," Mura said. "What's the plan?"

"Ah," Delly said, a bit taken off guard by this sudden call for action. "Hm. Well. Head down to Leiscourt and start snooping around, I suppose." She scratched her nose. "I don't suppose that you two might know anyone down there who, hm, might know a fellow who knows a fellow who might know how to track down a woman who doesn't want to be found?"

Mura and Vitna exchanged a glance. Vitna said, "We might know a fellow like that."

They proceeded with their lesson plans, then, with the two new women added into the mix. Vitna seemed to take a liking to Winn straightaway, which didn't do much to endear her to Delly. Beyond the occasional smile cast in Winn's direction, outside of lessons—they contributed knife-throwing—the two new younger Tothams mostly kept to themselves. They'd rented a room in the village and made their mother join them in it. Delly'd thought that was a bit rough of them at first, dragging an old lady out of a nice comfortable room in a manor to make her sleep with two other people in some cramped little room above a hat shop. That was until she spent half a night tossing and turning, went out into the hall to pace, and ran into Winn there, pacing up and down the same lonely track.

They squinted at each other.

"What are you doing up?" Delly asked.

"The same as you," Winn said. Then she grabbed Delly by the elbow and started tugging her down the hall, in the opposite direction from Delly's room. "Come on."

"Where are we going?" Delly asked.

"My room," Winn said. "I haven't slept a wink since the night I spent in your room. Can't stand being alone, I think."

"Oh," Delly said. "Me neither."

"Good thing that we ran into each other, then," Winn said, and pulled Delly into her room, shutting the door gently behind her. It wasn't a particularly interesting room: just a bed and a desk and a couple of trunks, both closed. Not that there should be very much to see, she reminded herself: this was just a room that Winn was staying in for a week, not one that would have much to reveal about her. Other than the fact that she was very tidy, which Delly already knew. Winn was the sort of gull who always carried the whiff of starch and laundry soap and wholesome hygienical habits about her. Delly cleared her throat. "What did you want to—should I read?"

"Oh, that'd be nice," Winn said brightly. "But I thought we could just sleep." She kicked her slippers off and climbed into bed. "You can grab a book, if you like."

"Uh," Delly said, and then mentally gave herself a sound shake by the scruff and went to make a selection. She decided to be very sly about it and selected a romance. There wasn't a chair next to the bed for her to sit in while she read, so she curled up closer to Winn than was really necessary to read it. Winn didn't pull away, at least, so Delly set to reading.

It was the sort of book that was full of sentences that started off with a lady, took the measure of her eyes, tramped across her bosom, and stopped by a scenic viewpoint over her plump arms, before ranging down along the bank of a long rushing stream of discussion on the Moral Character of Woman, in general, until you'd forgotten the name of the lady in question and had to shove your way through dense thickets of grammatical undergrowth to find it again. Engaging in such muscular literary explorations took up most of Delly's attention, but now and then she managed a quick glance at Winn to see how she was receiving Delly's efforts. Winn just lay there, still and contented-looking, a bit of a smile hanging around her mouth. Delly had barely broached the subject of the lady's long and turbulent clan history when Winn began emitting delicate whistling noises.

"Winn?" Delly whispered.

Winn didn't respond. "Good night, Winn," Delly whispered, feeling a warm surge of somethingness in her generally stony-hearted breast. Then she put the book aside and closed her eyes, and very rapidly fell asleep.

The next day was the wedding, though the happy event—as happy as it could be, considering the circumstances—took place entirely outside of Delly's view, for the reason that her disreputable self had not been invited to attend. She did, however, steal about seven of the nice little sandwiches that were intended for the luncheon party that followed the ceremony, and a bottle of wine intended for the same, and then dragged Winn out to the overlook she'd gone to alone the other day for an impromptu picnic.

"This is awfully nice," Winn said. She was smiling at Delly in a winsomely eye-crinkling way. "One last feast before we march off to war, eh? Shall we toast the bride and groom?"

"No," Delly said, and raised her glass. She'd lifted a couple of those, as well. "To Ermintrude."

Winn's expression went grave, and she toasted back. "To Ermintrude. May she be granted easeful relivings."

Delly clinked her glass against Winn's and downed half of her wine in one swallow. "You're an Elgarite?" she said then, a second before she could wonder if that was a rude question to ask.

"As much as the next gull," Winn said, and took a bite of ham sandwich. "I never attended Hall much, but I suppose I believe in the *Letters* and all. And it always gives you something to say when you don't know what else to say, eh? Useful for when you have to attend a funeral or visit an old lady in poor health." She ate some more of her sandwich. "It's an awfully nice view, isn't it? Thanks for bringing me up here, Delly."

"You're welcome," Delly said, and felt her face go warm. "I just thought that you might like it."

They ate and drank quietly for a while. Then Delly said, "Maybe once we've caught her and gotten our pay, I'll buy a place like this," gesturing toward the grand house below them and the wide expanse of green grass around it.

Winn laughed. "I think that you might need a bit more than a thousand tocats for that, old thing."

Delly's face went hot again, but not in a pleasant, stomach-fluttering sort of way. "I know that," she said shortly. "It was just a joke." She hadn't really known, was the thing. Or rather, she'd known once she'd thought about it but had opened up her mouth before she'd bothered thinking and once again revealed how fucking ignorant she was. Of *course* a girl who'd never seen more than twenty tocats at one time didn't know how much *houses* cost.

"I'm sorry, Delly," Winn said. There were faint lines between her eyes as she looked at Delly over the rim of her glass. "I was just joking, too." She cleared her throat. "Ever think about what sort of house you'd like to have, if you had all of the money in the world? I always thought I'd like one that was a perfect circle, and make the whole ceiling a window so I could look at the stars at night from the middle of my big round bed."

This was a dramatic enough change in topic and a peculiar enough vision for a house that Delly found herself successfully diverted, and they launched into mutual architectural efforts that smoothly cobbled over their earlier conversational ruts. From there they easily hopped from one topic to another, and Delly packed up the empty bottle and glasses and sandwich crumbs at the end of the meal, already envisioning the fine home that Winn's family money would be making for her in the very near future.

It was just as well that they'd had their private little luncheon together, because Delly certainly didn't have any time to make attempts at wooination over the ensuing hours. They had their lessons to attend to that afternoon, once Miss Dok was back from the wedding, and everything had to be done in half the usual amount of time, so there were no opportunities between the lockpickery and knifethrowery for tomfoolery. Then there was supper, followed by a spell of camaraderie-building card playing in the parlor, after which they all went up to their own rooms to pack. "I think I'll try to get my prayers out of the way," Winn said before she headed upstairs, earlier than the rest of them. "With all of the violence and intrigue it seems like we've planned, I don't know when I'll next find the time."

Delly, for her part, packed her single bag and then spent the rest of the night alternately tossing around in her bed like a halibut in the bottom of a rowboat, pacing up and down her room, and staring blankly at one page of a very boring novel. In the morning she made her aching-eyed way down to breakfast, ate two buttered rolls, drank three strong cups of coffee, and jangled her way to the large coaches in the drive that would take them to the train station. Miss Mayelle—or Mrs. Crossick now, Delly supposed—stood on the steps of the manor to see them off and hand each of them their pay, which came in a substantial linen pouch and which Delly sorely wished she'd been given a day earlier, so she might've had time to sew it into the linings of her bag and dress. Mayelle then trapped Miss Dok in a long embrace and whispered into her ear before she allowed her to climb into the carriage.

Delly eyed Miss Dok as she settled into the seat kitty-corner from Delly. "What did she say to you?"

"That's absolutely none of your business, Wells," Dok said, a point that Delly was forced to concede. It didn't stop her from wondering, though. You never knew what a couple of clanners might be whispering to each other.

"Shall I help everyone disguise their pay for the journey, then?" Winn asked. Delly was grateful: she was already fretting about her pay, and the interruption spared her from having to pretend that she was more annoyed with Miss Dok than she really was. Instead, she could just watch Winn make bags of cash look like bundles of soiled ladies' unmentionables, a pretty trick if Delly had ever seen one. Even Miss Dok was impressed, and quizzed Winn on her parameters for almost the entire duration of their trip to the train station.

Delly had insisted on their taking the train down to Leiscourt, despite the fact that she'd never actually ridden in one before. Her argument was that it would be faster and more convenient than their riding back, and that they would be at less risk from highwaymen. Winn, at this, had volunteered that they might be at much greater risk from train robbers, which earned her a kick in the ankle from Delly. In the end, though, all of Delly's scheming came to nothing: the newly forged Mrs. Crossick had barely heard half of her argument before she'd agreed to pay for all of their train tickets. So that was all settled, Delly's particulars would remain unimperiled by donkeykind, and after about an hour all crammed into the coach together, they made it to the station.

It wasn't at all what Delly had expected, mostly because what she had expected was entirely unreasonable. She'd imagined something like the central station in Leiscourt when she'd paid her two sen to go into it for the World's Exposition last year, with its crowds of pushing, shoving people eating inventively spiced nuts out of paper cones and gawping at troll-made magical constructions under the station's great arching glass-and-iron dome. This place was neither so grand nor so full of young boys trying to sell you commemorative plates. It was just a dull platform in a field, with a few dull-looking people on it and not so much as a dried-out old sandwich for sale, and the gray sky starting to spit out miserly little drops of rain. She looked around herself for a moment and sighed. "It has a markedly gloomy aspect, doesn't it? A mouse could fart on this platform and you might mistake it for gunfire."

The unliving mouse, which was perched on Mrs. Totham's shoulder, made a sound. Not a squeak, nor even a chitter. More of a deep, hollow boom, like a great bell tolling a few miles off. A quiet *bong*.

Everyone turned to look at it and, by extension, at Mrs. Totham. The hairs on Delly's arms were all standing up. Winn cleared her throat. "Mrs. Totham," she said, "begging your pardon if I'm out of turn, but is that sort of sound quite normal for an animal that is, erm." She paused, then said delicately, "Not, presently, in the very strictest of senses, *alive*?"

"Oh, dear me," Mrs. Totham murmured, giving the unliving mouse a gentle stroke. "I'm afraid that I don't know, Miss Cynallum. The inadvertent calling upon of certain magics by body scientists under great emotional strain often has very unpredictable effects. I think that I shall call upon my chapter of the Sororal Order of Wizardesses after we arrive in Leiscourt and consult with some other body scientists on the matter." She stroked the mouse again. "He's a very cunning little thing. I ought to name him, don't you think?"

"You should, Mother," Mura said in soothing tones. "Since you like him so much."

Mrs. Totham cast her mild, powder-scented gaze upon the assembled company. "What should I call him?"

"Graig?" Delly suggested. "I knew a fellow named Graig who resembled him exceedingly." An underwhelming gallop, Graig.

Mura shot Delly a quelling look. Winn ventured, "What about Buttons?"

"Buttons!" Mrs. Totham twittered. "How very charming!" She craned her neck to look at the mouse. "I'm sure that you would like *very much* to be called Buttons, wouldn't you?"

Buttons said, "*Bong.*"

As the sound died down, there was another sound. A humming. No, a flapping. The flapping of wings. Then the sky over them went dark, and the air was full of crows. Hundreds of crows, maybe more, flying low and tightly together, all heading in the exact same direction. There was no cawing, only the beating of their wings, which was so powerful that it made Delly's skirt whip around her ankles and blotted out all other sound in the station. Then, just as quickly as they'd arrived, they passed over, made a black cloud heading toward the horizon, and were gone.

The platform was silent. A small child began to wail.

"He likes it!" Mrs. Totham said. "And how dear of him to think of crows. He must have noticed yesterday when I fed one some bread crumbs and thought that I must like them. Crows are so very clever. Ah, look, the train's coming!"

The train was, indeed, coming, which at least gave Delly, Winn, and Miss Dok something to stare at that wasn't Mrs. Totham, the cursed *Buttons*, or each other. Once the train had finally finished pulling into the station, they all clambered on board, and quickly and wordlessly divided themselves up into two compartments: the Tothams in one, the other three in another. Once they'd closed the door securely behind them, they were barely seated before Miss Dok hissed, "*Buttons.* As if there wasn't *enough* for us to worry about."

"Do you think that if I got a big heavy cobblestone," Winn started, and then stopped. Miss Dok was shaking her head.

"*Please* don't. We'll just end up with a *flattened* unalive mouse gonging at us."

"Either that," Delly said, "or whatever cursed spirit is in that mouse right now will *leak out.*"

All three of them shuddered.

"It's probably best not to think about it," Winn said firmly, and they were all silent until the train made a groaning, wheezing sound and lurched forward. There was a long, tense stretch of time when none of them spoke, just peered quietly out the window as the train pulled out of the station, as if they were all poised to confront the next disgusticating apparition that they were all convinced might leap out at them. But nothing leapt: nothing remained in the compartment but them, three women on the edges of their seats.

Eventually they all sat back. Winn pulled a book out of her bag. Miss Dok, confoundingly, pulled out some knitting. Delly closed her eyes and leaned her head against the window, then immediately jerked upright again when her brains were half rattled out of her ears.

"Lean on me," Winn said.

Delly gave her a suspicious squint. No one *wanted* someone else's big heavy head on them. "Really?"

"Of course," Winn said. "I'm not using that shoulder for anything at the moment. And you look exhausted." She went a bit pink. "And it won't be much of a trial for me to be leaned on by *you*, Delly."

Delly squinted at her for a moment longer, taken aback by the suggestion that her own big heavy head might be less of a burden than anyone else's, even to a gull who'd expressed a baffling interest in householding her a few days previous. Winn gazed earnestly back. Delly sighed. "Thanks," she said, and leaned on Winn. It had finally started to rain in earnest outside, and the rain pattered against the window, and the train thrummed and rattled around them, and at some point Delly dropped off to sleep.

She slept through most of the journey, in fact: it seemed that trains must have some sort of uniquely soporific effect on Dellaria Wellses. She only woke up to drink large tin mugs of very weak, very milky sweet tea and eat the hard-boiled eggs and limp sandwiches that occasionally appeared before her. She thought, dimly, that this was what being sick in bed with a cold in the chest must be like for children with mothers. That this might be what her whole life would be like if she really could get her hooks into Winn for good.

She drifted in this way through an entire day and night, waking only briefly when Winn fell asleep too and their heads banged together until they readjusted themselves into a more salubrious drowsing position. She was only well and truly aroused from her slumber when they were pulling into the Leiscourt station, and even then only because Winn gave her a good shake. "Come on, old thing. No time for sleeping now. You can sleep after we've all been thrown in jail for engaging in wizarding battles with known murderesses in the streets of Leiscourt."

Winn, Delly thought, was doing a very poor job of extending her usual jolliness to the topic of their present employment.

Leiscourt station, even in the absence of an exhibition, looked much as Delly had remembered it: crowded and full of people who wanted to sell you teacups with pictures of the Leiscourt Arch printed on them. The truly strange thing about it was how the others fell into line behind her, clutching fearfully at their bags as they wound their way through the throng. All Except Mura and Vitna, of course, who flanked their mother like bodyguards and glared at anyone who chanced to wander close.

Right near the main doors that emptied out onto Dirnham Street there was an old lady selling maps of the city printed on cheap paper. Delly glanced one over, decided that it looked accurate enough, and bought six of them, much to the old lady's delight. Then she led her flock of martial ducklings out of the station.

"Right," Delly said, once they were out on the street and had navigated to a relatively peaceful corner. "I know that some of us already have a place to stay in Leiscourt. Who here *doesn't*?"

Mrs. Totham and Winn both raised their hands. Mura and Vitna exchanged a glance. "We know a place where we usually can take a room," Vitna said. "We were planning on bringing Mother there with us."

"Show me on the map," Delly instructed, and pondered the place that they pointed to. It was in a neighborhood not too far from Delly's room, about twenty minutes' walk in the direction of Elmsedge. Respectable enough to not frighten the ladies, but close enough to Delly's neighborhood and other parts of town where you could easily find red drip that they wouldn't be running across half of Leiscourt every day. "All right," Delly said. "We can work out of the neighborhood, so Mrs. Totham won't have so far to travel every day." And so Delly wouldn't have so far to travel, either, though she didn't say that bit aloud. She squinted at the map a bit longer, thinking. "There's a coffeehouse nearby. Damel's. Do you know it?"

Mura and Vitna nodded. Damel's was a nice cozy sort of hidey-hole, but not too expensive, and the staff never minded if you took up a table for hours on end to nurse a single cup of coffee and read all of the newspapers in the place. "Good," Delly said. "We'll make that our office, for now. Meet there every day at three, say."

Miss Dok arched her lovely eyebrows. They were a marvel, those eyebrows. Very black and very shapely. Delly wondered whether she might have a special barber for them, or if she gave them fifty strokes each with a tiny brush every night.

"You want us to start work at three o'clock in the *afternoon*?"

"That's right," Delly said. "If you figure that my mam makes a representative example of your ordinary dripper, which I do, then you have to expect that most of her colleagues don't get out of bed much earlier than that, and those that sell the stuff to them are likely to keep similar hours. We'll probably be up working at night, mostly."

Miss Dok went a bit pink under the powder on her cheeks. "I suppose that's very sensible," she said. "Three o'clock, then."

"Where are *you* staying?" Delly asked her. It occurred to her that she maybe ought to have asked that a bit earlier.

"In my rooms by Weltsir," Miss Dok said, in a tone that suggested that she'd like to add on an *obviously*.

"That's a bit of a journey," Delly said. It was all the way in the eastern quarter of the city, in the quiet old university district. "Sure you wouldn't rather stay closer by?"

Miss Dok looked at her for a long, uncomfortable moment. Then she said, "Yes."

"Oh," Delly said. "All . . . right, then." She looked at Winn. "You, ah. Know where you might like to stay yet?"

"No," Winn said. "I expect that I'll figure something out."

"You could stay with me," Delly blurted out, and then wished with all of her soul for the power of deblurtation. How the fuck was she going to let Winn *see* the inside of her dreary, dingy, miserable little room, let alone *sleep* in it? After a week in luxury at the manor, the realities of her room came writhing before her eyes like a vision from the releft: the sagging mattress, the peeling paint, the lack of any kind of color or comfort. How had she been *living* like that? How hadn't she *seen* it? It wasn't like buying a few cheap prints for the walls would have been so difficult, or cost more than half of one of her usual nights at a bar. She'd been living all this time like she was still stuck in the fucking home for wayward girls.

Or like she was living in that filthy squat she'd found her mam in.

Winn, unfortunately, couldn't see what all was happening in Delly's head. She looked delighted. "That'd be jolly nice of you, Delly, if you have the spare corner for me to curl up in. Save me having to find a place all on my own."

"It's nothing," said Delly's vile blurting mouth. "I have room." She didn't. "Especially for you." She was her own most hideous nightmare. She turned red, cleared her throat, then busied herself very importantly marking Damel's on all six maps. "Let's all go put down our bags and settle in, do whatever information gatheration that we can manage on our own, and meet at Damel's at three tomorrow."

The ladies exchanged glances. Then Delly was hit by a horrible smell. She gagged, then watched with a sort of creeping horror as the clasp of Mrs. Totham's reticule opened and Buttons emerged from within it. He looked more . . . swollen than he had when Delly had last had the misfortune of looking at him. Some of his fur had fallen out.

Buttons said, "*Bong.*"

There was silence until the last reverberations of the bonging had faded away. Even the passersby slowed their steps. The pigeons stopped burbling. Mrs. Totham gave a firm nod. "Wonderful! We're all in agreement, then. We shall see you all tomorrow!" And with that, she and her daughters turned and left.

9

Wherein Dellaria Expends a Great Deal of Energy
upon Various Pursuits Relating to Her Familial
and Domestic Affairs

They all split up then, to head toward wherever they planned on resting their weary heads that evening. Delly hailed a cab and gave the driver directions to her neighborhood entirely by instinct: her mind was once again wildly whirring after a solution to a problem she'd managed to get herself into. How in the releft was she meant to let Winn see her room in its present state? After a few moments of determined whirring, though, she thought that she might have hit upon a solution. Unfortunately, it involved spending some more of her hard-earned money. Even more unfortunately, it involved the cooperation of Mrs. Medlow, an uncooperative old cat if there ever was one.

Delly rummaged through the metaphorical dusty attic of her early religious education, found a heavily creased and yellowed prayer at the bottom of a metaphorical packing crate, and did her best to pray it.

They arrived fairly quickly, and Delly tipped the driver enough that he consented to help them carry in their bags and deposit them beside a table in the dining room at which Delly entreated Winn to sit. The bar itself, Delly was relieved to realize, was ordinary enough even through her new and more sophisticated lens: clean and plain, with only somewhat roughish customers. Dull, one might say, through the eyes of an individual as sober and upstanding as the newly reformed Dellaria Wells. "I won't be a tick," she said to Winn. "I just have to speak to my landlady." And with that she went barreling into the back room to find Mrs. Medlow.

Mrs. Medlow was slicing and buttering bread in the kitchen when Delly cornered her. "Dellaria!" she said. "How delightful to see you again!"

"You know very well that I'd be faced with pustules if I didn't come back, Mrs. Medlow," Delly said. "And *very* injurious to my sensibilities I still find that fact, Mrs. Medlow. But you'll be pleased to hear that I have your money."

"I *am* pleased to hear it," Mrs. Medlow said, and watched avidly as Delly counted the coins into her hand. She made as if to leave, to put the money wherever it was that she kept her dragon's hoard, but Delly stopped her.

"I'll give you more if you can do something for me."

Mrs. Medlow turned and smiled. "Of course, I would be *delighted* to help, Dellaria."

Delly restrained herself from any commentary. Instead, she only said, "I have a friend I'd like to stay with me for—"

"That will be another tocat a month."

"*Fine*," said Delly, through a jaw that felt toffee afflicted. "Like I was saying. She's a *nice* girl, and the room as it is ain't suitable. It needs cleaning and fixing up. A rug, maybe a chair or something, I don't know. If I pay you for your labors do you think you can have it looking respectable in two hours?"

Mrs. Medlow smiled. "Of course," she said. "Five tocats."

The toffee dissolved itself in an instant. Delly was sure her jaw was dangling near her ankles. "*Five tocats*, Mrs. Medlow? For *cleaning a room, Mrs. Medlow?*"

"And for buying the furniture," Mrs. Medlow said. "And the decorations. Ladies like them little statues and things, don't they?"

Delly imagined the sheer variety of little statues that Mrs. Medlow might purchase with five tocats and winced. "No statues," she said firmly. "Get some curtains, though. *Plain* ones." She suspected that Mrs. Medlow might be capable of inflicting any manner of dreadful chintzes upon Delly's person, if given her head. "Imagine that you're decorating a room for a nice gentleman boarder." She counted the tocats into Mrs. Medlow's hand, inwardly waving a tragical handkerchief at her departing wealth. "Two hours," she said again. "And ask a boy to carry up our bags. I'll leave them behind the bar." Then she went out to find Winn. "They're cleaning the room," she said. "Should we go have lunch?"

"All right," Winn said, all in innocence, and they went off to find some lunch together.

Lunch, at least, created no major difficulties: Delly steered them out of her neighborhood and into a nicer one nearby, where they sat down at a respectable restaurant and shared a lunch of roast lamb that Delly thought would pass muster with even a very daintitudinous member of the better classes. Winn, at least, seemed to have no complaints, though Delly was beginning to notice that Winn very rarely complained about anything at all. She ate heartily and then proposed a stroll in the nearby park they had passed on the way to the restaurant, "to stimulate the digestion a bit, what?" Delly agreed to this immediately—she'd been trying to think of a way to kill the rest of the two hours she had promised Mrs. Medlow—and they set out.

It was a nice day for a walk, and the park was very leafy and green and generally pastoral in its aspect. Winn went striding along with her hands in her pockets, her face turned up toward the sun, looking very boyish and, Delly thought, quite pretty. "One does like a nice tramp after lunch," Winn said. "Prevents sluggishness in the afternoon, what?"

"I guess so," Delly said, though she generally never took much note of her own sluggishness. Generally, she only paid attention to the state of her own well-being when she was so hungover that her knees ached. "You seem to have all sorts of very . . . healthy habits," she said eventually, for want of anything less boring to say.

Winn laughed at that. "You sound like my pop! He always pretends to fuss about having to get up early and eat wholesome meals and do physical exercise. Mother's very strict about that sort of thing. She used to march me around Lord-Mage's garden in Hexos for hours when I was little, teaching me how to identify all of the different insects and flowers and things. I found out later that she'd had to ask the gardeners what they all were ahead of time, since she didn't know anything about tropical plants. She always says that if you keep children going until they're exhausted, feed them, and put them in bed, then it doesn't leave them with any time to stick themselves with knives or fall down wells. So now that I'm grown up, I march *myself* around for hours, and I haven't fallen down any wells yet."

Delly thought of herself as a little girl, running wild in the streets and begging nips of gin off of the punters outside of the bars, and thought that she probably could have done with some forced marches of her own. "But your father doesn't go in for that sort of thing?"

"Oh, well, he'll *walk*," Winn said. "He has a bad leg, so he's not much for tramping around in the wilderness. He likes to have a walk down a busy street, and look in the shop windows, and stop for a coffee and a cigarette. He used to take me to museums and picture galleries, and when Mother took us on her forced marches he would bring along pencils and paper so we could both sketch."

"You can *draw*, too?" Delly asked. She'd always admired people who could draw.

"Oh, not very well," Winn said. "It's one of those accomplishments that one is meant to have, isn't it? Like dancing and playing the pianoforte. Though I must say that I draw better than I do either of *those*."

They were promenading around the fountain at the center of the park now, part of the crowds of clerks and young women taking their afternoon breaks from their shops and countinghouses. It wasn't a fine crowd, but it was a tidy and respectable one, and Delly suddenly found herself conscious of the terrible state of her own dress. "Maybe I should buy some new clothes," she said aloud. "With my pay, I mean. I've already paid off my rent for a while, so I won't have to worry about *that*, at least." Then she flushed. Now Winn knew for a fact that her rent was so cheap that she could pay off months of it with fifty tocats, and that she was still poor enough to worry about it.

Winn was nodding. "That would be nice. Having some nice new things to wear bolsters the morale, eh? Especially when you're going to meet new people."

"Like who?" Delly asked, a bit puzzled by this last bit. "Drip dealers?"

"Oh, well," Winn said, her cheeks going a bit pink. "You know that I—said a bit about my intentions, the other day. So I thought—when all of this is over, of course—that I'd like for you to meet my parents."

"*Me?*" Delly said, as if there had been some confusing aspect to Winn's very straightforward statement. "Meet your *parents*? Are you sure that's a good idea?"

Win was frowning. "Of course it is. I mean"—her cheeks went pinker—"I thought that I'd made my intentions clear?"

"Oh, no, I mean, you did," Delly said hastily. "I only thought it'd be more of the sort of householdry where we'd just pop over to some government office and have papers drawn up."

Winn frowned harder. "I don't want to elope," she said. "There wouldn't be any reason for us to have to do that." Then she added hastily, "I mean—if things were to, erm. Progress. In that fashion."

"Oh, right," Delly said, embarrassed. "I mean—let's not cross any bridges before they hatch." Then she winced.

"Right," Winn said firmly, after a moment of very evident confusion over whatever had just dribbled out of Delly's God-cursed mouth. "Well. Ah. Shall we walk some more?"

"Yes, right," Delly said, and they set off marching around the fountain with such determined vigor that a few clerks had to dive out of the way to save themselves from being bowled over.

Eventually they had nowhere left to march, and Delly led Winn back to her boardinghouse at a tortoise-chasing pace, stopping often to look at and comment upon objects they passed that, in fact, merited neither closer examination nor extended commentary. She kept stealing glances at her pocket watch. It had been about two hours by now, but she couldn't help but want to give Mrs. Medlow extra time to put everything in order. She had a sudden vision of herself leading Winn into a room full of burly fellows rolling out rugs and hanging up cheap pictures, and she winced.

"Is everything all right?" Winn asked. "You keep looking at your watch."

"Oh, it's nothing," Delly said hurriedly. "I'm just wondering whether or not they've finished cleaning the room yet."

"I should hope so," Winn said. "Unless the poor gull doing the cleaning has been equipped with a broom the size of a toothpick, what?"

Delly managed a weak smile.

By the time they had finally made it back to Mrs. Medlow's place Delly had worked herself into a near fever of nervous excitation. Once they were inside, she thundered up the narrow staircase at full tilt— "Steady on, there, Wells," Winn said from behind her—and unlocked and flung open the door as if she expected to find a robber behind it.

There wasn't a robber. Instead, there was a room that had been so effectively transformed by Mrs. Medlow's efforts that Delly was forced to merely blink at it for a moment in silent perplexity. The walls, at least, appeared to be the same in their size and shape as they had previously been, though the wallpaper had been stuck back into place where it had once been peeling, and several large framed prints of famous architectural marvels had been hung up to cover some particularly conspicuous stains. The bed was still there, but there was a new coverlet and plump-looking pillows on it, and the brass of the bed itself had been polished to a sheen. The washstand remained the same, but the cracked old pitcher and basin had been replaced by bright new ones, and the mirror had been cleaned, and there was a nice white towel on the hook and a fresh bit of soap in the dish. It only lacked for steaming-hot water.

The stove, on the far wall, had been polished as well, and it gleamed beside the newly filled coal scuttle in a way that seemed to say, *Won't we be cozy now?* There was a new copper kettle on the stove, too, and a little cupboard beside it that seemed to hint at more treasures within: cups, maybe, or a tin of cookies. Before the stove stood two sturdy-looking armchairs and a low table, which themselves stood upon a bright new red-and-blue rug. Winn's trunks were there, too, and Delly's carpetbag on top of it, all ready to be unpacked. The overall effect was so shockingly homey and cozy—like the room of a real, actual person who liked to curl up in a comfortable armchair and read books by the fire instead of guzzling gin with strangers on a cold winter evening— that Delly felt her eyes begin to suddenly sting.

"But what a snug little place you have, Delly!" Winn said, which brought Delly back to herself enough to step inside the rest of the way and let Winn in, too.

"Thank you," Delly said, blinking hard. Then, surprised that she meant it: "It's nice to be home."

They unpacked their things then, before settling into the new armchairs to plan their next moves. "I think I'll have to talk to my mam," Delly said. She wasn't particularly looking forward to the prospect. "Have to find her first, though."

"Do you not know where she is?" Winn asked. She sounded surprised about the idea, as if the thought of having misplaced one's mother was a concept entirely foreign to her experience. It probably was. *Respectable* mothers, Delly reckoned, tended to stay where one left them.

"Nope," Delly said, "I generally don't. No fixed abode. I know where she was the last time I saw her, though, so I suppose that's the place to start."

Winn was frowning. "That sounds very difficult, Delly," she said. Her voice was gentle. "Not knowing where your mother is, I mean."

Delly shrugged, thrown a bit off guard. "It's better than being *sure* where she is, sometimes," she said. "If I don't know where she is, then whatever chaos she's causing isn't *my* concern. As soon as I find her, I have to start cleaning up her messes. *And* she'll ask for money." She rubbed her hand over her face and sighed. "A very chaotic sort of person, my mam." She paused. "Maybe you could . . . make your own inquiries about the drip business? While I'm gone?" She was honestly not sure what kinds of inquiries Winn might be able to make. Everything about her shouted, *Nice young person from a respectable family.* She could pretend to be a nice young person from a respectable family who was slumming it with the drippers after having disgraced herself with an unsuitable boy, she supposed. More likely everyone would just assume that she was with the police and refuse to speak with her. Winn had a distinctly uniformed air to the set of her shoulders.

"Oh," Winn said. "But—I'll be absolutely *useless* on my own, but I might be able to make myself useful if I trot along with you."

Delly hesitated for a second. She hadn't expected that. And, truthfully, she wasn't sure whether or not Winn *could* make herself useful. She cleared her throat. "*How* would you . . . uh."

"Make myself useful?" Winn asked cheerfully, as if being asked to prove her own usefulness wasn't offensive to her in the least. "Well, I tend to get along like fresh cream with mothers, for one thing. Might sand a few edges off if I tag along, eh? And besides that, if you meet any unsavory types while you're looking for her, I might be able to intimidate them a bit."

"Intimidate them?" Delly asked, trying not to sound too skeptical of the idea. Winn was *big*, that was true enough, but so was that fellow down the street's enormous marshmallow cream of a dog, and the worst that that creature looked like he ever wanted to do to anyone was dribble all over their shoes in ecstasy when he was given a good healthy stroking. Winn had a face that everybody's mother could love. *Intimidating* wasn't the first word that sprang to mind, really.

"I can!" Winn said. "I'm *very* intimidating, really! Wait, let me show you. Look away for just a tick, won't you?"

Delly looked toward the wall, bemused, as Winn rattled around by her trunks. Eventually she piped up again. "You can turn around now, Delly!"

Delly turned around and then just gaped for a moment. Winn had changed into men's clothing: a knee-length pleated skirt—Delly was at pains not to gawp at her exposed bestockinged legs—and a white shirt with a jacket over it. Her skirt, jacket, and stockings were in sober black, as were her sturdy black boots. She'd also pulled her hair back into a severe plait. The jacket served to accentuate the broadness of her shoulders, and the hairstyle the strength of her jaw. She looked, if not like a man, then like a woman who could easily pick you up and toss you out the nearest window if you annoyed her. Which, Delly thought suddenly, she was. Winn was far, far stronger than most women, and probably most human men, as well, and out of her pretty dresses she suddenly looked it.

Delly licked her lips. "You look—positively terrifying, Winn."

Winn beamed. "Do you really think so?" she asked, and patted at her hair.

That made Delly want to laugh a bit, but she kept herself from doing that. Instead, she just nodded. "*Very.* And I'd like you to come with me to look for my mam at her old squat. That is, if *you'd* like to."

Winn blushed slightly, then smiled. "I'd like that very much."

They set off a few minutes later on the legs of two people who were determined to be highly efficacious motherhunters. Ol' Marvie's latest squat was about a twenty-minute walk from Delly's place, and the neighborhoods grew rougher as they walked through them. The roughness of a neighborhood had never bothered Delly much—being a fire witch meant that if any men tried to interfere with her, she could just set their skirts ablaze and flee, and she liked not having to worry about watching herself around the quality folks—but she found herself watching Winn now, and wondering what she was making of the places they were walking through. She tried to see them through Winn's eyes: the buildings that had been shuttered and abandoned interspersed with those that had too many people living all together in them packed up like eggs in a crate, the dogs and chickens and little children running aimlessly in the street, the washing hanging from the windows instead of hidden respectably away. Then there were the men who leaned: in doorways and in alleys, against front steps and out of windows, with cigarettes hanging from their mouths or bottles of beer from their fingers, and eyes that followed Winn and Delly as they passed.

Winn, at least, didn't look as if she was particularly bothered by any of it. She looked around as they walked with a very ordinary amount of interest, her shoulders back and her hands once again thrust comfortably into the pockets of her skirt.

"All right, Winn?" Delly asked after a while, when Winn's gaze seemed to turn inward for a time. There was nothing wrong in *asking*, at least.

"Me? Oh, yes, *I'm* all right," Winn said. "I was just thinking about supper."

Delly blinked. "But we only ate an hour ago."

Winn's cheeks went pink. "Unfortunately," she said, "having just eaten never seems to stop me from thinking about what my next meal will be. It's awfully embarrassing, I know."

"Oh, no, it's not *embarrassing*," Delly said hastily. "A sign of health is what it is."

"If you say so," Winn said. But she looked pleased, and Delly resolved to make sure to fill up the new cupboard in her room with things to eat, just in case Winn got hungry.

They arrived at Delly's mam's squat a few minutes later, and Delly showed Winn where the space was where you could wiggle through the fence. Winn eyed it for a moment. Then she said, "I think I'd rather go over it, m'self," leapt up into the air, grabbed ahold of the top of the fence, and swung herself over to the other side as easily as Delly might toss a rubber ball.

Delly gaped after her for a moment, already dreading what was to come. Then she sighed, handed her fate over to God, and got down into the dirt to wriggle under the fence in full view of Winn like a great filthy mole in a tattered old frock.

"Oh, dear," Winn said, and helped Delly to her feet, then started vigorously patting dirt off of her dress. "I'm awfully sorry, old thing, I ought to have waited and given you a leg up."

"That's all right," Delly said, though, since it had been brought up, she privately thought that Winn ought to have helped her, too. "I probably would have managed to fall off at the top and break my arm." She examined a new hole in the front of her dress with a resigned gust of air through her nose.

Winn's hands hovered in the air for a moment, then dropped back down to her sides. "I'd like to buy you a new dress," she said, and then colored. "Well—I don't know if it's *exactly* proper, when we aren't . . . y'know. But I think that it ought to pass muster just the one time, don't you?"

Delly gawped at her magnificently. If there were awards for gawping, the committee would have presented her with a plaque on the spot. "You don't have to buy me a dress," she said after a moment. What she was actually thinking was *You absolutely and with certainitude ought to buy me a dress*, and *This must mean that you really do like me*, and *I wonder if I could get away with asking for a hat*.

"I know that I don't *have* to," Winn said, "but it would make me happy. Especially since the dress you're wearing was damaged because I was an absolute brigand and let you go crawling around in the dirt like a worm, what?" Then, before Delly could begin to wonder whether or not this meant that Winn thought of her as especially wormlike in her aspect, Winn gestured toward the back door of the house. "Shall we have a look?"

Delly agreed that they ought to, and Winn held the broken old door for her in a way that seemed to apologize for the unfortunate fence incident. Then they were inside, in the filth and the gloom of the old house.

Delly immediately tripped over something. Winn caught her by the elbow before she hit the ground, gently set her back onto her feet, and made a light appear in her palm. Delly blinked against the sudden glare. "That's a clever trick." Delly hadn't heard her recite an incantation, or do any of the other things that academic wizards normally had to do to fire their spells. "And thanks for catching me."

"You're welcome," Winn said. "It's just a little thing that my uncle Loga taught me." She peered around herself for a moment. A line had formed between her eyebrows. "This is—really where your mother lives?"

Delly's face went hot. "Was the last time I saw her," she said, and then walked quickly into the next room, where she'd found her mam the last time. "Marvie Wells?" she called out. "Mam? Are you in here?"

"*Bitch*," a man's voice shouted, and a large shape came lurching out of the darkness and toward Delly. "*Told you not to come back, bitch!*" Or something like that: the words were too slurred to make out very clearly.

At first, Delly just stood there in a mist of befuddlement: she wasn't used to having obscenities screamed at her by large men in dark rooms, and it didn't occur to her to be frightened. By the time that thought had percolated its way through her body and into her muscles it was too late: the man had her by the throat and started squeezing. "*Bitch*," he said again. There wasn't any liquor on his breath. "*Bitch, you've been dead ten years.*"

Not true, Delly thought. *What a misunderstanding to have befallen us.* Though it might *become* true, in ten years' time, at the rate this fellow was going. She scratched at his hand, then concentrated with all of her rapidly diminishing strength and set his shirt on fire. He barely blinked. Delly's own dress started to smolder. "*Bitch*," he hissed.

Delly thought, *What a fucking undignified way to die.*

There was a sudden loud thwacking noise, and the man dropped to the ground like a rotten apple from a weak branch. Winn said, "*Blinkin' rilift,*" shook out her hand, and hastily rolled him over to extinguish the flames. Then she turned toward Delly and began slapping at her bosom, which Delly thought for a moment might indicate a very sudden but not unwelcome advancement in their courtship before she realized that her dress was still on fire.

"I think it's out," Winn said eventually, and then looked down at the man. "You don't suppose that he's—"

"Best not to know," Delly said quickly. A dead body was the last fucking thing that she wanted to add to the rapidly growing list of problems with **PROPERTY OF DELLARIA WELLS** written at the top.

Winn, her face illuminated by the little light in her left hand, gave her a look like she'd just grown a tail and barked. "We can't just *leave* him here," she said, and knelt down to feel for a pulse. "He's alive," she announced after a moment. "Is anyone else here, did you see?"

Delly made a cautious sojourn around the room, shook her head, then remembered that Winn couldn't see her, and said, "No. All clear. Let's get out of here."

"All right," Winn said, and stood up with a loud grunt, the big man in her arms. "Where's the nearest hospital?"

Delly stared at her, her nerves finally bubbling over into annoyance. "Just *leave* him, Winn. He'll sleep it off and wake up with a headache, that's all."

"People die from blows to the head hours later, sometimes," Winn said back. Snapped, really. Delly had never heard Winn snap at anyone before. "I'm not leaving a man to die just because you don't want to take the trouble to help him." Then, a moment later, "I'm sorry, Delly. I'm sorry, I didn't mean that."

"Yes, you did," Delly said. Her gut felt like it was the end of a five-gin night. "You were right, too." She turned toward the door. "The closest hospital's a mile from here. We're going to need to get a cab."

It was, it turned out, an extremely tricky thing to hail a cab while you were holding aloft an unconscious man who looked exactly as if you'd just lit him on fire and then punched him in the face after he'd attacked you in a drugged haze in a filthy abandoned building. They got one eventually, though, and once they'd gotten the man loaded into the back the rest of the ride went smoothly enough. He was just starting to come round by the time they'd reached the hospital, and though Delly had braced herself to be attacked again he was docile enough as they helped him through the hospital doors. He stared at Delly's face, his eyes flat and unfocused. "Mama," he said. "My head hurts, Mama."

His mam. Probably the bitch he'd tried to strangle, too. Delly gritted her teeth. "There, there, son," she said to him, and tried to fling him at the nearest nurse. "He attacked us," she said. "And he thinks I'm his mam."

"Oh, no," the nurse said. "Another one?"

Delly frowned. Something cold crept through her chest. "Another what?"

"Dripper," the nurse said. She was an older lady with a kind pink face and her hair shorn close: likely the member of some nice Daeslundic order that would feed you bread and soup with only a briefish bit of prayer over your misbegotten self. "There's something wrong with whatever stuff they're selling out there. We've had twenty come in just today. Frightened, seeing things, heart palpitations. Only half of them came in under their own power, the poor creatures."

Another cold slither. Delly said, "My mam's missing. Do you think you might have her here? Marvie Wells?"

The nurse pursed her lips. "I'll be back with you in a moment," she said, and then a couple of burly men came by and loaded the big man onto a stretcher, and the nurse went with them as they carried him away.

The wait felt a fuck of a lot longer than a moment. Winn squeezed Delly's elbow. "At least if she's here you'll know that she's being taken care of, eh?" she said. Delly didn't respond. If her mam was here, then that meant that something had gone wrong, and she was in no mood to look on the bright side about it.

Eventually the nurse came back. "We have no one here who has told us that her name is Marvie Wells," she said. "But there are a few who I suspect may have given us false names, and two who haven't given us names at all."

"Could I see 'em?" Delly asked. The nurse frowned. Delly persisted. "It's my *mam*."

The nurse softened. "I'll take you through the ward," she said. "No dawdling, and no bothering the other patients. If you don't find your mother, then you'll have to leave at once."

"All right," Delly said. She didn't care about any of the other people in there, anyway. "And my friend? Can she come with me?" She hadn't known she was going to ask that until it had already left her mouth. She didn't think that she regretted it, though.

"If she *behaves herself*," the nurse said, with a stern look at Winn. Then she gestured for them to follow her.

It was awful on the ward. There was no place to rest yourself: everywhere you looked was someone curled in on themselves in misery, and there was nothing to listen to but wails and groans, and every breath smelled like piss and vomit. Delly tried to breathe through her mouth and keep her eyes on the people whom she passed. Not her mam, not her mam, not her mam.

Her mam.

She almost walked past her before she recognized her. She looked—not shrunken, exactly, but *reduced* somehow. Not fighting or drinking or running a game. Just still and silent and gray in a hospital bed.

"Mam?" she whispered. Then, louder: "*Mam?*"

"You probably won't be able to wake her," the nurse said. "She was brought in like this. I'm afraid that when they come in in this state, all we can do is watch and wait and try to keep them comfortable. Most of them come around after a few days. Marvie Wells, you said her name was?"

"Yeah," Delly said, and wiped at her eyes. "What the fuck's wrong with her?"

"Watch your *language*, girl," the nurse said, "or I'll throw you out of here. And it's this new red drip they're selling that's causing it. Driving people mad is what it does." As she grew more indignant she started sounding less like a nice respectable religious lady and more like a tough old gull from West Leiscourt, like she'd grown up in the same sorts of neighborhoods that Delly had. "Damages the brain somehow, is what I think." Then she took a look at Delly's face and softened again. "Would you like to sit with her? Hold her hand for a while?"

No, Delly wanted to say. *Let the mean old cat rot*, she ought to have said. Instead she said, "Yes," and sat in the hard wooden chair beside the bed. "How long can she stay here? Who's paying for it?"

The nurse winced slightly. "We'll keep someone for two days," she said. "After that, if the family can't pay, we send them to the home for the poor on Cartwright Street."

Delly just nodded and squeezed her mam's hand without looking at her. "How much is it to stay here?"

"Five tocats a week."

Far more than Delly's rent, but she had enough left to pay for a few weeks, at least. She nodded again. Then she said, "And what if she gets better and leaves and just goes back to the drip?"

The nurse looked grave. "I don't know," she said. "But if her health has already been weakened by this first episode . . ."

Delly just kept nodding. She'd die, was what the nurse meant. Her mam would die. "Those places," she said. "Out in—out in the countryside, like they have in books, where they send rich ladies with weak lungs to take the air. How much do those cost?"

The nurse raised her eyebrows. "A great deal, miss," she said.

Delly persisted. "How much?"

"Well, I don't know exactly," the nurse said. "Twenty a week, or something like that, I expect."

Delly swallowed hard and nodded. "If I found the money, do you think you could help me get her into a place like that?"

The nurse looked sad, like she thought that Delly was a particularly tragic case. It made Delly want to slap her. "If you can find the money, I'll do my best."

"Thank you," Delly said, and squeezed her mam's hand. "Do you think I could just sit with her for a while?"

"Of course," the nurse said. "I'll be back in a few minutes to escort you out." Then she walked off.

"Delly," Winn whispered, once they were closer to being alone, "I'm awfully sorry."

"'S'not your fault," Delly mumbled. She regretted having asked if Winn could come in here. There was a distinct humiliating aspect to having an audience for this.

"I'm sure we can think of something," Winn said. "For the money."

Delly lifted her head to look at her. *We?*

Winn went a bit pink. "Well—I'd like to at least try to help, as much as I can. I don't have much money of my own, other than what we just earned, but I'm sure if we put our heads together we can think of something, what?"

"Maybe," Delly said, not sure whether to be moved by Winn's wanting to help or just annoyed by the fact that Winn was acting as if they'd just be able to have a bit of a think about it and then pull a few hundred tocats out of their assholes. Feeling moved won out. She had to close her eyes for a moment before she could speak again. "That's nice of you, Winn." Then she said, "That thousand tocats on Ainette's head sure would come in fucking handy about now."

"We'll get that," Winn said, all confidence. "And we'll figure something out for the interim, too." She looked down at the still figure on the bed. "She's awfully young, isn't she? Your mother, I mean."

"Suppose she is," Delly said after a moment. She'd never really thought about it. "She was about fourteen when she had me."

"*Fourteen*," Winn murmured. "That must have been awfully hard on both of you."

"I suppose so," Delly said after a moment. She had never thought too much about how hard it must have been for her mam, when she'd just been a little kid herself, and wanting her mam to act like a *mother*. Then she said, "What the fuck are we going to *do*, Winn?"

"Buy you two new dresses," Winn said.

Delly stared at her. "What?"

"If you try to wear that one for much longer, you'll be arrested for public indecency," Winn said. Delly glanced down at herself and winced. The dress, in addition to the holes, now sported several large singed spots that threatened to expose her soft, vulnerable belly to the judging eyes of society. "So we'll order you two new dresses, and maybe see if we can borrow one for until they're ready, and then we can have a nice hot supper before we settle in to try to decide what to do with ourselves next."

Delly had to close her eyes again. She felt—flayed, somehow. Like the flames that had singed her dress had been able to singe her skin, too, and now all of her insides were exposed to the air. "That sounds fine," she said after a long moment. "That—sounds awful fine, Winn."

"I'm glad," Winn said. Her voice was soft and low. "Do you want to sit with her a while longer?"

"Dunno," Delly said, looking down at her mam's hand clasped in her own. "Do you think it'd even make a difference?"

Winn tilted her head slightly and frowned as if she was really considering it. "I don't know whether or not it will make a difference to *her*. Mrs. Totham might be able to tell you more about that. But I suppose that it might make a difference to *you*."

Delly rubbed her thumb over her mam's knuckles. "I've been a real bitch to her," she said.

"Have you really?" Winn asked, and sat down in the chair on the other side of Marvie's bed. "How?"

"Got awfully snappish with her the last time I saw her," Delly said. "Getting on her about her using the red drip."

"Well, you weren't exactly wrong about that, were you?" Winn asked. "You were just worried about her, that's all." She was frowning again. "You know that this wasn't your *fault*, Delly."

"Course it wasn't my fuckin' fault," Delly said. "I didn't shove the fuckin' drip down her throat, did I?" Then she sighed. "Sorry."

"That's all right," Winn said, though she sounded as if she was maybe, finally, starting to lose her patience with Delly a bit. Or maybe that was just in Delly's head. It felt difficult to tell.

They sat quietly for a while then, or as quietly as they could within the clamor of the ward, until the nurse reappeared to turn them out. They were almost to the door before she thought to ask her something. "Were you here when she was brought in?"

"I was, as it happens," the nurse said. "Why?"

"Did you see who brought her? Did they give a name?"

"It was a man," the nurse said. She didn't say a gentleman. "Pale-complected. And very nearsighted, I would say."

"Because of his squint?" Delly asked. Her heart had started to beat a bit faster.

"Yes, exactly," the nurse said. "He ought to get himself some spectacles."

"Squint Jok," Delly said to Winn once they were out on the street. "That's what they call the fella that my mam's been keeping time with. It has to be him. If he was there when she took the stuff that put her into that state, then he probably knows who sold it to her. We've got to find Squint Jok, Winn."

"All right," Winn said. "That might be a bit of a lark, mm? A bit of an old-fashioned manhunt. We can get right to it after supper."

Delly stared at her cross-eyedwardly. "After supper?" she repeated.

"That's right," Winn said. "First those new dresses, then supper, and *then* we can set about hunting down this Squint Jok person. It's no good trying to loose the horses and hounds on a fellow on an empty stomach, what? We might find ourselves lagging in our pursuit for want of a good afternoon feed."

Delly conceded this point, though part of her felt as if she ought to argue, to insist on immediately charging after whoever had done this to her mam. The plain fact of the matter was that she was tired and hungry, and her dress was in charred tatters, and she wanted Winn to buy her new dresses and then pay for her dinner, too, and smile all the while like she was pleased to do it. That was what she wanted more than to seek justice for her mother: to have a rich gull treat her nice. Not a very noble impulse, but then again, Delly had never found herself unduly hampered by an excess of those. And she really was terribly tired today.

Winn took over from there, with an easiness that made it seem as if she hadn't taken over at all: more as if they were two placid little boats both being pulled along by the same inexorable current, and Winn's being a few breadths ahead was a matter of mere happenstance. They sailed first to a dress shop far nicer than any shop that Delly would have had the nerve to step into alone, but where Winn's warm presence and astoundingly bold-faced lies—she told them that Delly had just escaped from a house fire with only the singed clothing on her back—melted the ladies who worked there into fussing over her very kindly as they measured her and stuck her full of pins, and then as they let her wash the soot and grime off of herself in their basin and put on a borrowed dress to wear while hers were being made. By the time Delly walked out of the dressing room again, Winn and the ladies were sitting about with the placid air of people who had already completed all of the unseemly financial transactions and felt that it had all been a job well done.

"Why don't you pick out a hat, Delly?" Winn asked. "And a few new pairs of gloves."

Delly gawped at her for a moment—she'd never had *any* pairs of gloves: she wasn't that sort of woman—but Winn smiled at her so calmly that the current took ahold of Delly once more, and she picked out her hat and gloves as if she was in the sort of dream where money spurted forth from fountains and peppermints grew on trees.

Once they were finished with their shopping, they moved on to a very nice, cozy little restaurant, where the current compelled Winn to order three dozen oysters, bread and butter, an entire roast duck surrounded by potatoes that had been cooked in the duck's fat, and a dish of boiled and buttered carrots. Then she called for a bottle of wine as well, and tucked into her meal with all of her usual enthusiasm.

Delly, for her part, hadn't expected to find herself with much of an appetite until she started to eat. Then she ate, and ate, and drank more than her fair share of the wine. A month ago, the same amount of wine wouldn't have gotten her so much as a bit relatively relaxed, but now the world had gone as soft and woolly as one of her mam's old shawls. She beamed at Winn over the table, stuffed a bit more bread into her mouth, and declared loudly, "I haven't gotten drunk in weeks!"

Winn smiled back at her. "And are you now? Drunk, I mean?"

"Not *very*," Delly slurred out, and ate some more bread before abruptly recalling that they still had work to deal with and flinging down a big consternated sigh. "We still have to find Squint Jok."

"I know," Winn said. "Have you ever met him? What does he look like?"

"Never slapped my eyes on the fella," Delly said, before doing a bit of squinting of her own as she pondered the question. "Looks squint . . . ed, I suppose."

The corner of Winn's mouth twitched. Then she coughed, cleared her throat, and said, "Maybe we ought to look for him after a bit of coffee and dessert."

Delly readily agreed to this scheme, and after they'd dawdled over cake and coffee for a while she was sober enough to feel both prepared to go looking for Squint Jok and as if Winn had very possibly just been laughing at her. She didn't think that she minded being laughed at very much, though. Not by Winn, at least.

They headed out and spent an exhausting two hours visiting some of Delly's mam's favorite pubs and gin palaces, hoping either that Squint Jok would be there weeping for his dear Marvie over a foaming glass of beer or that someone who knew him would be willing to rat him out for the price of a glass of their own. Unfortunately, they had no such luck: nobody knew Squint Jok, and even if they had known him they wouldn't have known where he was this evening, and even if they'd known that, they wouldn't have told a couple of strange gulls like Delly and Winn. Even worse, Delly was being forced to tramp in and out of gin palaces without so much as a sip of the stuff to soothe her aching feet a bit.

By the time they eventually gave up and headed back to Delly's place, Delly was in a state of such intensive and uncompromising irritation, annoyance, and general fed-upation with her lot in life that she barely took a moment to appreciate how nice and cozy her room looked now as she lit the oil lamp, and instead only stomped over to the bed and started scrabbling at the fiddly little buttons at the back of her neck. The borrowed dress was a bit too tight around the middle, and she wanted it off of her more than she'd ever wanted a thing in her entire God-cursed life.

"You'll tear it like that," Winn said in her easy way. "Here, let me." Then she stepped up behind Delly and started to undo the back of her dress.

Delly submitted to an eternity of Winn that close, unbuttoning her dress, her breath on the back of her neck. Then she turned around and kissed her.

Winn gave a small squeak of surprise. Then she kissed back, and everything turned to softness and easiness and Delly's dress slipping down off of her shoulders. Winn sighed and put her hand to Delly's waist, and Delly surged up against her to kiss her deeper and hotter, her dress still falling without either of them needing to touch it. This time the sound Winn made was more of a groan, and her hands slid up toward Delly's chest. *"Dell."*

Delly gasped and strained onto her tiptoes to kiss her some more, her whole body feeling tight and coiled up with *wanting*. This wasn't at all like her ordinary lackadaisical gallops with old friends or perfect strangers. This felt like being a page of old newspaper caught up in a sudden gust of wind.

This completely new and not entirely unpleasant sensation was brought to an abrupt end when Winn pulled away from her. "Turn around," she said. Her voice sounded a bit hoarse. "I hadn't finished yet."

Delly turned. Her cheeks had gone hot. She let Winn finish undoing every last button, then stepped out of the borrowed dress and turned to look at her, feeling like an oyster scraped from its shell. "You ain't angry, Winn?"

"No, of course not," Winn said. "Why would I be angry?"

"Well," Delly said, "you didn't think I ought to be kissing you, before."

"Oh, I still don't think that you ought to be kissing me," Winn said. Her cheeks had gone pink. "Not regulation hammerball at all, Wells, leaping at a gull like that without prior warning. But I think we can let it go with a slap on the wrist, eh?" She blushed darker. "The law around here's notorious for letting good kissers off lightly."

Delly blinked, then ducked her head a little and smiled. "Guess you must always get away with everything, then."

Now they were both blushing and smiling stupidly at each other. Eventually Winn cleared her throat and mumbled something like "Well, yes. Ought to be getting to bed," and moved to a darker corner of the room and turned her back to undress, and Delly shook herself and went to the basin to wash up. A few moments later, they were climbing into bed together, and Delly reached out to turn down the lamp, and then everything was dark and warm and still.

"It was a—*dreadfully* nice bit of kissing, Dell," Winn said into the quiet.

Delly wanted, really, to reach out to her. To hold her. It was a very foreign impulse. Instead she said, "I'm glad," and wrapped her arms across her own chest to give herself a squeeze. *Good job, Wells*, she told herself. *You've caught a big fish.* Everything was going to change for her now: she would never have to scrimp and starve and scrabble around with the rest of the rabble to survive again. She was thinking about that, about the hat-and-gloves life she was going to lead from now on, when she fell asleep.

10

Wherein Some Discoveries Are Made,
and Dellaria Hits upon Her Worst Scheme Yet

Delly woke up feeling grand.

This was a novel enough feeling for Dellaria Wells that she sat up a bit to look about herself in order to attempt to locate the source of this very singular sensation. She didn't have far to look: there Winn was next to her in the bed, bathed in loveliness with her hair over her face and her mouth hanging open. *Wonderful.* Delly gazed at her, delighted, then eased herself out of bed. She wasn't at all stiff—she hadn't spent a day sitting hunched over a game in weeks—and her head wasn't aching from gin, and Winn thought that she was a good kisser. The air smelled fresh when it blew in through the window.

Delly popped her head out the door to snatch up the kettle of hot water that she had somehow slept through Mrs. Medlow's long-suffering hired girl plonking down outside the door in the predawn hours, then went bounding back inside with it and gave herself a good vigorous scrubbing at the basin. She took a quick glance at Winn—still sleeping—before getting dressed and darting out to buy her morning *Leiscourt Crier*—it was Delly's favorite of the Leiscourt papers, as it was generally the most thickly studded with invective against the better classes—and a few supplies for their room. Bread, butter, jam, coffee and tea and a pot to make them in, and a tin of cookies: the expensive kind with the dab of jam in the middle.

She'd hoped to surprise Winn with breakfast and was somewhat disappointed to find her already awake, fully dressed, and reading a book in one of the new armchairs when Delly walked in. When she saw Delly she smiled in a way that made Delly feel as if being late with breakfast was the greatest achievement of Delly's admittedly not particularly achievement-packed life thus far. "Oh, there you are, Dell!"

"G'morning," Delly said, and waved her parcels at her. "I'll make coffee if you'll see to the toast."

"You're a prince among gulls," Winn said, and they set to fixing themselves a nice breakfast with enormous good cheer.

Once breakfast was finished, Delly had dawdled over the paper for a bit, and they got everything cleaned up to Winn's somewhat bewilderingly exacting standards, they set out to have a last run at finding Squint Jok. Delly, personally, wasn't particularly optimistic that they'd find their man: based on the state her mam was in yesterday, she figured that the fella who'd brought her in was probably either lying low right now or half-dead himself. Still, there was no harm in asking around a bit, and so Delly and Winn went from bar to bar and cheap coffee shop to cheap coffee shop, asking whether anyone might have seen Squint Jok. It was a nasty day for it, with rain seeping down from the low gray sky and trying to get its cold hands under your collar. Whenever they stopped for a moment Winn would stomp her feet and blow on her hands and give a hearty "Brr!" while Delly would put her head down and scowl and try not to think about it.

The fifth place they stopped at was a particularly shabby sort of beerbucket with a particularly shabby sort of feller of Delly's acquaintance working behind the bar. They exchanged a few words of the usual and-how's-yer-mam sort—Delly had nothing positive to report on that front—which led Delly to the point in question. "Don't suppose you've seen her fella about? Squint Jok?"

"Oh, Jok?" the shabby feller said. "Sure. He's upstairs sleeping it off right now. Room number three. Want me to run up and bang on the door for you?"

Dell and Winn exchanged incredulous glances. "No, thanks," Delly said after a moment. "We'll just bang him up ourselves." Then she headed toward the stairwell at a gait a bit too close to a sprint, Winn following close behind her.

"Do you know what you're going to ask him?" Winn asked when they reached the landing.

"I suppose I'll think of a question or two," Delly said, and started pounding on the door with the number three painted on it in dark drippy blue.

After about a minute of pounding the door popped open, to reveal a very irritated-looking man in a patched dressing gown, with gray stubble over his jaw and the most squinted and bloodshot look to his eyes that Dellaria had ever had the misfortune to observe in a human personage.

"What the fuck do you want?" Squint Jok said.

"Morning, Jok," Delly said. "I'm Dellaria Wells. Marvie's daughter."

His eyes, remarkably, went a bit wider. Then he tried to bolt past Delly and into the hall. His progress was halted by Winn, who grabbed him firmly by his shoulders and said cheerfully, "We just wanted to ask you a few questions, that's all, Mr. Jok. Nothing at all to be alarmed about, what?"

Delly was momentarily distracted by the thought that Winn might think that Jok's mother, Mrs. Jok, had named her precious infant son *Squint* when he was born, and then shook herself slightly and recalled their mission. "Right. You brought my mam to the hospital, didn't you, Jok?"

"Might be that I did," the gentleman mumbled.

"Does that mean that it might be that you didn't?" Delly asked. "Because I'd intended on thanking whoever had helped my mam by giving them a half-tocat."

He turned his squint Dellyward at that. "If I said it was me, now, would you believe me?"

"I would," Delly said, fishing a half-tocat out of her reticule and holding it loosely in her palm so that he could see it. "As the nurse you handed her over to described you down to the last whisker. Don't suppose you could tell me a little more about what happened?"

"Not much to tell," Squint Jok said. His eyes were trained on the money now, his shoulders tense in a way that Delly found unpleasantly familiar. Like a hungry dog. "She went all funny and I brought her to the hospital."

"How'd she go funny, exactly?" Delly asked.

"*You* saw her. I'd thought she was *dead*, for a minute."

Delly tried not to grind her teeth. "I meant," she said, "what *caused* the funniness in the first place?" She knew that the nurse figured it was the red drip, but she thought she might as well hear Squint Jok's opinions on the subject.

"Dunno," said the gentleman in question. "She was fine all night." He gave a loud sniff. "Then she just fell right over and started flopping like a fish. Gave me a real nasty shock." He looked as if he thought himself the most injured party involved by far.

"And you have no idea what might have caused it?" Delly asked.

"Might have been that new drip she'd bought, I guess," Squint Jok said, as if he was in some doubt about the matter.

"The red kind, you mean?"

"Yeah, but," Squint Jok said, "this *new* stuff of the red. Stuff keeps getting stronger, seems like. She was fine doing the same the day before, with the old batch. Then yesterday she bought new, just took a little taste of it, and went into a fit."

"But it didn't harm *you* any," Delly said.

Squint Jok made a hideous face that Delly assumed was his attempt to demonstrate a sense of outraged dignity over the idea that he could ever be poisoned by red drip. "I don't do the red, miss. Won't touch the stuff. Everyone knows that it'll kill you quick as cats."

"You sat around and watched while my mam did it all right, though," Delly said, and then quickly followed that up with her next question before Squint Jok had a chance to dredge up a greater sense of outrage. "Do you know who she bought it from?"

"A boy," Squint Jok said. "Little squeaker. Eight or nine, maybe. Haven't seen 'im around the neighborhood before."

"Goodness rilift," Winn said. "You mean that *children* are selling that stuff?"

Delly was at pains to bite back a wince. "They use kids as runners," she explained. "Cops won't notice a kid hanging around, most of the time. Ain't that Leiscourt's under-tens are forming criminal organizations under their own power." She looked back at Squint Jok. "So do you think the stuff's coming from a different part of town, then?"

"I don't know *where* it comes from," Squint Jok said. "Just know that it comes from the Kind Companions."

Delly frowned. Squint Jok didn't even sound like he was from *Leiscourt*: she didn't see why he'd know a street clan that she'd never heard of. "The Kind Companions? I ain't had a seashell of the clan, so." Then she remembered that Winn was listening, and she reddened. "I mean, I haven't heard of 'em."

"They're who make the red drip," Squint Jok said. "That's what the kids say, at least. Say a Kind Companion sent them, and they're not allowed to say more." He shrugged, his eyes still fixed on the half-tocat. "Answered your questions."

"I've got more of 'em," Delly said. "You sure you don't know anything else about these Kind Companions?"

"I'm sure."

"Well, do you *know* anyone who might know more, then?"

He shook his head. Then he paused. "Rat might."

Delly frowned. "Who's *Rat*?"

"She's a fence who runs a pawnshop on Wheelwright's Alley. Rat always knows everything going on in that part of town." He held out his hand.

Delly handed over the half-tocat, and he immediately snatched it up, ducked back into his room, and slammed the door shut.

"I'll tell my mam that you send your best wishes," Delly said to the door. Then, more loudly, "I'll tell her that you're real fucking choked up thinking about her lying in that stinking ward alone for days on end." Then she turned and started heading down the stairs. Her eyes were stinging. Didn't make much sense, really. It wasn't as if her mam had ever gotten used to better treatment. It wasn't as if she'd expect anyone to worry about her, or pray for her, or sit with her at the side of her bed just to make sure that she was still breathing.

Winn followed her down the stairs out into the street and grabbed her by the shoulder. "Delly," she said, and then pulled her into an embrace right there in front of Squint Jok's boardinghouse. "You're a masterful interrogator, Dell," she murmured. "And that fellow was the nastiest bit of no-good I've ever seen in my life. Don't let him bother you, mm?"

"He was my mam's fella," Delly mumbled into Winn's chest, and then gave a loud sniff. "That's how she lives, Winn. With men like that. Treating her like that. Ever since—*always*." Delly, six years old, staying awake all night because she didn't want to close her eyes when her mam's latest fella was near.

Winn started to rock her, just a little, swaying back and forth with her on the street corner like they were at the center of their own private ball. "I'm sorry, Dell," she said. "I'm sorry. But things will come out all right soon."

"You think so?" Delly asked pitifully.

"I *know* so," Winn said. "It's almost time for lunch."

Delly gave a soggy laugh at that, and they headed off, Winn once more taking the lead without their having to discuss it. They had a hearty lunch—though Winn ate much more than Delly did—and then walked over to Damel's to meet the rest of their society for sorceresses, lady-necromancers, and other associated female reprobates.

Damel's, on a rainy day, was like honey to a sore throat. The windows were all steamed up as they approached, and when they opened the door there was a gentle billow of warm, smoky air, pleasantly larded through with the smells of coffee and orange cake and tobacco. No one looked up when they walked in: it wasn't that sort of place. It was the sort of place where old men nestled under their newspapers like they were down comforters and drank endless tiny cups of coffee to go with their afternoon cake, and artists and scholars squabbled contentedly with their friends in the corner booths over glasses of the cheapest hock on offer, and even the waiters seemed resistant to the idea of disturbing the peace of the patrons by asking whether they might like to settle the bill. The tables were all topped with chipped marble, the chairs were worn red velvet, and the wallpaper, a print popular in the earlier half of the century, had been turned a warming yellow from a generation of leisurely cigarettes. The stout little stove in the corner kept the room as snug as your bed just before you got up on a cold morning, and there were always at least four different kinds of freshly baked cake arrayed proudly on the front counter. Delly, as a little girl, had thought the place the absolute height of luxury and creature comfort, and now having spent two weeks staying in one of the grandest houses in Daeslund she was quite confident that on this point her younger self had been entirely correct. The door creaked behind her as they passed through it, as if it was heaving a sigh of contentment along with her to see her back again.

One of the corner booths was remarkably uninfested by painters, sculptors, or students of philosophy, and so she led Winn to it and settled in with another expansive sigh. Winn was looking about herself with what looked like a good amount of pleasure. "What a wonderful old place this is. My pop would love it."

"Do you think so?" Delly asked, delighted even though she didn't give a bent sen over what Winn's father might like. What she cared about was *Winn*, and what *she* thought of things. Since Winn loved her father, it seemed to follow that she would love the things that she thought he might like. Maybe if Winn thought that Delly liked things that her father liked, some of her feelings of fondness for her father would transfer over to Delly like blotting paper sucking up ink.

Or maybe Delly ought to order a drink and pull herself together a bit.

She flagged the waiter over to do exactly that, but somehow in the course of discussing what to order with Winn the wine was dropped and coffee and cake requested instead. These refreshments had only just arrived when Miss Dok came through the door, looking completely pristine and entirely undampened by the rain still coming down outside. She gave Delly and Winn a short nod when she walked in, spoke briefly to the waiter, and then settled herself at their table with the air of a queen taking her throne. "What a charming little room this is," she said. "I never would have wandered in here on my own, Wells, when it looks so wretched from the outside."

Delly rolled that one around her mouth for a moment and decided to take it as a compliment on her taste. "Thanks," she said. "I always thought it was the finest room in Leiscourt." Then she changed the subject. "Did you get up to much yesterday?"

"I took a lovely bath," Miss Dok said. "And sobbed a bit."

Delly blinked. She kept forgetting how much more personal this whole business with the Wexins was to her. Winn reached across the table to put her hand over Dok's. "I'm glad," she said. "I imagine that you needed it, Miss Dok."

"Oh, there's no need to fuss," Miss Dok said irritably, as if she hadn't been the one to present them with the image of her sobbing in the bath. Then she said, "Abstentia."

"Mm?" Winn said.

"My friends call me Abstentia," she said, and then directed her attention to the bag that she was carrying for just long enough for Delly to raise her eyebrows at Winn and then feel like an ass when Winn gave her a quelling look back. Winn, apparently, didn't think it was strange to hear that Dok thought of either of them as a friend.

Miss Dok—*Abstentia*, Delly supposed—placed a sheaf of papers on the table. "I broke into Ainette's rooms at Weltsir," she said briskly, "and went through all of her paperwork. I found more proof of how much debt she's in, though we already knew that. What's a bit more interesting is that I also found her diary."

Delly, who loved nothing more than to have a good nose through someone else's most treasured secrets, immediately pulled the papers over to have a healthy browse. What she saw was highly disappointing: nothing but a bunch of incomprehensible squiggles. Abstentia pulled the papers back, looking more like a satisfied cat than ever. "She kept her diary in shorthand," she said. "I've translated a bit of it. It's all very grim. Lots of poor—of Ainette running around trying to scrabble up some extra money to buy more drip. I don't know why she never came to me for *help*." This last bit was said in a rapid gust of frustration.

"She was ashamed," Delly said. She knew all about shame. She'd chewed through enough of it in her life to know how you choked on it when you swallowed, how the taste of it clung in your mouth and bits of it stuck in your teeth. "Probably figured she could sort it all out on her own and no one would ever have to know. I don't know how it went from that to her figuring that killing her sister would be a better idea than popping round her room some evening after the coffee and cake to ask her for a bit of a loan."

At almost that exact instant their own cake and coffee arrived. Abstentia practically dove upon her slice of cake to take her first bite, which Delly found unexpectedly endearing, and then sat back with a small sigh of contentment and said, "It *is* nice to have a piece of very good cake." Then she said, "Ainette was always too proud for her own good. And resentful of her sister, I think. She always talked about how her family had only householded her so that their precious Mayelle would have a loyal companion for the rest of her life. I never thought so much of it, really. She always seemed as if she really did *love* Mayelle."

"Funny thing," Winn said. "I can't make backs or fronts of it."

"I can," Delly said. The ladies both turned to look at her. She shrugged. "Love is complicated."

There was a bit of a commotion at the door then, as three people trooped in: the Tothams had finally arrived. Mrs. Totham looked contented enough, considering the circumstances. Her daughters, for their parts, looked as disgruntled as their mother was gruntled.

"Sorry we're late," Mura said as she clomped herself down into a chair. "Mama got us kicked out of our boardinghouse."

"She didn't do it *intentionally*," Vitna said, as Mrs. Totham twittered her way delicately into her own seat.

"Oh, dear, oh, dear, I really *do* apologize, girls," she said. "I never *imagined* that the odor would annoy the landlady so much."

Delly's eyebrows marched skyward. "The odor?"

"From Buttons," Mura said grimly. "She boiled him."

"You *boiled Buttons*?" Delly asked, utterly astonished. "Forgive me, Mrs. Totham, but I had thought that the two of you were fast friends."

"Oh, I wouldn't *dream* of speculating as to Buttons' feelings toward *myself*," Mrs. Totham said modestly. "I am, of course, very fond of Buttons. I only boiled him because he seemed to be growing uncomfortable with the process of decay, and I thought that I might be able to help hasten the process of skeletonization. He seemed to enjoy the bath very much. Didn't you, Buttons?"

There was a rustling from within the depths of Mrs. Totham's reticule then, and Delly watched, with a growing sense of dread, as Buttons emerged. He was very much changed, and not at all improved. Just bones now, arranged in space in the shape of a mouse, but with all of the fleshy and furry scaffolding that one might hope to see in a mouse dispiritingly absent. He clattered a bit as he walked across the table, came to a halt a few paces from Delly's coffee cup, and emitted a resonant "*Bong.*"

It said something for the soothing quality of Damel's as an establishment that the rest of the patrons barely looked up at Buttons' particularly cream-curdling contribution to the atmosphere. Once the last reverberations had died down, Delly cleared her throat. "Erm. Yes.

Miss Dok was just about to tell us all about what she learned from Miss Wexin's diary."

Abstentia inclined her head, then briefly repeated what she had already told Delly and Winn, concluding with, "The most relevant thing seems to be a person whom she only calls *C*. She writes that she's met C quite often, but usually without including any notes to herself about what happened *at* the meeting, and she mentions more than once her worries about C sending men to ask for money."

"C would be her faucet, then," Delly said. "That's good to know. A bit more information to start with. Thanks, Dok."

"You're welcome, Wells," Abstentia said in her silkiest tones, before offering Delly a very small smile.

Delly smiled back, wondering briefly whether Abstentia might have been hit on the head last night, and then turned her attention to the Tothams. "And you? Did you discover anything before the, ah, *boiling* got started?"

"A bit," Mura said, and then Vitna broke in.

"We asked around the neighborhood a bit. Seems that all of the red drip is coming from the same street clan."

"The Kind Companions?" Delly asked.

Vitna looked a shade disappointed that her revelatory thunder had been stolen so entirely, but she managed to rally herself enough to say, "That's right. They're new in town, but they took over the market pretty quick with the red. Made some enemies, but what I'm hearing is that they've got a lot of money and some strong wizards behind them, so no one's been able to take them out. Now their problem is that there's a run on supply. They can't make enough to keep up with demand, and the other clans are all trying to come up with their own red formulations, too. They might be in pretty tight straits soon if they can't hire on more wizards."

"Makes sense," Delly said. "Can't make drip without a wizard."

At that moment more cake and coffee arrived at their table, just as Winn said, "So what next?"

"I don't know," Delly said, with a bit of grimness about her edges.

"Well," Winn said, with nary a droplet of grim approaching even her most distant borders, "what if we all just took a moment to eat our cake and think it over?"

No one objected to this plan, so everyone ate cake and talked about where one could find a place for three respectable ladies and one skel-etal mouse to stay at a reasonable cost. This, to Delly, was safe ground: as a born-and-bred Leiscourter she was used to talking about rooms available to rent, the rising cost of rooms available to rent, and the lack of any suitable rooms available to rent at a reasonable cost in the same way that people from other towns might converse casually about the weather. There was, this entire time, the ghost of an idea echoing in the back of Delly's skull, until suddenly she said, in the middle of a conversation about whether a certain neighborhood that might have cheap rooms available to let would be suitable for a lady as respectable as Mrs. Totham, "I ought to try and work for them."

Everyone turned to squint at her. "You ought to try and work for who, Dell?" Winn asked.

"For the Kind Companions," Delly said. "Some people know me around town. They sure as hell know my mam. It'd be easy enough for them to look into me and see that I'm not with the constabulary or anything like that. Just tell 'em that I'm a wizard, hard up, behind on rent, and looking to work."

"Is that how it works, with street clans?" Miss Dok asked. "I wouldn't imagine that they'd be so very interested in hiring strangers to engage in criminal activity with them."

Delly pondered that. "Maybe I could tell 'em that I can help them make more of the red better and faster than they're doing it now, for a cut. Since they're having problems with their supply, and all. Having a stranger work for them would be better than having a stranger set up shop on their own."

Winn looked impressed. "Could you really?"

"No," Delly was forced to admit. "I wouldn't even know where to start with it. I never took chemicastry at Weltsir."

"I did," Miss Dok said. "And I might be able to formulate more of the stuff, if I was given a sample to work from."

"I might be able to help as well," Mrs. Totham said, "if the aim would be to create a drug that would function more effectively within the body. I would be far too afraid to approach those terrible Kind Companions, though."

"I could do that bit," Delly said. She was starting to feel excited. "You two stew up the stuff, I play the street clan head, and Winn, Vitna, and Mura play the muscle."

"I think I could manage that," Vitna said, sounding relieved. "Just stand around and look tough, you mean?"

"That's right," Delly said, a bit secretly pleased to think that Winn was bearing witness to both Delly's having had a wonderful idea and a gull who kept simpering unbearably in Winn's direction admitting that *her* chief area of expertise was standing around looking like her breakfast disagreed with her.

Delly was still being borne along on these winds of smugness when Winn brought her very suddenly back to earth. "I don't know if this is a good idea."

"Why not?" Delly asked, trying and failing to not sound as if she'd taken offense.

"I just don't think it'd come to anything good, Dell," Winn said. "If you make that stuff and offer to manufacture it for them, then they'll expect you to *do* it, and then you'll just be a drip dealer, exactly like them. Think of the poor people who might buy the stuff."

"But ours would be better," Delly said, warming more to her idea the more that it was argued against. "Safer. And we won't really have to do it for long, in any case. Just long enough to find Ainette."

"And then what?" Winn asked. "Do you think they'll take kindly to you stopping work and kidnapping one of their customers?"

"They won't be able to do much about it if we have them all arrested as soon as we've found Ainette," Miss Dok said. "If we tell the police what we know they'll be sure to help us."

"If *you* tell the police they'll be sure to help *you*," Delly said. "If *I* tell the police anything, they're likely to arrest me just under the assumption that if I wasn't responsible for the crime I'm reporting I probably *was* responsible for another crime that they haven't discovered yet."

Winn, Delly noticed, was frowning a bit. "It isn't really as bad as all that, is it?"

"Oh, no, no," Delly said hastily, even though it absolutely and unquestionably was worse. "Just got into a few scrapes when I was younger, that's all, so the magistrates know my name. Having you and Miss Dok speak to the police might smooth the way a bit better."

"I still don't think that it's a good idea," Winn was saying, but it was too late: the rest of them were off again, making plans, deciding where they could construct a laboratory and who would be responsible for finding a representative sample of the red to use as the basis of their own formulation. They had just decided that Mura and Vitna should be the ones to buy the stuff—the two of them weren't as likely to run into someone they knew as Delly, but Mura was comfortable enough speaking to strangers in rough neighborhoods, and Vitna was reliably capable of standing nearby and looking menacing—and just as Delly was congratulating herself on how well everything was coming along, Buttons walked to the very center of the table and said, in a deep, sonorous voice, "*Beware*."

There was a moment of silence as they all stared at Buttons. Delly cleared her throat. "Excuse me, sir, but would your elevated self care to add any elaboratory amendments to your most interesting and respectable remarks, sir?"

Buttons did not seem as if he cared to add any elaboratory amendments. He did not make any further remarks at all. Which was fortunate, as Delly was morally opposed to human speech produced by personages without a human throat. Or any throat at all, really, Buttons' own throat having apparently been boiled away several hours previous.

"You see!" Winn said triumphantly. "*Buttons* thinks that this is all a bad idea, too. I say that we toss it out and think of something else."

"Well, then," Miss Dok said creamily. "We'll mark you and the boiled rodent down as opposed. All in favor?"

The rest of them put up their hands, though Delly did so with a certain degree of guilt. And then they continued with their discussions, barreling closer and closer toward the execution of a clever idea that, if Delly had allowed herself more than a moment to really consider, she would have been forced to acknowledge was not a good idea at all.

11

Wherein Dellaria Encounters an Extraordinary
Quantity of Cherries, Does a Disagreeable Amount
of Cleaning, and Deepens Her Involvement
in Her Terrible Idea

With the duties mostly sorted out, everyone went their own separate ways: Mura and Vitna to try to find some red, Miss Dok and Mrs. Totham to the university library to begin to do some chemicastry research, and Winn and Delly off to try to find the fence in West Leiscourt that Squint Jok had mentioned. This was all fine enough, as far as Delly's plan went, but it was less fine as it came to Delly's hopes of being a householded woman within the year. Winn, usually so full of things to say, had barely so much as cleared her throat in the twenty minutes since they'd left Damel's. Eventually Delly cleared her own, and ventured, "You mad at me, Winn?"

Winn sighed. "No, Dell. I'm not mad. I'm just worried, that's all. What if things go badly? What if one of those people tries to hurt you?"

"I'm a fire witch," Delly reminded her. "If anyone bothers me—"

"You'll just set their skirts on fire. I know, you've said that before. But what if they're like that man who attacked you and can't feel the pain? Or what if someone shoots you? Are you good enough of a fire witch to stop bullets? Or how about a knife that someone's trying to stab you with?"

"I could stop a knife. I don't know about a bullet, though," Delly was forced to admit. "Never tried."

"Well, then," Winn said, a bit fiercely. "Then I suppose we'll just have to practice. Is there anywhere near your place where we can shoot a pistol without disturbing anybody?"

"A few places, but not if there happens to be a constable nearby," Delly said, which sent Winn off into an odd fit of frowning and mumbling about "noise-canceling parameters" and asking Delly questions about the lengths of the local alleyways, which occupied her until they arrived in West Leiscourt.

It was, it turned out, not at all difficult to find the pawnshop in question: everyone in this part of town seemed to know who Rat was. The shop was a small place with a great deal of dust in the windows, and a little bell that did its timid best to jangle as they walked through the door. It was dusty inside as well, and quite crammed with objects: furniture and pots and pans and hatboxes and other refugees from lives that had been disrupted. At the end of a narrow alley through this rubble was a large wooden desk, and behind the desk was the most extraordinarily dressed person Delly had ever seen. She wore a men's skirted suit in a virulent shade of green, paired with bright yellow stockings, a cravat in blue-and-purple plaid, and an enormous black hat so thickly laden with artificial cherries that you could use it to make a season's worth of artificial jam. Marooned between the cravat and the hat was an angular, dark-eyed, weathered face with a long scar across one cheek, and a luxuriant cascade of black curls that Delly strongly suspected of not having originally belonged to their current owner. The overall effect was of someone who was afraid that bright colors would soon be outlawed, and was therefore endeavoring to wear all of their soon-to-be-illegal articles of clothing at once in a sort of grand sartorial fireworks display. This explosive air was only heightened by the thick wreaths of smoke issuing from the large cigar that Rat was in the process of smoking.

"I beg your pardon," Delly said, doing her level best not to stare at the cherries. She had never in her life seen such a bounty of artificial fruit. The very sight of the hat was making her hungry. "Are you Rat?"

"I am!" Rat said, with such energetic emphasis that the cherries wobbled to and fro. "And how might I be of service to you two on this fine afternoon? An engagement ring, perhaps?"

Both Delly and Winn produced squawking noises of embarrassment that quickly dwindled into despairing peeps. Delly coughed. "No, ah, it was more *information* we were looking for. Would you mind answering a few questions—I'm very sorry, but is it *Miss* Rat or *Mrs.* Rat?"

"Oh, neither of those, if you please," Rat said modestly. "I'm only a very *regular* Rat."

"Oh," said Delly, who for a brief moment found herself to be a very irregular Dellaria. "Right. Well, Rat, do you think that you would mind answering a few questions?"

"That would depend on what the questions are about. And your name is . . . ?"

"Smith," Winn broke in. "Erm. We're *both* called Smith, I mean."

"Ah, no wonder the engagement ring is no longer necessary!" said Rat. "My hearty congratulations to you both!"

For one moment, Delly felt as if her entire being was curling in on itself like a dried-out leaf. Then she managed to uncurl herself sufficiently to say, "Thank you. What do you know about the Kind Companions?"

"Oh, a fair amount, Miss Smith," Rat said. "I could share everything that I know for, say, a half-tocat?"

Delly handed it over, resigned to spending her entire newly earned fortune on petty bribery. The cherries bobbled their gratitude. Then Rat said, "They're a newer bunch, and they're not West Leiscourters."

Delly frowned. "But most of the people doing the stuff are from West Leiscourt."

"That's true, too," Rat said. "The stuff *goes* to West Leiscourt, but it doesn't *come* from there."

"Well, where does it *come* from, then?" Delly asked, irritated at having found herself trapped on this particular conversational carousel. "Who are these Kind Companions?"

Rat didn't seem particularly ruffled by this outburst. The cherries remained serenely at their posts. "They don't send their runners to this part of town with their calling cards, but I'd say that they're from somewhere where the likes of you and I couldn't afford the rent. From what the runners tell me, the ladies that they've spoken to have accents like this one." Rat nodded at Winn.

Delly gaped. "They're *clanners*? And—*ladies*, you said?" She'd imagined a bunch of men from *her* class of society, not yet more *fine ladies*. She was in fine ladies up to her shoulders already, and now here were yet more of them. It was a regular fucking siege, it really was.

Rat shrugged. "That's what the kids they have working for them said. *Fine ladies*, they said. Though they *are* children, of course, and could be mistaken. They could be a pair of criminal actresses."

Delly squinted at Rat, wondering whether or not she was being led down the proverbial garden path with this *fine ladies* business. Rat and two-hundred-odd cherries gazed serenely back at her. "Fine," Delly said eventually. "Is there anything else you can tell me? Anything that you've heard about these fine ladies?"

Rat smiled. "I'm afraid not. But I'd be pleased to try and get you more information, for another half-tocat. Paid in advance, of course."

"Paid upon *receipt of the information*, Rat," Delly said.

Rat laughed, the cherries bobbing along with great amusement. "You can't blame me for trying! These are hard times, after all. Come back in two days and I'll tell you what I've found out."

"Hard times," Delly echoed. It was only polite. Then she said, "Thanks," and they took their leave.

They were quiet for a while as they walked. Then Winn suddenly burst out with, "Have you ever in your life seen such an *extraordinary* hat? I thought that her neck might snap from the weight of those horrible cherries, I really did. And that *cravat*!" Then she stopped and stared, clearly puzzled, as Delly practically collapsed in fits of laughter.

They made their way to Delly's place after that, and at Winn's suggestion took the rest of the afternoon off. Winn wrote letters, and Delly read a cheap novel, and then they had a nice quiet dinner in a nice quiet bar down the road before sitting in front of the stove and reading and having tea together before bed. It was such a civilized, peaceful way to spend an evening that Delly couldn't help but spin it out into a future: a kind, quiet, gentle future where there was always a hot stove, and a warm bed, and Winn.

The next morning led to a certain diminishment in her feelings toward Winn, when said person saw fit to yank Delly's newly acquired curtains open at half past sunrise, give Delly's shoulder a vigorous shake, and chirp out a number of loathsome phrases including "Up and at 'em!" and "Wasting daylight!" Delly upped and atted 'em only after making it clear to Winn that she was only doing so under extreme duress, but was still so muzzy from sleepiness that it took until she was washed, dressed, and halfway down the block before it occurred to her to ask where Winn was taking her.

"We're going to an alleyway to practice your being shot at and stabbed," Winn said, with a good healthy dose of that alarmingly sunny attitude of hers.

"Not that that doesn't sound like enormous fun," Delly said cautiously, "but don't you think that it might be rather dangerous, Winn?"

"Oh, no, don't worry," Winn said. "I've already thought it all out. You'll be perfectly safe."

Delly felt that she'd really like to argue against this, but she found herself in a bit of a bind: she and the others had practically *forced* Winn to participate in the drip-production plan, and Winn had only eventually agreed to it because Delly had so much as sworn on her mother's life that she'd be willing to go along with Winn's safety precautions. If she went back on that now it would be as good as inviting Winn to start arguing with her over her plan all over again. With that being the case, it seemed as though the only thing left to be done was to pin back her shoulders and march forward into what almost certainly would be Delly's swift, if accidental, demise.

Winn had selected an excellent alley for the endeavor, at least: it was an odd dead end of a thing between two abandoned houses, so no innocent local grannies were likely to accidentally wander into the path of a bullet. Winn prowled up and down the length of the alley first, reading out parameters from a notebook she'd had in her pocket. Then there was the faint buzz of magic, and she stopped, looking pleased. "There. That ought to do it. Would you mind stepping out of the alley for a moment, Dell? Thanks ever so."

Delly, who found Winn strangely irresistible when she was that polite, obeyed, and was treated to the unnerving sight of Winn visibly shouting something while no sound at all seemed to emerge from her mouth. She said, "What? I can't hear you."

Winn smiled and gestured her back in. "It worked! That's rather good fun, isn't it? Think how handy knowing those parameters would have been back in the old school days! Anyway, I thought that we'd start with a bit of stabbing." Then, without any further warning, she withdrew a knife from somewhere on her person and stabbed at Delly's shoulder with it.

"*Ow*," Delly said, once her brain had caught up with her. She rubbed at her shoulder—she was sure that she'd have a bruise there—and gave Winn an injured look. "You could have *warned* me," she said. "Not very sporting to just stab a girl before you've let her know that you have a knife. But you see, I did it, didn't I? You couldn't actually stab me."

"That's because the knife is blunted, you silly thing," Winn said kindly. "It's a practice weapon. And do you really think that these Kind Companions or their henchmen will stop to warn you before they give you a good stabbing?"

"Well, no," Delly admitted. "But what do you want me to do about that? I can't melt a thing before I know it's even there."

"Then you'll have to learn to notice that it's there faster," Winn said, and stabbed her again.

They proceeded on in this way—Winn stabbing Delly, and Delly complaining loudly over having been stabbed—until Winn finally relented a nail's width. "You can't just wait until the knife is an inch away from you, Dell. You have to pay attention to your opponent. I have to move to get the knife out, and as soon as you see me moving you should be preparing yourself as if you expect a weapon, even if you haven't seen it yet. Now, let's try again," she said, and very underhandedly stabbed Delly right above the particulars.

"*Ow*," Delly said, and then gathered herself together with the thought that she would, this time, actually attempt to follow Winn's instructions. She would do anything if it meant that she might have a chance of destroying that damn *knife*. She did her very best, then, to follow Winn's movements, to try to anticipate what she might do next. Her ability to melt the knife, though, was hampered by her worry. "If I get things hot enough to melt the blade then I could *hurt* you."

"Are you holding back because of that?" Winn asked. "Don't worry. I spelled these gloves for heat resistance a week ago." Then she moved to stab Delly again, and Delly saw the movement and lifted her hand to block it, and sent out just enough heat through the flesh of her hand to turn the knife into a twisted bit of scrap as it drove against her palm.

"*Ow*," Winn said, and dropped the knife to the ground with a clatter.

Ordinarily, Delly's impulse would be to say, *Ha! Serves you right for stabbing me all those times, and let that be a lesson to you!* Instead, what came out of her mouth was "Oh, *no*, are you all right? I *told* you that it might hurt you!"

"I'm fine, Delly," Winn said. She was smiling. "It was just a little hot, that's all. And you *did* it!" And with that, she flung her arms around Delly and gave her a sound kiss on the cheek.

Delly went pink. "I guess I did," she said. "Not bad, huh?"

"It was absolutely wonderful," Winn said, and pulled another knife from some mysterious inner compartment of her skirts. "Now let's do it again."

Delly had to ruin three more of Winn's practice knives—she

seemed to have an absolutely inexhaustible supply of the wretched things—before Winn was satisfied enough with how she was coming along to call a halt for the day. Delly, red-faced, sweating, and exhausted, still for some unholy reason chose to open her mouth and ask, "But what about the shooting?"

"That will have to wait until later today," Winn said, and then started marching off in the direction of the restaurant where they'd had their lunch the day before. "I'm absolutely famished. Nothing like a few hours of martial exertion to whet the appetite, what?"

"Sure," Delly said, though for her own part the only appetite that felt particularly whetted was the one that was whispering in her ear about the thought of how lovely it would be to take a cool bath followed by a long afternoon nap.

Once there was food in front of her, though, she found herself tearing through it with as much gusto as Winn, and the meal gave her more than enough energy for the walk over to Damel's. This time, when they arrived, the other ladies were all already assembled, and very eager to tell Delly about what they had all accomplished the day before. Mrs. Totham was the first to speak up, her eyes brighter than Delly had seen them since before the day that Ermintrude had died. "I believe that I have discovered some very interesting information about Buttons!"

"Oh, really?" Delly said, in her most civilized tones. "About *Buttons*, you say?"

"*Yes*," Mrs. Totham said, with enormous apparent delight. "I believe that the spirit that has animated Buttons is that of a long-dead but very powerful wizard!"

"Oh," Delly said faintly. This was, if she was entirely honest, the last bit of news that she would ever want to hear about Buttons, the first being *He has gone away and will never come back again*. "Do you suppose that that means that he has . . . a great deal of magical power, still?"

"Oh, I imagine that it's very likely," Mrs. Totham said. "Isn't that right, Buttons? Yes, yes, it is! You're a *very* powerful wizard, yes, you *are*!"

Buttons, who was curled horribly in Mrs. Totham's saucer, made a sound like an entire forest glade, complete with a babbling brook and chirping birds. Mrs. Totham beamed. "Isn't he a dear thing? He always likes to bring me birds."

Delly stared at Buttons. Buttons turned his skull in her direction, and the holes where his eyes used to be began to glow a faint, ominous crimson. Delly cleared her throat. "Yes," she said. "Very . . . dear." Then she looked away from Buttons and hastily changed the subject. "How about you, Dok? How did you get along with the research?"

"Quite well, thank you," Abstentia said, and patted contentedly at the large stack of extremely dull-looking books on the table beside her. "I still have a great deal of material to work through, but I think that I've put together a general theory of how the stuff ought to be . . . put together. I really *do* need that sample, though, to see whether or not my theories are correct." She looked positively delighted at the idea that she still had hour upon hour of staring at musty old books to look forward to, which in Delly's experience was perfectly normal, for an academic wizard. They were wonderfully strange creatures, like the sorts of things that you heard about fishermen finding washed up on beaches after storms.

"Then you'll be pleased to see this," Mura said, and passed a little bag across the table.

Miss Dok opened it, peeped inside, and started to pull out whatever was in it before glancing around the crowded coffee shop and thinking better of it. "Is this—"

Mura nodded. "Cost a few bright sen, too. Seems like half of Leiscourt is hungry for the stuff."

"And we're about to make more of it," Winn murmured, and took a sip of her coffee.

A bit of a silence fell over the table at that, and Delly felt as if it was practically her sworn duty to step in. "Only in order to stop it once and for all and see all of the people responsible thrown into prison," she said, inwardly twitching a bit at the sheer fraudulence of her presenting herself with such a law-and-orderly aspect. It did the trick, at least: Mrs. Totham especially looked visibly cheered by the reminder that they were going to make sure that her daughter's murderer was punished for her crimes.

Then Abstentia spoke up. "There's still the matter of our needing a laboratory to formulate the stuff in."

Delly chewed at her lip. "Couldn't you use the laboratories at Weltsir?"

"No," Abstentia said immediately. "That would be out of the question. What on earth would I do if one of the chemicastry lecturers walked in?"

"Hm," Delly said, and chewed on her lip again. "Can't have it where any of us live, either. Too easy to get ratted out by our landlords." And besides, the Tothams had already been kicked out of one boardinghouse: she didn't want to see them made homeless again for conducting arcane experiments. Then she had an idea. "How would an abandoned building work for it?"

"I don't see why an abandoned building *wouldn't* work for it," Abstentia said. "Provided that there's an even floor and adequate light and ventilation."

"Hm," Delly said again. "How would you like to look at a bit of real estate?"

Abstentia allowed that she would like that, and the rest of the crowd piped up to say that they'd like to come along, too. Delly frowned. "It'll be a bit attention-grabbing, though, having a whole flock of strange gulls all come tramping through that neighborhood at once. D'you think you might see your way to doing something else this afternoon and letting me show you the way to the building tomorrow, Tothams?"

The Tothams agreed to this, though the younger two seemed less pleased about it when Dok presented them with a shopping list of various chemicals and bits of equipment she would need to begin her experiments and recommended that they go to Reclid Lane in the university district to find them. Mrs. Totham, for her part, was very cheerful about it. "But what fun! It's been years since I've gone shopping on Reclid Lane. And it will be just the thing to try to find some of the materials that I need in order to attempt to establish better communication with Buttons."

Winn shifted in her seat a bit. "Do you really think that attempting to, ah, *rouse* Buttons is entirely wise, Mrs. Totham?"

"But whyever wouldn't it be?" Mrs. Totham asked, gazing fondly down at the dreadful unliving creature currently gnawing fruitlessly on a sugar cube that she had left in her saucer. As he gnawed, little granules of sugar fell through his hollow jaw and dropped to the table below him. It was, Delly thought, one of the most simultaneously comical and tragical things that she had ever seen. "I'm very eager to get to know him better. Won't having a nice chat be *lovely*, Buttons?"

Buttons said, "*Bong.*"

As usual, Buttons' bonging filled everyone except Mrs. Totham with an immediate and urgent sense that they would like to be as far away as possible from the source of the noise, and within a few minutes they had all finished their cake, gathered up their things, paid, and left the building as quickly as they could manage.

Delly, Winn, and Abstentia started to gossip the instant that the Tothams were out of earshot. "What in the releft are we going to do about that *Buttons* thing?" Delly asked.

"Nothing at all in the releft, I should think, considering that it would seem that we're dealing with an angry spirit fallen out of the cycle of reliving and forced to abide within the mortal remains of a house mouse," Abstentia said, sounding considerably more amused by the idea than Delly really thought that a nice young lady ought to be.

"It gives me the hot shivers," Winn said. "Do you think we should call in some haltonites and have them chant prayers over Mrs. Totham's reticule?"

"I don't know about that," Delly said. "Seems to me that that would just be inviting the cursed creature to chant *back*."

All three of them shuddered.

"Why don't we talk about something nicer?" Winn asked, and made a noble effort to change the subject. They quickly discovered, however, that there didn't seem to be a single subject that they could all manage to converse about: Abstentia didn't follow hammerball, Delly didn't ride, and Winn had never been to Weltsir and was therefore unable to share reminiscences about the odder professors. At last they settled on cheap novels, and spent the rest of their walk arguing about one particular romance that Winn had liked very much but both Delly and Abstentia agreed had turned into an inadvertent tragicomedy at about two hundred pages in. They banded together a bit to make fun of Winn for her terrible taste in books—Winn, as usual, took it with nothing but laughter and good cheer—and by the time they reached Delly's mam's old squat Delly was starting to feel as if maybe she and Abstentia could get to be friends after all.

This feeling evaporated at almost the instant Delly explained how they were to get into the place. "You've been crawling around in the *mud*?" Abstentia asked, her perfect eyebrows making themselves into perfect arches. "Like a *pig*?" Then, before Delly could grind up a suitably peppery retort, she stepped toward the fence, consulted a little notebook that she drew from her pocket, incanted a bit, and then rapped at the fence with her knuckles. A few boards of the fence swung inward like a door being opened for guests, and Abstentia gave Delly a loathsomely smug look over her shoulder before stepping daintily into the overgrown garden.

She didn't go to any particular efforts to make herself agreeable once they were inside the building, either. "Good God, it's *horrible*," she said, looking around the filthy, dark sitting room as if she'd never seen anything worse in her life. Which, to be fair, she probably hadn't. *Quality* girls never spent time in places like this.

"Well, it's what we have," Winn said, her tone suddenly and uncharacteristically firm. "So we can either stand around complaining about it or roll our sleeves up and see what we can make of the place." And with that, she pulled on her fireproof leather gloves and started pulling the boards down from the windows to let the light stream in. "Oh, look at that! There's a broom," she said, pointing at a cobweb-shrouded form in the corner of the room. "Abstentia, how about you do a bit of sweeping? And, Dell, can you start carrying some of the garbage out? I'm going to see if I can fix the window frame."

It was difficult, in the face of such efforts, to not start bustling around as if one was oneself a very active and industrious personage and not a woman who generally conducted herself with the energy and enthusiasm of the skin someone had just peeled off the top of a hot pudding. Delly set to carrying garbage out, with energy if not enthusiasm, and after a half an hour or so the room began to look remarkably like a room.

Winn had even managed to fix the window frame, presumably with either subtle magical arts or a hammer and nails she had pulled out of a secret compartment hidden in her skirts, and had taken the boards down from the other windows and wiped the glass as well, so they could better see what they were working with. In bright light the ominous shapes that loomed in the corners were rudely exposed as nothing but a wobbly table and a dirty old armchair, and they were able to easily find and dispatch the worst of the cobwebs. Even Abstentia looked vaguely pleased about their progress. "I suppose that I might be able to work in here, given a bit more scrubbing."

"I'm sure that we're all overjoyed to hear it," Delly said, very politely. "Have you given any thought to what you might need to set up your laboratory that wasn't on that list you gave the Tothams?"

"Oh, not much," she said. "A table, a chair, a bright lamp, some thick leather gloves and a leather apron——"

"I beg your pardon," Winn broke in. "You mean the kind that a butcher wears?"

"Yes, exactly," Abstentia said. "To keep the substances I'll be working with off of my skin and clothing." Then she cocked her head. "Make that two chairs, two pairs of gloves, and two aprons. You'll be assisting me, won't you, Winnifer?"

"*Me?*" Winn said in a high bray. Then she cleared her throat. "I mean—I never did much in *chemicastry*. I'm more of an illusionist. I might pull a rabbit out of a beaker, what? Isn't Mrs. Totham going to assist you?"

"Would you really trust Mrs. Totham around a table of volatile chemicals?" Abstentia asked, widening her eyes like a bad actress playing a shocked ingenue. "She's likely to see an interesting bird fly by the window and drop a beaker on her shoe. Not that she won't be very useful when it comes to developing a strong theory as to how we can improve upon the current formulation."

Delly blinked. "To *improve* upon it?"

"Yes, of course," Abstentia said. "Why in the world would they be interested in hiring us on as suppliers if we present them with a purely mediocre product? They might just decide to murder us and eliminate the potential competition."

Winn looked uncharacteristically aggravated. "Are you trying to suggest that if I don't help you to produce powerful illegal drugs that we might all be *murdered*?"

Abstentia's eyes went more innocent than ever. She might have been born just minutes previously. "Oh, no, of course not. I would take complete responsibility for the failure of our product, as I *am* the one in charge of this aspect of our venture. But, by the same token, I do feel as if it's my duty to perform to the very best of my ability for as long as we're working together, and it might be difficult to run a laboratory of this type without any assistance."

Winn gave Abstentia a long, steady look. Then she sighed. "All right, then," she said. "I suppose that I did say that I agreed to make Dellaria our leader, and she has appointed you to work on the . . . product."

"Wouldn't really be regulation hammerball if you changed your mind now, would it, Winn?" Delly asked, trying to make her eyes as grapelike as Abstentia's.

Winn turned her own eyes into arrow slits. Then one corner of her mouth curled up. "You wouldn't know regulation play if a hammerball hit you straight in the eye, Dell," she said. She said it fondly, Delly hoped. "All right, I'll do it. The two of you can stop badgering me now, what?"

"My intent was certainly never to *badger*," Abstentia said, at the same time that Delly said, "I'd never try and *badger* you, Winn." Then the two of them caught each other's eyes and exchanged a very ladylike smirk.

Winn glanced between them. Then she laughed and shook her head. "I'm off to find a mop and a bucket, if you two want to make yourself responsible for the table, chairs, and leather aprons," she said, before marching out the door.

Abstentia and Delly both spent a long moment staring rather stupidly at the doorway that Winn had just left through. "I'm afraid that we've annoyed her," Abstentia said.

"I dunno," Delly said slowly. "I'm not sure if Winn *gets* mad." She certainly hadn't expressed much annoyance so far, and if Delly was sure of anything, it was that her presence was a sort of final exam of unflappability: if you were unflapped by Dellaria Wells, you were almost certain to remain similarly unflapped in any other possible scenario.

Abstentia gave her a pitying look. "Oh, *really*. She only acts so perfectly serene around *you* because she has a desperate pash on you."

"You think so?" Delly asked, her face gone warm.

Abstentia gave an extremely inelegant snort. "Don't fish for reassurance of things you already know, Wells, it's unattractive. Do you have enough money on you to buy what we need?"

"I won't have enough to buy food for my own cursed self, at this rate," Delly told her. Abstentia looked unmoved. Delly groaned. "Yeah, I suppose I have enough."

"Oh, good," Abstentia said, in sweetly frosted tones, and put on a pair of spectacles that she pulled out of her reticule. As soon as she put them on, she was someone else. There was no period of shift or change: she was herself and then she was someone different. Or rather, when Delly looked again, an elderly version of herself: a bit stouter and more stooped, with white hair and a modest and faded version of the dress she was wearing. "As a young lady going alone to a tannery to purchase leather gloves and aprons might leave an impression upon the shopkeepers, I think that a disguise might be in order."

Delly found herself impressed despite herself. "Not bad work. Did you make that construct on your own?"

Abstentia smiled, which made her face bloom into a profusion of wrinkles. "Of course. Last year, for a costume party." Even her voice sounded old and wavery. "Ainette pretended that I was her elderly aunt, and I went around acting like an awful old busybody all evening until we unmasked at midnight. It was wonderful fun: Ainette nearly laughed herself sick." Then her smile faded, and she cleared her throat. "I'll go and buy what we need, then," she said, and walked off, perhaps a bit too briskly for a woman of her advanced years.

Delly worked on picking up the bigger bits of refuse in the room until the others came back, and then they all dedicated themselves to silent and solemn focus on first carrying the furniture and leather goods into the house, then scrubbing the place down until their knuckles went red, and finally setting up the table and chairs at the center of the room before standing up to catch their breath and stare at what they had accomplished.

"Sakes," Delly said, looking around herself. It was bare, true, but that was respectable enough for a laboratory, and nothing about the clean boards of the floor or the stout solidity of the table legs invited particular criticism. "I wouldn't be at all ashamed to bring Mrs. Totham in here now."

"Oh, yes, you would be," Winn said, more dreadfully cheerful than ever. "We still have to clear a path through that back room, unless you want Mrs. Totham to trip over a heap of garbage and land next to the dead body of one of Buttons' elderly relations, what?"

Delly and Abstentia both groaned. Then they hauled their weary forms to the stinking garbage pile that had once been the kitchen to see if they could manage to locate the floor.

12

Wherein Dellaria Indulges Her Most Romantical
Instincts, and Is Also Shot At

It was a hard, stinking, sweat-drenched hour or so before they'd
more or less cleared the kitchen, after which they all collapsed into
the new chairs around the table and tried their best not to smell each
other. Abstentia was inspecting a rend in her skirt with a resigned air.
"Between this and the stench, I'll have to burn this dress."

"Oh, don't be so dramatic, Abstentia," Winn said. "Just send it out
to be washed and mended if it bothers you so much. And speaking of
which, I think that it's probably best for us to get some rest now, eh?
We'll just spend the rest of the daylight hours pretending to work and
bickering with each other if we try to push on any longer. I say we all
hail cabs back home and have a scrub and a feed before an early bedtime."

Abstentia and Delly both voiced their hearty agreement with this
plan, and they spent a few more frustrating minutes trying to muster
up the energy to magically ward the building before finally declaring
it secure and their day of work over. Delly flagged down a cab at record
speed, and then, on impulse, offered it to Abstentia. "We got a lot done
today, Dok. And that was a clever idea of yours, that disguise for buying the peculiar stuff."

Abstentia looked surprised, but only for a moment. "Thank you," she said. "I thought it was clever as well. See you at Damel's tomorrow, then." And with that she was off.

"That was jolly nice of you, Dell," Winn said, once they were securely settled in a cab of their own.

Delly shrugged, feeling unaccountably uncomfortable. "It's always easy to hail another cab around here. And it *was* a good idea that she had." Then she told Winn about the enchanted spectacles.

Winn smiled at her. "It *does* sound like a riliftin' clever bit of illusion. And it was still nice of you to tell her so."

Delly flushed and changed the subject.

When they got back to their place they decided that a quick scrub at the washstand wouldn't be nearly good enough considering the stink that they'd both managed to build up over the course of the afternoon, and that they each ought to have a bath. There not being enough hot water in the kitchen to accommodate two baths at such short notice, they each made a change of clothes into a tidy bundle and walked three blocks to the nearest bathhouse.

"You know," Winn said, "if we *are* courting, it wouldn't be the proper thing to bathe in the same room." She went a bit pink. "As much as that might be a jolly way to spend the afternoon."

"We can stay at opposite walls," Delly suggested. "And keep our eyes averted. As much as we might be inclined to peek." Seemed a bit ginny to her, but Fine Young Ladies had their ways.

"Shake on it?" Winn said, and they shook on it very gravely before paying their half-sen each and entering the bathhouse.

Delly always liked a visit to the bathhouse. It was like another world in there, as if the stout front door with the stout old lady posted at it to take your money and warn you not to get into the water if you were bleeding presented a gateway into fairyland. There were, of course, first the changing rooms to contend with, full of elderly ladies with sharp elbows who needed to hold conferences with their dearest friends directly in front of the cubbyhole in which one most wanted to hide one's dirty underthings.

But then one passed through this crowded testing ground and entered into a realm of joy, where the steam wreathed the elderly ladies in glory and everything was warmer and wetter and pleasanter than it was outside. Delly sank into the water and then settled toward the bottom like a fistful of sand. She even heated the water around herself in order to make it perfectly comfortable for a fire witch but decidedly too warm for anyone else, which made a nice comfortable space around her in which she could spread out her limbs a bit. There she lolled for some time, her eyes half-closed, occasionally sinking entirely underneath the hot water for a moment before resurfacing again to breathe in great gulps of hot, steamy air, until she had entered into a state that was closer to sleep than it was to wakefulness. So thoroughly relaxed was Delly that it took her longer than it probably should have to realize that two women nearby were talking about the Wexins.

"Missing, that's what they're saying. What I heard from Tetra is that they sent one of *their* men over with the message, and Her Ladyship and Miss Clairelle were talking about it over breakfast before the gentlemen came in. Her Ladyship said that she thought that the Wexin girl might have gotten herself in trouble with a gentleman, and Miss Clairelle said, Oh, *no*, she couldn't *possibly*. Doesn't want to think ill of her friend, I expect. Some gentleman is probably what it is, I say. Probably got herself into a family way and then ran off before it could cause a scandal. She's a householded daughter, you know. Not real Wexin blood. Who knows what sort of creature the mother might have been. Never pays to let strangers into your house, that's what *I* say."

The other woman made noises of agreement over these rare coins of wisdom, and the two of them moved on to other topics as Delly filed the name they'd mentioned into the appropriate desk drawer of her mind so that she could ask Abstentia about it. *Miss Clairelle.* They hadn't really bothered to try to find out if Ainette had gotten in touch with any of her friends. It seemed unlikely—presumably anyone who knew Ainette would also know her sister, and contact with anyone they both knew would be clearly dangerous for Ainette—but it wouldn't hurt to ask around a bit.

Delly floated for a while longer, wondering idly whether or not Her Ladyship, Miss Clairelle, or their gossiping maids would find Ainette's having gone missing because she had attempted to murder her own sister and then successfully murdered her sister's young bodyguard during an escape attempt more or less shocking than the thought that she might have had an unwise gallop or two and gotten herself knocked up out of wedlock. She finally roused herself, a bit reluctantly, and bought a bit of soap from one of the sellers circulating the room. She then gave herself a nice thorough scrubbing before getting out, drying off, putting her clean dress on, and combing her hair, after which she sailed back out of the bathhouse and into the freshish evening air, feeling as if she was an entirely reconstitutionalized woman, ready to face whatever new and peculiar torments the world might thrust upon her.

Fortunately, the only thing thrust upon her in this particular moment was a paper cone of roasted chestnuts being vigorously proffered by one Winn Cynallum. "I'm always starving when I get out of the baths, aren't you? Swimming always works up such an appetite."

"Were you *swimming* in there?" Delly asked, astounded. She knew, of course, that there was a swimming pool in the bathhouse where one could take exercise, but it had never occurred to her that anyone would do so who wasn't some sort of religious ascetic or under specific orders from their doctor to suffer through regular cold baths.

"Oh, just for half an hour or so before my scrub," Winn said. "Let's go find some supper—I could eat a *herd*."

Delly followed Winn, feeling oddly peaceful as she led the way to the nearest restaurant that suited her standards. There was something pleasant about allowing oneself to be simply carried along in Winn's wake: one knew that one would never be led into bad decisions when Winn was at the head of the battalion, and that there also might be a delicious pie at the end of the march. Winn seemed to possess a unique genius for finding very good pie.

By the time they sat down for their evening meal it was already dark, and almost as soon as they finished their feed they stumbled home, fell into bed, and slept soundly until the comfortable and natural awakening of the next morning. That was, at least, what Dellaria hoped would happen. She was bitterly disappointed when instead she was once again shaken awake by Winn at an hour when, as far as Delly was concerned, no self-respecting person should be forced to hear another person saying the phrase "Wakey-wakey!" Followed immediately by "Time for you to be shot at a bit, Dellaria!"

"But I don't *want* to be shot at," Delly said in a quavering voice that she hoped might inspire a bit of pity in the stern breast of her interlocutor.

"Too bad," Winn said. "It's either be shot at now, by m'self, in the interest of your learning how not to be killed, or be shot at later by someone else in the interest of your being right and *properly* killed."

"You don't *know* that I'll be shot at," Delly said sulkily. "I might not be shot at at all."

"If you didn't want to be shot at at all you shouldn't have gotten into this business, Dellaria," Winn said. "You might have considered taking in laundry instead, what? A much safer sort of career. Noble profession, too. Making everyone smell nicer without any violence. Anyway, up and at 'em, Wells!"

Delly obeyed, though not without entering a few more complaints into the official record. They breakfasted on bread and butter with cress, and then Winn dragged a resisting Dellaria to their violence alley, where she proceeded to draw her pistol in a decidedly unnerving fashion. "Steady on, Cynallum," Delly said, hoping that the use of some of the Cynallum vernacular might steady what seemed to be the agitated Cynallum nerves. It was probably Delly's fault: a nice gull like Winn could only take so much before a wretch of a Wells drove her to addlement.

"Oh, don't worry," Winn said. "I'm not going to shoot at you. I'm going to shoot *past* you." Then she fired.

Delly only stood there staring at her, utterly stupefied. Her ears were ringing. "Why?" she asked, after a long moment.

"To give you a chance to try and melt it without your being in any real danger," Winn said patiently. "Though it didn't go very well, did it?"

"How in the releft am I supposed to melt a bullet?" Delly snapped, and then cleared her throat. "Begging your pardon for my language, but considering as that the eye moves more slowly than bullets, and magic moves more slowly than the eye, and I, myself, am a slowish sort of person, generally, I don't—and I'm being very clear and honest with you, Winn, out of consideration for our fondness for each other—I don't think that it's relefting well possible."

"You really do go on when you're trying to wriggle your way out of something," Winn said. If good cheer was generally like the warming rays of the sun, Winn's good cheer, at this moment, was like the warming rays of the sun to a man in the middle of a desert wearing a thick coat. "But we can try to start a bit slower." And with that, she extracted the bullets from her pistol and lobbed one directly at Delly's head.

Delly ducked. Winn sighed. "You're meant to melt it, remember?"

"I panicked," Delly said. "Do it again?"

Winn tossed another one. Delly threw a messy wall of heat bulletward. The bullet bounced off of Delly's chest, and Winn's hair blew back a bit. "Look out, Dell," Winn said. "You nearly gave me a nice golden sear."

"Sorry," Delly said. "Another one?"

Winn tossed a few more. Delly failed to melt a single one, and then had to gather them up to give them back to Winn. "They're too small," she complained. "And they move too fast."

"They move a riliftin' lot faster when someone's firing them at you out of a revolver," Winn said, and chucked another one straight at

Delly's head. Delly, tired and frustrated, threw up a barrier of heat all around her body, and then blinked when something wet splattered against her head. Winn shrieked.

Delly said, "Was it a bird?" She had a vague notion that a bird might have just shat on her.

"No," Winn said. "You have molten lead on your forehead."

"Oh," Delly said, and wiped it off with her hand before shaking it onto the ground. She always forgot that things like molten lead were likely to injure other people. "Good thing it didn't get on my clothes." One really did go through dresses quickly when one was a professional fire witch. "Do you think that it would be within the capabilities of your average working wizard to create a dress that wouldn't burn with the same rapidity as your more ordinary clothing?"

"I'll ask Abstentia," Winn said. "We ought to be able to put something together between the three of us. I'd say that enchanting an existing dress would be easier than creating an entirely new fireproof dress, wizarding seamstresses not being so very thick on the ground, what?" Then she said, "Delly, you *did* it."

"What?" Delly said. "Oh. I suppose that I did."

"You did," Winn said, and bounded over to give Delly a nice solid squeeze against her nice solid bosom. "You're a miracle, Delly Wells, you really are." Then, to Delly's grave disappointment, she released her. Delly would have been perfectly content to have been squeezed and told how wonderful she was into the late afternoon. "You should pick where we have lunch. To celebrate, I mean."

"Oh," Delly said. "Well—I'd say that I'd be better off letting you pick a celebratatory meal, considering the fact that whatever you pick is usually what I like best."

Winn went gratifyingly pink. "I'm awfully glad to hear it," she said, and then took ahold of Delly's hand, casual as could be, to lead her out of the alley.

Delly found herself in a strange state. Maybe it was the squeeze, or the sudden and unexpected handholding, or the way that Winn kept smiling at her, but somehow the joy, excitement, delight, and other associated emotions that these unusual occurrences brought forth in the Wellsian breast were enough to completely discombobulate your garden-variety Dellaria for the following hour or so. Presumably, they ate, though Delly barely attended to what she was shoving into her mouth. She was watching Winn, instead, wrapped up in the small details of her: the lock of silver hair that had fallen out of its chignon and she kept pushing out of her face, her big, sturdy hands, the specific honey color of her eyes. She was so entranced that they were halfway through their meal—Winn had, of course, found more excellent pie, which Delly in this moment found almost inconceivably delightful—before it occurred to her that her staring was probably exceedingly uncomfortable for Winn, and forced her gaze down to her plate.

By the time they were finished with their meal they had just enough time to pick up Delly's new dresses before they would have to report in at Damel's. She popped into the back room to change into one of them—it was a very dark green, which according to Winn set off Delly's complexion admirably. Delly was herself somewhat skeptical of this—she didn't really know how one could tell whether or not dull brown hair and freckles had been set off to their best advantage. Her skepticism, however, was rapidly put to rest when she stepped out of the dressing room and Winn's eyes went wide. "Oh, Delly," she said. "You look absolutely *beautiful*."

Delly blushed. Winn blushed. The shopgirls might have blushed, for all that Delly knew. She wasn't attending to much but staring at Winn, who was staring back at her.

They somehow made it to Damel's—astonishing, really, considering how distracted they both were—and deliberately sat with some space between them at the same table they'd claimed last time. Winn ordered coffee and cake, and they settled in to watch the goings-on among the regulars in a warm, buzzing silence.

This time the Tothams were the next to arrive, Mrs. Totham floating along to their table as serenely as a queen, while her daughters staggered behind her with their arms laden with packages. Mura flung her packages onto the table, herself into a chair, and a furious glare at her sister. "I *told* you that we should have gotten a cab, *Vitna*."

"There was nothing at all stopping you from paying for a cab for yourself with your own money, *Mura*," Vitna said.

"Now, now, girls, let's not argue," Mrs. Totham said. "Think of what your dear sister Ermintrude would think to see you squabbling like children."

"She'd join in the fray in a second," Mura muttered.

Vitna pinched her. Mura slapped her in retaliation. Buttons, a strange red light emanating from his eye sockets, marched up Mrs. Totham's sleeve, starting from her wrist, took a firm stance upon her shoulder, and screamed, in the voice of a terrified woman, "*Beware!*"

That settled things down quickly enough. Winn, who had been placidly eating cake the whole while, carefully set down her fork and said, "Goodness golly, that was absolutely *horrible*."

The normally imperturbable denizens of Damel's seemed to agree. They were attracting outraged glances. One elderly gent was moved enough to stand and speak to a waiter, who then cautiously edged toward their table, looking deeply unhappy at the prospect of having to converse with a customer. "Thousand pardons, ladies," he said. "But I'm afraid that if your familiar continues to disturb the other customers with its screaming, we'll have to ask you to leave the premises."

"Oh," Mrs. Totham said. "Buttons isn't my *familiar*. He's an entirely independent personage, I assure you. In fact, I suspect that he may have been a member of the high headmanship, in his own time!" She looked very pleased about it. Delly supposed that was fair enough: it wasn't everyone who went about with a skeletal mouse who might or might not have previously been a wizard who might or might not have met the First Headman in her handbag.

The waiter didn't look nearly as happy to hear this droplet of informational nectar as Mrs. Totham had been to impart it. "Well, then," he said. "If you could tell His Lordship that the management would appreciate it if he screamed a bit less, I would be very much obliged." Then he shuffled off with the air of a man who had seen far too much that he would never be able to forget throughout his years of working in a coffee shop famous for its apricot crumb cake.

Mrs. Totham was frowning slightly. "Do you know, I think that that young man"—the waiter was fifty if he was old enough to put his own trousers on—"was taking an ironical tone with me."

"Oh, *no*, Mother," Mura said, her own honeyed tone so tinged with acid you could serve it up as a refreshing lemonade. "I imagine that he was just overwhelmed to learn that he was in the presence of a personage of such excellent breeding."

Mrs. Totham looked as though she wasn't sure how to respond to this statement, and Delly was enormously relieved to see Abstentia walk through the door. Though Abstentia would be worse than useless at smoothing over an argument, her presence generally seemed to have the effect of causing people who might otherwise bicker amongst themselves to band together in order to bicker with Abstentia instead. "Ah, look, here's Miss Dok!" Delly said heartily. She found herself, to her surprise, genuinely pleased to see her.

"Hello, Wells," Abstentia said. "Winn. Tothams."

"We each have our own names, you know," Mura said.

"I know," Abstentia said. "Oh, good, you bought the things that I asked for." She started to open up one of the packages, then stopped when Winn cleared her throat.

"Do you really think that it's a wise idea to flash that stuff about in public?"

"It's not as if anyone in here is very likely to see that I have a few perfectly ordinary chemicastry supplies and draw radical conclusions," Abstentia said, though she also stopped unwrapping the package.

"Not really *such* radical conclusions, considering that they'd be true," Winn said. "Shall we all put the sturdy young backs to work and carry this stuff to the laboratory, then?"

The younger Tothams both groaned loudly. "We just carted all of that stuff over *here*."

"Well, now it's time to cart it elsewhere," Winn said. Then she paused and glanced at Delly. "That is, if Delly thinks we ought to."

Delly just stared at her for a moment, nonplussed. Then she remembered that she was meant to be the leader of their merry band and cleared her throat. This was a bit tricky. Delly, frankly, thought that it was a bit hard of Winn to demand that they all get back to work when she personally felt as if she'd barely had a chance to sit down, and the Tothams were still red in the face (in Vitna's case) and visibly bedewed with perspiration from their package-carting efforts (in Mura's). At the same time, it seemed fairly discourteous for Delly to disagree with her (charming, adorable, altogether incomparable) future householder in front of a group of their peers. She would have to be very delicate about it. "Ah, right. Yeah, let's do as Winn says after we've all finished our coffee and cake. We could probably all use a few more minutes of recuperation before we go marching back over half of Leiscourt."

Mura and Vitna looked relieved, and immediately signaled to the waiter to order more sweets. Delly tried communicate to Winn that there ought not be any hard feelings through the very vigorous waggling of her eyebrows. Winn looked perplexed for a time, then began smiling and nodding as someone might to a little child telling a very long and exceedingly tedious story: a look that said something like, *Yes, yes, you* are *doing your best, aren't you?*

Delly flushed and stopped her eyebrow contortions, satisfied at least that Winn didn't feel too betrayed by Delly's having decided against immediate and vigorous productive effort in favor of eating cake with ass firmly encushioned upon a velvety Damel's chair. They tarried for about another half an hour—even Winn gave in and had a bit more cake—until Delly was finally forced to sigh, say, "Time to start getting things done, I guess," and heave the Wellsian figure to its feet. "We should do this in shifts so we're not such a crowd all tramping through the neighborhood together." She chewed at her lip, thinking. "Abstentia, if you pick out what you need the most, you and Winn can go ahead with those and get started, if you remember how to get there all right. I'll take the Tothams around the other way with the rest of the packages so that the same people won't see all of us."

Everyone agreed to these arrangements, and they divided up the packages. The route that Delly used to bring the Tothams to the laboratory was circuitous enough that she was tired and sore-footed by the time they arrived, and disinclined to engage in any educational endeavors. This mattered not a speck to Abstentia, who waved her over impatiently the instant she stepped into the room. "Good, you're finally here. Come here, Wells, you'll need to learn a little basic chemicastry and laboratory protocol if you're going to be of any use."

"Excuse me," Delly said. "Without any intention of being rude to your respectable self, but I don't recollect having volunteered myself as your assistant."

"There's no need for you to have said it aloud, Miss Wells," Winn said, heartier than a hot bowl of oatmeal. "We knew you'd be keen to help the instant you were given the opportunity. We both admire your dedication as a leader to pitching in and keeping up company morale, what?"

Delly glared at her. Winn smiled. Delly sighed. "Yeah, all right. Did you at least get me another apron?"

"No," Abstentia said. "Presumably, as a fire witch, you're more likely to escape unscathed from an explosion than the rest of us, regardless of what you're wearing. Now, come over here so that I can show this to you." Then she added, more politely, "Mrs. Totham, would you care to watch as well? It might be helpful for you to have some basic understanding of the materials before we embark upon testing on live subjects."

This last sentence did very little to fill Delly with warmer feelings toward learning the art of chemicastry.

"Next thing you know you'll be volunteering me to act as the live subject, as well," she murmured to Winn. Winn only laughed, which at the moment Delly found musical, delightful, and deeply irritating.

Once they really embarked upon the lesson, however, Delly was surprised to find herself quite genuinely absorbed by the subject. Today all that they would be doing was analyzing the sample of red drip that the Tothams had acquired so that they could find out what it was made of. This, apparently, necessitated a great deal of weighing and measuring minute quantities of various substances, mixing them together, encanting until they changed colors or boiled over or did something else mildly interesting, weighing and measuring some more, and then doing all sorts of extremely dull mathematics in order to try to determine the proportions involved, while Winn furiously took notes and argued with you over whether or not you'd gotten all of the figures down correctly. Mura and Vitna, the lucky creatures, were entirely unblessed with magical talent or training and unable to participate in the chemicastry, and so Delly handed them two tocats and assigned them to attempt to finish cleaning the kitchen and buy some items that would turn it into a space in which they might all actually be able to sit down and fix a pot of coffee.

The chemicastry was extremely tedious, but there was also something soothing about the fussy exactitude of it. Accidentally spill a bit of powder or mispronounce a word as you encanted and you would be left with nothing at all to show for your efforts—or, in Delly's case, accidentally heat a beaker a degree or two higher than what had been requested and cause a small explosion. She didn't know why Winn and Abstentia got so fussy about it, really: Delly thought that it livened up the atmosphere a bit. It was the most exciting thing to happen in the laboratory for the entire afternoon.

The explosion, however, didn't slow them down for long: after Delly was subjected to a thorough and somewhat invigorating round of criticism from Abstentia on the subject of how her carelessness could result in someone having their fingers blown off, hair singed to cinders, or skin horribly blistered, Delly, suitably chastened, promised to do better going forward, and their next attempt was carried out without any maimings, singeings, or blisterings to speak of. Then there were more tests, and more mathematics, and finally Abstentia sat back with a loud, satisfied sigh. "*There*," she said, and tapped a stack of papers with her finger.

Delly squinted at the top paper on the stack. It was a much denser thicket of parameters than she'd ever hacked her way through during her one trying year at Weltsir. "That's our recipe for the drip, then?"

"*Recipe* is a jolly nice way of putting it," said Winn. She didn't sound very happy about it.

"Mrs. Totham and I will take over for now," Abstentia said, sounding pleased enough to make up for half a dozen unhappy Winnifers. "Mrs. Totham, what do you make of this?"

Mrs. Totham—and Buttons, who had been watching the chemicastrical proceedings in a way that Delly found very discomforting—approached. "Ah, how interesting," Mrs. Totham said after a moment. "I can see how this would induce very pleasurable sensations." She sat down to examine the stack of papers more thoroughly, Buttons venturing around to sit near the edge of the table and peruse them as well.

Mrs. Totham turned the page. Buttons made the sound of a strong wind whipping through the branches of a dead tree.

"Yes, I quite agree," Mrs. Totham said, and turned to the next page.

Delly, Winn, and Abstentia all exchanged worried glances. "What was that, Mrs. Totham?" Delly ventured.

"Oh, Buttons was just commenting on how the combined effects of some of the elements in the drip might cause restricted blood flow to the brain, which would explain some of the dreadful side effects that have been reported."

"*Buttons* said that, Mrs. Totham?" Winn asked, her eyes gone rather wide.

Delly, for her part, was interested in a different aspect of Mrs. Totham's statement. "So do you think that you might make a better version, Mrs. Totham? One without the dreadful side effects?"

Mrs. Totham frowned slightly and looked down at Buttons. "*Reduced* side effects, perhaps. To eliminate them would likely result in the negation of the pleasurable effects that make the product worthwhile to its users. Unless you disagree, Buttons?"

Buttons said, "*Bong.*"

Mrs. Totham smiled. "We think that we'll be able to formulate a version that will be a *significant* improvement."

"Good," Delly said, feeling a wave of relief wash over her. If her mam did get onto the streets again, and did get back onto the drip, maybe she'd be able to keep her ornery old carcass alive long enough for Delly to have another chance to send her out to that place in the country. "When can we start?"

"Not until we've worked out some decisions about the formulation," Abstentia said firmly.

Abstentia and Mrs. Totham—and Buttons, unfortunately—huddled together over the papers in a way that seemed to indicate that they were finished with their discussions. Delly and Winn exchanged a glance, then retired to the kitchen, where Mura and Vitna were drinking coffee with their long legs stretched out in front of them. Mura looked up and smiled when they walked in. "Not bad for three hours and two tocats, is it?"

The transformation wasn't, to be fair, quite as dramatic as what Mrs. Medlow had achieved in Delly's room, but Delly's room hadn't started out with stray dead rats and broken chairs in the corners. The rats and broken chairs had now been banished and the floor and walls scrubbed clean, and Mura and Vitna had brought in a sturdy new table and a few mismatched chairs to put around it. There was a small fire in the grate that they had presumably used to boil water for the coffee. "We'll probably have to hire a boy to go down the chimney, but it's a solidly built old house," Vitna said. "I went out onto the roof and it all looks sound. Someone could live here and make a nice home out of it after the rest of the trash was cleared out."

"It looks grand to me," Delly said.

Winn sat down next to Vitna. "Do you know very much about building houses? I always thought that seemed like a very interesting thing to know how to do."

Delly, personally, thought that fixing roofs and things sounded wretchedly dull, and drank coffee and listened with sour spirits as Vitna expounded upon her history of earning her bread as a woman-of-all-work. It was, Delly realized with dismay, exactly the sort of thing that she imagined that Winn's terrifying mother would approve of in a prospective daughter-in-law. Delly would have to do something truly impressive to turn Winn's attention back onto Delly's own under-whelming self. Then she had an idea. "Vitna," she spewed forth, "do you think that the three of you might like to live here? We could all pitch in to clean it up a bit, and I'm sure that Winn would be able to cast an illusion to make it look as if the windows were still boarded up, and then you wouldn't have to worry about losing another room be-cause of Buttons . . . being as he is."

The sisters both sat up a bit. "That would be fine," Mura said. "Would you really be willing to help us clean up the place?"

"Of course," Delly said, bolstered by the smile from Winn that she could see in the corner of her eye. "You're part of our little company, after all. And if you're staying here, you'll be able to make sure that no one else wanders in here and discovers the laboratory, so it will work out better for everyone, really."

"I think that it's a wonderful idea," Winn said. "Has anyone looked at the second story? Maybe there's a room up there that we could fix up into a cozy little nook for your mother."

"And Buttons," Delly added, amused by the idea. "Maybe a basket for him to sleep in. Do mice sleep in baskets?"

"I think when it comes to Buttons, the more relevant question is whether he sleeps *at all*," Winn said, and stood. "Right. Shall we have a look around upstairs?"

They all tromped up the stairs to have a nose around, which was a very unpleasant nose until Winn found the unusually large dead rat responsible for the odor and tossed it out the window. They then opened the rest of the windows and embarked on more cleaning—which mostly consisted of carrying loads of refuse out to the street for the trash pickers to carry away—until Abstentia popped her head in to say that she and Mrs. Totham were done for the afternoon, and what on earth were they all doing up here?

It then fell to Delly to explain about how they wanted to fix up the upstairs so that the Tothams could stay in the house and guard the laboratory. "We thought that we could fix up one room for Mura and Vitna and another for Mrs. Totham. And a basket for Buttons."

Mrs. Totham burst into tears. Buttons made a sound like the ringing of hundreds of delicate bells. Delly waved her hands through the air as if she thought that this might accomplish something while Mura and Vitna gathered around their mother to comfort her. "Oh, come on, now, don't cry, Mother," Mura said. "We've gotten everything sorted out now."

"I know," Mrs. Totham said. "I'm very sorry, so very sorry. It's only that—after all of these terrible things that have happened—so very *kind*—and Buttons will have his *very own basket*. Miss Wells, was this your doing? Bless you, I really must—bless you, Miss Wells. How very *kind*."

Delly cleared her throat, embarrassed at the lump in it. Mrs. Totham was such a nice old thing, even if she *was* a necromancer engaged in dread communion with some ancient wizarding demon trapped within the skeleton of a mouse. "Really, Mrs. Totham, it's selfish of the rest of us to want you to stay here. So that you can keep an eye on the laboratory, I mean. So I won't have any more thanking from you."

"I understand," Mrs. Totham said, and wiped at her eyes with her handkerchief. "The girls and I will do our absolute utmost to protect the laboratory from any invaders, I'm sure."

"I dunno if it will take that much effort, Mrs. Totham, considering that most of the fellas who might consider breaking into a place like this will be mostly distinctly wan and weedy types, Mrs. Totham,"

Delly said. "But I have every faith that you and your lovely daughters will do a very fine job of keeping an eye on the place."

This, unfortunately, set Mrs. Totham off in tears again, and after they'd all banded together to comfort her for a while, they all set about scrubbing down the room with renewed vigor, while Mrs. Totham marched off to the closest market with Vitna after declaring that she would cook supper for all of them at the house that evening as a token of gratitude for their kindness to her. That pretty well set the schedule for the rest of the evening: Mrs. Totham labored away at the stove in the newly respectable kitchen while the younger generation worked to bring the second floor up to standard. Except for Abstentia, who made excuses about having to go over the figures for her formula again and darted off to the laboratory, where she'd be safe from the horrors of communal cleaning. Delly couldn't blame her, really.

Eventually Mrs. Totham called them all down to eat, and they pulled all of the chairs in the house into the kitchen and lit some candles so that they could gather around for what Mrs. Totham called a *family supper*. Mrs. Totham had cooked a simple meal of chicken and dumplings with carrots and peas in it, and fresh bread for mopping up the last bits of gravy. It tasted so good that Delly suspected Mrs. Totham of having applied some of her dark arts to the cookery, but after a moment of hesitation over the thought, she decided that she was too hungry to worry too much about demons in the dumplings and simply settled in to a nice hearty meal. It was all very cozy, really, with everyone all huddled up around the little table with their elbows knocking together while Abstentia and Winn discussed magical theory and Mura and Vitna fought over the crusty end slices of bread.

Eventually everyone was full enough from their supper and aching enough from the labors of the day that they agreed that the only thing left to do was to get some rest, with the goal of getting the Tothams moved in and starting on drip production the following day. So they all left to go search for some scraps of rest in their own little berths, and for the first time in hours, on the long walk back to Delly's little place, Delly and Winn were entirely alone together.

"It was really wonderful what you did today, Dell," Winn said, almost the instant that they could speak privately.

"What do you mean?" Delly asked, even though she knew exactly what Winn was talking about. She had offered to move the Tothams into the house mostly in order to impress Winn with the kind, generous, and altogether virtuous personality of Dellaria Wells.

"You offering to fix up the house for the Tothams like that," Winn said. "Mrs. Totham was practically beside herself, the dear old thing. It was *awfully* considerate of you, Dell."

Delly attempted to avoid preening too visibly. Then she said, "It wasn't that considerate, really. I was just worried about the laboratory being broken into with no one there." Modestly objecting to something always made it much more convincing.

Winn gave her a fond look. "It's just like you to say that," she said. Then she very gently took Delly's hand and squeezed it before drawing it through her own elbow.

Delly's hand, that cursed appendage, immediately began to sweat. "Is this really proper, Winn? Holding hands and linking arms and the sort, I mean. I wouldn't know, having been raised by a person as generally improper as my mother. I wouldn't want to jeopardize my relationship with you over some improprietous grasping of inappropriate limbs, Winn."

Winn was still smiling at her. "You're awfully funny sometimes, Dell," she said. "I don't think that anyone who might disapprove of *anything* that we do is very likely to suddenly appear on this street at this time of night. And it's completely proper for two friends to walk down the street arm in arm. Nothing at all to worry about on that score, what?"

"If you say so," Delly said, and they walked quietly for a while.

"Dell," Winn said eventually, "what do you think you'd like to do after all of this is over?"

"Do?" Delly asked, and immediately felt quite the dunce. There was nothing particularly difficult about comprehending the word *do*. "I don't know. I suppose that I haven't had time to think about it."

"I don't know if I really have time to think about it, either," Winn said. "So instead I waste time when I should be doing something else." Her voice went more sun-warmed as she spoke. "My mother used to take me up to her clan's summer seat for a month every year, right before the weather started to turn cold. Maybe that's what I'll do. Go up north and see the relations, and wade in the brooks during the day and look at the stars at night. Get some of the city out of my hair."

It sounded pretty nice to Delly. Dull, but nice. "Don't you get bored out there?"

"Sometimes," Winn said. "But it's a nice thing to be a bit bored sometimes, what? After a while you start learning to be interested in watching the wind blow through the grass, and all of the other pastoral whatsit."

"I don't know if I'd be able to manage that," Delly said. "Becoming as one with the chirpicating crickets, et cetera."

Winn really, genuinely threw her head back to laugh at that. Then she looked down at Delly and smiled. "You could find out," she said. "If you came with me."

Delly looked up at her, startled. Winn hadn't really formally proposed yet, and though that made very little difference to Delly when it came to accepting a free holiday to the countryside, she was quite sure that it made a difference to *Winn*. "Do you mean it? But—if nothing's settled, really, with our—you know—"

"No matter what," Winn said. "As a friend, if nothing else. Which we are regardless, Dell. And you'll deserve a nice holiday in the countryside after all of this madness is over. Either there or off to Hexos. It's nice and warm there. Better in every way than Leiscourt over a long winter."

"I don't know if it will ever be over, for me," Delly said, before she could think better of it. "I mean—I don't mean to be needlessly dramatical. It's just that my mam will still be my mam, afterward. I don't know if I'll be able to flit off to the mountains with her in the state she's in right now." Her mam would be a weight around Delly's ankles no matter what Delly did. *Unless she dies*, said a voice from the back of Delly's head, but she shied away from that. She didn't want her mam to die. Not even if part of her thought that she might be better off that way.

"We'll get her all settled into a nice place first," Winn said, with the comfortable confidence that Delly always found so baffling in her. "And once she's good and comfortable and settled in, I'll whisk you off for that nice boring holiday."

"Do you promise?" Delly asked, feeling a bit pitiful and embarrassing even as she asked it.

"I promise," Winn said, and Delly, who had apparently learned nothing at all about what promises were worth from nearly thirty years of experience in disappointment, found herself believing her.

13

Wherein Dellaria Enters More Deeply into What She
Insists on Pretending Is Not a Criminal Enterprise,
and Is Vigorously Threatened

The next few days settled themselves into something like a pleasant workaday routine. Up at dawn to be shot at by Winn a bit, then lunch, then off to the house to work on either cleaning or drip production. Winn was very firm about the fact that she vastly preferred trying to put together a cozy room for Mrs. Totham to anything having to do with the drip—she still hadn't changed her mind about Delly's scheme, unfortunately—and so Delly found herself thrust more and more into the role of Abstentia's assistant.

It was aggravating, mostly, was what it was. There were too many numbers to deal with, and too many things that could go horribly wrong if your mind wandered for a moment and you mistook the third vial from the left with the fourth (which Delly had only done once, so it was very unfair of Abstentia to keep talking about it, really). Delly would have quit and wandered off to do something more interesting— that had been her general approach toward steady employment for most of her life so far—but making Winn do it instead seemed as if it was practically guaranteed to dispel the pink and dewy haze that had cloaked the two of them over the past few days, and she was too dedicated to this particular scheme to try to come up with a new one now. So she clung to her task like a burr on a stocking and discovered, to her astonishment, that as the days went by the words and numbers that had all struck her as incomprehensible gibberish began to seem increasingly familiar.

She also went back to see Rat again, Rat having promised to provide more information on whatever wretched fine ladies were the cause of Delly's current state of familial woe. This time, Rat's hat had an enormous bird on it, while Rat's face bore the serene smile of a person who had managed to uphold their end of the bargain. "I have a very interesting bit of information for you, I think. One of the runner-boys swears back and sideways that he heard one of the fine ladies call the other one *Clare*."

Clare. That sounded a bit familiar, but Delly couldn't for the life of her recall why. Then it came to her: the maid in the bathhouse who had been gossiping about Ainette had mentioned a Miss Clairelle. Not exactly the same thing as Clare, perhaps, but easy enough to mishear, or one might be the shortened version of the other. "Thanks very much," Delly said, and handed over the sum that they'd previously agreed on as payment. Then she paused. "Begging your pardon, Rat, if this would be outside of your honorable personage's general scope of labor and sundry services, but I don't suppose that you might see your way to letting me speak to one of these fine young runners my own self?"

"That might be possible," Rat said. The enormous bird nodded its agreement. "For two tocats."

Delly gave Rat her very widest and most unbelieving eyes. "*Two tocats?*"

They haggled back and forth for a while and eventually settled on one tocat, which made Delly feel like quite the accomplished young woman of business. Then they arranged the time—noon, in three days—for their meeting, and Delly trotted off to meet Winn and the other ladies at Damel's.

There was a new, special apple cake available today, which was a good bolster to Delly's nerves when she presented her plan to Abstentia. "We need to have a sample of our product ready to send to the Kind Companions in three days."

"*What?*" Abstentia said.

"Oh, gracious me!" Mrs. Totham said.

"Well, *fuck*," Mura muttered.

"Oh, *Dell*," Winn said.

Buttons said, "*Bong.*"

Delly waited for the clamor to die down a bit before she attempted speech again. "I'm awfully sorry," she said. "I know that it's very short notice, but my contact"—she thought that the word *contact* also made her sound like a very accomplished woman of business—"can only guarantee that they will be able to convince one of the Kind Companions' runners to wait for me for half an hour on that particular day." Then she added, in what she hoped was a pacifying manner, "We don't have to make very *much* of the . . . substance." It had occurred to her only very belatedly that saying the words *we don't have to make very much red drip* in a public café might not be the cleverest of possible actions that could be undertaken by a Skillful Woman of Business.

"The *quantity* isn't the issue, *Wells*," Abstentia said, in a tone withering enough to kill off a small grove of trees. "We haven't even finalized our formula yet, let alone created something that we can be positive will be safe and effective."

"Then we'll have to finalize the formula," Delly said. "And make *something*. We're supposed to be using this as a pretense to get in touch with the Kind Companions so that we can find Ainette, not revolutionizing the . . . *particular* industry in Leiscourt. Any effective product will be good enough."

"Not for me," Abstentia said. "Don't you have any sense of standards, Wells? And in any case, as I've said before, it seems to me that presenting an inferior product to a group of dangerous, violent criminals isn't a particularly clever plan."

"And *I* don't know if these Kind Companions are really as dangerous as they've managed to convince the populace that they are," Delly snapped back. "I don't suppose that you know someone named Miss Clairelle?"

Abstentia's expression immediately went thundersome. "What *about* Clairelle?"

Delly explained about what she'd heard at the bathhouse, and then what she'd heard from Rat, as Abstentia's face grew steadily paler. "I don't believe it," she said. "*One* classmate becoming a hardened criminal is unfortunate, but *two* of them begins to suggest some type of conspiracy." She paused. "Or a gas leak."

"So she was a classmate of yours?" Delly asked.

"She *is* a classmate of mine," Abstentia said. "Of mine and Ainette's. But, more pertinently, she's the daughter of Lord Tredworth."

Delly herself didn't care whether this gull was the daughter of a boat captain from Del Sem Berg, but Winn gave the sort of gasp that you'd normally hear from the audience of a horror play. Delly looked toward her, startled. Winn wasn't normally the gasping sort. "What?"

"Lord Tredworth is a *second headman*," she said. "The Tredworths are one of the oldest families in Daeslund."

Delly endeavored not to gawp. Her endeavors failed. "What in the releft would a girl like that need to get into selling drugs for?"

"We don't know that she's involved in selling drugs at all," Abstentia said. She sounded a little tired. "Clairelle has been worrying over her father having to sell some land up north. He's apparently made some unwise investments, and between that and the crop failures over the past two years . . ."

"Hard times," Mura said sympathetically.

"Hard times," everyone else echoed. It was the right thing to say, after all.

Delly, being a noted expert in saying the *wrong* thing, said, "If they have land to sell, they're rich. No need to get together with Ainette to form a young ladies' society for crime and necromancy."

Abstentia rolled her eyes. "You have the empathetic capacity of a soiled stocking, Wells. It isn't as if they have an unlimited amount of property to sell off. At a certain point it will be Tredworth Manor. Isn't it quite natural to want to keep one's family home off of the auction block?"

"I wouldn't know," Delly said, feeling more annoyed by all of this than she probably ought to be. "My family home was a room above a brothel on Six-Bend Island that burned down after the trash heap out back caught on fire six years ago." Then she changed the subject. "There's no use in our jabbering on about it, anyhow. We have three days to put this stuff together so that we can get in contact with whoever these Kind Companions actually are, instead of sitting around at Damel's gossiping about some clanner's financial problems."

"Because of *you*," Abstentia burst out. "*You're* the one who went off and created this absurd deadline for the rest of us without so much as asking what we thought of it. It isn't as if I can just pop over to the library and consult a copy of *The Ruthless Young Lady's Guide to Felonious Wizardry* to make sure that I'm doing this properly. If I can't manage to create something up to standard in three days and it leads to trouble for us all, that's on *your head*, Wells."

Delly's face went hot. She wanted to scream at her, to tell her what a sour, haughty cat she was. Then she caught a glimpse of Winn's face from the corner of her eye and thought of what she would think to see Delly cursing in her friend's face like the poor ignorant trash that she was, and took a deep breath. "You're right," she said, though it pained her exceedingly. "I'm sorry. I should have consulted with you first. And I'll be sure to try and keep the rest of you out of it when I meet with them. But I still want to have the product ready in time for the meeting that I've arranged, and I'm willing to work as hard as I have to over the next three days to make sure that it's ready and up to your high standards."

This seemed to mollify Abstentia a bit. "Maybe not up to *my* standards," she said. "But something that might pass muster with *Clairelle Tredworth*, at least."

"Is she a bit of a dim light, then?" Delly asked, curious despite herself.

"Oh, no," Abstentia said. "She was sixth in our class last year." She paused, and then added, "I was first."

"Of course," Delly said. Then she said, "Shall we go to the house?"

They went to the house and immediately dove back into their labors, now with the unhappy and somewhat frantic vigor of a group of women on a firm deadline. They determined that they would have to take the formula that they had now and immediately create a sample of the product, in order to establish what Abstentia called "a base upon which we can build."

This, strangely enough, was the easiest thing that they'd done so far. Just a bit of mixing and heating, really: compared with all of the discussion and argument and mathematics that had preceded it, it seemed like nothing at all. Delly stared at the resulting little flask of red liquid, nonplussed. "Is that it, then?"

"That's it," Abstentia said. "In theory, at least. Not that I have the slightest doubt that my formula might be inaccurate. Whether or not it's an *improvement* is what remains to be seen."

"But how in the blink are we going to be able to tell?" Winn asked suddenly.

They all looked at each other.

"Well, *I'm* certainly not going to take any of it," Abstentia said, and looked hard at Delly.

"What the fuck are you looking at *me* for?" Delly asked, offended. "Just because my mam's a dripper doesn't mean that I'm out to start taking it."

"Did I say anything of the kind?" Abstentia retorted. "I don't recall having said anything of the kind. My only thought was that, as the leader of our group and the person who was responsible for the creation of a three-day deadline for the finalization of our product, you ought to bear the responsibility of testing it."

"Abstentia," Winn said, moving a bit closer to Delly's side. "Do you really think that that's entirely fair? Considering Delly's family situation, don't you think that it's a bit strong of you to ask her to take drip herself?"

Delly went a bit warm-faced. Herself, Dellaria Wells, being once again defended by a woman with a family name. It hadn't gotten tiresome yet.

"No, I don't," Abstentia said. "I think that it's entirely fair. And just because the two of you are *involved* in some way—"

"I'm terribly sorry, Miss Dok," Mrs. Totham said. "Really most terribly sorry to interrupt—you know that I *never* like to interrupt. But I wanted to mention that I would be capable of performing just the merest bit of body science in order to quickly return a person who has taken the drip to sobriety. If you would allow me to perform body science upon you, of course. I would never dream of using magic upon an unwilling person, indeed I would not!"

"Of *course* you wouldn't, Mrs. Totham," Winn said. "You're the dearest old bean in the world. And if you really think you'd be able to do that, I'm willing to march myself out onto the plank and take the stuff myself. It's not as if a little bit of drip is likely to do me much damage, even if there's something wrong with this batch. Sturdy troll blood and all, what?"

"There most certainly is *not* anything wrong with this batch," Abstentia said. "As you should certainly know, as you've seen all of the same figures that I have."

"Well, I'm not as good at mathematics as you are, Abstentia," Winn said in her amiable way. Abstentia blushed slightly. Delly could hardly blame her. Sometimes being irritated with Winn felt a bit as if you had suddenly found yourself on a busy street corner in a shouting match with an oak tree.

"In any case," Delly said, "pardon me if I seem suspicious of your abilities, Mrs. Totham, but how exactly will this de-drippification procedure work?"

"Well, you see," Mrs. Totham said—clearly delighted to have been invited to expound upon the subtle art of body science when generally people started wincing and edging away from her as soon as they detected a whiff of necromancy in the room—"the effects of the drip are caused entirely by its effect on the brain. If I influence the brain so that it no longer recognizes the drip, then it will have no effects on you whatever. Other than the side effects of the cessation, of course."

Delly raised her eyebrows. "What sorts of side effects, exactly?"

"Oh, dear, nothing very severe, I assure you," Mrs. Totham said. "Only a bit of light-headedness, headache, excessive perspiration, vomiting, looseness of the bowels—"

Winn was beginning to look somewhat pinched around the eyes. "You mean all of those? At the same time?"

"Not *necessarily*," Mrs. Totham said. "It may be dependent upon the individual. In any case, the symptoms are very unlikely to last for longer than a few hours."

"A few *hours*?" Winn asked, now in very obvious despair.

"I'll do it," Delly blurted out. "I mean—I don't want you to have to suffer, Winn."

Winn gave her a smile wreathed in the gentle mists of gratitude. "Oh," she said. "It's very kind of you to offer, Dell, but I don't want to see you suffer, either."

"I don't know that anyone is suffering more than I am, at the moment, watching the two of you," Abstentia said. "And if you're done staring at each other like two milkmaids holding hands behind a haystack, we do have work to do."

"Right," Delly said, partially spurred by her own embarrassment. What was wrong with her? Winn (despite being bathed in an ever-wafting perfume of beauty, wisdom, and effervescent delightfulness) was only a fairly ordinary person, after all. She was a fine prospect, not the First Headman's daughter. There was no reason for Delly to go wandering around beaming like she'd been bashed over the head with a gold club encrusted with diamonds, but here Delly was volunteering for several hours of looseness of the bowels on another gull's behalf.

She needed to get herself together. Being fond of her prospect was all well and good, but being so fond of her that she lost her instinct for self-preservation could only lead to ill. Until Delly had legal documentation that Winn would take financial responsibility for her as her householder, Delly was as vulnerable to her whims as any other clanless girl in Leiscourt having pretty words whispered into her ear, and she was engaged in a potentially very dangerous plot to find and detain a murderess. Delly had to keep her wits about her. Thus, with the conviction that she must at all costs maintain a sense of keen and sober judgment now firmly ensconced within the Wellsian bosom, Dellaria opened up her ignorant gawp and said, "I'll take the drip."

"You really don't have to, Dell," Winn said, but Delly, determined to remain steadfast in the face of Winn's charms, remained unmoved. Abstentia handed over the beaker, and Delly dipped her ring finger into the drip as she'd seen others do a thousand times before, opened her mouth, and let a large drop fall from her finger onto her tongue. It tasted like what vinegar would taste like if it was distilled at the bottom of a pile of dirty clothes.

All of the other women leaned in a bit. "Well?" Abstentia said.

Delly rolled her eyes. "It takes time to kick in," she said, and sat down in the nearest chair, trying not to look as anxious as she felt. From what she'd seen, it was better not to be standing up when it hit you.

"Oh," Abstentia said, and reached for her notebook. "Is that generally considered good or bad?"

"Bad, I'd say," Delly said. "People would rather have it quicker."

"Interesting," Abstentia said, and scribbled down a note. "Did you just swallow?"

"Yeah," Delly said. "It tastes terrible. The real seasoned drippers say it starts quicker if they hold it under their tongues, but I'd rather not have the taste of it in my mouth for long enough to let it start making itself at home."

"How interesting," Mrs. Totham said. "I imagine that by holding it under their tongues they allow it to absorb directly into their blood-streams instead of it having to bypass their digestive system first. How very clever of these seasoned personages!"

"I'm not sure if *very clever* is exactly the phraseological construction I would put to it, Mrs. Totham," Delly said.

Abstentia was still writing notes. "What would you say is the worst aspect of the flavor?"

"Every aspect," Delly said. She might have snapped a bit. "I'd imagine that any alteration you could make would only be an improvement. As it is, it tastes like the side effects that Mrs. Totham was just so kindly informing me that I have to look forward to in about twenty minutes." She was, at the moment, fighting back a completely useless impulse to stick her fingers down her throat and vomit it up before it could take her over like it had done to her mam. It was too late for that now. She'd already gone and fucking *taken* the stuff, and now she'd have to rely on nothing more than her own will to do better than her mam had done with it. Considering how far in life Delly's will had gotten her up till now she didn't have particularly high hopes.

"You'll be all right, Dell," Winn murmured, and squeezed her shoulder. "Should I nip out to the other room and make you a nice cup of tea?"

"That would be very nice of you, Winn," Delly said, suddenly struck by visions of herself in the near future, waking up in a broad, clean bed while Winn cooed the same question at her and servants added logs to the roaring fire.

"I won't be half a blink, then," Winn said, and trotted off, while Delly gazed foolishly after her.

"Isn't young love so wonderful to see," Mrs. Totham said.

"Not in a laboratory," Abstentia said. "Especially in this case. The look on your face right now is positively unsanitary, Wells."

"Oh, shove it up your particulars, Dok," Delly said. She felt very cheerful. "You're just jealous that you ain't got a prospect of your own."

Abstentia looked even smugger than usual at that. She practically purred and kneaded the floor with her pretty little paws. "I would disabuse you of that notion, Wells," she said, "if it weren't extremely unattractive for a young lady to brag about the number and quality of her suitors."

"Are there really so many of them?" Delly asked, immediately interested. "You can't just mention all of your suitors and then not tell us about them."

"Oh, well," Abstentia said, "if you all really insist." Then she dove merrily into describing the gents in question—there were three of them, one of them the son of a family whose various scandals Delly had read about with great interest in the society papers—in detail that would have, if included in one of said society papers, resulted in said paper being sued for libel. When Winn came back into the room she nearly dropped a full pot of tea onto the floor in shock.

Abstentia was about halfway through a description of one particularly notable gentleman's particularly notable physical attributes (she didn't say a thing about his body, just his green eyes and thick brown hair, which Delly both respected—it seemed like fine young ladies really *did* abstain from frivolous galloping outside of the bonds of marriage—and found baffling) when Delly started to feel funny. Not a drank-too-much-the-night-before sort of funny, or a saw-a-pretty-girl-and-don't-know-what-to-do-with-myself funny, which were two types of funny with which Delly was very intimately acquainted. This was something different entirely. A warm and soft, butter-melted and honey-dipped, kissed and cradled feeling. The best feeling, maybe, that she had ever had.

"Oh," she murmured, very quietly. She felt that she absolutely had to be quiet. If she made too much noise it might frighten that feeling away.

"Dell," Winn said, crouching down beside her. That was terribly nice of her. As nice as cream. As nice as pudding and port and plums. As nice as avoiding penury. "Are you all right?"

"Oh, yes," Delly said, and then shivered, her eyes locking onto

Winn's face. She could go for a gallop, really. Her mouth started to water. Then she smiled. "Winn. It's so nice, Winn. It's the nicest, spectacularest good."

"All right, Dell," Winn said in a soothing voice that made Delly's neck tingle. Winn tilted her head up to look at Mrs. Totham. She had such a beautiful head. "Mrs. Totham, do you think we could sober her up now?"

"Not yet," Abstentia said quickly. She was taking notes in her notebook. She was so beautiful, too. All of Delly's friends were confoundingly beautiful. "We haven't had enough time to make observations of the effects of the drip. How do you feel, Dellaria? Do you notice any unpleasant effects?"

"No," Delly said. She was very busy staring at Winn again. There was a little blue to her skin. Just a very little. Like a linen curtain with the blue sea behind it, Delly might say, if she was the sort of person inclined toward saying that sort of thing. Then she swallowed and noted, "Mouth's a little dry."

Winn handed her a cup of tea. Delly goggled at it. "Where did it come from?"

"I made it for you earlier, Dell," Winn said, and reached up her hand to push a bit of Delly's hair behind her ear. She was smiling. "Remember? For in case you get sick?"

"Oh, right," Delly said. She remembered now. She took the cup and took a sip. "You're so kind," she said. "The kindest, the very kindest. You made me strange tea. Could you do that again?"

"Do what?" Winn asked. "Make you tea that you don't like?"

"What's so strange about it?" Abstentia asked. "Is it more bitter than usual?"

"Yes," Delly said. "No. Touch my hair again, like that?"

"All right, Dell," Winn said, and did it again. Delly sighed and shivered.

Abstentia sighed, too. It wasn't nearly as happy a sigh as Delly's, though. Poor Abstentia. She was too proper to have her prospects touch her hair. Though maybe she could sneak off and have her hair touched, anyway, in secret. That might improve her mood. "Is it more bitter than usual, Dellaria?"

"Don't be bitter, Abstentia," Delly said. "You can go see the gentleman with the green eyes as soon as we're finished here and have all of the scandalous secret gallops that you like." She took another sip of tea, then frowned. "It's very bitter tea, Winn."

"I'm very sorry," Winn said. "I'll put more cream and sugar into it next time." She looked at Abstentia. "*Now* can Mrs. Totham sober her up?"

"I suppose so," Abstentia said. "It doesn't seem as if we're likely to get anything remotely useful out of her."

"Well, Abstentia, that seems like a very good reason for you to be the one to take the drip next time," Winn said, in her nice, lovely, wonderful voice, as Mrs. Totham stepped in closer to Delly's chair.

"Just hold still, my dear," Mrs. Totham said, and rested one hand on the top of Delly's head. "This will only take a moment." Delly was just thinking about how dear and soft and delightful Mrs. Totham was when the world slammed shut.

That's what it felt like. Like a heavy door clanging shut. Like a book being closed. Like a light turned out. The joy and warmth and ease were gone, and in their place was nothing at all. Nothing at all for just a moment, and then every horror that Delly had pressed onto the crowded shelves at the very back of her skull tumbled out to fill the empty space. Ermintrude's dead twisted face. A screaming woman near her mam's hospital bed. Her mother's still, waxy face. Delly, a child, the damp room they slept in, the men who came and went. Ermintrude again, and the dead cat behind the inn, and that man still choking her as he burned, and Delly now, in this moment, lurching to the side to be sick all over the floor.

Abstentia shrieked and leapt back. Winn said, "Oh, Dell," and moved in. Wiped her face with a cloth. Held the teacup to her mouth. Touched her hair. "It's all right, Dell. It's all right."

It wasn't all right. It wasn't all right. She said, "It's fucking awful, Winn." She wanted, more than anything, to take the drip again: to be where she had been a few moments ago and not where she was right now. *This must be how Mam felt*, she thought. Something like this feeling might have been what brought her mother to the place where she was now. The thought made her sick again. "I want my mam," she heard herself saying. "I want to go see my mam."

"All right, Dell," Winn said back. "All right. We'll go see her as soon as you're feeling a bit better."

"This seems like a worse reaction than what you described, Mrs. Totham," Abstentia was saying. "Are you sure that you accounted for everything that might go wrong?"

"I felt certain that I had," Mrs. Totham said. She was actually wringing her hands. In another situation Delly would have found it funny. She'd thought that people only did that in plays. "Only—I suppose that I had been thinking in terms of the effects that would be expected if someone sobered up over a period of several hours."

"You didn't take *time* into account?" Abstentia asked. She sounded furious. "You could have *killed* her, you silly thing!"

"I could *not* have killed her," Mrs. Totham said immediately. "I know that with absolute certainty. And I do not appreciate being spoken to in that tone, Miss Dok, indeed I do not! I would *never* do something that had any risk of putting Miss Wells in danger."

"Don't shout at each other," Delly mumbled, though part of her was a bit touched that they cared enough about her to feel compelled to shout. "Makes my head hurt. M'all right."

They immediately stopped shouting. "You don't *seem* all right," Abstentia said. "Winnifer, why don't you bring her home? She's not going to be any good to anyone like this."

"I can hear you talking," Delly said, but Winn was already sliding an arm under her shoulders and lifting her to her feet.

"C'mon, Dell," she said. "Let's get a cab and go home."

Home, Delly thought. What a funny thing for Winn to say. How funny that it sounded like a thing that she really meant.

They got a cab and went home. Delly cleaned her teeth, and Winn helped her into bed.

When she woke up again, she did so with a flail. "Mam," she said. "I have to go see my mam."

"Yes, I know, it's all right, Dell," Winn said, standing up from one of the armchairs by the stove. "You only slept for an hour. It's only six in the afternoon, there's still plenty of time. Are you feeling any better?"

Delly's face went warm. "Yes," she said. "Was I sick on you?" Winn was wearing a different dress than she had been before.

"Only a little," Winn said. "Nothing that won't come out in the wash. You got rather more on yourself. Lucky we got you those nice new dresses, what?"

"I guess so," Delly said, and carefully pried herself out of bed. Her head still ached. "I feel like shit."

"I'll make some more tea," Winn said, and started doing so as Delly got dressed in the clean new dress that had been draped over the back of a chair for her. That Winn had draped over the back of a chair for her. Because Delly mattered enough to her that she cared to do that. Maybe this was what her whole life would be like after they were householded. *If* they were householded. If Delly didn't manage to drive Winn away first.

They drank their tea, then got another cab to go to the hospital where Delly's mother was being kept. "I'm running out of money," Delly said, a few minutes into the ride. It was true. Day after day it was trickling through her fingers.

"That's all right," Winn said. "I can easily help you to pay for things until we finish this job and you come into that eight-hundred-odd tocats, what?"

"What?" Delly asked. "You can't do that."

"Of course I can," Winn said. "There's no laws against it, are there?"

"But I might not be able to pay you back," Delly said.

"That's all right," Winn said. "I won't starve." Then she gave Delly's hand a gentle squeeze.

"Oh," Delly said, feeling rather foolish. Then she squeezed Winn's hand back.

When they arrived at the hospital it took some time before anyone paid them any notice. Delly, her head still aching, just stood there like a stump while Winn marched off to find someone to help them. She watched, still stumpified, as Winn caught a passing nurse and began to speak to her. The conversation seemed to be lasting rather longer than it really ought. The nurse left, then came back with a large ledger to show to Winn. It didn't occur to Delly that she maybe ought to be worried until Winn started to wave her hands around in the air as she spoke. It was when the nurse started to look upset, though, that Delly walked over herself, just in time to hear the nurse say, "I really am sorry, miss, but how were we meant to know that there was any reason why the woman shouldn't be allowed to leave?"

"What?" Delly said. Her heart started to pound. This wasn't part of her fucking plan. "She's gone? You let her *leave*?"

"*I* didn't do anything," the nurse said. "And I'll thank both of you not to speak to me in that fashion. I don't know nothing at all about this Wells woman. I just saw here that she signed herself out this morning, that's all. I had nothing else to do with it, and if you want to shout at someone you can go shout at her. It's none of *my* business."

Delly started to cry. She didn't plan on it. It just happened on its own. Her head was pounding, and her mam was missing again, and the tears clawed their way up her throat and came out of her in a sound like she was trying to cough a fish bone out of her throat. The nurse said, "Really, there's no need to fuss. If she could sign that book and walk out of here on her own two legs, then there's nothing all that wrong with her." Then she walked off.

Delly rubbed at her eyes with her knuckles. "Fuck," she said. *"Fuck."*

"Come on, Dell," Winn said softly. "Come on." She took ahold of Delly's elbow and started steering her out of the hospital.

"I should have come for her sooner," Delly was saying. It was just coming out of her mouth. "I should have come to see her before. I can't believe I let this fucking *happen*—"

"Relax," Winn said. "Relax, Dell. She's your ailing mother, not the fastest filly at the Auf Dem Mare races, what? We'll find her. How far could she have possibly gone?"

"You're right," Delly said, relaxing a hair. "You're right. But—fuck—where should we even *look*?"

Winn frowned slightly. Then she said, "You know—didn't she used to live in our laboratory?"

They got back into another cab and headed straight back toward the laboratory. They didn't talk along the way. Delly had gone brittle with fear. She'd lost her mam again, and it wasn't just a bit of bother this time. Mam had almost died once from the red drip already. If she was let loose on the stuff again, she might manage to do herself in for good.

Delly dove out of the cab once they arrived at the address near the laboratory they'd given to the driver, flung some money at the man, and practically sprinted down the street toward their building. There she stopped, confounded. In the few hours since they'd left it, the building had somehow gone further to seed. The boards were up over the windows again, and there appeared to be a new hole in the front wall near the roofline. Everything about it looked sadder, dimmer, and grimmer than it had ever been.

"What in the releft do you suppose happened?" Delly asked, as Winn came jogging up to her side. "Have they all left?"

Winn gave her a sidelong look. "Dell," she said. "Abstentia and I had been talking about spelling the place to make it look abandoned still, remember? She must have gone ahead and done it on her own. And jolly fine work, too, for a gull who isn't a dedicated illusionist."

"Oh," Delly said, feeling decidedly foolish. "Right. But how can we see to get in now?"

"Just a tick," Winn said, and mumbled a quick incantation, then took hold of Delly's hand.

Delly, embarrassingly, had a moment of feeling exceedingly excited over Winn holding her hand again before realizing that the gesture was practical and not romantical: as soon as their hands touched, the house was back to its old self again, with a warm light gleaming a hello from the windows. "Did you take down Abstentia's spell?" she asked, half hoping that Winn would say yes. She imagined that Abstentia would be very entertainingly outraged by having her spells disrupted.

"No, just made it so that we can see through it. Come on, then," Winn said, and gently tugged Delly along to the back, and through the hidden door Abstentia had made through the fence, and into the kitchen, where Dellaria's vile reprobate of a mother was sitting at the table in a clean new dress, drinking tea and eating cake with Mrs. Totham.

"*Mam*," Delly said, ran to her, and flung her arms around her like a child who'd never learned better. "Mam, I was scraping *mud* for thee. I thought you were being *box-measured*, so."

"Hullo, Delly," her mam said, as if there was nothing at all unusual in their meeting this way. Talking strange, too, nice and proper for the clanners. "*I'm* all right, there's no need to make a fuss about it."

"Your charming mother was just telling me all about how clever you were in school as a child, Miss Wells," Mrs. Totham said. "And as she also mentioned that she has nowhere to stay at the moment, I told her that of course she must stay here with the girls and me. Mura and Vitna have already made such wonderful progress upstairs, and there's plenty of space in my room for one more to stay with Buttons and me!"

There was the sound of the tinkling of dozens of little bells from the vicinity of Delly's mam's lap. Delly looked down and had to choke back a delicate shriek. Buttons was perched on her mother's knee, up on his dreadful skeletal haunches, his red gleaming eyeholes gone a passionate rose-petal pink.

"Mrs. Wells and Buttons have become *very* fast friends already," Mrs. Totham twittered.

"Oh," Delly said, and then, with all of the force and vigor available to her in this moment of trial, changed the subject. "Are you off the drip now, Mam? Only I don't know if this is the right place for you to be, if you're avoiding the stuff?"

"*Dellaria*," her mam hissed. "I don't know what's gotten into you, telling tales about my business in front of—"

"They know already, Mam," Delly said, cutting her off. "Mrs. Totham looked into me before we'd even properly met, so she knows all about your—activities. Are you on the stuff or not?"

"I'm not *now*," Marvie said, a bit of alleychat slipping in. "Not that it's *your* junction, Dellaria."

"It *is* my junction if you're in *my* bolt-for," Delly snapped back.

"*Your* bolt-for?" Marvie said, sitting up straighter in her chair. "This is the same house that I was staying in not two weeks ago! You just came along and took it! It ought to be my house, by all rights!"

"That's right, I *did* take it," Delly said. "And I intend on buying it all nice and legal, soon enough." She'd just decided that this very moment, but she thought that she liked the sound of it as soon as it passed her lips. "And as long as it is mine, I don't want you bringing any of that stuff into it!"

"Excuse me," Mrs. Totham said, as sweetly as the prettiest little bird she'd ever admired back when they were staying in the countryside. "But I had thought—do forgive me if I'm at all rude, Mrs. Wells—that if you are very much in need of the use of the red drip, you might be willing—I do hope that I don't presume too much—to act as our tester for the product that we ourselves are currently in the course of developing."

"Absolutely *not*," Delly said. "I *forbid* it, I absolutely *forbid* it—"

"You can't forbid things of *me*," Marvie said. "I'm your releftin' *mother*."

"I'll not have thee *dripping filth* while I have fuckin' *mirrors* on thee," Delly said, her face gone all hot with fury.

"Miss Wells," Mrs. Totham said, like a snake made of spun sugar. "Pardon me, of course I *never* like to intrude upon the private matters of another family, but I really *do* feel as if I ought to say this—don't you think that, if there's a choice between dear Mrs. Wells using red drip that we have made ourselves with every possible attention given to the quality and safety of the product, and used here under the watchful eyes of those who care about her—"

"The fuck do *you* care about her?" Delly broke in. "You only met her half an hour ago!"

"As I was saying," Mrs. Totham said, carrying on as if Delly hadn't said anything at all, "wouldn't it be better for her to be doing it here, with us, than out on the street using drip made by goodness knows what sort of villainous personages? And then we'll have someone with experience in the red drip to act as our tester for our version, which will be *so* much better than you becoming so dreadfully ill again, won't it?"

"It would be *better*," Delly said, "if she *didn't do it at all*."

"You don't get to tell me what I do or don't do, Dellaria," her mam said. "If you want to tell me what to do I'll walk out of here before you're finished getting the words out of your mouth."

Delly felt herself slump. It was true. She knew it was true. Her mam didn't want to stop. Didn't love Delly enough to stop. "All right," she said. "I suppose—all *right*, Mam." Her throat ached. "But you promise that you'll stay here, won't you? You'll stay here, and just take the stuff that we give thee, and not get into any gargle or nothing, too, Mam? And you'll—you'll eat the mess I bring thee, and—"

"Of course I will," Marvie said. "Of course I'd rather be here, where I can chatter at thee, pup."

Delly stared at her. Her face looked like she meant it, like she wasn't lying. Like she really did care about seeing her daughter every day. Maybe right now, in a warm kitchen with a cup of hot tea and the promise of free drip coming to her tomorrow, she did. "You want to see me?"

"You're my *daughter*," Marvie said, as if that was an answer.

"Always have been," Delly said. She felt—she didn't know—like a cleaver that had been used to cut through too much bone. Blunted. "I always have been your daughter, Mam." She swallowed. She had to get ahold of herself. Then she said, "D'you think you'd like to have breakfast together in the morning? I could—bring by some of those iced raisin buns you used to like. The ones from that bakery on Trent Street." Pitiful. Pathetic. She still wanted her mam to say yes.

"*Ooh*, that would be lovely," her mam said. "I haven't had those buns in years." Then, before Delly truly had time to absorb the sting of her being more eager for buns than to sit down for a meal with her daughter: "And I haven't sat down for a meal with you in almost as long. How about I pop out tomorrow morning for eggs and bacon and cook up a nice spread for us to go with the buns? Burn the bacon up just like you used to like it?"

Delly, for a moment, felt herself transforming into a credulous little girl whose mam had promised her, once again, to cook her a nice breakfast in the morning like the mothers of other little girls did. *Really and truly this time, Mam?* the little girl wanted to ask. *Do you really, really mean it?* Delly put her hand over that little girl's mouth. Nothing good would come of letting her say her piece. Instead she just said, "That sounds nice." She cleared her throat. "This is Miss Winnifer Cynallum, Mam. Miss Cynallum, this is my mother, Marvie Wells." She didn't know if that was the right way to introduce a fine young lady to one's mean, lying dripper of a mother. She was just doing her fucking best.

"It's a pleasure to meet you, Mrs. Wells," Winn said, and held out her hand to shake.

Marvie shook her hand and looked Winn over with a considering air that Delly found exceedingly disagreeable. What right did Marvie

Wells have to look at someone like Winn as if she knew anything about her? "Oh, the pleasure's all mine, I'm sure, miss, for me to be meeting such a fine young lady as yourself, miss."

It was disgusting, hearing her simper and fawn. It was even more disgusting when Delly realized, with an icy jolt of revulsion, that she herself had spoken to her betters about a thousand times in exactly the same way. As if she was pleading with them not to crush her underfoot.

"I'm not so very fine, Mrs. Wells," Winn said, just as gentle and kind as she ever was. "And it's an honor for me to meet the woman who raised such a wonderful daughter."

Delly half wanted to argue with that. Not like Marvie Wells had raised her, really, any more than a tree raised the seeds that fell from it. Instead she held her tongue and listened as her mam did a bit more simpering, and Winn delivered a few more compliments and finally said, "It's getting late. I think that I ought to escort Miss Wells back to her room, now. She's had an awfully long day."

Delly's mam's eyes lit up the second she heard the word *escort* in relation to her daughter. Delly knew exactly what she was thinking: that her daughter had really and truly hooked a good rich householder. Delly piped up before her mam could say anything that would make Winn regret her tendencies toward gentlewomanly escortation. "Yes, I think that we all ought to get some rest," she said. "Good night, Mam."

"Good night, Dellaria," her mam said. Delly could feel her watching them as they walked out.

"*Fuck* me, Winn, this ain't a particularly favorable turn of fucking events," Delly said the second they were out on the street, the number of syllables in her personal lexicon being proportional to her perception of egregious enfucktation in her current, present, and unfortunate familial circumstances.

"It certainly isn't the sort of thing in which one would want to see one's mother engaging in her golden years," Winn said. "At least she's getting up to no good somewhere safe and warm where you'll be able to keep an eye on what she's getting up to, what?"

"I suppose," Delly said, dispiritedly. "I'd rather she'd decide to take up needlepointing pictures of kittens." Mrs. Medlow, Delly's landlady, had a sitting room thoroughly enkittenated on nearly every surface that was not already too thickly barnacled with ribbons, doilies, and porcelain shepherdesses to be an appropriate canvas for kittenization. Though Delly disapproved of needlepointed kittens as an element of home decoration, she approved mightily of the creation of them as a wholesome occupation for middle-aged ladies who might otherwise be inclined toward raining chaos and devastation upon the lives of innocent young persons such as herself.

"Well, you never know, do you?" Winn said. "Maybe Mrs. Totham will be a good influence on her, and the next time you see your mother she'll be knitting hats for babies and identifying interesting birds like the placidest old puss on earth."

"*Mrs. Totham*," Delly said. "*Mrs. Totham* isn't a placid old puss. She's a flesh-eating weasel who's learned to bat at yarn and lap cream. Do you think she asked my mam in for tea when she came wandering in, wondering what had become of her squat, knowing all along she wanted to use her as a relefting *test subject*?"

"Oh, I don't know about that," Winn said. "She's the sort of woman who would invite the milkman in for tea if he stayed on the steps long enough for her to catch him."

"That's just what she *wants* you to think about her," Delly said sourly.

"Well, maybe," Winn said. "But—and I hope you won't be too annoyed with me for saying so, Dell—she might not be *completely* wrong, you know. About your mother being safer this way than she would be out on her own, I mean."

"But I don't want her to be dripping *more safely*," Delly said, turning once more into a whining, wretched little child. "I don't want her dripping *at all*." She was clutching at Winn's elbow as they walked. It felt better to have something solid under her hand. "As soon as I get the money together, I'm sending her out to a sanitarium in the countryside. I don't care if she doesn't releftin' well like it. If I tell them she's lost her head from the drip and shed some tears over her well-being, they'll drag her off whether she likes it or not."

"She won't thank you for that," Winn said, mild as warm porridge.

"My mam," Delly said, "has never thanked me for a releftin' thing in my entire God-cursed life, and I've scraped her out of trouble of her own making more times than she's cooked me a hot breakfast. I imagine that she'll be a bit grateful sooner or later, and if she isn't, it won't be so very releftin' much of a change from our usual course of relations."

"I'm sorry," Winn said. "I'm sorry it's been so hard between you. I do think that it might be a very grave mistake to try to force her to stop what she's doing, though. It doesn't seem like the sort of thing that a woman would take very kindly to from her own daughter. Don't you think it might be better to let her stop the drip on her own?"

"Maybe that's true," Delly said. "But I'd like to say, and meaning no disrespect to you, Winn, that you don't know Marvie Wells. The only way that she's stopping drip is if she drinks herself to death before the drip gets her first."

That was grim enough to pour a large bucket of water over the dim coals of their conversation, and they were silent for the rest of the walk back home.

They went up to the room in silence, and undressed and put on their nightgowns in silence. Then, instead of climbing into bed, Delly stoked the fire and then sat down in one of the armchairs. Winn sat down in the other one and reached out to take Delly's hand. Then she tugged gently on it to pull her closer.

Delly went to her, and Winn put her hands to the sides of Delly's hips and lifted her into her lap. Delly sucked in a breath, all of her suddenly and entirely awake. "What do you—"

She couldn't finish the question. Winn had covered Delly's mouth by putting her own mouth onto it, which was about the best way of shutting up Dellaria Wells that anyone had ever devised.

They kissed for a while. There was more urgency to it than there had been the last time that they'd kissed like this. One of Winn's big hands gripped at Delly's back. Delly wriggled to straddle Winn's lap, the skirt of her nightdress hiked up around her hips. Winn's hand slid to her side. Then, just as suddenly as Winn had pulled Delly in, she pulled herself away. "We really shouldn't," she said, and then tumbled back in to kiss Delly again like she couldn't help herself. That's how Delly felt, too. Helpless to her. Winn's hand was between her thighs now, and they were kissing again. Delly got her fingers into Winn's hair and then yelped and clutched at Winn's shoulder as Winn carried her to bed.

There was a bit of a tussle then, between Winn and Delly's chemise. Winn, to Delly's delight, won, and there was a faint ripping noise before Winn finally got it peeled off of her and dropped it unceremoniously off the side of the bed. Then Winn was kissing her breasts and heading downward, and Delly was on the verge of shoving her head the rest of the way there when Winn popped up with a face like a tomato and said, "I'm sorry. I shouldn't."

"Why the fuck shouldn't you?" said Delly, who was feeling a mite dizzy. And irritated. Like a dog who had just watched a group of feasters inconsiderately clean their plates and then carry the bones away.

"I'm sorry," Winn said again. She certainly looked it, at least. She was squirming. "I just—I care about you so much, Dell. And I don't want you to ever think that I'm—I know that people of my class sometimes—" She stopped. "You deserve to know that I'm serious about you. That I'm not just using you to pass the time."

"Oh," Delly said. "You don't want to take advantage." It was a nice thing to hear, she supposed, but not at all what she *wanted* to hear at this particular juncture. "There's no need to worry about that, Winn. I'd be glad to be taken advantage of. There's nothing of which I'd be gladder, in fact."

Winn was shaking her head. "I know that you must think that now," she said. Then she cleared her throat and got a dreadfully sincere look on her face. "Had a bit of a—fling with a gull two years ago. Didn't go too well, in the end. I don't *ever* want you to feel that way, Dell."

"Well, we won't let things go that way, then," Delly said.

"I don't know that I believe that we can just decide that neither of us will have our feelings hurt," Winn said. "I'd rather be careful about it, if you don't mind too much. And I'm awfully sorry for having let things get so far, just now. Not very gentlewomanly of me, eh?" She pulled the blanket up over Delly to cover her, then gently stroked Delly's hair out of her eyes. "I'm starting to feel as if I've mucked things up with you already."

"You haven't," Delly said, and, on impulse, tugged at Winn to get her to lie down with her and tucked her face into Winn's neck. She smelled like soap and lavender oil. "You haven't even a bit."

"That's good to know," Winn said. Delly put her head onto Winn's shoulder. She'd never done this before, not really. Gotten this close to someone without giving them a gallop first. She felt warm and wide awake. Winn put her arm around Delly's waist. They stayed like that until Delly's neck went stiff, and she rolled over and turned to face the other way. She didn't expect Winn to follow her and put her arm around her again. She didn't expect to fall asleep.

In the morning, Delly woke up to the smell of coffee already made, which was as new of an experience as any that she'd had of late, with the exception of any experiences that she'd had involving Buttons. She sat up.

"Thanks," she said.

Winn popped her head up from fixing the last hooks at the top of her dress and beamed. "No need to thank me! Someone's got to crank the sun up, what?"

"S'pose so," Delly said. Then she cracked her neck, yawned, got up, and sat down in an armchair to prepare for coffee to be delivered to her like she was a queen.

After they'd dressed and had their coffee, they went to buy a dozen sweet rolls, then trundled over to the increasingly crowded Red Drip Laboratory and Home for Wayward Women to try to see whether or not Delly's mam might really have made the breakfast that she'd promised. Whether she might have kicked off a whole life's worth of being herself and been magically transformed into a mother.

Either way they would have their rolls, at least.

14

Wherein Everything Ceases to Be Theoretical
and Becomes Terrible Instead

When they arrived Delly's mam was looking clean, mostly sober, and very pleased with herself. The kitchen smelled of coffee and bacon, and there was the sizzle of frying eggs. "You're just in time to have your eggs while they're still hot, pup," she said. "Did you sleep well?"

Delly could not have been more surprised if her mother had suddenly begun bonging like Buttons. "Well enough," she said after a moment. "Did you?"

"Better than I used to when I lived here," Marvie said, and began assembling food on a plate. "You bunch have fixed this place up to a regular delight, so." Then she added, with a barely noticeable simper, "Won't you sit down, Miss Cynallum?"

Winn and Delly both sat. Delly was profoundly befuddled. This barely seemed like her mam at all. More like the mam that Delly had spent most of her childhood hoping that her mam might suddenly become. She continued in her state of enfuddlement as they started to eat and her mam made surprisingly polite small talk with Winn, until Abstentia came striding into the room and said, "We have that sample ready for you, Mrs. Wells." Then she added a casual little "Good morning, Miss Wells. Miss Cynallum."

"Oh, *wonderful*," Delly's mam cooed, and practically leapt to her feet to follow Abstentia to the other room.

Delly stared after her, feeling a bit dull. Of course, that was it. Her mam was on her best behavior because she wanted to stay here and have all of the relefted drip that she could ever want hand-delivered to her for free. Of course. Of course that was why she was acting different. *Marvie fucking Wells.*

"She seems very well," Winn ventured after a while.

"She seems well because she's found a way to get a hot meal, a warm bed, and her poison for free, and she doesn't want to risk us kicking her out," Delly said, and took an enraged bite of her roll.

They took their time over breakfast—Delly suspected Winn of thinking that she needed a few minutes to stop gnashing her teeth so loudly—and when they went into the laboratory they found Abstentia and Mrs. Totham were hard at work on a new batch of drip, and Delly's mam was sitting in the corner absorbed in untangling a bunch of yarn. Abstentia looked up when they walked in. "Good of the two of you to finally arrive."

"No need to thank us, Dok," Delly said, attempting to emulate some of the paint-peeling good cheer that Winn regularly leveled against those who displeased her.

Abstentia barely blinked before she fired back another round. "We've gotten plenty done in your absence, at least. Your *mother*, being such an expert in red drip, had some excellent bits of feedback to give us on yesterday's batch, so now we're trying three different variations on the original formula. I don't suppose you might deign to lend a hand?"

"Oh, leave off of it, Abstentia," Winn said, as Delly went red from embarrassment. "You're just annoyed that both of the Wellses have made themselves more useful than *you've* managed."

Abstentia apparently did not have any responses to that statement already wrapped up and ready to be presented, so they all stopped squabbling and got to work: Abstentia and Mrs. Totham finishing one of the variations, and Delly and Winn the other. Abstentia and Mrs. Totham completed theirs very quickly, as they'd started long before the other two had arrived, and within less than an hour they were offering Delly's mam a taste. Delly left the room to go outside for a smoke for that part. She didn't fucking well need to see it.

Her mam was alive, well, and untangling yarn again when she walked back into the room, and Abstentia was looking as satisfied as an old man after a heavy supper and a glass of port. "It seems that we've eliminated the third line of the incantation as the reason for the unusual oral side effects, so we can move on to the next possible culprit."

"Oh, wonderful," Delly said. Winn cast her a worried look. Delly nudged her aside to get back to work.

They labored away in silence for a while. Long enough that Delly's mam started wriggling around like she had ants up her particulars, then got up and started walking toward the door. "No wandering off too far," Delly said.

"None of your—" her mam started, and then stopped. "Will you have finished with the next bit soon?"

"Give us a half an hour, Mrs. Wells," Abstentia chirped. "By then we should have the second sample ready for you."

"If you go to the kitchen, there are still plenty of those sweet rolls, Mrs. Wells," Winn said, and Marvie went trotting off.

She reemerged after very little time had passed at all, and stood around staring hungrily at the rest of them until Abstentia handed her the next sample, which settled Marvie right back into her yarn-winding chair as if she was born to sit in it.

Delly bothered watching, this time. She made herself watch. She watched as her mam's eyes went all dull and abstracted, and how she started smiling down at her hands working the yarn like they were a little child she loved. That's what Delly assumed, at least. Not like she was all that familiar with seeing that look on her mam's face.

The day wore on. Delly's mam told them how they ought to fix their product to make it more like what drippers liked. She was useful to them. Delly hated it, but that was a plain fact. Her mam was making what they wanted to sell far better than it would have been without her. Delly tried to tell herself again that it was all for the good, that Delly was going to use the money from that reward to get her mam away from Leiscourt and off to some nice place in the countryside where she'd be cleaned out and scrubbed up and turned into a nice responsible matron. It was harder to convince herself of the idea than ever, right now. She was getting her mam tangled up in the drip faster than her mam was detangling that relefting hank of yarn. She had to get that money for sure now, now that she knew what her mam looked like half-dead in a hospital bed. Delly had trashburned every opportunity that had ever been set in front of her, but there was no more room for that now. She had her shot at her prospect, and saving her mam, and making a future that wasn't burned to the ground by the invading force of her own turnip-headedness. It was enough to drive a gull to gin, especially when she thought about the fact that she'd only be able to pull this off if she remained utterly and dismally sober.

They paused for luncheon, which struck Delly as somewhat ridiculous at a time like this, and then worked on through suppertime. Then it was time to eat, and go back to her room, and sleep, and wake up in the morning to do it all over again. She and Winn didn't do any kissing this time. Maybe all of the kissing sorts of instincts had been worked right out of her.

By ten in the morning on the third day, Delly had a little sample of their product in a little bottle in her hand. That morning her mam had tasted a bit of their final product and pronounced it "like licking heaven, almost." Delly figured that was about as good of an endorsement as they were likely to get, and Dok was confident that there were no foreign ingredients in it that might induce sudden death or spontaneous bouts of stranger strangling. So she put the little bottle into the pocket of her pretty new green dress along with a note outlining her business proposal, and, all alone—she didn't want the Kind Companions' runner getting his eyes on Winn, if she could help it—she set out for Rat's place, telling Winn that she would see her back at their room that evening.

When she walked through the doors of the shop, she saw a young boy there right away, pretending to be interested in a stack of leather-bound books. He was such a young boy that it gave Delly a bit of a pang: a little freckle-faced creature no bigger than she had been when she'd first started begging for change. What he was into was worse than that, but she didn't have any room for misgivings now. She sidled up to him and murmured, "You waiting for me?"

He shrugged his narrow little shoulders. "You got something to give me?"

She passed him the bottle and the note. "Send word back through Rat before the shop closes tomorrow," she said. Then she waited for him to leave first before leaving herself, her eyes darting about for the whole walk back in fear that someone might be following.

She didn't see anyone, at least, but just in case she took a winding route to a resounding non-Damel's mediocrity of a coffee shop in order to very slowly read that morning's *Crier*, before taking another equally winding route back to her room, where she found Winn sprawled across the surface of the entire bed, resplendently bebathrobed with her hair twisted up in bits of rag. "Sakes," Delly said. "Are you expecting to go to a party tonight?"

"No," Winn said. "My social calendar isn't all that blinkin' crowded at the moment, what?"

"Then why have you . . ." Delly started, and then trailed off, waving her hand vaguely in the direction of Winn's head.

"Well," Winn said, her cheeks darkening a bit. "I thought, erm. Just might be nice to do something different with my hair tomorrow."

"Oh," Delly said, and felt her own cheeks heating. "Would you like me to pop out to hunt up some supper? I'm absolutely famished."

Winn smiled at her. "That would be absolutely cream-topped of you, if you don't mind," she said, which obviously spurred Delly into charging right back out the door again for fear of being thought of as anything less than utterly and entirely cream-topped.

She ran down to the closest market then, and bought a few things based on what made her mouth water when she looked at them, which meant that she ended up with all manner of bread and cheese and butter and a packet of sausages and a bottle of wine, as well as an evening edition *Leiscourt Crier* to look over after supper. Then she carried the whole feast back to Winn to present it to her like a triumphant returning huntress. "Let's have a picnic on the floor and roast sausages over the stove like it's our campfire."

Winn gave a smile so wide that it looked like it might not fit through the bedroom door. "That's an absolutely *silver-plated* idea, Dell," she said, and got up to help Delly spread out a blanket on the floor and then put down plates and glasses and everything else they'd need for a good hearty run at the trough. Then they huddled down and got to work on their supper.

It was altogether a very cozy scene. The two of them drinking wine and eating cheese, roasting sausages over the stove and giggling when the fat spat, Winn in her curling rags and Delly in a pair of tattered old slippers. They ate until they were full, then each had a cup of tea while Winn read a book and Delly absorbed some scandal from her paper. Then, thoroughly exhausted, they scrubbed their faces, pulled on their nightdresses, and went immediately to bed.

Delly woke up with a hand over her mouth. A man's voice whispered, *"Don't make a sound."*

Delly, agreeably, did not make a sound. Instead, in her sleep-muddled state, she panicked, lit the man's sleeve on fire, panicked again, and then took the opportunity of the time *he* took to hop around the room in a silent panic of his own to snatch Winn's pistol up from under the bed. He must have seen her moving, though, because in almost the same instant he managed to extinguish his sleeve and draw his own gun, so they ended up both drawing on each other in the same moment: Delly reclining in bed in her nightgown and cap, and the man standing in the corner of her room, smoldering unhappily.

"Bet that I'm a better shot than you, witch," the man whispered.

"I'd guess you're right," Delly whispered back. "But if you'd wanted to shoot me, why did you have to go and wake me up first?"

The man was quiet for a moment. Then he said, "You need to come with me."

"Well, give me a minute to put my robe and slippers on," Delly said, and then made a show of placing the gun on the bedside table before raising her hands and slowly standing up. She could tell that Winn, in bed beside her, was only pretending to sleep: her breathing had changed a few moments after Delly herself had woken up to that hand over her mouth. Delly was pretty sure that if Winn was sharp enough to know not to let this man know she was awake, she was pretty sure to have recognized the sound of Delly putting the gun down as well, God bless her. Having your girl know that you'd let a man catch you snoring was a bit embarrassing, but Delly figured it wasn't half as embarrassing as having her find you dead in an alley the next morning still wearing your slippers and nightdress.

The man kept his gun on Delly while she took her time over putting her slippers on and pulling on her robe, then herded her out into the hall, down the stairs, and into the street. Delly dragged her feet. "Where are you taking me?"

"Shut up," the man said.

"I think that it's a very relevant question, sir," Delly said, and stopped walking entirely. She didn't want to get too far ahead of Winn. "And very rude of you to tell a young woman to shut up, sir, when you have already cruelly wrested her from her bed in the middle of the night and—" She had to stop talking then, because the man had started hitting her. In the back of her head, to be precise. With his revolver, probably, to be preciser. The pain was a sputtering fountain. Delly staggered a bit and watched the elaborate display in front of her eyes with a detached interest for a moment before giving a loud, pained groan.

"Will you shut the fuck up now?" the man hissed.

"S'pose so," Delly slurred out. Her tongue felt thick. "Just— gimmya moment." She sank to her knees. She didn't need to, exactly. She wanted to give Winn time to catch up. Where the fuck was *Winn*?

"Get up," the man hissed at her. *"Get up."* They were at the edge of the circle of light cast by the gas lamp nearby.

"How about *you* get *down*, sir?" said Winn's voice. "On your knees, I mean. And put the gun down, too. I, erm, suggest that because I have a gun pointed at your head, which puts *you* into a demmed awkward situation, what?"

Delly thought that Winn could perhaps work a bit on the decided-ness of her manner when issuing instructions to armed brigands, but she didn't want to overcriticize her savior. She could weep with relief. She came very close to it. Instead, however, she kept her chin up and waited for the sound of a pistol being put down onto the cobblestones before she wobbled her way back up to her feet. "Thanks, Winn."

"Don't mention it!" Winn said, and kicked the gun away from the brigand. "Would you mind grabbing that, Dell? And you, up on your feet. Time to take a little walk back to our room, eh?"

The reprobate obeyed, though he didn't look entirely delighted about it. Delly fell into step beside Winn, and Winn immediately started whispering at her. "Are you all right, Dell? He didn't hit you too hard, did he? I'm awfully sorry I didn't stop him sooner, I really am. I thought that I might be clever and follow you all the way to wherever he was taking you so that we'd know where the Kind Companions'—oh, I don't know, *secret lair* was, but of course when he *hit* you I couldn't carry on just dawdling on at the rear, what?"

"Oh, sorry," Delly said, dismayed. She hadn't thought of taking her abduction as an opportunity to learn more about their foes, which she now saw was very shortsighted of her. "It wasn't *too* hard." He had, in fact, hit her fairly fucking hard, but she didn't want to rub salt in the wound.

"I'm sorry that he hit you at all. And what are we going to *do* with him?"

That stumped Delly for a moment. "Interrogate him, I suppose." Then she paused. "Do you know how to interrogate someone?"

"I don't know the slightest thing about interrogations," Winn whispered back. "I suppose we'll have to improvise." Then she stuck her pistol into the kidnapper's back and said, in a much gruffer voice than her usual toast-and-marmalade tones, "Get moving, man, we don't have all night."

The criminal seemed very impressed by this—or at least unnerved by Winn's sudden shift in demeanor—because he speeded his steps, and they were soon safely back inside their room. Delly kept her newly stolen pistol on him while Winn lit the oil lamp, and then they made him sit on the floor while they both sat in the matching armchairs, the better to loom over him. He was, a big, strapping fellow, with thick dark hair and a dark mustache. He glared at them. They glared back. They all, collectively, glared. The wastrel was the first to give up and say something. "What do you want from me?"

Delly blinked. "What do *you* want from *me*? You're the one breaking into young ladies' bedrooms in the middle of the night."

"You ain't no lady," the man muttered.

"Steady on, that was un-blinkin'-called-for," said Winn. "And if you don't answer our questions Miss Wells will light your stockings on fire."

"That's right," Delly said immediately, giving Winn an admiring glance. What quick thinking!

The man quailed a bit. Then he rallied and said, "You haven't asked me any questions," in a way that Delly thought might be meant to sound defiant but actually just sounded exceedingly sulky.

"Oh, right," Winn said. "Erm. Who sent you here?"

"Won't tell you," the man said, sulkier than ever.

"Oh, come now," Winn said. "You just as good as said that you would answer questions once we asked them, and now you're not holding up your end of the bargain."

"Didn't *make* no bargain," the man said.

"Well, let's make one now," Winn said. "It's answers or the flaming stockings. What do you say to *that*?"

The man squirmed. "They'll kill me if they find out I squealed on 'em."

"So take the first train to Monsatelle," Delly suggested. "You can start a new life and shave that mustache off."

He squinted at her. "What's wrong with my mustache?"

"Oh, nothing," Delly said. "If that's the way that you *want* to look. Anyway, what's your name and who sent you?"

"Whaddya need to know my name for?" he demanded.

"So we know what to *call* you, cleverboots," Delly said. "It's either give us a name or we'll give you one. Like . . . Mittens."

"Ooh, lovely," Winn said. "Mittens suits you. Who sent you here, Mittens? Tell us or it'll be your toes first. Toasted right off." Delly, taking her cue from Winn, called up a little flame in her palm and advanced toward him threateningly.

"It was the Kind Companions," Mittens blurted out. "The Kind Companions sent me to bring you in. And my name's Wren. Kail Wren."

"Oh!" Winn said. "My pop's middle name is Kail. Jolly small world, what? Mind telling us who the Kind Companions are, exactly? Don't suppose that one of them is a lady called—oh, drat it all, what was that lady's name again? The one they were gossiping about in the bathhouse?"

"Oh, shit," Delly said. "I mean, pardon me. I don't remember. It was, ah—" She dug about desperately in her memory for a moment, like a rat terrier on a scent. "Claret? No, that can't be right."

"Claret's a *drink*, you silly bitch," Kail Mittens said. "Her name's—"

Then he stopped and looked a bit like he'd like to toast his own toes off and save Delly the trouble.

Delly pulled the flame back into her palm and moved it toward his face in a pointed fashion. "No, go on," she said. "We're very interested."

He swallowed. "Heard the other one call her Clairelle."

"The other one? Who's the other one?" Winn asked, as Delly took a moment to feel very pleased with herself over the so-far-stunning success of her interrogation techniques. Clairelle was that exact name, the woman whom Dok knew and whose name Delly had overheard in the bathhouse. She'd been on the right path after all.

Kail Mittens, in the meantime, appeared to be mulling over what the best response would be to being questioned by one strapping lass while another shorter and stouter personage threatened him with a ball of flame. In the end, he decided to answer Winn's question. "Dunno," he said. "Honest, I don't. Haven't even seen her face. They were in their office together and I just happened to overhear them talking, like. The Clairelle one called her *Wex*, which ain't even a proper name for a lady."

Delly and Winn exchanged a glance. Wex was most certainly not a proper name for a lady, but it could be a nickname for a girl whose surname was Wexin. "Listening at keyholes, were you?" Winn asked. "Did you manage to hear anything else of note? Names? Dates? Did anyone happen to push a signed letter detailing their crimes under the door and into the hall?"

Kail Mittens looked first perplexed, then offended. "I wasn't *listening at keyholes*," he said, as if a bit of eavesdropping would be a course of action entirely beneath the high moral stature of a fella who'd just attempted to kidnap a young woman out of her bed in the dead of night. "And I didn't hear *nothing*. They were arguing about some party, that's all."

"What kind of party?" Delly asked, though as soon as she did so she wondered a bit why she had bothered. It wasn't as if it'd be the kind of party that *she* might have been invited to.

"How the fuck should I know?" replied the scornful Kail Mittens. "I wasn't invited. Some party with some Lord Fuckedhisname."

"Of the *Pembleton* Fuckedhisnames?" Winn asked, and then snorted at her own joke. Delly and Kail Mittens both stared at her. She cleared her throat. "Erm. Anyway. Where's this office where you do your eavesdropping, then?"

Kail Mittens goggled. "You can't just ask me that!"

"Why not?" Winn asked.

"I'd say that we can," Delly said, feeling distinctly embarrassed that she hadn't thought to ask earlier. "Seeing as that we both have guns, and you don't."

Kail mittens went a bit red in the face. Then he said, "Two-eighteen Torrent Street."

Delly gave a soft whistle. "Nice address." A lot of rich lawyers had their offices up on Torrent Street. Then she frowned. "Do they know *this* address?"

He shook his head hard. "No. I just found out when I followed you today. I won't tell 'em, I swear I won't."

"You won't be able to," Winn said, very gravely. Kail Mittens went ash-faced. A moment later Winn blinked. "Oh, for goodness' sake, we're not going to *kill* you. We're going to put you on a train with a hard promise on you."

"A hard promise of mostly-on-the-face pustules," Delly added.

"You don't got to bother with the hard promise," Kail Mittens said. "I'll be fucked before I come back here with a whole pack of wizarding she-beasts after my neck."

"*Pardon?*" Winn said.

"Not *you*," Kail Mittens said hastily. "The Kind Companions, I meant. Bunch of *Unkind* Companions, more like, the nasty things."

Delly recoiled slightly at this regrettably unimaginative insult. "I should have called them a bunch of wicked wizardesses, if I was to take a critical tone toward the ladies in question," she said. "First train to

Monsatelle isn't until six, Winn. Killing him'd let us get back to bed earlier."

"Not once you factor in getting rid of the body," Winn said, and checked her watch. "Gosh. It's only three. Dell, do you think there's anywhere around here where the three of us could pop round for a cup of coffee at this time of night?"

"I don't know about coffee," Delly said. "Unless you want to stand up at a cart to drink it. We'd be able to dredge up a glass of gin that comes with a chair, though." She paused. "They might have sherry." Based on the faces she always made when she drank it, Winn didn't seem to be very fond of gin.

"Oh, that might be nice," Winn said, and then patted at her hair and sighed. "I'll have to take my curlers out."

They must have made a very strange little group, once they made their way onto the streets: one man walking ahead of two women with pistols not entirely concealed in their reticules. The bar they picked wasn't the sort of place where they kicked out the customers for looking a bit peculiar, though, and within very short order they were furnished with two glasses of gin and one of sherry poured from the dustiest bottle Delly had ever seen in her life. Then they all sat around a table and stared at each other.

"Well," Winn said. "What did you do before you got into the kidnapping business, Mr. Wren?"

Kail Mittens cleared his throat and took a hearty guzzle of his gin before he responded. "Used to be an ashman."

"Oh," Delly said. "Not much money in that, is there? Hard work, too."

"Not much money in anything, these days," Kail Mittens said gloomily. "And I threw my back out. That was what led me to a life of crime. Hard times."

"Hard times," Delly agreed, and they clinked glasses in a spirit of mutual suffering under the current economy.

The minutes didn't flow so much as they seeped. Eventually Delly dug up a pack of cards, and they made a run at a game of whist, which was made more difficult by the fact that they were three cards short of a full deck. Delly ordered them another round. Kail Mittens started to become expansive in his conversation and complained at length about what a tyrant Miss Clairelle was as an employer. "Not so much as a tip on Elgarsday!" he exclaimed. "Tightfisted releftin' creatures, these clanners. Don't know what an honest day's work's worth, they don't."

Delly decided that it wasn't worth her time to suggest to him that kidnapping people in order to present them to the leader of a drug-production ring was not the most honest form of labor that she'd ever heard of someone making into their career. Instead she only asked, "Do you know what they wanted from me?"

He shrugged. "Wanted to get your formula out of you and then slit your throat, I reckon," he said. Then he finished off his glass of gin.

"Well," Delly said after a moment, "doesn't that fill the heart with warmth?"

"Oh, certainly," Winn said. "Like tucking your toes up against the grate, really."

"You're *sure* that they don't know where we live?" Delly asked suddenly. "As long as they don't know anything and you don't tell them about it, we won't have any cause to track you down in Monsatelle and light your bed on fire."

Kail Mittens nodded so hard that Delly feared for the long-term stability of his neck. "Don't worry about me. You won't see me back here. I've hated this God-fucked ash heap of a city for years."

Eventually time managed to progress in the usual fashion, and Delly and Winn, drunk and bleary-eyed, escorted Kail Mittens to Leiscourt Central Station, where Winn put the hard promise on him. Then, as subtly as they could, they frog-marched him onto the first train to Monsatelle and stood on the platform waving their handkerchiefs and pretending to weep until the train was finally out of sight.

Once the train was gone, they left the station together, silent and hand in hand. Delly wasn't quite sure which of them had reached out for the other first, but they were both gripping at each other as if they were afraid of being swept away by a strong current.

Winn was the first to speak, once they were out on the street. "We could have both died tonight, Dell."

"Oh, I don't know about that," Delly said. "Considering how inefficient ol' Mittens was at kidnapping, he probably wouldn't have been any better at getting a murder done. He seemed like a rare unprofessional fella, as murderers go."

"Don't be funny, Dell," Winn said, very quietly. "*Don't*. You came damn close to being killed tonight."

Delly hadn't ever heard Winn say the word *damn* before. It shook her up a bit. "I'm all right, though," she said. "And he's gone and out of the way, and no one else knows where we live."

"Do you really think that they'll just give up?" Winn asked. "They'll send *someone else*, Delly. You *know* that they will. We have their attention now, whether we like it or not. There's no—shoving this back into the bottle." She squeezed Delly's hand even harder, until it started to almost hurt. "We could do what he just did. Get on a train and leave. My pop would be glad to have us in Hexos, and there's nowhere on earth safer than our house there."

"I can't just *leave*," Delly said. "I have to deal with my mam. And anyhow, I promised Mrs. Totham." Talking about how she had promised poor dear old Mrs. Totham to help her avenge her murdered daughter sounded better than telling the truth, which was that she wanted that fucking money, and wanted it very badly at that. Winn might be a prospect so plump with promise that they were in this very moment holding hands, but there still wasn't a gold ring on Delly's finger yet. If she had that money in hand, she'd be able to get her mam sorted away whether her prospect played out or not.

"Then you have to be more careful," Winn said, then stopped walking and turned to seize both of Delly's hands at once. "You have to be more *careful*, Dell. I don't know how much more plainly I can put it to you. You could *die* if you're not more careful."

"I *am* careful," Delly said mulishly. "I trotted through half of Leiscourt trying to keep anyone from following me yesterday. How much more careful can I possibly fucking be?"

"I don't *know*, Dell," Winn snapped, loudly enough that a few weary early-morning travelers turned their necks to peer at them through the early-morning gloom. Winn sighed, then took a deep breath. "I don't know. But I'm awfully tired and hungry, and I think that we ought to first have a good breakfast and then go back to bed."

"All right," Delly said, and took a deep breath of her own. "All right." Their fingers were still tangled together.

They went to a coffee shop, and Delly ate too much in the way that she always did when she was too tired to properly feel her own stomach. Over breakfast they spoke, a little, about how Delly could be more careful. Winn would make her a pair of enchanted specs like the ones that Abstentia used to go to the leather-goods shop. No, not just one pair, multiple pairs. They would each carry a pistol at all times: in addition to Delly's practicing melting bullets, she would now have to practice her marksmanship as well. Or better yet, Winn would just go everywhere with Delly to keep an eye on her. Winn was talking fast, her big hands busy with shredding a bit of bread into tiny crumbs onto the table. Eventually Delly had to break in. "Winn," she said, "that all sounds fine. But if we're going to get all of that done, we'll have to try and get some sleep."

Winn slumped a bit. Then she rubbed at her eyes. "I think I might be too frightened to sleep."

"Me too," Delly said, even though she wasn't sure if she was, exactly. Maybe part of her wasn't all that afraid of being murdered. "But we'll just have to do our best with the unfortunate circumstances, I guess." She paused. "Your hair looks pretty like that. With the curls, I mean."

"Oh," Winn said, and reached up to pat at her hair. "They would have looked better if I'd been able to keep them in the rags all night."

"They look good enough for me," Delly said firmly. "And the next time you try it you'll be able to keep them in all night, now that we've shipped Mittens off to Monsatelle."

Winn gave a weak giggle. "*Mittens of Monsatelle* sounds absolutely ridiculous."

"Maybe he can use the name to make a grand new life for himself," Delly said. "Mittens of Monsatelle, the—noted actor of tragical roles."

Winn was smiling now. She raised her coffee cup. "To Mittens," she said, "and the success of his career on the stage."

"To Mittens," Delly agreed, and lifted her own coffee cup so that they could have a toast. Then they paid the bill and trundled back to their little room.

15

Wherein Dellaria Learns More Than She Ever Hoped
to Know About Buttons, and Enters into More Than
One Possibly Ill-Considered Agreement

The walk to the laboratory that afternoon was so furtive and elaborate that it felt as though they were ladies engaging in courtly
intrigue in a more glamorous age, if ladies engaging in courtly intrigue
in a more glamorous age had frequently found themselves hiding
in public toilets in order to change their disguises midway between
their rented room and the abandoned building they were using as the
base of their criminal enterprises. In any case, they eventually made it
to the laboratory, where they were greeted with shock, fear, and an
infuriated Mura wielding a broom in one hand and a knife in the
other.

Winn, being surprisingly nimble of foot for a gull of her size,
dodged a swipe from the broom and hastily shouted out the phrase
that ended the illusions she had cast to disguise them. Delly, for her
part, bounced away from Mura like a cat leaping out of a bathtub and
shrieked, "Stop! It's us!" with even more grace and gravitas than was
the usual Wellsian mode.

"Oh, for fuck's sake," Vitna said as her sister dropped her broom in
disgust. The other women were filtering into the room as well, clearly

wondering what all of the shouting was about. "Why didn't you take the disguises off before you came in? Nearly made my heart stop."

"I *forgot*," Winn said. "And I didn't think that you would *hit me over the head with a broom*."

"I didn't *hit* you," Mura said, all full of indignitude. "I drew back at the last moment. I know how to keep control over my weapon. What were you two wearing disguises for, anyway? And why are you so late getting here?"

Delly cleared her throat, feeling oddly self-conscious as her mother wandered in, with her new bosom companion, Mrs. Totham, close behind. Mam looked dull and sleepy—they'd probably been feeding her more drip—but it still felt odd to have to talk about having been attacked by a strange man in front of her mother. She swallowed the feeling back. Maybe it would be good for her mam to worry about her a bit. "We might've been—a *bit* attacked in our bed last night."

"You were attacked?" Abstentia said. "By who? What happened? Were either of you hurt?"

"*Your bed?*" Delly's mam said, and Delly immediately felt foolish. Her mam, of course, didn't give a grasshopper's tit that her daughter had been in mortal danger. All she cared about was whether or not she was sharing a bed with her rich clanner prospect.

It wouldn't do any good to pay attention to her, so Delly didn't. Instead, as quickly and clearly as she could, she explained to Abstentia all that had happened the night before, with particular emphasis on the mention of the gull called *Wex*. Abstentia's expression grew continuously more pinched as Delly spoke, as it always seemed to when her friend's criminal activities were the topic of conversation, until eventually she burst out with a loud "Well, you certainly can't go back to that room tonight."

"Like rabbit shit we can't," Delly said, almost as loudly. "Where else are we going to go?"

"You can stay here," Abstentia said. "It will be far safer, and there will be less need for you to go tramping back and forth across the city every day, drawing unnecessary attention to yourselves."

"No," Delly said. "I *absolutely* object. I won't stay here, and we ain't *drawing attention* to ourselves. We had disguises and everything, and we *sent Mittens to Monsatelle*." The indignity of being told that she would have to bunk with her mam after she'd gone to all of that trouble to send Mittens off to start his new life on the stage was too tough a bit of gristle for even Dellaria Wells's iron guts to digest.

"Dell, you have to admit that she has a point," Winn said. "Us walking back and forth from here to our room all the time makes it much more likely that someone will follow us here, and then our birds really *will* be roasted."

"She *doesn't* have a point," Delly said sulkily, even though Abstentia very clearly did. "We've been perfectly all right in our room so far."

"We were *attacked* in our room *last night*," Winn said. "Listen, how about we take a room at a hotel, at least, just for a few nights. Just in case that Mittens person was lying about not having told anyone else the address. We can ask your landlady to keep an eye out for any strangers lurking around the place while we're gone."

"A *hotel* costs *money*," Delly said. "Which I am, in all exactitude, *out of*."

"So I'll pay for it," Winn said breezily. "Or send my pop the bill, at least. No harm in leaning a bit upon the steady arm of one's father in one's hour of need, what? If anything, my sending him bills would just be proof that I'm still spry and able enough to book a room at a hotel and order hearty meals on a regular basis."

Delly only stared at her for a moment, utterly astonished that any living personage had ever, was currently, or could ever live in such confidence that another living personage would be so eager to pay for their hearty meals. All she could do, in the end, was shrug. "All right," she said. "If you really think your pop won't send the constabulary after you to drag you back to Hexos the second he sees the first bill."

"Oh, I wouldn't worry about that," Winn said, before her expression turned somewhat troubled. "The only thing that I *might* worry about is that if he was worried enough about me to tell my mother."

Delly was about to inquire as to what exactly might happen if Winn's father told her mother about his worries—from Winn's expression, the results might be exceedingly dire—but was interrupted by Abstentia. "If you two are quite finished with making your domestic arrangements, do you suppose that we might talk about whether or not we'll need to start making more of our product for the Kind Companions? If they were willing to kidnap you to get our formula, they *must* be interested in the stuff. Miss Wells, I don't suppose that you thought to arrange for some way for them to communicate with you other than allowing them to break into your room in the middle of the night?"

"Oh, *shit*," Delly said, and fumbled her pocket watch out of her reticule. "I'm late to meet them."

She turned to head toward the door, but Winn grabbed her by the elbow before she could get more than a step away. "Don't you *dare* go running off there on your own, Dellaria," she said. "I'm coming with you."

"So am I," Abstentia said. "Since the two of you obviously can't be trusted to take care of yourselves on your own."

"And what good are *you* going to do?" Delly asked, feeling distinctly irritatized. "I don't see *you* throwing any punches at a brigand."

"Obviously I wouldn't *throw a punch*," Abstentia said, as prim as a rose. "But as you might recall, I am more than capable of defending myself with magic, if need be. Only just yesterday I memorized the condensed parameters to produce an *extremely* powerful electric shock."

"Have you memorized the parameters for making sure that you only shock your intended target?" Winn asked.

Abstentia looked, for a moment, as if she wanted to bite her own nose off. Then she said, "I have other parameters memorized as well. And I can bring my notebook. And I can let Miss Wells borrow the new protective construct that I've been working on."

Delly blinked. It seemed as though Abstentia had built more magical constructs in her shortish life than Delly had swilled glasses of cheap gin. "Another construct? What does this one do?"

"Afflict anyone who comes too close to you with severe dizziness, in theory," Abstentia said. "I haven't had a chance to test it yet." Her eyes had taken on an alarming gleam. "I'll just pop up to the laboratory to fetch it," she added, and darted off.

"Well, if everyone else is going, we might as well come along, too," Mura said, as Vitna nodded her agreement. Then a new voice broke into the conversation, low and hollow and horrible. A cup on the table rattled in its saucer. The door to the sitting room creaked in its frame.

"*Beware*," Buttons said, and then crawled back into the broken teapot that the residents of the house had been using as a sugar bowl.

There was a moment of silence. Mrs. Totham cried out, "Oh, *please* don't go, girls," and burst into tears.

Vitna rushed to soothe her, while Mura attempted to be the voice of reason. "Come on, Mother, don't cry. What does that stupid *mouse* know, anyway?"

"Buttons is *not* stupid," Mrs. Totham said through her tears. "And you *mustn't* go, you *mustn't*. Buttons is warning you, and he was there when poor Ermintrude—" She was crying too hard to speak now. Delly grimaced and watched with a sense of deep unease as her own mother opened her arms and gathered Mrs. Totham up against her bosom to comfort her. That drip Mrs. Totham was making, Delly thought, must be truly incredible stuff.

"I won't go, Mother," Vitna said. "And Mura won't, either."

"Yes, I will," Mura said. "We came here so that we could get revenge for what happened to our sister, not to sit around cowering like *mice*." At this she shot a meaningful look toward the sugar bowl, where Buttons could be heard rustling about amongst the sugar cubes. A moment later, from inside the sugar bowl, came the sound of a prolonged and resonant fart.

Winn giggled. Mrs. Totham sniffled. "Oh, don't fight amongst yourselves, *please*," she said. "I can't make you stay here, Mura, of course. I only wish that you would take dear Buttons *seriously*, when he only wants the best for us."

Buttons made another extremely rude noise. Mura glowered at the sugar bowl, then directed her attention to her sister. "Vitna, why don't you take Mother to the aviary in the botanical gardens today? I'm sure that she'd enjoy that very much. And then we can all join you to have supper in the Palm House restaurant. Wouldn't that be a lovely treat?"

"That *does* sound nice," Delly said quickly. The Palm House restaurant had been very popular with the smart set about twenty years ago, which meant that it was currently just right for members of Delly's set when they wanted to impress a sweetheart.

"I think it's a wonderful idea," Winn said.

Mrs. Totham looked hesitant. "Oh, dear me," she said. "You won't come, Mura? I did hear that there's a breeding pair of crested ironbills at the aviary at present . . ."

"Then that's settled, then," Delly said. "You can bring my mam with you. I'm leaving now, so anyone who wants to come with me needs to start scuffing some shoe leather."

There was, for a moment, a flurry of shoe scuffing as everyone raced to find their handbag or parasol or experimental magical construct or favorite revolver. Mura and Vitna got into a brief squabble over who ought to carry their sharpest pair of knives. Then they all donned their disguises and went marching off together to meet their enemies—or to receive a note from their enemies passed on by the owner of a pawnshop, which would be an awfully steep drop in the excitement of the afternoon.

They headed toward Rat's shop at a bit of a trot, and everyone took a pause directly outside to check for lurking brigands and pat their hair back into place. Then they marched inside with Delly in the lead, the bell over the door jingling cheerfully at them as they entered.

"Is that you two?" Rat called out from behind her desk. Her hat today had about five more ostrich feathers than any normal hat should be expected to bear. "*Lovely* disguises. And you've brought company!"

"Thank you," Delly said. "Just one of our most intimate friends." She was trying not to stare at the woman sitting next to Rat behind the desk. There was something very strange about her. Delly had a vague sense that she was beautiful, but her eyes kept on skidding over her face like feet on icy pavement. There was nothing solid to cling to, just a blurry, watercolored impression of dark curls and bright eyes.

"That's a terribly clever illusion," Winn murmured as the woman rose.

"I believe that you've been trying to get my attention," she said. "You have it. What did you do with my man?"

"Your man?" Delly asked. She'd been distracted by the woman's voice. It was a lovely, low, musical voice, with a thoroughly pressed-and-powdered accent that she was attempting to cover up with an extremely poor stab at West Leiscourt. Clanners never really knew how people like Delly talked. "Oh, you mean Mittens? I mean, Kail what'd'ye'call'im? He decided to start a new life on the stage."

Though it was difficult to see, exactly, with that strange illusion on her face, Delly thought that she could detect the arch of two eyebrows through the blur. "Very well, then," she said. "If that's the way that we're to play this game."

Delly wrinkled her nose. "You sound like a penny blood villain," she said. "I'm not here to play games, miss. I just wanted to do business. My mam's ailing and I have bills to pay, and I frankly found it very hurtful that you sent a man to follow and abduct me, very hurtful indeed."

Winn chipped in then. "Not the sort of behavior that one likes to see when one's attempting to embark upon a fruitful business relationship, what?"

The woman cocked her head. "My goodness," she said. "*You* went to a decent school, didn't you? How did you get mixed up with *this* bunch?"

Winn cleared her throat, and Delly knew without looking that she must be blushing. Delly decided to step in. "Forgive me terribly if I'm rude, but I was wondering if we might possibly cut through the dough and into the roast of the matter, as it were. What did you think of our product?" She paused. "And what shall we call you?"

"Nothing at all," the woman said. "Why would you need to call me anything? And your product was—adequate, I suppose."

Abstentia, cloaked in her old-lady disguise, gave a creaking yelp. "*Adequate?* If you can describe a single thing about my formulation that was less than *completely*—"

Delly cut her off. "Excuse me. Historically, miss, if we haven't known what to call someone, miss, we've called them Mittens," Delly said. "I hope that being called Mittens won't be too upsetting to you, Miss Mittens, as we have to call you *something*. What exactly was wrong with our product, Miss Mittens?"

Miss Mittens grimaced dramatically enough that it was visible through the illusion. "You may call me—Miss Cat," she said.

"I feel threatened!" Rat cried, the ostrich feather wriggling with the force of her amusement. She'd been watching the proceedings as if she'd never seen a more entertaining show in her entire hideously be-hatted career. "I hope that you won't hunt me down in my humble hole, Miss Cat."

Miss Cat carried on as if Rat hadn't spoken, which Delly also felt was probably the only really reasonable way of dealing with Rat. "As I said, the product was perfectly adequate. What was your purpose in sending it to me?"

"Begging your pardon once again, Miss Cat," Delly said, "but I would have thought that our purpose was obvious, Miss Cat. We want to go into business with you. No competition, nothing like that. More like—like how they keep the tanneries at the outskirts of town, but fine ladies such as yourself can still buy their leather gloves at nice dainty stores in proper neighborhoods. We would produce the product, you would buy it from us, and then you would distribute it at whatever price you thought was reasonable, Miss Cat. That end of things would be no business of ours. Unless, of course, you were in need of extra hands, in which case I'm sure that we would be able to make ourselves available. We're a group of ready and able workers, Miss Cat, and very keen to make ourselves of service to you, Miss Cat." Then, after this torrent of language, Delly stopped to catch her breath. Her heart was beating too fast. She wasn't at all sure that Cat—Miss Clairelle, maybe—would agree to any of this, and if she didn't agree then Delly would be in a very awkward position indeed. None of them had planned for a scenario in which she refused them.

Miss Cat flicked open her fan and stirred the air with it a bit. The illusion around her face blurred even further. "It might be possible for us to come to an arrangement," she said after a moment. "As there is a *very* great demand for our product, despite our recent production increases. One sen for twenty drops."

Delly was about to open her mouth to agree to that—she wasn't sure exactly how many drops of drip were in the one-ounce bottles that it was generally sold in, but she was fairly sure that it was far more than twenty—when Abstentia broke in in the creaking old-lady voice granted to her by her enchanted spectacles. "Absolutely not," she snapped. "We might be amateurs in this enterprise, Miss Cat, but we aren't the dunces that you seem to think we are. I could walk down to the corner chemist in five minutes and buy the weakest cough syrup on the market for the price you just named."

Miss Cat fanned herself more vigorously. "You seem to forget, *madam*, that you are the ones requesting my cooperation in this matter. The sales apparatus is mine. It is, you will comprehend, perfectly usual for wholesale prices to be lower than what might be found on the high street."

"It certainly would be the *high* street, considering the product," Winn said, and snickered quietly to herself until she noticed the expressions on the faces of her fellows and cleared her throat. "Sorry. Carry on."

"Be that as it may," Abstentia said, as if Winn hadn't spoken at all, "you have tested our product, Miss Cat. You're aware of the quality. How much would you say would be an average price for an ounce of red drip on the street, Miss W—Whelk?"

"Miss *Whelk*?" Delly repeated, rather offended. She didn't consider herself to be even remotely whelkish in appearance, personality, or odor. Arguing about it, however, would probably only serve to draw attention to her actual surname, so she gathered herself. "Erm. About two tocats, I should say. Expensive stuff, red drip. Especially when it's of exceptionally high quality, as ours is."

"Indeed," Abstentia said. "There are approximately five hundred drops in a one-ounce bottle. At one sen per twenty drops, we would be earning only a quarter-tocat per bottle, which is such a paltry sum that it would hardly be worth our while to produce the stuff. We might as well use our abilities to perform magic tricks on street corners to amuse schoolchildren. One tocat per ounce would be far more reasonable."

Miss Cat threw back her head and laughed. Her laughter didn't sound very convincingly mirthful: unlike her man Sir Mittens, Delly thought that Miss Cat would be very unlikely to find a new career on the stage if her crimes proved less than fruitful in the long term. The laughter then came to a very abrupt halt, and Miss Cat leaned forward in her chair. "You forget yourself, miss," she said. "You engage in this endeavor only upon my sufferance. It is *I* who determines what is or is not *reasonable*. You may work with me on my terms, or find yourself eliminated as an obstruction to business, also on my terms. The choice is yours."

"That's very reasonable of you, Miss Cat," Delly said, before Abstentia could open her mouth and further aggravate an already sufficiently aggravating situation. "You must admit, though, that we would be free to remove ourselves from competition with you by taking our drip production to another city, which would sadly deprive you of the ability to easily increase the strength of your operations here in Leiscourt, Miss Cat. Do you suppose we might come to some compromise in terms of price that would be mutually satisfactory, Miss Cat?"

The fan became a blur. "One sen per ten drops," she said finally. "A half-tocat per ounce. Take it or take yourself away from Leiscourt. I wouldn't press my luck, if I were you. The production of manufactured laudanum is a very serious crime, you know, and one that I'm sure that the police might be very interested in investigating."

Delly felt her stomach swoop. "I'm sure that it won't be necessary for the police to be involved, Miss Cat," she said quickly. "A half-tocat per ounce sounds very reasonable to me, Miss Cat."

Miss Cat's smile gleamed through the blur.

They came to an agreement fairly easily after that—Delly didn't feel as if she had much room to engage in a spirited debate on the subject—and got out of the shop as quickly as they could, having agreed to deliver fifty ounces of drip to Rat in one week's time. Abstentia had squawked a bit at that number, but it wasn't a violent squawking, so Delly assumed that producing this quantity of drip in a week was, at least, within her capabilities. As they filed out through the front door of the shop they heard the sound of Rat's laughter mingling with the jingle of the bell.

Delly was silent for a while, as Winn and Abstentia both mumbled out the parameters for spells to change their appearances and alert them if they were being followed. They'd been walking for several minutes before she finally worked up the nerve to speak. Even then it was in a hiss. *"She's in with the police."*

"Well, she *says* that she is, what?" Winn said. "I could easily march down to the police station tomorrow morning in my best frock and accuse someone of stealing my diamond tiara, as well. It doesn't mean that I have a man in the force."

"I don't think that it's unlikely that she does have connections within the police force," Abstentia said. Her voice was measured and calm, which, from Abstentia, was somewhat extraordinary. "I recognized her voice. That was, almost undoubtedly, Clairelle Tredworth. It wouldn't surprise me at all to learn that she's managed to get some officer of the law in her pocket, considering who her father is."

"*Shit,*" Delly mumbled. "*Relefting fucking—*"

"Goodness, Dell, you're setting my ears aflame," Winn said. "There's no reason to panic. She doesn't know who we are, where we stay, or where the lab is. For all she knows Abstentia is an elderly lady with very strong opinions about the cost of cough syrup."

"Maybe so," Delly said, "but she didn't seem to me like the kind of cat who would give up too quick catching her mouse."

"Unimaginative animal metaphors aside," Abstentia said, "I don't know that her having connections with the police ought to alter our course, particularly. It isn't as if the fact that what we're doing is both dangerous and illegal is a secret to any of us. We'll just have to do our best to avoid making any mistakes."

Delly, who had never in her life, in her recollection, managed to avoid making any mistakes for longer than the duration of a severe cold in the chest, found herself nodding. There was not very much that could be done. This boulder had already rolled halfway down the hill and was currently picking up speed and aiming itself at an innocent villager prancing about in a pastoral fashion in the flower-strewn meadows below. At this point, Delly (who was, in this analogy, simultaneously both the downward-hurtling boulder and the frolicking agrarian personage) could only grit her teeth and hope to the releft that she made it out of this mess in one piece.

"And," Abstentia added, "there was something else that I think we ought to take an interest in. Miss Cat mentioned that they'd recently increased their production. Didn't you also say that that nurse you spoke to at the hospital had said that she'd noticed a very recent increase in the number of people poisoned by red drip, Cynallum?"

Winn nodded, looking a bit guilty over her sudden exposure as a person who had enjoyed a bit of a gossip on the subject of Delly's mam's hospitalization. "A sudden flood of the stuff in the streets starting about a week ago, it sounded like."

"Interesting, isn't it?" Abstentia said. "That the increase of red drip in the streets of Leiscourt coincides so neatly with the time when our dear Ainette might have arrived here. It would certainly be a way to work off her debt if she started helping to produce the stuff, wouldn't it? And she's certainly enough of a wizard to be able to quickly and radically increase the amount of drip that the Kind Companions are brewing."

"And enough of a—*personage* to not care who she hurt if there were problems with the quality," Winn said, at which reminder of poor Ermintrude's demise a gloomy silence settled over their entire company.

Mura cleared the fog of unspeakability by clearing her throat. "Hate to make all of this worse," she said, "but we promised to meet my mother and sister at the botanical gardens for supper."

There was a chorus of groans. Abstentia wrinkled her nose. "A drink," she said. "I think that all of us could use a stiff drink."

"*I* sure as fuck could," Delly said, and led the charge in the direction of the nearest coffee shop that might serve a respectable glass of wine to a respectable young woman on a respectable late afternoon.

What they ended up in was a coffee shop heartily velveted and becandled in an attempt at a decadent Esiphian atmosphere, which was, thank God, reinforced with the availability of three different types of fortified wine. Delly immediately fortified herself with a glass, which she drank too quickly while the others were still trying to decide whether or not they wanted any food or if that would spoil their appetites before supper. Delly, emboldened by her drink, flapped her hand at the waiter. "Bring us some bread and olives and a round of vermouth for the table," she said, and the waiter, evidently impressed by her air of leadership, hurried to obey.

Delly felt relatively relaxed after her second glass. Relaxed enough to sit back in her chair, at least, and eat a few olives. After half of her third glass she rubbed Winn's ankle under the table with her foot. Winn frowned at her. She herself had eaten a great deal of bread and olives, ordered a cup of strong coffee, and barely touched her vermouth. "Are you all right, Dell?"

"Oh, I'm fine," Delly said. "Fit as a fig tree, in fact."

"I don't know if that's the phrase, old thing," Winn said, and rubbed Delly's ankle with her foot right back. There was still a deep worried line between her eyebrows. "Please don't drink too much. We still have a visit to an aviary to get through. And with everything—well. We ought to keep our wits about us."

"Oh, don't worry about me," Delly said, sitting up a bit. "It takes more than a lap of vermouth to put *me* under the table."

"I know," Winn said. "Even so, Dell." She pushed her cup of coffee in Delly's direction.

Delly sighed and picked it up to take a sip. "That woman seemed mighty comfortable with the idea of killing people."

"I know," Winn said. "Which is why we're going to have to stay sharp as we can until all of this is over."

"Until all of this is over," Delly repeated, and took a gulp of coffee that she hoped was big enough to banish the warm glow of the vermouth. Winn was right. She had to stay sharp. She had more than just herself to think about now. All of them were dug into this shit so deep that it would take a whole crew of shoveling workmen to extract them. They had to get their job done, get ahold of Ainette, and get the fuck out before all of Leiscourt's criminals and officers of the law came down around their ears.

It was enough to drive anyone to drink, and then right back out of drink to a tense and horrible sobriety.

Once all of the olives were gone, they made their thoroughly disguised and wary way to the botanical gardens, where they duly paid their penny each to be admitted. The gardens themselves looked a bit wan, at this point in the autumn, but the aviary was something else entirely: a hot, wet, stinking paradise unto itself. It was inside of an enormous glass house filled to the brim with palm trees and dark creeping vines and strange plants with pink fleshy flowers, and swooping through the warm, wet air were hundreds of peculiar birds, each more gaudily attired in its variegated feathers than the last.

Delly's initial intent had been to stick with her group, with the thought that she would be less likely to get herself into trouble if she was sufficiently chaperoned. But the place was too beguiling to spend the whole while with one's eyes locked on the back of Abstentia's head, and Delly could have sworn that she had only stopped to gawp at an artificial waterfall for a moment when she looked up again to find herself alone. Alone except for a young couple, that is, who took a moment away from gazing admiringly at each other to glare unadmiringly at Delly until she slunk off.

She ambled along aimlessly for a while, just looking. It was nice to be somewhere so wet and warm and green, even if it did stink of bird shit. It occurred to her, as she wandered, that these birds had come from somewhere, and that the somewhere that they came from was just as steamy and soft-edged as this.

"Oh, *there* you are," Winn said.

Delly only jumped and shrieked a very little bit. Then she cleared her throat and stepped to the side to allow Winn to fall in beside her. "It's nice in here," she said, as they began to stroll together. "I was just wondering about where they came from. The birds, I mean."

"Somewhere like this," Winn said. "It reminds me a bit of Sango."

Delly turned to goggle at her. "You've been to *Sango*?"

"Only once, years ago," Winn said. "My uncle Loga invited us to spend the winter with him at his estate in the southwest. I mostly remember the smell of the air, and getting caught in the rain every afternoon."

"Sakes," Delly murmured. "Maybe *that's* what I'll do, when this is over. Take the money and run off to Sango. I always thought I'd like to live somewhere warm."

They walked quietly for a moment. Then Winn said, "You could always come home to Hexos with me, instead of my mother's summer village. It's not a jungle like this, but the weather is better than

Daeslund. It's sunny for most of the year, and the sea is a nice deep blue, and there are orange trees everywhere you look. You have to be careful sometimes when you walk down the street about not slipping in orange pulp."

"*Orange trees*," Delly repeated, amazed, and then made up her mind on the spot. "All right," she said. "That's what I'll do once we've caught Ainette. Or if we *don't* catch her and I have to run from the Kind Companions before they slit my throat."

"That's just what I think," Winn said, and gave Delly's hand a squeeze. "Just you and the orange trees, eh?"

"And you," Delly said. "You and the orange trees and me."

Winn went slightly pink. "I'd hoped that I'd be there, too," she said. "I just didn't think it would be my place to make wanton assumptions over who you'd want to find dawdling amongst the groves, what?"

"I'd want *you* dawdling in the groves, obviously," Delly said. "Who else? *Abstentia?*"

They both giggled, though Winn did so with a somewhat guilty air. Then Delly heard a very familiar voice. "Look, Buttons! There she is! The crested ironbill!" Then, in response to this, a muted and melliluous "*Bong.*"

Delly and Winn exchanged a glance. Then, without a word, they turned in the direction of the voices and headed down the path a bit farther, until they came upon a bench that had the questionable fortune of supporting Mrs. Totham, Buttons, and Dellaria's unconscious mother. Mrs. Totham looked up as they approached, and beamed. "Look, girls!" she said, in an exaggerated whisper. "There she is!"

Delly looked up at where Mrs. Totham was pointing, to see a large, bright red bird with an enormous orange beak. "Very pretty," she said, though truth be told she didn't see how this particular bird was worthy of so much more excitement than any other pretty bird in the aviary.

"And very *special*," Mrs. Totham said, all aflutter with delight. "This is a *female* crested ironbill. You can see the male over there." She pointed out a dull brown little creature perched on a nearby branch. "In most species the male displays his beautiful plumage in order to attract the female, but for the crested ironbill it's the *female* who is the gaudy, and the male the drab!"

"That *is* interesting," Delly said. "It's a wonder that the females bother with the males at all, really. Though I sometimes think the same about the women in my neighborhood. Might be better off if they sent all of the fellas off to work on farms."

"Oh, dear," said Mrs. Totham, in a twitter more delicate than that of a single rare bird in the building. "Wouldn't that be a pity? Wherever would we ladies be without the gentlemen?"

"I'm sure that we wouldn't know what to do with ourselves, Mrs. Totham," Delly said gravely. Winn tittered, then cleared her throat. Then Delly turned her attention toward her mother and whispered to Mrs. Totham, "Did you give her some of the new product before you left?"

"Only a very small drop," Mrs. Totham said. "I think that dear Mrs. Wells finds the warm heat very soothing to her joints. They were giving her a great deal of trouble last night, I'm afraid."

Delly frowned. "Her joints? What's the matter with her joints?"

Mrs. Totham's gentle brown eyes went wide. "Oh, dearie me," she said. "Poor dear Mrs. Wells must not have told you for fear of worrying you. A mother *never* likes to worry her daughter." She lowered her voice. "I'm afraid that she has very severe arthritis in her left wrist and right knee. I did my best to ease her condition as much as I could this morning, but there's only so much that body science can do. No *wonder* she's been using that drop, the poor dear."

"Drip," Delly said automatically. "Is *that* what she said? That she uses drip because of her *arthritis*?" It made her angry just to think of it. All of those years of gin and laudanum blamed on *arthritis*.

"Oh, no, she didn't *say* that," Mrs. Totham said. "That was only my guess. Arthritis can be exceedingly painful, you know. My dear husband has developed arthritis in his hip. It came on quite suddenly: I suspect that it might have been all of that damp weather we had this past spring. As I recently said to my neighbor, Mrs. Dorus . . ."

Delly and Winn sat down on the bench beside the one occupied by the older ladies. Delly felt her eyes start to drift shut. It was the heat, maybe, or the three glasses of vermouth, or the squawking of the birds, or the soothing drone of Mrs. Totham talking about her husband's arthritis. She had almost nodded off completely when she was jolted awake by a sudden and excited squeal. "Oh! I forgot to tell you!"

Mrs. Totham's excitement was resonant enough to wake up not only Delly, but her mother as well, and for an uncomfortable moment Delly found herself staring directly into what was very close to being her own squint-eyed, sleep-bleared face. "Oh, dear, did I wake you?" Mrs. Totham asked. "I'm terribly sorry, I didn't mean to annoy you. It's only that I'd forgotten to tell you what I've learned about Buttons!"

"Oh?" Delly croaked out, and tried to subtly crack her neck. It had gone all stiff while she was dozing. "What did you learn about Buttons?"

Mrs. Totham leaned forward slightly on the bench. Delly tried not to stare at Buttons, who was making his creepsome way across Mrs. Totham's lap and toward the lap of Delly's mother. Mrs. Totham looked even more excited about this new bit of news than she had over the glamorous she-bird. "I found a manuscript at the clubhouse of the Sororal Order of Wizardesses," Mrs. Totham said. "A most interesting volume about noted wizards who have died in magical accidents."

"Oh?" Delly said, hoping desperately that this story would not end up buried in the target at which it was presently aimed. "Sounds like a real thrill of a book, Mrs. Totham."

"Oh, it *was*," Mrs. Totham said. "Particularly one case of a wizard named Collius Trell, who died over one hundred years ago. Mr. Trell was employed as a tutor for the youngest sons of a great family, but in his spare time he was also engaged in the study of, ah, creative body science."

"Necromancy, you mean," Delly said. "How did he die?"

Mrs. Totham, who had gone a little wilted-looking upon hearing the word *necromancy*, gave an eager nod at being invited to continue with her horrible tale. "*Well*," she said, "one summer the whole family left to go on an extended holiday to the seaside, and most of the staff went with them. Mr. Trell stayed behind, as his pupils were having their holiday, too, and so he determined to work on his own projects. He ordered all of the servants to stay far away from his quarters, which they were glad to do, considering the strange sounds that often emerged from within his laboratory, and the fact that most of the young girls working there didn't at all care to have to look at all of the mice that Mr. Trell kept in cages in his rooms for use in his experiments."

"Oh, no," Winn murmured, looking just as uneasy as Delly felt.

Mrs. Totham had a strange exalted gleam in her eyes. "It was over a month before the family came back and the eldest sons forced open the door to Mr. Trell's room. Inside, they found all of the mouse cages empty, with their doors hanging open, and the only things left of Mr. Trell were his skeleton, his belt buckle, and the soles of his shoes." She paused for a moment to allow the tension to build in the hearts of her horrified audience. Hang Mittens: it was *Mrs. Totham* who'd been born for a life on the stage. "Where do you suppose that this fearful event occurred?"

Delly licked her lips. "Crossick Manor?"

"*Yes!*" Mrs. Totham cried, and clapped her hands together in delight. "So you see what I mean about Buttons?"

Delly cast a glance at Buttons, who was presently perched upon her mother's knee. Her mother, Delly was pleased to note, was not so far gone as to be unmoved by Mrs. Totham's story. She was looking at Buttons as if she was afraid that he might be inclined to bite. "Do you really think that *Buttons* is this—Mr. Trell feller?"

"Yes!" Mrs. Totham said again, as Buttons made a sound like a babbling brook. Mrs. Totham beamed. "You *see*?"

"Well, in *that* case," Delly said, "if you don't mind, sir, I would prefer it if you would remove yourself from my mother's knee, sir."

Buttons, at this, made his now customary farting sound. Delly's mam grimaced, and hissed at Delly, "Don't *aggravate* him, Dellaria."

Delly was about to become argumentative on the subject, before it occurred to her that her mother's objections might be less motivated by a desire to defend an unalive wizard-possessed mouse over her daughter, and more by the fear that the unalive mouse might unleash vile acts of necromancy if his temper was roused. With this in mind, Delly cleared her throat, in order to dislodge and then swallow a lump of pride. "I apologize, Mr. Trell," she said. "It's only that I'm very protective of the unimpeachable virtue of my dear mother, Mr. Trell."

It might have just been Delly's fancy, but for a moment Buttons' glowing red eyes seemed to narrow. Then he emitted a terse and muted "*Bong.*"

"Mrs. Totham," Winn said, after the traditional moment of uncomfortable silence that always followed one of Buttons' bongings, "if Buttons is Mr. Trell . . . do you suppose that he *enjoys* being, erm. A . . . not *entirely* alive mouse?"

Buttons, at this point, made a new sound: like a drop of water falling from a height into a half-full bucket. Mrs. Totham gave a thoughtful nod. "He finds it much preferable to where he was before."

"Oh," Winn said, rather faintly. "And—where was he, before?"

Buttons made the sound of a creaky gate slamming shut. This, really, needed no translation, but Mrs. Totham provided one nevertheless. "He would prefer not to discuss it."

All of them, at that juncture, found themselves extremely interested in observing the tropical birds. A moment later they were rescued by the arrival of the rest of their merry band of female catastrophes: Vitna was in the lead, placidly eating roasted chestnuts out of a large paper cone, while Mura and Abstentia trailed behind her, both looking distinctly ill at ease with their jungly surroundings. Abstentia was still holding up her parasol. Delly raised her eyebrows. "I don't mean to tell you your business, Miss Dok, but what do you need a parasol for indoors?"

"You always mean to tell everyone their business, Miss Wells," Abstentia said. "It seems to be an inescapable aspect of your nature. And I need the parasol to protect me from bird mess. I saw some drop down onto the path in front of me not two minutes ago."

There was a loud rustling, then, as all of the ladies hastily opened their parasols. Winn leapt to her feet and said, with a degree of good cheer that struck Delly as somewhat excessive even for Winn, "Well, then! Shall we leave here and have our supper?"

There was a chorus of general agreement, and they immediately proceeded to troop their way out of the aviary and toward the Palm House restaurant, which benefited from all of the advantages of the aviary—the warm air, the glass enclosure letting in the light from the setting sun, the vines and towering palms—without the threat of falling bird mess. In the Palm House one could also order wine, which was really all that you needed to make a place appealing to Dellaria Wells.

They were seated by a handsome fellow dressed up like a footman, and then a more elderly and distinguished footman glided up to ask them what they would like to drink. Delly quailed a bit—all that she knew about wine was that it came in more than one color and that she enjoyed guzzling it of an evening—and was deeply relieved when Winn cut in to ask very learned-sounding questions about what the distinguished gent had to offer, and then sent him off to fetch two bottles of something or other. Abstentia looked almost as impressed as Delly felt. "Gracious me, Cynallum, I didn't think that you had it in you."

Winn, as usual, seemed more amused than offended by Abstentia's sallies. "I learned how to order wine at my pop's knee. Not like it's *difficult*, what?"

Delly felt herself flush. It probably *didn't* seem difficult, to someone like Winn. It occurred to her, suddenly, that if Winn became Delly's householder there would be things that she would be expected to know. That it would be more than just her accent that might serve to embarrass Winn and her family: that Delly would likely expose herself as trash at every turn. It was practically enough to put a gull off of her wine. Or it would have been, Delly supposed, for a gull who wasn't Dellaria Wells: the Wellsian thirst was not so easily eliminated. What *did* do the trick was the thought that Winn might observe said thirst displayed by Delly's mother, and that the direct comparison of the two would cast Delly in a less than flatterating light. With this in mind, she allowed the distinguished gentleman to pour her only half of a glass, and took one small sip every few minutes as she waited for the food to arrive.

It might have been Delly's imagination, but it seemed to her that Winn was very happy that night. She certainly smiled a great deal, and ate a great deal, and laughed a great deal. She certainly cut the choicest bits of meat from her own plate to give to Delly, which she said was a "troll custom" she had learned from her mother. She certainly let their knees touch under the table.

After they had all eaten their fill, and the heads of the older women were beginning to nod over the table, it was Winn who asked for the bill, and Winn who paid for it without so much as allowing anyone else to take a peek. She then asked whether Mura and Vitna might be so kind as to escort their mother and Mrs. Wells home while she and Delly took a turn around the rest of the botanical gardens. Considering that Winn had just paid for all of their suppers, none of the ladies seemed interested in arguing against this plan, and the youth soon gathered up their elders and departed.

Delly allowed Winn to lead then, and they headed out into the gardens. It was all lit up at night, with the gas lamps blazing and the orchestra playing in the band shell. Winn drew Delly's hand through her arm. "Shall we visit the hedge maze?"

Delly agreed that this sounded like a fine idea and they walked away from the lights and the band shell to the quieter end of the park, where the maze was. At the entrance there was a bored-looking girl selling candles so that visitors could see the path ahead of them. Winn bought one, and they headed into the maze.

The maze had a strange air to it at night. They passed a great number of people as they walked, but in the darkness and flickering candlelight they seemed ghostlike and insubstantial, appearing for a moment and then vanishing into the gloom. It seemed that everyone else in the maze had the same feeling, as if everyone around them had the same sense that no one around them was real and nothing they did really counted. There were shouts of sudden wild laughter and the sound of running feet. When they turned one corner they practically tripped over two young fellas with their hands up each other's skirts. Winn gave an embarrassed yelp. Delly just laughed and pulled her on by.

"This *is* fun, isn't it?" she asked, once they'd turned another corner to a quieter stretch of hedge.

"I'm awfully glad you like it," Winn said. "I always like a maze. Gives the brain a bit of exercise, what?" She cleared her throat. "Anyway. I—had something that I wanted to ask you. Uh. I suppose I've *already* asked, in a way, but I wanted to, ah. Y'know. Ask *formally*."

"Winn," Delly said. Her heart went straight from a dawdle to a trot. "Begging your pardon, but don't choke to death on it. Ask me *what?*"

Winn cleared her throat. "I wrote to my parents," she said. "To tell them that I wanted to ask a girl to let me household her. Well, ah, I told my mother that I'd found a human vahn who I wanted to take to clan, but it's—close enough to the same thing, really. You don't need to worry about that. And—anyway. Oh, *blast* it." She fumbled in her pocket for a moment, then pulled out a long, thin golden chain. "It's from my mother's family," she said. "My father wears one, too. You can loop it around twice if it's too long, and wear it under your clothes if you'd rather. Oh, *dash* it all, you haven't answered yet. Will you have me, Dell?"

Yes! Delly's brain screamed at her. *Say yes, you silly tit!* She *should* say yes, she *wanted* to say yes, but her mouth didn't seem willing to form the words. She kept thinking about how she didn't have the first fucking idea of how to behave herself around people who knew which wine was what. She kept looking at Winn's dear, earnest face as she asked Delly so sweetly and uncomfortably to be her householded, entirely innocent of what a wretched, scheming, money-gobbling creature Delly had been this whole time. Delly knew that she ought to say yes, but her cursed mouth flapped itself like a sheet in the wind and unleashed a mumbled "I don't know."

If faces could be said to fall, then Winn's plummeted. "Oh," she said.

"I'm sorry," Delly said quickly. "I mean, *yes*."

"Oh," Winn said again. "Really?"

"Yes," Delly said. "Yes, of course. We've talked about it before, haven't we? I just—panicked." She had to fix this. It wasn't going to do a bit of good to her if one weak moment ruined the prospect that she'd worked so hard to cultivate.

"Well," Winn said after a moment. "If you're sure?"

"Yes," Delly said again. Her face had gone hot. "Sorry for, uh. Saying that I didn't know." She chanced a smile. It made her feel a bit better, as if the smile on her face meant that this was something to be excited about. It ought to be something to be excited about. She didn't understand why she couldn't work up a decent amount of excitement.

"I don't know if it's the sort of thing that you ought to apologize for, Dell," Winn said. She was smiling as if she was trying not to. Then she stuck her candle into the dirt and held up the chain in both hands. "May I?"

Delly ducked her head and swallowed as Winn gently looped the chain around her neck. The gold of it glimmered in the candlelight. When Delly looked up again Winn startled her with a kiss.

Everything made much more sense while they were kissing. This was a universe that was comprehensible: just their mouths and their breath, Delly's heart pounding, her hands at Winn's hips. It was all hot and good and simple while they were kissing, and then another pack of people came around the corner and Winn sprang back with an embarrassed little laugh, and Delly found herself firmly bound to the earth again.

"I'm sorry," Winn said. "Got a bit carried away there, what?"

"When you apologize it makes it seem as if you regret it," Delly said, and smiled, and threaded her hand through Winn's elbow, just as sweet as she could be. She wasn't going to fuck everything up for herself. Not this time. "And I hope you don't regret kissing me."

"Never," Winn said, and bent to pick up the candle. It illuminated the furrow between her eyebrows. "And you don't regret saying yes to me?"

"Of course not," Delly said, and swallowed her worries, and kept smiling, and let Winn lead her deeper into the maze.

16

Wherein Dellaria Immerses Herself in Work to
Dull Her Misgivings, and Is Exposed to the
Corrupting Power of Money

The evening of Delly's engagement was lovely. It really was. Finding her way through the maze with Winn was lovely. Stopping by the band shell and swaying together to the music was lovely. There was nothing in the whole evening that any young woman could possibly find to criticize: a kind, wealthy suitor draping you in gold under the romantic beams of the moon. Winn's proposal had, all together, been irreproachable in every way, which made Delly feel that much worse about being so completely discomfortable and uncombobulated about it.

She was still thinking about it as the deep indigo of the night sky leached away into the metaphorical wash water of the firmament. It was a puzzle. There was no *reason* for her to be so panicked over the prospect of a lifetime with Winn, no good reason at all. Winn was good and kind and clever, and probably the handsomest gull that Delly had ever successfully engaged in conversation. The only reason that anyone could possibly object to their union was if they thought Delly wasn't good enough for Winn. This was, Delly thought, undeniably true. Delly was an ill-mannered, ill-tempered, money-hungry slattern with a decidedly potato-like aspect to her personal appearance. Her having swindled Winn into proposing by pretending to be a better person than she was in actuality was nothing short of fraud. Delly could readily admit to all of this. The concern wasn't that Delly had committed a fraud—she'd done that plenty of times. It was that she was currently lying awake at night in their nice respectable hotel feeling sick to her stomach over it.

The unease stuck with her for the next several days, trotting along at her heels as she accepted the congratulations of the other women in their group and endured the joyful tears of her mother. Worst of all was Winn's happiness, as it only made Delly feel as if she ought to be feeling the same. She did her best to *act* as if she felt the same, for Winn's sake if for no other reason. She hated the thought of how crestfallen Winn would look if she ever discovered the truth.

It probably wouldn't have come as a shock to any longtime observer of Dellaria Wells when, as she cast about looking for something to make herself feel better, she cast herself into the bar she and Winn had gone to with Kail Mittens and looked for solace in a bottle of gin. What did come as a shock to Delly was the strange sense of relief she felt when Winn came striding into the place just before Delly hit the bottom of the bottle.

"Oh, Dell," Winn said. "Did you just drink all of that yourself?"

"*Mmph*," Delly said, and clung to her chair more tightly. She felt distinctly in danger of being bucked off, and *mmph* was the most articulate thing that she could presently seem to force out of her mouth.

"Oh, dear," Winn said. Then she leaned over Delly, wrapped her arms around her, and picked her up with a quiet "*Oof.*"

Delly made a muffled yawp. Winn shushed her. "As if you're in any condition to walk, *really*," she said, and carried her out of the bar and to a waiting cab.

Delly leaned against Winn in the cab and clung to Winn's hand, and eventually managed to convince her tongue to do something other than loll about uselessly in her mouth. "I have a secret, Winn," she said.

"Mm? Is it that you were just alone in that awful bar working your way through most of a bottle of gin? Because I'm sorry to tell you that it isn't a secret any longer, old thing."

"No, not that," Delly said, and gripped harder at Winn's hand. She was ashamed. She was all dizzy from the gin. She was just like her mother. "D'you think that I'm going to end up like my mam?"

"No," Winn said. "No, I don't think that. You're not very much like your mother at all." She kissed the top of Delly's head. That was nice. "Is that your secret? That you're worried about turning out like your mother?"

Delly shook her head. "That's not the secret," she said. "The secret's something that I haven't told you. That's how you know it's a secret. From not knowing about it." She was surprised that such a person as thoroughly clever as Winn would need to have the meaning of the word *secret* explained to her.

"Oh, I *see*," Winn said. "That makes sense, thank you." Then she said, "Why don't you close your eyes, Dell? I'll keep an eye on things for you while you get a bit of rest, eh?"

That sounded very sensible to Delly. "All right." She yawned. "You're *wonderful*."

"Thank you," Winn said. "You're a bit of a nice cut of beef yourself, what?"

"Confusing," Delly mumbled. Winn was always using confusing turns of phraseology. This one was so confusing that she had to close her eyes to think about it. She was still thinking about it when she nodded off.

She woke up, very briefly, when the carriage came to a stop and she was once again picked up and carried away in her betrothed's alarmingly powerful arms. Winn carried her all the way up the stairs, then whispered, "Sorry, old thing," and briefly set Delly down onto her wobbly hindquarters to unlock the door before scooping her up again, briskly de-booting her, and tucking her into bed.

The next thing that Delly knew her head was pounding, her mouth felt as if it had been left out on an exposed cobblestone for an hour after noon in midsummer, and she was gripped by the conviction that she had done something embarrassing. A moment later the recollection of her terrified clinging to the chair in the bar returned to her, and she gave a low groan that sounded, even to her own ears, dispiritingly similar to the lowing of an especially downtrodden cow.

"Good morning!" Winn trilled, and practically skipped across the room to draw back the curtains and welcome the battering rays of the morning sun. "It seems like *you* had a nice sleep. I think I could have hammered nails directly into the bed frame without waking you this morning."

"Feels like you're hammering nails directly into my skull right now," Delly muttered. "Is there water anywhere?"

"Plenty in the oceans, I expect," Winn said, and chortled heartily at her own joke before presenting Delly with a glass of water.

Delly drank it down in a few eager gulps, then sat up in bed. She still felt very much as though she'd been dragged backward through a garbage pit. In that sense, at least, the fact that Delly planned on producing red drip to be sold by a violent gang of gentlewomen made her less of a menace to society than Mrs. Medlow, who sold gin by the gallon every evening in her fairly respectable pub before retiring to her doily arbor just before dawn. It was a comforting thought, despite the fact that Delly found it entirely unconvincing.

"You look better already," Winn said. "Breakfast?"

They breakfasted on enough food for a smallish battalion with Winn's usual relish, then hoofed it down to the laboratory, where Abstentia was already hard at work producing the drip that Miss Cat had ordered, a task that managed to completely occupy all three of them for the next few days. It was just as well: Delly would have happily spent two days breaking rocks with a mallet if she'd thought it might help take her mind off of her personal life. In any case, with all of them working at full tilt, they managed to produce the amount of drip that Miss Cat had demanded with time to spare. When they went to meet her at Rat's place to deliver the goods, Delly thought that she caught a hint of surprise through the blur as they handed their parcels over.

She confirmed that impression a moment later, as Miss Cat opened up the package right there on Rat's desk, as bold as pepper. "I'm surprised that you lot managed it. I had thought that I would be spending my evening cornering you in whatever bolt-hole you've hidden yourself away in."

Delly tried to look as if she wasn't rattled. "Begging your pardon, Miss Cat, but I don't know why you would think such a thing, Miss Cat. I myself am a woman who honors her agreements, Miss Cat." This was a particularly shocking lie, but Delly thought that it suited the occasion.

Miss Cat opened up one of their bottles, dipped her little finger into the drip, and then dipped that finger into a bottle of clear liquid on the table. The liquid turned red. She gave a short nod. "It will do," she said, and started counting coins out into a small drawstring bag on Rat's desk. Delly tried not to watch with too much visible eagerness and had to school her expression when Miss Cat abruptly looked up. "How much more do you think that you'll be able to consistently produce per week?"

An opportunity. There it was. An opportunity to get closer to doing what they'd spent all of this time working toward. It was too bad that Delly's gut was swooping over it. She cleared her throat and did her best to say more or less what she, Winn, and Abstentia had planned on, and leave out any of her own creative enhancements. "Not any more than we did this week in the space that we have, Miss Cat, as we're operating out of very cramped quarters, Miss Cat. If we were given an opportunity to work out of a more expansive laboratory we would, of course, greatly improve our productivication, Miss Cat."

"*Productivication* is not a *word*," Miss Cat said. "And you needn't repeat my name so frequently, Miss Whelk. Once per sentence is *quite* enough." There was, through the blur, the suggestion of a thoughtful frown. "Are all five of you directly involved in the work of production?" Mura and Vitna had both come along this time, for the purpose of intimidation.

The sisters shook their heads. "*No*," Vitna said loudly, and moved her hand to the hilt of her knife as if she was concerned that she might be conscripted into performing dangerous feats of chemicastry against her will.

"And it's just you three, then?" Miss Cat asked, gesturing toward Abstentia, Delly, and Winn.

Delly thought for a moment of Mrs. Totham—she had made herself very useful during Abstentia's original creation of her formula, and would likely be even more useful in the case of any chemicastrical accidents—but then thought better of it and nodded. Usefulness notwithstanding, she didn't think that Winn would consider dragging an elderly lady straight into the Kind Companions' lair to be entirely regulation hammerball. "Yes, Miss Cat." Then, just to make sure that Miss Cat wouldn't mistake her for a woman who would allow a clanner to tell her how to speak: "Just the three of us involved in the *productivication*, Miss Cat."

"You are very impertinent, Miss Whelk," Miss Cat said. Delly, once again, internally cursed Abstentia for having chosen such an entirely unfortunate name for her. "Be here tomorrow morning at six. I'll have a man lead you to the place where you'll work. I'll expect to receive exactly quadruple this first order in a week's time." Then, all of a sudden, she tossed the drawstring bag of coins, hard, straight at Delly's head.

Delly yelped and ducked, but she hadn't truly needed to worry: Winn shot out one hand and caught the bag out of midair. When she spoke, her voice was like a stranger's: low and gravelly and well studded with menace.

"Bad fucking form, Miss Cat."

The illusion over Miss Cat's face rippled. It was from startlement or fear, maybe, but for a moment Delly caught a clear glimpse of a pretty, pointed, foxlike little face, the dark eyes gone very wide. Delly heard a muffled hiss behind her: Abstentia, she assumed, recognizing her classmate and not liking that she had. Then the illusion dropped down over her face again like a thick curtain, and when she spoke there wasn't so much as a tremor of nerves in her voice. "As I am the one paying you, I am also the one who shall determine what is and isn't bad form," she said. Then she waved a hand at them. "You may leave."

Winn actually growled at that, like a wild animal, and took a step toward Miss Cat. Delly took a moment to enjoy watching Miss Cat shrink away from her before grabbing at Winn's wrist. "Let's go," she said, and then snatched the bag of money out of Winn's hand and herded her out of the pawnshop, with the rest of their group crowding after her as if they couldn't wait to be free of the place.

"She wants *two hundred fucking ounces*," Delly hissed, as soon as they were out on the street. The bag of money was heavy in her hand. Twenty-five tocats in cash for a few days' worth of easy work. "That's one hundred tocats in a week. How shall we split it up? A quarter for each of us doing the production and the last quarter for the Tothams?"

Winn gave her a pop-eyed look. "You're going to *keep* it?"

Delly popped her eyes right back at her. "Of *course* I'm going to keep it. What else would I do with it, throw it into the river?"

"It's *drug* money," Winn said.

"I wouldn't take that money if you paid me," Abstentia said, and then winced.

Mura snorted. "Two-way split between us and you, then, Wells?"

"All right by me," Delly said, and they shook on it before Delly handed over twelve tocats to Mura and then slipped the rest into her own coat pocket. Delly thought it was some kind of rich cake that the clanners were getting on her tits about their scruples over where their money came from, considering that their cash came from their dear old relefting dads. She felt as a-jitter as if she'd just drunk a pot of strong coffee. All of that *money*. A few weeks of this and she could get her mam into that place in the countryside whether she tracked down Ainette Wexin and got ahold of that thousand-tocat reward or not.

It bothered her a bit, if she was perfectly fucking honest, that Winn was being such a foot cramp about it. She knew about Delly's mam, and Delly's having trouble making rent, and all of the rest of Delly's irritatingly enurchinated personal history. Or she knew enough, at least. She knew what Delly had told her, at least. She knew enough to be *understanding*, at least. Even if Delly hadn't exactly given her every detail. Delly didn't *owe* her any relefting details. The more Delly thought about it, the more she felt as if Winn had practically thrown rotten eggs at Delly for daring to want to earn money to help her poor ailing mother. She stewed over that for a few minutes as they walked and was taken off guard when Abstentia spoke up. "So now that we've managed to get access to the laboratory, do any of you have the slightest idea as to how we're to extract Ainette, if we find her there?"

"*I* have an idea," Delly said, and proceeded to make up a plan on the spot. "Befriend her with our disguises on, get her off somewhere on her own, Dok will hit her with some sort of—sleeping spell, and Winn will sling her over her shoulder and carry her off."

"*Sleeping spell*," Abstentia said, as if she'd never in her life heard something half as thickly bearded with absurdity. "You do know that it's *illegal* to distribute parameters for knocking out an unwilling person, don't you? Do you want me to write the parameters for this sleeping spell on my own, in addition to firing two hundred ounces of red drip?"

"Sure," Delly said. "If anyone was capable of it, it would be you, after all."

There was a moment of silence as Abstentia's desire to win the argument warred with her equally powerful urge to preen over her own brilliance. Eventually, to Delly's satisfaction, the second urge seemed to win out. "A modified type of drip might be a more practical solution than a purely parametrical approach," Abstentia said. "We know that Ainette takes drip, so it should be easy enough to get the stuff into her, I would imagine." Then, as if she couldn't help herself, she stuck in the knife and gave it a saucy wriggle. "I'll run some tests this evening and test the results on your mother, Wells."

"Oh, *fuck* you," Delly spat out, more stung than she would like to be by the dig.

"Don't fight, you two, it gives me a headache," Winn said. "And there's no reason to waste time with fighting when we're already late for lunch."

It was difficult to argue with this nutritional wisdom, so Delly and Abstentia managed to come to a truce for the duration of their luncheon, and by the time they'd finished eating, there seemed little point in reengaging in verbal combat. At that juncture, Delly made a silent commitment to herself: she would do her very best to avoid scrapping with Abstentia again, as much as she possibly could, until this whole endeavor was over in one way or another. There was nothing at all to be gained from antagonizing her at this point, and if she ever decided to walk out of their little informal pact, there was no way in the releft that Delly would be able to make their production quota on her own. Seeing as that Abstentia was refusing to take any pay for her labor, Delly would have to be even greater of a walking roof-collapse of a personage to annoy Abstentia into leaving before she'd had a chance to help further weigh down Delly's pockets.

With this in mind, Delly dove back into her work that evening with gusto, determined that the best course to keep herself from committing any shockingly irritating acts was to keep her hands unceasingly busy and her babble-hole uncompromisingly shut. She managed to surprise herself by making a success of it, even when her mother came slinking into the laboratory to float around the room like a dust mote and gaze at the drip they were making like a dog staring at a juicy roast resting on a countertop. Abstentia smiled at her.

"Don't worry, Mrs. Wells, we'll have something for you in just a moment. I'm making something very *special* for you to test for us this evening, as it happens."

And here, Delly thought, she had been doing so very well with her policy of silence. It really was very fucking like Abstentia to draw the urge to engage in mortal combat out of the people around her. "You mean that knockout stuff, Dok?"

Abstentia gave the sort of smile that Delly was more used to seeing from piemen assuring her that their wares contained nothing but the most natural and wholesome of ingredients. "The more *relaxing* formulation, yes," she said. "It's meant to provoke heaviness in the limbs and the inducement of deep, restful sleep along with the usual effects, so that it might be taken once in the evening and the user awakens feeling very pleasantly refreshed."

"Ooh, but that sounds just lovely," Delly's mam cooed.

"It sure does," Delly said. "You oughtta try it out yourself tonight, Abstentia. That way you'll be nice and well rested for our early start tomorrow morning."

"I only wish that I could," Abstentia said. "But I'm afraid that the state of my health makes it quite impossible for me to indulge in any drip or strong drink."

"That's a releftin'—" Delly started, and then caught herself just in time. She wasn't going to fight with Abstentia. "—pity. What if I paid a lad to catch you a few rats to test the stuff on before you let any people drip it? It's always best to be cautious when it comes to a new formulation, don't you think? It would be terrible if something went wrong."

Abstentia looked like she'd bitten down on a pebble in her bread, which was always how she looked when she knew that she'd been outmaneuvered. "You're right, of course. What a terribly clever idea, Miss Wells. Do you think that you *could* find a boy to catch rats for you?" Then, just as Delly opened her mouth to respond: "Ah, never mind, but of *course* you'd know boys who catch rats for a living. How very silly of me."

Abstentia Dok, Delly thought, really did have a hatchet where her tongue ought to have been.

"You're a very interfering creature, Dellaria," her mam mumbled. It was awfully like Delly's mam to complain about Delly having saved her from being tricked into swallowing something they were intending to use in a kidnapping.

"Don't you worry, Mam," Delly said, aiming to emulate Abstentia's jammy tones. Her mam seemed to respond well to being insincerely wheedled, even if it made Delly's throat burn to do it. "The latest batches I've made have been good and strong. Would you like a drop now, Mam?" Delly could be sick, saying it, but if she gave her mam a drop now and she toddled off for a sleep, she'd be less likely to come floating around Abstentia again later to ask for some of the new stuff. That was always how it was with Delly's mam. You were always stuck fussing around the edges of things, steering her toward a bad decision now because you hoped it'd keep her from a worse one tomorrow. Delly was tired to the fucking grave of it. Not that *that* was anything new, either.

"Oh, that would be *lovely*, Delly," her mam said. Cooing like a releftin' pigeon. Calling her *Delly*, too, all nice and sweet and cozy. Delly wanted to be mad about that. Instead, what slipped out of her mouth was, "Can I sit with you for a while after you drip, Mam?"

"I don't see why not," her mam said, and then stared at the little bottles of drip on Delly's work space until Delly scooped out a measure of the stuff for her with a dripping spoon. She watched as her mam took it, watched her face for changes even though she knew that it would be a while before the stuff started to do its work. Part of her wanted very badly to be able to see the moment when it changed, when she passed over from the woman her mother was when she was craving for something to the woman she became with gin or drip in her. Those were the two mothers Delly had grown up with, and though she wasn't a little girl ruled by her mam's moods now, there was still that kernel of a child in her who was always anxious to know which mother she'd be confronted with next.

At this moment, at least, she was a relatively calm and gentle mother, who gazed with kindness upon the daughter who'd just given her exactly what she wanted. "Let's go up to my room," she said. "I want to lie down. Get off of my feet."

Delly bit back any questions she might have wanted to ask about what exactly her mam had done today that she found so tiring, and followed her meekly up the stairs to the room she shared with Mrs. Totham, who was presently out engaging in her usual horrible Buttons-related research at the Sororal Order. The room was tidier than she had expected—Mrs. Totham's work, no doubt—and shabbily but fairly comfortably appointed, with a thick quilt on the bed and a little table with two mismatched chairs by the window. As soon as they had the door closed her mam gave a loud, undignified groan and fumbled to loosen her stays. "Releftin' things digging into my back—"

"Let me," Delly said, and rushed in to help make her mam comfortable. She was moving before she even had the chance to think about it. "Are you going to sleep, Mam, or just resting your eyes a bit?"

"Just resting my eyes," her mam said, which meant that she had the intention of having a full and proper sleep. Delly helped her undress down to her chemise, then pulled off her own shoes and sat down on the bed.

"Maybe I ought to lie down myself."

"No reason not to, if you're feeling tired," her mam said peaceably. "Want me to plait your hair for you? Ain't done that in an age."

Delly swallowed. Her mam had done that for her, sometimes, when Delly was a little girl and both of them happened to be in the right place at the relatively sober time. "All right."

Her mam hopped up to fetch a hairbrush, and Delly, without being told what to do, sat down on the floor next to the bed. Her mam sat on the edge of the bed and started to brush her hair. It felt nice. Delly sighed. "Mam," she said. "Did I tell you that I went to the countryside? And stayed in a manor with a bunch of clanners?" She didn't know why she was saying it. Probably hoping that her mam would be impressed by it, she supposed.

"I'm not surprised," her mam said. "I always knew you were clever enough to make it with the swells. Like your new *householder*."

"She ain't my householder yet, Mam," Delly said, feeling strangely embarrassed. "Still plenty of time for me to muck it all up."

"You won't muck it up," Delly's mam said, as dismissive as a cat told that she might not be very good at chasing rats. She started on the first plait, on the right side of Delly's head. She always used to do two of them and make them into a crown. "What was the manor like, then?"

Delly told her about it. Only the good parts, obviously—despite the fact that her mam had never expressed much of an inclination toward worrying about her in the past, it didn't seem like it would be very nice daughterly behavior to intentionally risk inciting an unprecedented bout of maternal concern. So she told her the good parts—about the sweeping lawns and the enormous trees, and how the air smelled strange and good and sweet. She told her about the different fine desserts every night, and the small parlor with all of the cushions and pictures and draperies in it, and the honest-to-fuck liveried footmen, though she neglected to mention that she had honest-to-fucked one of them. "It's nice in the country, Mam," she said. "It really is. The air really is better, like how they say. I figure it really could fix you up to breathe it, if you were feeling poorly. And the food tastes better. The vegetables were all fresher, and the fish didn't ever stink. You'd like it out there." She didn't know that for a fact. She was hoping, more. Hoping that her mam still had it in her to like the same things that anyone else would.

"That does sound nice," her mam said. She sounded a little funny. *Wistful*, maybe, was the word. Delly felt an exotic sense of optimism bubble up in her bosom.

"You could go," she said. "To the countryside, I mean. Have a nice rest in the peace and quiet."

Her mam snorted. "How? You want me to go labor in the fields? If I went out to the countryside I'd starve to death before I managed any *peace and quiet*."

"I would pay for it," Delly said, feeling very bold about herself. "You wouldn't have to worry about that, Mam. I'm making money now, ain't I? And—well, there's Winn. Or there will be, soon. You won't have to worry about paying for it, if you wanted to go."

"You're too eager about it," her mam said. She was starting to slur her words together. "Whaddya want me to go to the countryside for?"

"I just think you would like it, that's all," Delly said. She wanted to be annoyed at her mother being such a suspicious old cat, but really she was more impressed by her perceptiveness than anything else. "Have you ever left Leiscourt, Mam?"

"Not unless you count eight months in Lossgate Prison," her mam said, and finished Delly's last plait before lying down on the bed and pulling the blankets over herself. "You ought to lie down, too, Delly."

"It'll mess up my plaits," Delly said. Maybe it was a stupid thing to say. She wasn't entirely positive.

"Lie down, anyway," her mam said, and Delly obeyed. Her mam rolled over onto her side. "Tell me more about that manor," she said. She was slurring so badly now that it was difficult to make out the words. "About the gardens. Tell me about those."

Delly obeyed. She told her about the lawns and the ordered hedges, and the folly at the top of the hill. She told her about walking through the kitchen gardens and smelling the creeping thyme as she crushed it under her feet. She told her about the rose garden with the dropping petals, and the groundskeeper's cottage at the edge of the dark woods. She kept talking about it until her mam went silent. Delly felt a jolt in her gut and leaned in closer to her. "Mam?"

She didn't respond. Delly couldn't hear her breathing. She reached out and gave her a gentle shake. "Mam, are you all right?"

No response. Delly felt cold. It couldn't be like this. Not now, not with Delly right here to watch her, not after she'd made sure she'd only taken the safer kind of drip. This couldn't be the way it went. She shook her harder. *"Mam!"*

Her mam groaned then and swatted at her with a feeble hand. "Geddoff, Dellaria, m'*sleeping*."

Delly let herself collapse down onto the bed next to her. "Sorry, Mam," she said. "I won't do it again." That was a lie, though. She did do it again. She did it over and over again, checking that her mam was still alive and breathing until she thought that it was safe for her to sleep.

17

Wherein Dellaria Takes a Step Closer
and Encounters a Locked Door

Delly had her supper and went to bed not long after she finally left her mam. It wasn't her usual preference to go to bed early, but she felt far more than usually wrung out and decided that she ought to go to bed at a grandmotherly hour for the sake of getting a good night's rest and being able to meet Miss Cat's man at the appointed time the next morning in a state of well-rested glory. That was the plan, at least. The reality was that she ate her supper with Winn, lay down in the bed while Winn snoozed in an armchair over her book, and stared at the ceiling for an hour or so before silently climbing back out of bed, getting dressed, and heading down into the alley behind the hotel to smoke. Then she realized, to her annoyance, that her cigarette case was entirely empty, so the only thing left to do was walk a few blocks to a bar she liked to try and buy one off of the bartender.

When she walked into the place, though, she was almost immediately thrown off of her intentions. Her curly-headed friend Elo was there, as firmly planted as he ever was next to the stove in the corner. She tried to sidle up to the bar without him spotting her—she wasn't in the mood for a chat—but that was no good: she figured the fella had a bit of a nose for the scent of gallops past. He gave her a little wave. She sighed and walked on over. It felt inevitable, in a way.

"Hey now, Delly," he said.

"Hey, Elo," she said. "Don't suppose you could spare a cigarette?"

He handed her one. She lit it up and took a drag. He eyed her. "Don't suppose you came here looking for me?"

"Nope," Delly said. "Just came here looking for an asher."

He laughed. "Guess I could provide you with what you wanted either way, then." He cocked his head. "Don't suppose I could provide you with anything else? Seeing as how we're both here, I mean."

Delly shrugged and took another drag on her cigarette. "I'm betrothed," she said, "to a clanner." She felt herself being pulled toward a gallop with him anyway, straight toward exactly what she shouldn't do. There'd always been an inevitability to the fuckups of Dellaria Wells.

"Shit," he said. "Congratulations, then. That same prospect you told me about before, you mean? How'd you manage the game?"

"Fucked if I know," she said. "Where's your bolt-for now?"

"Down below the theater on Bride's Lane," he said. "I'm in a production there now with some fellas I know. The pay's shit, but it's free rent if you stay in the old catacombs. Ghosts don't bother us much, at least: I expect they're worried about a bunch of actors asking them to borrow money." He stood. He felt that inevitability, too, she knew. They were both used to living their lives this way.

She smiled at his joke, then nodded. Winn would still be asleep when she got back, if she went with him. All in innocence.

She stuck out her hand to shake with him. "I'll see you around, Elo. Chatter you up if any of her clanner pals are looking for a decent young fella with a fine singing voice."

He blinked, then sighed and smiled and shook his head, and wrapped her small rough hand in his bigger rougher one, then wrapped her whole self up in a squeeze. "That'd be a laugh," he said. "I ain't a decent enough fella for a clanner, so."

"Sure you are," she said, squeezing him back. Her eyes had started to sting, and her speech slipped further into what it had been when they were kids together. "*Fuck*, Elo. Th'art a ladder over 'em most. You don't know what they're like, those people. Most not a half-sen to thee, so."

He pulled back to look at her. "You all right? Your clanner ain't striking on thee? You know you've got folks in the neighborhood who'll help if you're in trouble, Dellaria. There's me, at least. Always room for one more down in the crypts, so."

"I know," she said, trying to pull herself together. "And I'm all right. My gull's all right. I guess—I dunno. That I thought I could jump into something better. But I dunno if there's anything on earth that's better all the way through. It's all just rotten in different parts. You wouldn't *believe* what some of those people are like, pup." All of those people in the hospital out of their minds on tainted drip. Ermintrude's dead, twisted face.

"Yeah, well," he said. "There's bad folks down here, too. At least with the clanners you'll eat all right. Hard times out there."

"Hard times," Delly echoed, and leaned in to give him another squeeze. "I'll keep my mirrors out for thee, pup."

"Might it so," he said. Didn't believe it, she knew. She didn't know if she believed it, either. When people around here left, they didn't come back because they'd planned on it. They came back because they'd gotten somewhere higher and then fallen. "Good luck, Delly Wells."

"And to thee," Delly said, and left. On the walk back, her cheeks felt cold. It took her a while to realize that it was because she'd been crying. Strange. She wasn't really sure why.

When she got back to the room, Winn was sitting up in bed, clearly waiting for her. She looked a little pale. "Where were you?"

She sounded sharper than she normally did. Delly frowned. "Out for a smoke," she said. "Needed to clear my head."

"Was it a man?" Winn asked. Her voice sounded tight. "Like that footman back at Crossick Manor?"

"What in the *releft*?" Delly said, astonished. "No, it wasn't a man. I had a damn *smoke*. And—how do you know it was a footman, anyhow?"

"I'm not as stupid as you think I am, Dellaria," Winn said. "I riliftin' figured it out. Was it *really* just a smoke?"

"*Yes*," Delly said. She really was getting annoyed now. "And you can go and ask the bartender at the Stag's Leap if you don't believe me. I was in there for all of five minutes, and left on my own."

Winn sagged like an old mattress. "I'm sorry, Dell," she said. "It was just—a bit scary, really. Waking up and not knowing where you were, I mean."

"That's all right," Delly said, a bit stiffly. "I ought to have left a note." And Winn ought to have trusted her, even if Delly, historically, had not been worthy of that trust. She wanted to be *treated* as if she was worthy of it, in any case. What was the point of having behaved in a moral and dignified fashion if one's betrothed would accuse one of having fucked the nearest footman in any case?

Delly carried her wounded dignity over to the basin to splash water onto her face, then undressed and put herself to bed at Winn's side. There she tenderly nursed her poor injured ego until it was improved enough for her to say, "I'm sorry that I frightened you."

"I'm sorry that I spouted unfounded accusations at you the instant you walked back through the blinkin' door," Winn said. Then: "Really, Dell. I'm awfully sorry. It was absolutely beastly of me."

"That's all right," Delly said, and expressed her pleasure at being the recipient of a good, healthy apologetic grovel by snuggling up closer to Winn's side. "Say," she said, her voice thoroughly syrup drenched. "I don't suppose that you might like to let me—"

"Not until we're *householded*, Dell," Winn said firmly.

Delly sighed. "I don't know if I'm really cut out to be such a thoroughly moral person."

Winn gave her arm a comforting pat. "You're doing beautifully at it," she said. "G'night, Dell. Try to get some sleep. We've all sorts of crimes to commit in the morning."

Delly laughed. From under the bed came an odd, cacophonous jingling sound, like the doors of several hat shops all being opened simultaneously.

Winn and Delly both froze. The jingling faded into silence. Delly, with a sense of mounting horror, whispered, *"Buttons?"*

There was a delicate scrabbling noise, and Delly watched with dull despair as Buttons made his gut-churning way out from under the bed, climbed up the thick hotel quilt, and came to rest upon her beblanketed knee. Delly and Buttons regarded each other. Buttons, the sly thing, gave a not-very-convincingly mouse-ish squeak.

"What on earth are you doing *here*, Buttons?" Winn asked. "Is something the matter with Mrs. Totham?"

Buttons gave a dismissive whistle, then marched up the bed and curled himself into a bony ball between their pillows. Delly recoiled. Winn smiled. "He's really a rather cunning little thing, isn't he?" she said. "*Oh*, do you know what would be awfully nice?" She hopped out of bed and rummaged about in her trunk for a moment before returning with a short scrap of pink ribbon in her hand. "I'd been wondering what to do with this," she said, and then tied it in a neat bow around Buttons' skeletal neck. "There. You look *wonderfully* smart, Buttons!"

Buttons purred like a cat, which struck Delly as a particularly flesh-prickling offense against nature, though she decided that, in this instance, she would not at all be served by the contribution of any clever commentary on the subject. Winn patted her arm again. "Well! Now that all of the excitement's over, we really should try to get some sleep."

"If it's at all possible," Delly said darkly, eyeing the wicked unliving creature currently preening in his new ribbon a few inches away from her nose. Buttons made a sound like the cooing of an unusually self-satisfied dove. Delly rolled over and endeavored, with all of her might, to pretend that Buttons was nothing more than an extremely irritating figment of her imagination.

She must have eventually drifted off, because what felt like a moment later she was jolted awake by the sound of one of the hotel maids knocking on the door as Delly had requested the previous day. She and Winn groaned their drowsy ways into their clothes, then tossed some coffee and toast down their throats. They were about to head for the door when Buttons emerged from underneath a pillow and honked like an imperious goose.

"Oh," Winn said. "Did you want to come with us, Buttons?"

Buttons honked again. Delly frowned. "I don't know if Miss Cat would look too kindly on our bringing a . . . *Buttons* with us."

"Miss Cat doesn't have to know. I'm sure that he'll be as quiet as a mouse," Winn said, and chortled heartily to herself as she placed her reticule onto the bed so that Buttons could crawl inside. He did so, though not before making a distinctly rude noise at Dellaria. Delly made a rude noise right back. "Don't squabble, you two," Winn said, and the three of them donned their magical disguises and hunkered more deeply into the comfort of Winn's reticule, respectively, before sallying forth into the relative peace of Leiscourt just before dawn.

When they arrived at Rat's shop, Abstentia was already there, her obvious irritation at having to be here at this house only emphasized by the deep wrinkles of her old-woman face. "How kind of you to finally join me," she said.

"Oh, *hush*, Ab—*Miss Apple*, we're here with time to spare," Winn said cheerfully.

"*Miss Apple?*" Abstentia repeated, and looked as if she'd like to argue about her new moniker—Delly didn't see why: it was certainly a sight better than *Miss Whelk*—when a young boy appeared from the alley beside Rat's shop. The same boy, in fact, as the able young person whom Delly had handed over their product sample to the week before.

"Hey there," Delly said, friendly-like.

"Hey," the Able Young Person said back, and held out three lengths of blue ribbon. "Miss says that you're meant to tie these around your necks, miss."

"Oh, *does* she say that? Well, you can tell your *miss* that—" Abstentia began, and then gave a muffled yelp as Winn kicked her in the shin.

"It's not nice to kick old ladies, miss," said the Able Young Person, his eyes as full of reproach as his knees were covered in scabs.

"I'm *not*!" Abstentia said, just as Winn said, "I *didn't*!" Then they both winced, shut their mouths, and reached out to take a ribbon.

Delly took a ribbon as well, though she waited for Abstentia and Winn to do some mumbling of parameters to identify what magic had been done to them before she was willing to wrap it around her own neck. The instant she did she deeply wished that she hadn't. The thing was very clever and deeply awful: it blacked out everything in her field of vision except for the people and the street directly below her feet. She'd be able to follow the boy and avoid running headlong into strangers, but she wouldn't be able to get so much as a peep at a street sign or distinctive bit of local architecture.

"Goodness, what sort of maniacal personality do you think might have written these parameters?" Winn asked. She sounded almost pleased. "It gives me a headache just to *think* about it. I say, boy, do you think that your mistress would let me borrow one of these?"

"Not *likely*, miss," the boy said, and started walking off.

"Ah, well. It doesn't cost anything to ask," Winn said, and went striding on her long legs after him.

It was, it turned out, fairly relefting dizzying to go charging down a busy street following a young boy with no way to see anything around you. After a few minutes' worth of it, Delly had to stop and take a few deep breaths to keep from being sick. There was no time for too much of that, though: they were still moving, dodging through crowds of decently dressed people as they went. Delly tried to focus on that, on what she *could* see instead of what she couldn't, and what she could hear being said around her. The accents. The kinds of shops mentioned in passing conversation. Delly Wells might be an ignorant piece of trash who couldn't make it through a full year at Weltsir, but she knew her damn city. The cobblestones were mostly square-edged here, and dark gray. Some girls were exclaiming over new Esiphian hats they could see. There was the trickle of water from a fountain.

Then, there: the clanging of a fire truck bell. Ardwin's Square, with the fountain at the center and the fire station at the east side. Walking forward then. Not too far, five hundred feet or so, and then a right turn. More walking, and then a left. The crowds thinning out now, and the cobbles getting older and rougher as the neighborhood got poorer. More walking. A turn. A stop. The sound of a door that the boy led them through, and the door closing. "You can take the ribbons off," he said. Delly did. She was trying not to smile. They were somewhere around Penitent's Way, by the Elder Hall, she'd bet a tocat on it. Let her take this trip a few more times and she'd have it down to the fucking number on the door.

In the meantime, she would have to settle for taking a good peep at the house they were presently in, which was entirely unlike what Delly had expected. She had, she supposed, expected some sort of abandoned warehouse. This was just an ordinary house—or ordinary, she supposed, by the standards of rich people, even if it was in a ragged neighborhood on the edge of West Leiscourt. It made sense, when she put a moment of thought into it: a Fine Young Lady renting a warehouse on the outskirts of town might raise a well-bred eyebrow or two, but no one would think twice about a Fine Young Lady renting a house in a respectable neighborhood to live in to do . . . whatever it was that Fine Young Ladies did when they were in town instead of in the country. She would have to consult with Winn on the subject later.

The Able Young Person was leading them down the hall now, which gave Delly more of an opportunity to survey the terrain. It was a very strange place. There were signs, here and there, of it being lived in—she spotted fresh flowers in a vase, and packages and calling cards on a table in the front hall—but there was an oddness to it, too. For all that Delly was ignorant of the usual ways of the rich, she was fairly sure that those packages ought to have been whisked away by the servants, and not just left there in the front hall, and that their disreputable crew shouldn't have been let in by the front entrance to begin with. And while the front hall and the few rooms that she caught a quick glimpse of as she passed them looked fine enough, with thick curtains at the windows and flowers on the tables, the farther they passed into the house, the more it looked like a place that had been closed off for a summer in the country and never opened up again. There were paintings or mirrors in the hall that had been shrouded in cloths to keep off the dust, and there was a funny, musty smell to the air as if it had been a long time since anyone had opened a window.

The Able Young Person led them up a grand staircase then, and through a tall, wide set of doors, and into a ballroom. That's what it was. A ballroom, empty but for three big, wide tables with three sets of laboratory equipment atop them, exactly like their set back at the house except triple the size. "Good God," Abstentia said, in her creaking old-woman voice. "This is certainly the best use of a ballroom that *I've* ever seen."

"You *would* think that," Delly mumbled. It really was exactly like Abstentia to think that using a ballroom as a laboratory was a jollier use of the space than *throwing parties in it*.

"I'm very glad to hear that you think so," said Miss Cat, and all three of them twisted around as if they'd been caught rifling through her closet to watch her come gliding into the room in a very smart red dress. "As you'll be spending a great deal of time in here." She made a very conspicuous show of checking her pocket watch. "It's just before seven now. I expect that you'll have to be here until at least eight in the evening if you want to keep to the production schedule that you've agreed to."

"Oh, sure," Delly said, when neither of the others spoke up in response to this laughable statement. It made sense, really: it occurred to her that she was the only person in the room to have ever held down an actual relefting *job*—even if she had only managed it for a few weeks at a time. "When will we have our lunch and supper breaks, then?"

Miss Cat's befuddlement was visible even through the blur. "I *beg* your pardon?"

"I'm a card-carrying member of the pipelayer's union, miss," Delly said. This was, technically, true, even though the card she was carrying had a fellow named Arran Beckle's name on it. "Generally, miss, if you're going to dictate the hours that we work in addition to our production quotas, miss, then I'd expect regular breaks to be written into our contract, miss."

"I didn't say that I would *dictate* anything," Miss Cat said, even though she had very clearly just tried to. "Work when you like. Just have my two hundred ounces ready on time, and there will be no call for there to be any unpleasantness between us. When you're ready to leave, my boy will lead you out. Do *not* attempt to leave independently: I have warded the doors and windows." And with that she marched out of the room just as abruptly as she had sailed into it.

They were all quiet for a moment. Then Delly whispered, "Is she still in the house?"

Abstentia pulled a notebook from her pocket, paged through it, and encanted from the parameters that she found. Then she grimaced. "She's warded the place against basic scrying work. I could dismantle the wards, but she'd likely be alerted to— What on earth is *Buttons* doing here?"

Said skeletal creature, who had clambered from Winn's reticule up onto her shoulder, warbled like a canary. Winn shrugged. "He wanted to come along this morning," she said. Delly's betrothed was getting as bad as Mrs. Totham when it came to the ascribing of complex opinions to a dead mouse. Winn looked down at Buttons. "I say, Buttons, I don't suppose that *you* might be able to tell whether or not Miss Cat is still in here?"

Buttons meowed like a cat. Then he made a sound like a brick being dropped into a mostly empty well. A splash with a great deal of echo to it.

Winn looked pleased. "She's gone, you mean?"

Buttons said, "*Bong.*"

It sounded, to Delly, like a particularly affirmatory bonging.

"Right!" she said. "I'll have a look around to see if I can find any signs of Ainette, then."

Abstentia looked as if she had just smelled a rotten egg. "Oh, really, are we taking our cues from *Buttons* now?"

Buttons made a noise that ought to have produced a smell like rotten eggs. "If anyone tries to stop me, I'll say that I was looking for the privy," Delly said. She was feeling eager to have a good, healthy snoop. Buttons, for his part, gave a high-pitched whistle and flung himself off of Winn's shoulder, landed on the floor with a loud clatter, and galloped over toward Delly's feet. There he went up onto his haunches and gave Delly what she could only consider a *beseeching* look. "Ah," she said. "Did you want to come with me, Buttons?" Despite her usual feelings toward Buttons, she thought it would be pretty hard of her to be rude to him after he'd helped her out with the Miss Cat detection services.

"That sounds like a good idea to me," Winn said. "Safety in numbers, what? You two have a look round while we get things set up in here, and we can all have a jaw about it while we get the production started, and take more time to all hunt around together while the drip is settling later." The drip had to be filtered, separated, and given time to settle out again twice before it reached Abstentia's exacting quality standards.

"Sounds like a good idea to me," Delly said, and crouched down and held out her hand to let Buttons climb up her sleeve and onto her shoulder. She even managed not to shudder. Then she and Buttons went back downstairs to have a nice leisurely look through the place.

There wasn't much to see, really, on the first floor. A bit depressing. Just a lot of dull, mostly empty rooms, once you got past the front parlor, where a lady might entertain guests of an afternoon. She returned to that grand staircase to head to the second story and noticed the dust on the balustrades. That feeling of strangeness returned to her, and this time she managed to grab ahold of what the place reminded her of: it was a stage set. Just enough of everything to make it look like a fine lady's home from the outside to someone who wasn't looking too closely.

Things didn't get any cheerier upstairs on the level of the laboratory, though they did get a bit more interesting, with most of the interest coming from a number of doors that Delly couldn't open. Three of them, to be precise about it. Delly glanced down at Buttons, who was still perched on her shoulder like something out of a pirate's most rum-sodden nightmares. "I'd say that *this* looks a bit promising, eh, Buttons?"

Buttons said, "*Bong.*" It was an unusually agreeable-sounding bong, as the bongings of Buttons went. Delly, thus encouraged, soldiered onward and started inspecting the locks. The first one or two, at the end of the hallway closer to the main staircase, were nothing particularly extraordinary. She recognized the make of the physical locks, and there was only the ordinary hum of very ordinary warding spells around the doorframe. Doing her little melting trick would be no good here—she needed to be able to come back tomorrow, and Miss Cat would certainly notice if one of her nice modern locks suddenly stopped working—but Delly had other ways of getting past a troublesome lock.

"I just need to come back tomorrow with my lockpicks and this will be half taken care of," she said to Buttons. "I suppose I'll have to ask Abstentia for help with the wizardy bits."

Buttons made another of his very rude noises and followed it up with a high-pitched "*Bing!*" like the sound of a bell you would use to summon someone to wait on you in the sort of shop that Delly was generally too embarrassed to enter. For a brief moment, as the *bing!* floated in the air, the subtle humming of the doorway wards went silent. Then, a moment later, they returned, buzzing along as if they hadn't just been temporarily o*bing*erated into nothingness.

Delly craned her neck in order to eye Buttons more effectively. He looked just as he always did, which was to say that he looked absolutely horrible. "Have you been able to *bing* like that this whole time?"

Buttons said, "*Bong.*"

Delly waited for a moment to see if any further explanation might be forthcoming. No further explanation forthcame. *Bong* was, apparently, it. "Well," she said eventually. "Let's have a look at that other door, then."

This was the door that she was dreading looking at more closely, though she couldn't say why, exactly. She'd only given it a quick look before, squinting up the dark narrow stairwell to the attic just for long enough to see a door with a heavy padlock on it. Maybe that was what gave her a bad feeling about it. From what she'd heard from her friends in service, the servants' quarters should ordinarily be up there under the roof. Not something that would need a big padlock on the outside of the door, unless Miss Cat was such a nightmare of an employer that she had to keep her maids under lock and key to prevent them from slipping away in the middle of the night.

If that was it, though, then it made no sense that Delly's dread only increased as she climbed the stairs. There was something wrong about that door, something that churned her guts like butter. Something familiar that she was having trouble placing. "I don't like this," she said aloud.

Buttons, unnervingly, did *not* say, *bong.*

They reached the door, and Delly leaned in to inspect the padlock, which was a big, complicated, modern thing that she didn't know whether or not she could pick. She was practically nose to keyhole with it, trying to figure out the make, when she noticed the noise. At first she thought it was the not-sound buzz of Miss Cat's wards, until she started listening more closely and realized that it wasn't that at all. It was a strange, grinding, chattering hum, with the occasional screech of metal on metal. She couldn't stop hearing it now. It almost seemed to be getting louder, along with the rising sense of *wrongness* that seeped through the doorframe, and suddenly Delly remembered where she had felt this before. The suit of armor. The spider-things. The strange devices that Ainette had killed to bring to life.

Then, just next to her ear, Delly heard a man's voice. It was a low, rasping voice, as if it had gone unused for a very, very long time. *"Dellaria Wells. Beware!"*

Delly screamed, startled, and tried to whirl around to see who had spoken. She just had time to think, *Mr. Trell?* before she lost her balance and fell.

18

Wherein Fires Are Started

The next thing Delly knew, she was lying on her back, staring up at the ceiling, listening to a noise like a steam engine on the express line from some pagan hell shrieking directly past her right ear. She winced, which she immediately regretted—it made her head pound even harder—and gave a small muffled sob. She had fallen down the stairs, obviously, and given her head a good wallop and knocked the wind out of herself on the way down, and now she felt shaken and weak-limbed and pitiful. She rolled her head a bit to the right in order to look directly at Buttons, who was sitting up on his bony haunches, making a sound like a teakettle's vengeful ghost. "Buttons," she managed. *"Please stop."*

Buttons stopped. Then he put one repulsive little paw gently onto Delly's cheek, which Delly thought was either a wonderfully tender gesture, as gestures from unliving mice went, or a sign that Mr. Trell planned on leaving his current puny form and entering Delly's body via her right nostril.

Fortunately, she wasn't forced to discover the answer one way or another, as a moment later there was a clatter of running feet and

Winn and Abstentia loomed above her. From this angle, at least, they looked a bit concerned. "Goodness, Dell, what are you doing on the riliftin' floor?"

"Oh, for God's sake, Cynallum, she *obviously* fell down the stairs," Abstentia said, which roused Winn from her fog of befuddlement enough to offer Delly a hand up. Delly held out her own hand to let Buttons clamber into it before allowing Winn to haul her to her feet. Abstentia was glowering. "What on earth were you doing that led to you tumbling down the attic stairs?"

"Looking at that evil door up there," Delly said. She still felt very much as if her brain had endured a vigorous whisking. "And then Mr. Trell startled me."

Winn's eyebrows leapt like hairy pole-vaulters. "*Mr. Trell?* Do you mean—*Buttons*, you mean?"

"I *think* it was Mr. Trell," Delly said, suddenly uncertain. "He said my name." She looked at Buttons. Buttons looked back at her, then gave a squeak as unassuming as any emitted by the most ordinary house mouse to have ever nibbled biscuits.

"*You're* being awfully coy," Delly told him. "It was nice of you to call for help, though. Who *knows* how long I would have spent on the floor if you hadn't."

Buttons put his horrid paw onto her cheek again and said, "*Bong.*"

The rest of them waited for the customary uncomfortable moment to pass before they spoke. This time it was Winn who broke the post-*bong*etary silence. "What was so evil about the door, Dell?" The furrows between her eyebrows indicated that she thought the only evil thing in the vicinity was how hard Delly had just banged her head.

Delly explained about the enormous padlock and powerful wards, and the strange, sickening, familiar feeling it had given her. "It's worse here, though," she said. "Worse than the armor and the spider-things." She swallowed. "Much worse."

Winn had gone a little pale. "If the other two were bad because she'd used a dead animal to animate those . . . *things*," she said. "Then what do you think could *possibly* be behind—"

"I think that there's no use in our speculating about it," Abstentia said briskly. "We'll need to study the lock and wards, *calmly*, and make a plan for getting past them as well as a plan to defend ourselves against *anything* that we might find inside. In the meantime, Wells, what did you make of the other doors?"

Delly shrugged, a bit thrown off course. "I dunno. They weren't too strange. Get me a pick and between me and Buttons we'll get you in there in two minutes."

Abstentia looked puzzled. "What does *Buttons* have to do with anything?"

"Oh, he can take down wards by *bing*'ing at them," Delly said. Her head still ached.

Winn was staring at her. "Are you *sure* that you feel all right, Dell?"

"No," Delly said. "I feel awful. I *do* know what I'm relefting well saying, though. I guess you probably don't have a lockpick on you?"

Winn immediately started pulling the pins out of her hair. "Will any of these work?"

Delly, after a moment in which she dully admired how nice Winn looked with her silver hair tumbled carelessly around her shoulders, reached out to take one of them. "Would you mind if I bent the tip of this a bit?"

"Not at all," Winn said, and Delly got to enjoy a few lovely moments of Winn watching her and looking impressed and admiratious as Delly pulled just enough heat into her fingertips to bend the pin into the shape that she needed at the tip. Delly blew on it for a few moments to cool it off, then walked over to the nearest door to take her shot at the lock. She glanced down at her shoulder before she got started. "Are you ready to *bing* after I get this lock open, Buttons?"

Buttons said, "*Bong.*"

Abstentia spoke up then. "I'm going to lay down an alarm on the front door, in case Miss Cat comes back. God knows that the last thing we need is for her to reappear when we're elbow-deep in her linen cupboard."

Delly winced, annoyed at herself for not having thought of that. She'd like to blame the blow to the head, but it could probably be just as fairly put down to her being naturally heedless and incompetent. "Thanks, Dok."

Abstentia nodded and strode off, and Delly got to work on the lock. She didn't encounter any surprises in it, unpleasant or otherwise. It was a very ordinary lock, just like a few others she'd worked on before. The only real difficulty she faced at the moment was not fumbling this from the pressure of being watched. She'd never attempted to pick a lock for an audience before, except for one incident when the audience was a police officer who happened to be walking home from his beat and her performance ended with a wild sprint down a number of alleyways.

Eventually she got everything lined up correctly and smiled at the satisfying sound of the bolt sliding free. "I'm ready for your *bing*, Mr. Trell."

Buttons *bing*'ed. The humming of the wards stopped. Winn jumped. "Goodness, that's quite a riliftin' party trick, eh? How do you suppose he does that?"

"No idea," Delly said, and pushed her way through the door. She didn't think that any good could possibly come of thinking too deeply about the *bing*s and *bong*s of Buttons.

It was a study, or maybe an office—whichever sort of room high-quality types sat in when they needed to write letters or read long, dry books or count their money. It was dark inside, with the thick curtains drawn, and the space was cluttered with bookshelves and two armchairs and a desk that all seemed too big for the room. Winn looked toward Delly. "Shall we start with the desk?"

They started with the desk. The desk drawer had been warded as well, but Buttons *bing*'ed it open with no apparent difficulty, and the cheap lock only took a few seconds of delicate jiggling with the pick before the drawer popped open.

The desk, to Delly's extreme disappointment, wasn't full of stacks of banknotes for thousands of tocats. Just letters, mostly, and a small black ledger. Delly grasped a handful of letters to browse through, while Winn started flipping through the ledger.

The letters were far less boring than they'd looked at first glance. They were, in fact, *love letters*, and the kind of love letters that from a fine gentleman would probably be called *passionate*. If a fella from Delly's neighborhood had written them, they'd probably be called *dirtier than the bottom rungs of a barstool*. No wonder Miss Cat kept them under lock and key. Delly kept reading them for a while despite the fact that she was fairly sure that the gentleman was extremely unlikely to slip any information as to Ainette's whereabouts between rapturous descriptions of dear Clairelle's creamy bosom. Delly wrinkled her nose. "Winn, *you're* an educated personage. Would you say that you'd ever found a gull's bosom to be particularly *creamy*?"

Winn's head popped up from the ledger. Her expression appeared generally confounded. "I don't know about *creamy*," she said after a moment. "You mean—in the pale sense, or in the . . . *liquid* sense?"

"I couldn't say," Delly said after a moment of consideration. "In the silken sense, maybe."

"That would depend," Winn said firmly, "on whether or not the cream had clotted. Oh, I *say*, Dell, have a peep at this!"

Delly had a peep. Winn was pointing at a bunch of numbers. "Very numerical," Delly said after a moment.

"Oh, come on, Dell," Winn said in a surprisingly Abstentiated tone. "Let's heave to and focus on something that isn't creamy bosoms for a moment, shall we? I think these are production numbers here, and income over here at the far right. There's a few months in a row where it looks like she was producing about twenty ounces a week. Then *this* happened about two weeks ago." She pointed out one of the entries in the ledger.

Delly stared at it for a moment before it registered. "Five *hundred* ounces?" It didn't make any sense. "But even if she's got Ainette working for her, too, how the fuck could two people *possibly* make *five hundred ounces* of drip in a *week*?"

"I don't know," Winn said. "But, Dell—maybe making someone work like that would be a reason for needing a padlock to keep them in."

"Oh," Delly said. She suddenly felt sick. "Aw, *fuck*, Winn. Do you really think she's locked in that horrible attic right now?" She chewed on her lip for a second, thinking. "But why would there be necromancy leaking out around the door? You don't need to kill any cats to fire drip. She could easily just do everything that Dok can do without necromancy coming into it."

"I don't know," Winn said after a moment. "I can jolly well assume that it's not being done for any reason you'd like to tell your Elgarite great-aunt about, though."

"The door is alarmed," Abstentia announced as she walked into the room. "What would offend my Elgarite aunt?"

"Doing necromancy in the attic," Delly told her.

"Spoken like a woman who's never met any of my aunts," Abstentia said. "Aunt Veritasa would gladly sacrifice any number of other women's children in an attic if it meant she could secure a decent marriage for one of my spotty-faced cousins. Have you found anything of interest in here?"

Winn showed her the ledger and briefly explained the conclusions they had come to, including their strong suspicion that Ainette, Abstentia's friend, might be chained up in the attic and forced to produce drip day and night for Miss Clairelle, Abstentia's peer and classmate. Abstentia's expression barely flickered. Instead, she glanced down at her pocket watch and said, "That first batch will be ready to be filtered soon. If we want to check that second door, we'll have to hurry."

Winn frowned. "Abstentia," she said, after a moment, "are you all right?"

"Of *course* I'm *all right*," Abstentia snapped. "Come on, Wells. You can work on that lock while I look at that attic door. I'll have to examine the wards before I can start writing parameters to take them down." Then she whirled around and strode back out into the hall.

Delly and Winn exchanged a glance, then silently began putting everything back into the desk exactly as they had found it. Then they left the room, making sure that it was locked properly before they closed the door.

The next room was nothing but storage for drip ingredients, and a cursory search of the place didn't yield any further information. They were already out of the room, double-checking the lock and resetting the wards, when Abstentia came down the attic stairs, her face the color of snow in a city street three days after it had fallen, a notebook clutched tightly in her left hand. "You're right, Wells," she said. "It's— a very striking sensation, at that door." She cleared her throat. "I tried to—make some notes on the wards, or what I could learn from them after firing a basic Reclid's query. I . . . think that she might be using several interlocking layers of—of Morgan's—" Her voice broke and she stopped. "I'm sorry," she said, and cleared her throat again.

"Abstentia," Winn started, but Abstentia was already heading down the hallway toward the ballroom.

Delly and Winn followed her, and the three of them set back to work in their nice new laboratory, silently setting up the second filtration and starting up the next batch. They worked like that for a few hours, all of them a bit tense and quiet. They worked until past noon, until the sound of Winn's stomach growling grew too loud to easily ignore. "Dreadfully sorry, old things," she said. "Do you think that we might be able to send that young lad out to fetch some sandwiches?"

"If we can find him, maybe," Delly said, and then promptly volunteered herself to lead the hunt. She would have taken a much worse excuse to get out of the laboratory and stretch her legs a bit, but going off to fetch food for her householder-to-be seemed like a nice, well-behaved, wifely use of her time. She didn't find the Able Young Person, though: instead she only found a Harried Aged Housekeeper, who allowed for the possibility that she might send up a plate of sandwiches later, if she had the time. She also seemed to be under the impression that the strange women working upstairs were a portrait painter and her two assistants, which was so absurd an assertation on Miss Clairelle's part that Delly found herself perplexed. How on earth had she gotten away with committing crimes for this long when she was so counfoundingly bad at making up lies about them? It must, Delly thought, be a side effect of being a clanner. Any sort of outrageous lie sounded more like the most crystalline of truths when spoken in an expensive-sounding-enough accent.

Delly made her way back up to the laboratory, and a platter of horribly dry ham sandwiches and a large pot of very weak tea arrived not long after. Winn, ordinarily so full of vigorous good cheer, appeared quite deflated. "Gracious," she said. "We knew that Miss Clairelle was feeling a bit of financial strain, but it seems a dashed shame to economize on tea and butter." She still ate three sandwiches despite her disappointment, and seemed slightly cheered when Delly reassured her that they would have a really good hot dinner after they'd knocked off work for the evening.

The time for leaving work came earlier than expected: Winn had emitted only the most indirect of musings on the better restaurants near Rat's shop when the Able Young Person appeared in the doorway, where he leaned pitifully against the doorframe as if to suggest he had within the past few hours contracted some horrible wasting disease that prevented him from standing upright on his own. "Say," he said. "Don't suppose you'll be finishing here anytime soon? My ma's expecting me for supper in an hour, and she'll give me a good wallop if I'm late."

"Well!" Winn said. "We'd certainly want to avoid any wallopings, wouldn't we, Miss Whelk?"

"Oh, sure," Delly said. "I never like to see a child walloped. Excepting, of course, when he *absolutely* deserves it." At this juncture she and the

Able Young Person exchanged a bit of an eyeball of understanding, both of them either currently being or having previously been children who deserved a good solid walloping during at least half of their waking hours.

This evening, at least, the Able Young Person would abide unbe-walloped: Abstentia announced that they had made several ounces more drip than they needed to in order to meet their goal for the day, which meant that they could clean up and then go home immediately. The walk home, in the dark, was even more dizzying than the walk to work, though it also yielded more information: the dinner carts were out, and Delly recognized the booming voice of one fellow who sold fried fish in Poorman's Square every other night. Delly resolved to ask him tomorrow where he went every *other* night. Then she concentrated on looking at her shoes before she got sick.

The next day, Winn got up even earlier than she had the day before, in order to purchase provisions for their luncheon before they set out for Rat's. She was so eager and early, in fact, that she dragged Delly to Rat's shop about half an hour before either Abstentia or the Able Young Person had arrived. It was raining that morning, the sort of distinctly Leiscourtian rain that could be better described as a mist bent on vengeance. They lingered there in cold, damp silence, stamp-ing their feet and blowing on their hands, until a very amused-looking Rat popped her head through the door. Today's hat was decorated with a furry animal of some sort. Delly tried to avoid looking at it for too long, for fear of making eye contact. "*Hullo* again, you two!" Rat said. "Come on in. I just made a pot of coffee."

Winn opened her mouth as if to make a polite excuse, which pro-pelled Delly into diving through the door before she could be forced into standing in the hostile mists for the next half an hour for the sake of politeness. Rat laughed and held the door for Winn to come scur-rying in as well, her whole big body steaming with apology. "*Dread-fully* sorry to put you out like this, Rat."

"I'm not put out," Rat said. "Having a couple of pretty young gulls in the shop before dawn does me good."

Winn blushed. "Erm. You're very kind, I'm sure," she said after a moment, and Delly and Winn allowed Rat to urge them into two of the many chairs crammed into the room and to accept cups of coffee and plates of generously buttered toast soldiers.

Rat herself poured something from a small silver flask into her own cup of coffee, put her boots up onto her desk, and said, "You two have gotten yourself into a real mess of trouble, haven't you?"

And there it was. Delly figured that a woman like Rat very rarely offered coffee and toast to relative strangers without looking for something in exchange, even if it was just information. Delly ate a piece of toast, took a sip of coffee, and asked, "What makes you say that, Rat?"

"Anytime you're letting some young lad put an enchanted ribbon on you that doesn't let you see where you're being led to commit your crimes, you're in trouble," Rat said.

Winn bridled. "Who says that we're committing crimes?"

Rat actually laughed aloud at that, which didn't do anything to soothe Winn's very evident unease over this unanticipated early-morning interrogation by a woman wearing an infuriated weasel on her hat. Then Rat looked straight at Delly. "Listen, kid," she said. "You remind me of me when I was your age, so I'm going to offer you some advice, free of charge. Don't try and fool yourself into thinking that you're safer now that you're in deep with them. You ain't safer. You're worse off than you were before, because now you've got their attention. If your neck ain't getting tired from looking over your shoulder, then you ain't worried enough yet."

Delly ate some more toast. "Thanks, Rat," she said. "I appreciate the free advice. Might I ask if you're speaking from any particular experience with the personages in question?"

"Nope," Rat said, and drank some more of her fortified coffee. "But in my experience, personages like that Miss Cat are all pretty much alike."

Delly took a moment to absorb this, along with the toast and coffee that she was also rapidly absorbing. "Well, thank you, anyhow," she said. "I aim to wear out my neck, Rat."

"See that you do," Rat said. "It would be a real pity if you had to call off your wedding on account of being dead."

Delly, for once, found herself entirely at a loss for words. She was saved from the ensuing silence only by the arrival of the Able Young Person, who was followed moments later by an uncharacteristically tardy Abstentia. Winn frowned when she saw her. "Goodness, Abstentia, did you get any sleep last night?" she asked. Abstentia did look unusually rumpled and wild-eyed this morning, as if someone had been stroking her glossy fur in the wrong direction.

Abstentia's only response to this was to give Winn a very withering look. Winn sighed and thanked Rat very prettily for the coffee and toast, and they threw themselves onto the mercy of the Able Young Person for another long and sickeningly beribboned walk to work. It was almost a relief to be elbow-deep in drip making again once they arrived. This, at least, was something predictable.

Abstentia seemed to feel much the same: after an hour or so of work she even unwound herself to the point of speaking civilly to her colleagues again. "I did some analysis of my notes on those door wards from yesterday, and I think I may have been able to work up some diagnostic parameters that will clarify things a bit. Wells, did you learn anything more about that lock?"

"Ah," Delly said, caught out entirely by these sudden and unjustified accusations of potential industry. "No. I'll need to buy a lock of the same model, for that."

"And you didn't do that *yesterday*?"

"No," Delly said, doing her level best to sound as if she didn't find Abstentia aggravating in the slightest. "I was otherwise occupied, Miss Dok. If I have your *leave*, Miss Dok, I'll leave early this afternoon in order to purchase one, Miss Dok."

"Oh, for all of the rilift, how many times do I have to tell you two to stop *bickering*?" Winn asked, and banged a beaker down onto the table with a somewhat worrying degree of force, considering the unsettled drip's tendency toward spontaneous combustion. Delly had not, it seemed, done as well at concealing her feelings about Abstentia's temper this morning as she thought she had.

The day still wore on, though, despite their squabbles, and after a brief break to eat the sandwiches Winn had packed it was really only the briefest of sprints to reach the point in the evening when Delly could reasonably declare herself finished with her work for the day, wheedle the Able Young Person into leading her back to Rat's, and then toddle off in search of a lock like the one on the evil door.

This ended up being far more of an expedition than Delly had planned on. The first two shopkeepers had either never heard of a lock matching her description or were simply uninterested in doing business with a suspicious-looking gutterwitch describing expensive locks based on their general outward appearance. At the third shop her luck turned a bit: they didn't carry said lock but suggested another shop where said lock *might* be purchased. Another turn to her luck: the luxurious lock emporium that might or might not carry the lock that she needed was just a few blocks away from their hotel. If all went well, for a change, she'd be able to buy the lock and then pop by the room just in time to meet Winn for a nice late supper.

It was rather shocking to her when things went just as planned, when she acquired exactly the right lock without any particular struggle—beyond the loss of an entire half-tocat: the lock was releftin' *expensive*—and then tottering on over to her room to practice a bit of light lockpickery while she waited for her betrothed to make her delightful appearance.

The lockpicking proved to be less than enlightening, and when Winn came through the door she was greeted by the presumably less than delightening sight of Dellaria Wells, red-faced and frizz-haired, cursing vividly at an inanimate object that had probably hoped for much better from its so-far short and highly eventful career. "Goodness," Winn said, carefully hanging her nice coat on the hook by the door. It was chilly out this evening. "Did that poor lock do something to offend you personally?"

"*Yes*," Delly said, and slammed the cursed thing down onto the table with a satisfying *clonk*. "I need something to eat. And a *drink*."

"I think it's a night for a nice stew," Winn said, immediately recoating herself. "And mulled wine."

Delly consented to this, and Winn went so far as to hail a cab to deliver them to a pub that could provide a stew that would meet her exacting standards. There she ordered enough to stew and mull Delly into utter equanimity, placidity, and facial floridity. Even her hands felt warm and contented. "I think I'll have another go at that lock when I get back," she said. "Couldn't be any worse than the first try."

"A second try's as good as nine," Winn said proverbially. "Shall I ask the waiter to flag down another cab for us?"

"If you like," Delly said, and lolled about like a First Headman's wife while a young man flagged down a cab for her, a young lady paid her bill for her, and the same young lady helped her into her coat and out the door and up the step into the cab as if she was the most precious and delicate creature on earth. She leaned against Winn's shoulder once they were safely in the cab, feeling safe and warm and—she wasn't sure. Comforted, maybe. "You make me feel positively—like a queen, Winn."

"Do I really?" Winn asked. "I'm awfully glad to hear that, Dell." Her voice was soft. She squeezed Delly's knee through her skirt.

"Winnifer," Delly slurred out, "how positively scandalous of you."

"Oh, ah, dreadfully sorry," Winn said, and jerked her hand away as if Delly's knee was on fire. Which, to be fair, wouldn't be outside the realms of possibility for a tipsy fire witch.

Delly gave a muffled cackle and dragged Winn's hand back to its post. "Didn't tell you to *stop*."

Winn mumbled something very polite and embarrassed-sounding. It might have been, "Not really the *thing*, what?" She didn't move her hand away again, though. Dellaria felt deeply pleased with herself.

Then, on impulse, she put her own hand over Winn's. After a moment, Winn turned her hand so that her palm faced up, and they laced their fingers together.

They stayed like that for the whole ride home, holding hands in the dark, snug and cozy as could be. Then they got up to their room and made themselves even snugger in warm robes by the hot stove, drinking tea and feeling perfectly content and comfortable. Delly worked on her lock some more. Winn read aloud from a novel even more scandalizing than their cab ride had been. Buttons said, "*Bong.*"

Delly blinked, then looked about herself until she spotted him. He was perched atop the stove, presumably warming his bony hindquarters. "What are *you* still doing here?" she asked. "I should have thought you would have wanted to go home to Mrs. Totham by now."

Buttons said, in the whispering, raspy voice of a man, "*Beware.*"

Winn gasped. Delly shivered. "Is that you again, then, Mr. Trell?"

Buttons said, "*Bong.*"

They went to bed after that, beaten down by a barrage of Buttonsical *bong*ery so late in an otherwise perfectly pleasant evening. They cuddled a bit, which was awfully nice. They slept.

They were woken up by the sound of Mrs. Totham screaming.

It was the worst sound that Delly had ever heard. It was so terrible that it jolted her out of bed and sent her tumbling to the floor. She lay there for a moment, stunned, then jolted up again to look around for the source of the screaming. Eventually she found it. The skeletal culprit was perched on the bedpost, still making enough noise to haul himself out of his own God-detested grave. "*Help!*" he was screaming in Mrs. Totham's quavering voice. "*Help! Help! Fire!*"

"*Shut the fuck up, Buttons!*" Delly screamed back.

Buttons shut up. There was a moment of beautiful, perfect silence. Then Winn was on her feet, too, and yanking her clothes on. "Come *on*, Dell."

Delly gawped at her. Her ears were still ringing. "Come on where?"

"To the *laboratory*," Winn said. "Didn't you hear? There's a *fire*."

Buttons gave a loud, decisive *bong*.

"Shit," Delly said, abruptly and horribly shaken out of her daze. "Fuck. My *mam*." She rushed to the foot of the bed to start yanking her own shoes on, then threw on her coat over her nightdress. Her mam was a dripper. Drippers died in fires. They died in fires all the time. They'd die before they even knew they ought to run. Buttons came racing toward her, and she scooped him up and jammed him into her coat pocket before racing to the door and down the stairs, Winn right at her heels.

The street was almost empty when they got outside. It was late: too late for there to be many cabbies out in the streets looking for drunks to ferry home. They ran for a few blocks, desperately waving at any passing carriages. None of them stopped. Then they ran past a pub with a horse and cart tied up in front of it. Not a cab: one of those little things that rich fellas drove, and no coachman in sight. Delly was still running when Winn grabbed her arm and nearly yanked her off her feet. "Come on," she hissed, and then climbed up into the cart's driver's seat before holding out her hand for Delly.

Delly grabbed ahold of her hand and scrabbled inelegantly after her, ignoring the muffled, distressed bonging emerging from her coat pocket. Then she held on to the seat of the coach as Winn urged the horse into what Delly could only assume ought to be called a *gallop*. Certainly the jouncing Delly was receiving as the cart clattered over the cobblestones at a gut-cramping speed gave Delly's hindquarters a battering. Somewhere in the distance she could hear a man shouting, "*Stop! Thief!*" But that was soon behind them, drowned out by the clamor of the cart and the pounding of Delly's heart in her ears.

Then they drew closer to the laboratory, and Delly, who had previously felt as if she hadn't breathed once since the terrifying ride had begun, was abruptly confronted with the fact that she had been mistaken. The air was thick enough with smoke that she could taste it at the back of her throat, and every breath turned conscious and hard fought. Winn started to cough. Delly could see a great column of it now, rising over the tops of the buildings. The horse shied away from it, too, and Delly remembered being dragged by that damn donkey and grabbed at Winn's arm. "Stop the cart," Delly said. "Winn, *stop*, before the creature bolts."

Winn worked whatever magic she generally used to make the horse stop running—tugging at the reins and soft sounds from her mouth—then leapt from the cart, Delly slithering down after her. Then they both started to run toward the flames.

They found Mrs. Totham from the sound of her. She was weeping loudly, standing between her two daughters, who were holding her up by her elbows. When she saw Delly she gave a louder wail. "*Miss Wells*," she cried out. "*Miss Wells*, there was a *boy*, he threw something through the window, it set the laboratory alight—and your dear *mother—upstairs—*"

Delly didn't stop moving long enough to acknowledge her. She just kept running straight toward the house, until she registered that Winn was following her and went still as a rock. "Don't fucking *follow* me, Winn."

"I certainly blinkin' *will* follow you," Winn said. "Fire witches only can't be *burned*. Doesn't mean that the *smoke* won't get you. If you deal with the heat, I'll provide the light and fresh air."

There wasn't any time to argue with her. Delly ground her teeth. She'd never had to hold flames away from two people in the middle of a conflagration before, and she'd never been any fucking good at un-announced exams during her single year at Weltsir. "*Fine*," she said after a moment, and started to run again. Winn ran after her, encant-ing as she went. A moment later there was a rush of wind, and sud-denly Delly could breathe easily again. A light was glowing in Winn's palm. The sweat gleamed on her face.

"Delly," she said. "Getting rather warm, what?"

"Oh, right," Delly said, and concentrated until she felt the heat around them drop. Her head started to hurt almost immediately. They were through the fence now, and into the back garden. "I won't be able to keep this up for long, Winn."

"Then we'll be quick about it," Winn said, and kicked in the back door.

The smoke washed over them right away, like a wave crashing over their heads. Even whatever parameters Winn was using to keep the worst of it off of them weren't enough to keep the smell of it out of Delly's nose, or the burn out of her throat. They pushed farther into the house, Winn a step ahead to light the way, though the little light in her hand did next to nothing in the face of the curtains of smoke and the wild shadows cast by the flames in the next room. The laboratory. The laboratory was burning, and Delly's mam's room was right above it.

They headed toward the stairs, where the heat was so intense that even Delly started to sweat. Winn muttered, "Bit blinkin' warm, what?" and started pounding up the steps two at a time, as Delly scrambled after her and the stairs creaked ominously beneath them. The damn things hadn't been all that sturdy underfoot at the best of times, and now with the flames lapping at them from below, Delly was just hoping that they'd keep connecting first floor to second for long enough to prevent Delly from being left suspended 'twixt the two.

They made it, at last, to the second-story hallway, and from there into Delly's mam's bedroom. The smoke was even thicker up there, so thick that it was hard to see anything but dim shapes rising out of the gloom. She stumbled forward, hands extended, until she hit the bed, and felt around some more until she grasped a foot. It didn't move, didn't jerk away. Didn't so much as twitch. "She's *here*," she said. "Winn, she's here, I think she's—"

Winn didn't say anything, just picked her mam up and slung her over her shoulder like a sack of laundry and turned toward the door, Delly sticking close to her side. They were both tiring, Delly knew: the air around them was growing thicker as it grew harder for Winn to keep firing her parameters, and Delly could feel her own hands shaking from the strain of holding back the flames. They were almost to the stairs. Delly's foot hit the top step, there was an ear-scraping, floor-shaking crash, and Winn's hand closed on Delly's shoulder and jerked her violently backward as the stairs crumbled away and the flames closed around them. Delly gave a hoarse, shocked little cry. Her heart was battering at her ribs like a bad piano player at the keys. Then Winn cried out, too, from pain, and Delly hissed and slammed all of her power into holding back the fire. She felt sweat trickling down her back. The air smelled like burnt hair. "Dell," Winn said. Her voice sounded strained. "C'mon." She turned and headed back toward Mam's room. Delly followed. She wouldn't be able to breathe without her.

"How are we going to get *out*?" she asked Winn's back. Wanting someone to save her. Like a child. Like a fucking child. Her teeth were chattering.

Winn didn't answer. Maybe she was just saving her breath: the air was getting close, the smoke too thick to see through even with Winn's spell keeping back the worst of it. Then there was the sound of fabric tearing and, a moment later, glass shattering. The smoke cleared a bit, enough to see Winn find the latch and yank open the window. Then she picked up Delly's mam from the floor and rattled off an incantation. A second after that she sat down on the sill, Delly's mam in her arms, swung her legs around with a grunt, and dropped.

Dell screamed and bolted to the window, only to be greeted with the sight of Winn floating downward like an autumn leaf, alighting very elegantly on her two feet, Delly's mam cradled in her arms. Then she set Marvie on the ground and yelled out, "Dell! Jump!"

"I can't!" Delly yelled back. "I'll break my legs!"

There was another crash from inside of the house, and the roar of the fire. The heat was getting harder to hold off. She could barely hear Winn's response over the din. "I'll catch you! Just *jump*!"

Delly swallowed hard. "Well, fuck," she said. Then she closed her eyes and jumped.

Winn caught her, after a fashion. She did catch her, really, except the force of the impact nearly wrenched Delly's arm out of its socket before Winn lost her footing and they both hit the ground with a loud *oof.*

Winn got up first, then picked up Delly's mam again and reached for Delly's hand. "Come *on*," she said. "Before the whole blinkin' thing comes down on top of us."

Delly got up, her whole body aching, and started hobbling her way down the street as fast as she could. "*Mrs. Totham!*" she called out. She was trying not to glance toward her mam where she was cradled in Winn's arms. They needed to find Mrs. Totham. She would be able to help. "She breathing?" It came out strange. Gruff. She blamed the smoke still in her throat.

Winn didn't say anything, just broke into a jog. "*Mrs. Totham,*" she called out. Delly's chest went tight. Smoke in her lungs.

"*Here!*" It was Mrs. Totham's voice, and Mrs. Totham's slight figure emerging from the gloom. "Oh, thank *God.* Lay her out somewhere dry. Here, over here." She gestured to a bench at the side of the road. She wasn't twittering now, or wailing, or weeping. She sounded like a person in command. Winn obeyed her, laying Delly's mam out on the bench. "Stand back, give me room," Mrs. Totham said, and stepped in close and put her hand on Mam's chest. Then there was that feeling in the air. Like the spider-things. Like the suit of armor. Like the attic door.

Dread clogged up Delly's throat. There was something creeping up her arm. At first she thought that it was just in her head, just a side effect of the terror in the air. Then she looked down and saw something white, and nearly screamed and swatted it away before her mind caught up with her. She let him climb up to her shoulder. That low, rasping voice whispered in her ear. "*Death,*" Mr. Trell whispered. "*A slow death, Dellaria Wells.*"

Delly shivered. "I don't understand, Mr. Trell," she whispered back. Buttons made no reply. Then Mrs. Totham groaned, and Delly's mam gave a loud, pained wheeze of a gasp and rolled over to vomit onto the cobblestones.

Mrs. Totham staggered slightly, but Winn caught her before she could fall. "Mrs. Totham," she said. "What's wrong? Are you—unwell?"

"Oh, no, no," Mrs. Totham said faintly. "I'm quite well. Mura, dear, could you—" Her daughters stepped in then to take ahold of each of her elbows. Delly hadn't even heard them come up. Too focused on the horror show around her, probably: wasn't as if the genus Totham trod upon particularly velvety paws. "I'm quite all right," Mrs. Totham continued. "It's only that I had to burn a bit more of myself off, for want of any other—*material*, for the body science. Little scrapes and accidents hardly take anything at all, but I'm afraid that more serious injuries can be—dreadfully taxing." She swayed on her feet very slightly. "You ought to take dear Mrs. Wells to a hospital, as quickly as you can," she said. Then she burst into tears. "Oh, our— lovely *home*!"

"It was just a place to stay, Mother," Mura said. Then she said, "You ought to go home. *Really* home. Ermintrude wouldn't want all of this. You could go home and see Father, and rest."

"You all ought to," Delly said. The words felt as if they were coming from outside of herself. "I'll still share the money with you, same as I said I would. I'll catch the Wexin girl. She won't get away with what she did to Ermintrude. You can put a hard promise on me for it, if you like. But there's nothing left for you to do here, I don't think. And these people—" She thought of what Rat had said to her. "You ought to get out while you can."

"I'm sure that there's no need for anyone to have a hard promise put on them, Miss Wells," Mrs. Totham said.

"*Yes*, there is, Mother," Mura said.

"Right," Delly said. She didn't care about what kind of fucking hard promise they put on her. Mrs. Totham shouldn't be here anymore. No one's mother should be here anymore. Probably no one's child, either. Leiscourt was a cold, misting, motherkilling place. Delly would want to leave here and go back home, too, if she'd had a home to go back to. "There's a theater on Bride's Lane," Delly said. "If you're not about to leave to get on a train, I want you all to disguise yourselves as best you can, then head there in time for the show tomorrow night. Should be one at eight o'clock. Pay for your tickets and watch it with everyone else. I'll try to find you at the intermission. If I'm not there, then stay behind and find someone who works there who you can ask for Elo. Tell them it's urgent and Delly Wells sent you, and that I'll be there as soon as I can. Don't let anyone but Elo take you anywhere. He's a tall fella, curly red hair. You can put that hard promise on me after I get there tonight."

She felt, for a moment, strangely peaceful, as if her moment of conviction was a salve for the horrible jittering confusion of the past hour. Then her decisiveness ground up against the rocky shoal of the fact that she wasn't strong enough to pick up her wheezing, vomit-bespattered mother and stride purposefully toward the nearest hospital. She shot Winn a pleading look, and Winn, without having to be asked, stepped forward and scooped Delly's mam up into her arms. Then they strode off purposefully together, in pursuit of a horse and cart that had long since run away from them.

19

Wherein the Fires Rage On

They got her mam to the hospital and bribed a man who worked there into getting her into a bed. Then Delly started looking for a nurse. Winn trailed after her, quiet at first, then piping up a bit. "What are you looking for, Dell?"

"I need to talk to someone," Delly said. She needed to find that nurse. She didn't even know her name. She wandered around with Winn following after her like a tail—a tail tucked between the legs, not a tail high and wagging—until a broad, stout fellow asked them what they were doing, and Delly described the nurse she was hunting, and the broad, stout fellow directed them to a windowless room on the first floor, where they found the nurse in question bending bleary-eyed over a cup of hot tea.

"No visitors in here, miss," the nurse said when she saw them in the doorway.

Delly barged in, anyway. "I talked to you about my mam last week," she said. "She's back now."

The nurse stared at her for a long moment, with the look of someone who had worn her eyes out on the jagged faces of miserable people. Then she said, "Oh! You're that girl who set that man on fire."

Delly acknowledged this. The nurse frowned. "I'm sorry to hear your mam's back. Is there something you wanted, miss? I'm having my break."

"Yes," Delly said, and pulled out the bag of money still in her coat pocket. "I need you to have my mam sent to one of those countryside places. You said you would, if I could find the money. I've got ten tocats here. That should be all right for a few days, shouldn't it? Just get her there, and I'll get you the rest of the money as soon as I can."

The nurse took a sip of her tea. She looked tired. "I can't do anything for her with ten tocats, miss," she said. "You'd have to pay for at least two weeks in advance. And what happened to you, anyway? Did you set someone on fire again?"

"But," Delly said. Her throat hurt. Her eyes hurt. "She's here now. And I didn't set the fire. Someone burned my mam's house down. She almost died. *Again*." Miss Clairelle had done it, she was sure. Sent someone to burn down their laboratory. She hadn't given a tin sen about who might be inside it.

"I'll pay for it," Winn said suddenly, and stepped forward. She was still disheveled and smelled like soot, but the nurse sat up a bit straighter when she heard her speak. "Have you a pen and paper?"

"Yes, miss," the nurse said, and stood hurriedly to produce them from a shelf behind her. Winn leaned over the table to write, then folded the page in half, wrote down an address, and handed it over to the nurse. "There's a lawyer at that address called Mr. Craws. He'll take care of the finances. Just tell his secretary when you walk in that the note is, erm . . ." She cleared her throat. "From Lord Cynallum's daughter."

Delly, from a distance, heard herself give a muffled croak. The nurse, who had been seated, leapt to her feet. Winn flapped an embarrassed hand at her. "No, please sit, Sister. You're having your break, what? And I've asked him to make sure that you're paid for your trouble as well. If you could only try to arrange things quickly? Mrs. Wells really does need to be out of Leiscourt as soon as possible."

"Of course, miss," the nurse was saying. "Of course I will." Winn already had Delly by the elbow, though, and she was dragging her out of the room and out of the wing and out of the hospital as if she thought that admitting to being the daughter of a *fucking lord* was an arrestable offense and wanted to make a clean getaway.

"*Lord*," Delly said as soon as they were out on the street. "*Lord Cynallum.* Your *pop's* a *lord*? Does that make you a—a fuckin' *lady*, then, or—"

"*No*," Winn said. "It's an—honorary title, that's all. Just what they call you in Hexos if you're on the Directress's Advisory Council. It's not *inheritable*. I only ever call him that when I need to get something done faster. And it jolly well *worked*, didn't it?"

"You lied about it," Delly said. "You said—he worked for the government, you said. I thought you meant—you said he was a *secretary*."

"He is, sometimes," Winn said. "I didn't lie. He's personal secretary to the Lord-Mage of Hexos, when Uncle Loga's gotten his affairs into a complete muddle and he needs Pop's help to straighten things out. And he runs a shipping company that Uncle Loga owns. He just has this ginny *title*, as well. It doesn't *mean* anything, Dell."

"Fucking course *you'd* say that," she said, and then started walking fast. "Write up a payment plan for me."

Winn looked bewildered. "What?"

"So I can pay you back for my mam's care," Delly said, and started walking even faster, hoping that Winn would take the hint.

"Dell," Winn started. "I'm not going to—"

"Leave it alone, Cynallum," Delly snapped. "We're already late for Rat's."

They were late. Late enough that Abstentia started laying into them the instant they arrived. "We've been standing here for almost an *hour*, what excuse can you *possibly*—good God, were you in a fire? What on earth happened? Are you all right? Is everyone safe? Where are the Tothams?"

"There was a fire," Delly said shortly, a bit dizzied by the sudden twists and pivots of Abstentia's questioning. "*This* one's"—she nodded at the Able Young Person, who was standing nearby eating a piece of toffee in an utterly loathsome fashion—"employer knows all about it, I'm sure. If not the lad himself." Mrs. Totham had seen a boy, she said, throwing something through the window to set the building on fire. "Everyone's all right now, though. Including the Tothams."

Abstentia's pretty brown eyes went very wide. "Ah," she said after a moment, and glanced at the Able Young Person before looking back at Delly and clearing her throat. When she spoke again it was all business. "Let's go, then. We're late enough as it is."

She was a clever enough girl, Abstentia Dok.

Delly filled her in on everything that had happened once they got to the laboratory and started to work, keeping her voice low as they bent their heads together over the beakers. Once Delly was done with her narrative, Abstentia stared down at the table for a moment, frowning. "We need to finish this soon, don't we? As soon as we can."

Delly nodded. Winn spoke up then, for the first time in what felt like hours. "We need to make a plan."

"Not here," Delly mouthed. She wasn't taking any more risks. Not now that she knew more about the kinds of things that Miss Cat was willing to do.

Abstentia inclined her head at that, then moved to make some adjustments to the flame under one of her beakers, then bent to make a note before tilting the notebook slightly toward Delly. *At your theater tonight at midnight.* Then she looked over her drip table again, frowned, adjusted the flame, and thoroughly crossed out what she had just written, so that no spying eyes could possibly read it, even if a set of sticky toffee-coated fingers pinched the book.

They got their way through a few hours of work, somehow. At about three in the afternoon, Winn closed her hand gently around

Delly's wrist. "Dell," she said. "Your hands are shaking. Why don't you sit down for a while? Just rest your eyes a bit, mm?"

She led her to a chair in the corner of the room. "Just for a moment, Dell," she said, and Dell allowed herself to be led, to sit, and the next thing she knew she was being shaken gently awake again. "C'mon, Dell," Winn murmured. "Time to go home."

"Don't have a home," Delly mumbled. It was true. She'd day-dreamed about buying the laboratory and living in it, but she'd never had a home, not really. She probably never would.

Delly and Winn walked to the theater and made it there just in time to buy their tickets and find their seats before the curtain rose. It was hard to really focus on the play, once it got started, except the parts with Elo in it. He was playing one of the leads. He hadn't told Delly that. The seductive villain who was more interesting than the hero and spent more time than him on the stage. He was wearing all black and putting on a clanner accent. The accent was good. *He* was good. The sometimes-rowdy audience got quieter when he was talking and cheered at his best lines. Delly felt herself biting her lip all through his parts, hoping to keep him up on the high wire he was walking, keep him from plummeting back down into the ash heap they'd both climbed up from. *He'd* be all right, if a clanner wanted to household him. *He'd* be able to put on the accent and wear the clothes and walk into the fucking *drawing room* without infuriating anyone's mother-in-law.

"Is that your friend?" Winn was whispering. "The wicked lord? He's quite good, what?"

"Yeah," Delly said. "That's my pal Elo." She was proud of him, she realized. She was proud of him. Doing something legal, doing some-thing that kept him clothed and housed and fed. Doing something that he was good at. Doing it *himself*, without having to tie himself to any living person, without having to scrape and simper, without hav-ing to lie except for on a stage when everyone knew he was doing it. "He's damn good."

There was an intermission. They found the Tothams drinking cheap hock and eating little sandwiches in the lobby. Vitna was looking dewy-eyed. "Ermintrude would have loved this play," she said. "She always liked a good high-class villain."

Delly decided not to comment on the irony of that.

Second act. Elo was killed by the hero in a duel, which was only to be expected, but the crowd jeered at it anyhow. Then the curtain again, and the bows and the applause, and Delly getting up while the crowd was still milling around and chatting, her associates in tow, to find someone who could let her backstage. She nearly got carried out the door by a burly stagehand at first, until she said in her strongest West Leiscourt, "Grab a pin, I'm friends with Elo, so. Tell 'im Delly's here to see him?" and the burly fellow went to fetch him, the whole bunch of them safely hidden behind the worn red curtains.

Elo came out a few minutes later, stripped down to his skirt and shirtsleeves, face still painted and powdered, red curls damp from his having sweated under his black wig. "Delly!" he said. He looked glad to see her. "How'd you like the play, then?"

"You were the best part," Delly said, and gave him the kind of squeeze that women like Winn didn't give to men they hadn't married. Then she said, "I'm in a real releftin' scrape right now, Elo." Women like Winn didn't call men by their given names, either.

"Are you?" he asked. "Well. Come on down to the crypts and tell me about it over a drink."

"Ah," Delly said. "Could my—friends all come with me?"

Elo looked over the assembled throng with wide eyes. Then he shrugged and smiled. "Why not? The more the merrier," he said, and gestured for them to follow him.

The crypts under the theater might not have ever been crypts. They probably hadn't been, really. They'd probably been something else: a bathhouse, maybe, or a covered market, or any other kind of building that had been knocked down and then built over again sometime in the past thousand years. There were warrens like them all over Leiscourt, remnants of cities that had been here before and that the city Delly lived in would turn into one day. Delly didn't figure it mattered much. When it came to being given the hot shivers, the rules worked about the same both above the theater and below: it was the idea of the thing, not the reality. They were *called* crypts, and so they were, and they felt like that as they made their way through them.

The theater stored things in the tunnels. Looked like they'd been doing it for about a hundred years. Racks of dresses, wigs, artificial beards. Axes and swords and a suit of armor that made Delly think of Ermintrude and her white twisted face, the pig's snout, the pain that she must have felt before the end. She shoved that away. There were other things to look at. Crowns. Top hats. A crystal ball and six artificial palm trees. A coffin. They were descending deeper into the crypts. It didn't look like a prop, the coffin. It looked like it was about to be lowered into the dirt. Though it didn't need that, probably. They were already far more than six feet under.

There was something wriggling in Delly's coat pocket. After a moment Buttons poked his head out. *"A slow death, Delly Wells,"* he whispered. *"Beware."*

"Oh, *shut up*, Mr. Trell," Delly hissed back. "Talk to me when you have something *helpful* to say." Then she shoved him back into the bottom of her pocket again.

Elo cast her a concerned look. "Are you all right, pup? Who's talking to thee?"

"Oh, nobody," Delly said, and gave her pocket a vicious pat. Then she gave a theatrical shiver. "Bit creepy down here, isn't it?" It made it better to say it aloud.

"Oh, yeah," Elo said. "But like I told you, there's nothing that frightens off the ghosts more than the threat of being haunted by actors. If we see a specter, we just try to convince it to help fill the seats on opening night and then ask to borrow five sen for a drink."

Delly laughed, maybe a bit longer and harder than the joke deserved. She could feel the unease crawling just under her skin. Her eyes felt like they were throbbing. Elo frowned at her for a moment, then clapped her on the shoulder. "How about we kick the gargle and you veil the mirrors for the trip, so?" He was West Leiscourting at her harder than he really needed to. Neither of them usually bothered with that much alleychat between the two of them. She understood the impulse, though, with clanners around. It made you want to strap on your breastplate.

"Might it so, pup," Delly said, and rubbed at her eyes. She was tired. She was so *fucking* tired.

They finally got to the part of the crypts where the actors had their rooms. A few dozen little cells that might have held a cheesemonger's stall once, or a monk's cell, or a crypt for some clan that had long since died out. There were a few empty, at least, and Delly dove into one and started to strip the second she got the door shut, Winn just managing to slip in after her. Her clothes stank of smoke.

"I'll go and see if I can scrounge up some hot water for us," Winn said. Her voice was soft. "So that you can have a bit of a scrub. Were you, erm, going to lie down?"

"Yeah," Delly said shortly.

"Oh," Winn said. Then, "How long have you known Mr. Elo?"

"Mr. Farrow," Delly said. "His name's Elo Farrow. Known him since we were kids together. Grew up in the same neighborhood." She paused. Then she said, "We used to fuck. Did the day I met you, actually. That very night."

There was a pause.

"Delly," Winn said. "What— Why would you say that to me? There's no—blinkin' use to it, what?"

"Sure there is," Delly said. "Figure you could use a chatter on how you ought to have your mirrors clear before you let Wester trash like me 'n' Elo near your clink, so."

"*Dell*," Winn said. "I can't understand what you're riliftin' *saying*."

"That's because you're a clanner," Delly said. Her heart was pounding. "Your *pop's* a *lord*, and I'm a West Leiscourt gutterwitch who started talking sweet at you the day I met you because I knew you had money from the second you opened your mouth to talk. That's why I went after you, Winn. You smelled like cash and I didn't have enough left to pay rent, and I figured I could probably fuck a few presents I could pawn outta you before you got bored of me. And now you want to household me and let me—alleychat in front of the fucking dukes at your father's dinner parties. It's a *mistake*, Winn. Just figured I ought to let you know now. Not like it'll cause a fuckin' scandal if you break the engagement. You can't ruin a woman like me. I never had a damn reputation to begin with."

Winn didn't say a word at that. She just turned and walked through the door.

Delly got into the narrow cot by the wall and passed out.

When she woke up it was to Winn shaking her and an overwhelming sense of panic, her mouth already flapping like a cheap gate in the wind. "Winn, I'm sorry, I didn't mean it, I was just in a nasty temper—"

"Oh, hush, Dell," Winn said. "Here." She handed Delly a cup of steaming tea. "Sorry for waking you, but Abstentia will be here in half an hour. Best not to face Abstentia Dok with a dirty face and empty stomach."

Delly stared at her, baffled, and then took a big gulp of scalding tea. "You ain't angry at me?"

"No use in talking about any of that right now," Winn said. "Bit silly to be attending to personal matters in general, when we're in the middle of this mess and not at top form, what? Should have known better from the start." She clapped her hand onto Delly's shoulder and gave it a firm squeeze.

"Oh," Delly said, and gulped some more tea, then got up to make a serious attempt to rid herself of some of her coating of soot. Winn was right. She must be right. It would be better not to talk about it. It would all—blow over, probably, if she gave it a bit of time. It would end in one way or another.

They walked back up to the higher levels of the crypts, where they found a sort of party taking place under the artificial palm trees. The Tothams were there, as was Abstentia. And Elo, who was sitting with Abstentia, laughing and drinking wine. Delly scowled and strode on over to warn him off.

"Hold goat, Elo, before you have cat-sticks in thee."

Abstentia wrinkled up her nose at her. "Goodness, Wells, how very *colorful* of you. You're practically at one with your setting." She took another sip of her wine. "What's our plan?"

They started to work out their plan. So far none of their plans had gone like greased marbles, and from what Delly could tell this one didn't beat any of their other ones for ingeniousness. Nothing ingenious at all, really. They'd keep their heads down and brew for a few more days, giving Delly time to work on that lock, Abstentia time to examine the wards on the evil room, and Miss Cat time to assume that they'd taken the message of the burning laboratory to heart and were on their best behavior. Then they would return at night to open the room up. If Ainette was there, then that was that: they'd gotten what they'd come for, and they could pay to use the calling-tower at Weltsir to get a message to Mayelle Crossick within the hour. If she wasn't, then the rest of them could wander around Leiscourt whistling for Ainette all they wanted. If she wasn't sleeping on a hard cot in that attic, Delly was hopping on the next train to Monsatelle to start up her own drip manufacturing, and into the damn releft with all the rest of them. If she didn't get that reward money, she was going to have to find the clink to pay off that nurse for her mam's care some other way, and she'd have to do it fast. Getting other people hooked on the same damn drip that had nearly killed her mother more than once now was about the only avenue for earning that much money that Delly could see remaining to her. Now that she'd fucked things up to Hexos and back with her rich prospect, at least.

Delly hadn't shared that last bit of her plan with the rest of the group. She figured they'd be able to figure it out when they noted the cloud of dust produced by Dellaria Wells vanishing over the horizon.

They went over the plan a few times, looking for leaks and seams. There were a few of them. There was plenty that could go wrong, between the wards, the lock, the danger of a servant waking, the danger of Ainette herself kicking up a fuss about being rescued from bondage in an attic against her will. Abstentia rubbed at her eyes with her fingertips. "I would insist on creating some sort of magical way to subdue Ainette," she said, "but I'm afraid that we might be reduced to chloroform."

"*Chloroform*," Winn repeated. "Where would you even find the stuff?"

"I'll formulate it myself," Abstentia said.

"No, you won't," Delly said, and endeavorated to sound less meanly pleased than she felt. "Our lab's burned down."

"Oh, for *fuck's* sake," said Abstentia, and then just sat there for a moment looking deeply astonished at what had just popped out of her mouth.

"How *colorful* of you, Dok," Delly said, unable to prevent herself from sounding thoroughly gleeful. "I can hardly see you, you blend in so well with the palm trees." Then she remembered what they were talking about and scowled. "Guess the chloroform's out, then."

"I could get you some," Elo said. They all turned to look at him. He shrugged. "I might know a feller who knows a feller."

"That'd be grand of you, Elo," Delly said. "I'm good for the clink for it." Then she said, "We have to figure out where exactly Miss Cat's place is. Any of you have a map?"

Winn did: the same cheap map Delly had bought for her about ten thousand years ago on the day they arrived in Leiscourt. Delly circled the block where she was almost positive Miss Cat's place was. "It's one of these, I think," Delly said. "We just have to—narrow it down, somehow."

"*How?*" Abstentia asked, and they launched into a nice squabble about it for a while until Winn intervened.

"Why don't we all do our best to remember the look of the cobbles out front, but I drop a button on the steps as well, just in case?"

They all went quiet for a moment.

Delly said, "That could work."

They went over everything a few more times in any case, as if discussing it to death would help to hold together a plan that might as well have been held together with wishes and wallpaper paste. At some point, amidst the tumult, Mrs. Totham gave an especially delicate "Ahem!" When that failed to grab anyone's attention, Buttons, whom Mrs. Totham had been dandling on her knee, sat up on his haunches and gave an especially loud and notificationary "*Bong!*"

Elo jumped and stared at Buttons with every ounce of the horror that Buttons so richly deserved. "What the *fuck* is—what *is* that thing?"

"That's Mr. Trell," Delly said. "But we call him Buttons."

Elo said, a bit faintly, "Oh, *no.*"

Into the ensuing silence Mrs. Totham fluttered like a butterfly. "Forgive me," she said, "for interrupting. But Miss Dok has very kindly offered to perform that hard promise for me, Miss Wells."

Delly glared at Abstentia. Abstentia smirked at Delly. Delly sighed. "All right. Do your worst, Dok."

Abstentia did the work of setting up the hard promise, then grabbed ahold of Delly's hand to set the curse onto her. Delly shook out her hand after. "Fuckin' releft, any reason you have to make it *sting*? And what did you curse me with, anyway?"

"You know, Wells, I'm surprised at you. I should have thought you were clever enough to ask about what you were promising to and how you would be held to it *before* you allowed me to curse you," Miss Dok said. "And it was only a disease of the type that ladies oughtn't hear mentioned. Please don't worry: it isn't fatal." She paused. "Not immediately, at least."

Winn, suddenly, was on her feet. "How *dare* you," she said. Her voice had dropped down lower than Delly had ever heard it. There was a menace to it. A growl. "You—you are *no gentlewoman*, Dok."

"I hadn't thought that whether or not a person was a gentlewoman was something that you particularly cared about, Cynallum," Abstentia said, as cool as a fresh pint. "Considering."

Winn's hand twitched. Delly grabbed her wrist before she could grab her pistol and they ended up with clanner all over the artificial palm trees. "Sit *down*, Winn."

Winn sat. Delly gave her knee a hard squeeze, in the hopes that it would prevent her from popping up again like an honor-bound jok-in-the-box. "Dok," she said, "what do you mean about *what you were promising to*? It was the money I'll owe to the Tothams if we get that reward, wasn't it?"

Mrs. Totham spoke up then. All sweetness and delicacy. She might as well have been borne into the conversation on the wings of butterflies. "I do beg your pardon, Miss Wells," she said, "but Miss Dok and I have made the very *smallest* alteration to what you and I had originally agreed on. The hard promise is that you will give my family the money that we're owed, should you receive it, but it also requires you to do your utmost to bring my daughter's killer to justice, whether that justice comes from her sister, the law, or God. The hard promise will only be released when that woman no longer walks free." Mrs. Totham looked directly into Delly's eyes then, and there were no butterfly wings in her gaze. Only granite, or marble, or an entire frozen mountaintop. Something that the best fire witch in Leiscourt wouldn't have the merest hope of melting. "Failure at this juncture won't settle your debt, Miss Wells. Only justice will do that."

"Revenge, you mean," Delly said. "Only revenge will do it." She felt . . . calm, strangely enough. Settled. As if she could stop frantically scrabbling at the bars of her prison and set herself to break the rocks in front of her.

Mrs. Totham tilted her head slightly. There was such a coolness to her. An evenness to her gaze. "Call it what you like," she said. "As long as that bitch suffers like my daughter did." Then she stood, with Buttons in her palm. Her daughters stood with her. "We must be going now," she said. "Our train leaves at midnight."

Buttons made a loud trilling sound. Mrs. Totham looked down at him. "Buttons? Whatever is the matter?"

Buttons took a flying leap then, from Mrs. Totham's hand to the table. Then he turned to face her, sat up on his haunches, and gave a soft snuffling grunt. Like a pig. Like Ermintrude rubbing her tusks in the dirt.

Mrs. Totham's eyes went suddenly bright. "Oh, Buttons," she whispered. "You want to stay behind? To—to help avenge her?"

Buttons said, "*Bong.*"

Mrs. Totham wiped at her eyes with her handkerchief. "Thank you," she said. "*Thank you*, Buttons. You've been—such a wonderful comfort to me. Such a *wonderful* friend."

Buttons made a new sound then. A rushing of water first, like a fast-moving brook. Then the patter of soft rain. Then the birds: any number of them, a whole forest full of them, trilling like the ribbon-colored creatures they'd seen in the aviary. A jungle, that was what it was. A whole bird-bedecked jungle for Mrs. Totham, warm and living and far away from everything.

Mrs. Totham was weeping openly now, not bothering to wipe the tears away. "Good-bye, Buttons," she whispered.

Buttons raised his bony little paw. A wave.

Mrs. Totham's daughters took her by the elbows to gently lead her away. She tottered when she walked. From the back she looked small and bent and frail. An old woman. An old woman battered down by grief.

Delly scooped Buttons up in her hand to whisper to him. "You sly creature," she whispered. "What the fuck's *your* angle, then?"

Buttons said, "*Bong.*"

For the next few days they followed the plan. Delly practiced with that infernal lock she'd purchased for hours every night until she could crack the thing in under a minute every time, then bought another model of the same lock and learned to do the same with that one. She figured she should be able to get Miss Cat's lock in under ten, if nothing went wrong.

Elo bought the chloroform. Abstentia growled and cursed over her ward-breaking parameters. Winn went down into the deepest part of the crypts and shot through decades of empty wine and gin bottles left behind by the unfulfilled dreams of generations of actors. Shooting wasn't part of the plan, exactly, but Delly didn't feel the need to discourage her. Maybe Winn thought that she ought to be prepared, if it came to that. Maybe she was imagining Delly's face on every bottle.

They hadn't talked about that. Their betrothal, and what Delly had told her, all the shit she'd admitted to. Delly'd slipped the gold chain into Winn's coat pocket two nights back. Winn hadn't given it back.

On the morning that they received their pay for all of their hard work for Miss Cat, Winn dropped a small white button onto the steps of Miss Cat's house. When Miss Cat dropped by to hand over their earnings, she didn't mention that. She did mention the fire, though. With a smirk. "I'm very glad to see that my message about your producing any product independently was well-received."

"Yes, Miss Cat," Delly said. She'd had plenty of practice with bowing and scraping. She'd had a lifetime of it. "We're very thankful, miss, for the opportunity to have work at all, miss."

Miss Cat smiled. When they left that evening, the button was still exactly in its place on the step, just another bit of trash in the street by the steps to her grand house. Delly figured Miss Cat must be far too fine a miss to have taken note of it.

They went back that night, the three of them: Delly, Winn, and Abstentia, no disguises now, no ribbons around their necks, walking quietly down the street Delly had circled on the map. It was strange walking down it when you could see the whole thing. A nice, genteel, elegant sort of street. Only a bit shabby at the edges. A last determined petal clinging to the edge of the flower that West Leiscourt had been, before it went to seed.

Delly wouldn't give a shit if the whole block burned down to ashes.

They went down the block house by house, with Winn's little palm light directed toward the ground. They didn't see the button. They doubled back, tried again. On the third pass, they found it: it was in the mud between two cobblestones, halfway between one house and another. "Shit," Delly murmured. "Someone must've kicked it."

"Coin toss?" Winn asked.

Delly squinted at the two houses. There was a light shining from the second-story window of the house on the left. Someone up late. Reading, maybe, next to the roaring fire. "No need," she said, and headed up the steps of the house that was completely dark.

The front door was locked and warded. Delly pulled her lockpicks and Buttons out of her pocket. "Ready to go, Mr. Trell?"

Buttons said, "*Bong.*"

They picked and *bing*'ed their way through the front door with little difficulty, and then they were inside. It was the right building: the right flowers on the table in the entryway. They made their way down the hall, up the stairs, down another hall, up the stairs again. To the attic door.

The fog of evil hadn't thinned since the last time that Delly had stood by this door. Her stomach roiled. She swallowed, then set Buttons atop the lock and got out her picks.

"Blinkin' rilift," she heard Winn whisper. "The thing has a real blinkin' atmosphere, doesn't it?" She cleared her throat. "How long do you—"

"As fast as I can," Delly said. Then she said, "*Shh.* I need to listen."

Abstentia and Winn went quiet. There was still that sound from the attic, though. Humming and clanking and grinding. The horrible, oppressive stink of dread. Then Buttons whispering. "*Death,*" he said. "*A slow death.*"

"Shut the *fuck* up, Buttons," Delly hissed, just as the lock gave its final, satisfying click. She stepped back from the door, as Buttons leapt off of the lock to land on her dress and stick there, the filthy clinging thing. "Your turn, Dok."

Abstentia stepped forward, pulled her notebook from her pocket, and started to incant. Delly felt the wards begin to thin. Then there was something odd. A sort of distant *pop*.

"*Shit*," Abstentia said. "Shit, *fuck*."

"What?" Delly asked. "What was that?"

"An alarm," Abstentia said. "It tripped an alarm. We have to hurry."

"*Shit*," Delly said. "*Fuck.*"

Buttons said, "*Bing!*" and the weakened wards fell. Abstentia grabbed the handle and pushed through the door.

The sound got louder when they walked in, and so did the clamor of that feeling. Death. Dread. The squeal and clank of metal. The sweet, sickly smell of decay. Delly wanted to turn back, to get out, to run. Then Winn raised her hand with the light in her palm so they could see what was in front of them.

It didn't make sense at first. Delly couldn't understand what she was looking at. Then it started filtering through, one piece at a time. There was a long table with drip-making equipment on it, the same beakers and burners they had downstairs, the burners alight, the beakers bubbling. And—*things*. Metal things cooking the drip. Like the spiders. They were like the metal spiders Ainette had made before, creaking and groaning at their hinges, weighing, measuring, stirring, and pouring. Each had a task. Each had something flowing from its center. Blood, Delly thought at first, and then realized that they were ribbons. A pretty red ribbon wrapped around each spider, like a bow around a present, and Delly turned her head to see how the ribbons extended away from the spiders, how they drifted and turned in the air as they moved, how they moved through the air until they reached the place where they were anchored, the cot where they were anchored, the still body where they were anchored. Ainette.

She was dead. That was Delly's first thought. They were too late to bring her to justice: she was dead already. She was thin, far thinner than she'd been a few weeks ago, and her skin looked almost transparent where it stretched over her skull. She was dead. She didn't even look like a particularly well-preserved corpse.

Then someone ran past Delly, and there was a gleam of metal. Abstentia, with a knife in her hand. Delly was just about to dive forward to try to wrest Abstentia away before she could stab Ainette's body through the heart like a vampire when Abstentia started using the knife to slash through the ribbons, snarling at the corpse the whole while. "You *stupid*—you hateful, selfish, *stupid* girl!"

It was only the work of moments for her to have cut all of the ribbons away, and only a few moments longer for there to be a change in the room. The horrible creatures slowed in their work, then stopped entirely, frozen in their places. One of them was stuck midpour of a particularly nasty chemical that they added to the stuff in order to cancel the effects of another, even nastier ingredient: Delly rushed over to yank the bottle from its claw and turn the burner off before the whole thing bubbled over and ignited.

When Delly turned around, Abstentia had her face a few inches away from Ainette's. Then she drew back, scowling. "She's in a drip sleep," she announced. "Dead to the world, but not to her Maker. We'll see her in prison yet. Cynallum, do you think that you could carry her?"

"Don't see why not," Winn said, and scooped Ainette up in her arms as if she weighed nothing at all. Which she didn't, it looked like, or at least close enough to that. Then they left the attic, Delly determinedly not looking back at the spider-things where they stood still in the dark.

The servants' stairway was too narrow for Winn to carry Ainette down it, so they went out the way they'd just come. Delly came to an abrupt stop in front of the door to Miss Cat's office, then said, "Just a tick, ladies," and melted through the lock on the door.

"What on *earth*, Wells?" Abstentia said, as Buttons *bing*'ed the door open. Then they burned and *bing*'ed their way into Miss Cat's desk, and Delly snatched up the ledger and the passionate letters and shoved them into her coat pockets.

"What was all of that about, Dell?" Winn asked as Delly emerged.

Delly started walking down the hall again and spoke over her shoulder as Winn and Abstentia followed her. "Just taking out a little insurance policy."

They were hurrying through the laboratory in the ballroom, heading toward the stairs, when someone spoke. "What on earth do you think you're doing with *her*?" Then: "Stop where you are and put her down at once, or I'll shoot."

They stopped where they were. Winn lowered Ainette to the ground. Then they slowly turned to face Miss Clairelle Tredworth, who was standing beside one of their drip-making tables with a pistol aimed straight at Winn's head.

She was in her dressing gown, which struck Delly as funny: she must have been in a real relefting hurry to get here. So much of a hurry, in fact, that she had also not bothered to put the illusion onto her face as she usually did. The face that she'd been hiding was pale and delicate, with a sharp chin and wide, dark eyes. Her prettiness was marred only by the look of fury on her face, a look that quickly veered into extreme astonishment. "Miss *Dok*?"

"Hello, Miss Tredworth," Abstentia said. "What a *lovely* criminal enterprise you have."

Miss Tredworth's face made another sudden shift from astonishment to irritation, which was about what Delly would expect from someone conversing with Abstentia Dok. Delly wished dearly that she could pinch the woman to get her to shut up. Tredworth had a *gun* pointed at Winn's head: the last thing they needed was to bait her. It was an enormous relief when Tredworth suddenly moved to aim her pistol at Abstentia instead. "I'd say the same about yours, but it seems to me that it's altogether a very shabby operation. Was this all a rescue attempt, then? Is that all? Because I can assure you that Miss Wexin is as happy as can be, up in her cozy garret. She's paying off her debt to me, and her little spiders feed her drip once an hour. All she has to do is feed them in return."

Delly felt sick. Abstentia, for her part, sounded completely calm. "It's not a rescue attempt. Her sister wants her brought to justice. If you allow us to leave with her now, we won't breathe a word of your operation to the police. You can put a hard promise on us to hold us to it, if you like. Just give us Ainette."

Miss Tredworth laughed. She really did. Like a villain in a sen blood. "The *police*?" she asked. "You're going to go to the *police* and report the criminal organization being operated out of a house rented out in *Lady Tredworth's* name?" She cocked her head slightly to the side. "I will offer to set a hard promise on you, though. If you return Ainette upstairs to her little cot, you may all take a hard promise to never speak of this to anyone, and to continue making drip here, to my specifications, for as long as I require your services. In return, I'll let you live."

"All right," Delly said quickly. "I agree."

Miss Cat turned to her and smiled, training her pistol toward Delly. Abstentia whirled toward her and squawked. And Winn, whose hand Delly had noticed inching slowly toward her pocket, drew her pistol and aimed it straight at Miss Tredworth's head. "Don't move, Miss Tredworth," she said. "So much as a blink and you'll be down a blinkin' eyeball. Abstentia, *run*."

Abstentia turned to run. Then a few things happened all at once. Miss Tredworth jerked her arm to fire at Abstentia. Delly threw up a hasty barrier of heat to try to block the bullet. Winn fired, dropping Miss Tredworth where she stood. And a spatter of molten lead from Miss Tredworth's bullet sailed through the air and landed in one of the open beakers that they had left out on the laboratory table to cool.

For a moment the whole world upended itself and shook up and down like God himself was salting his dinner. Then Delly was on her back on the ground, her ears ringing. For a moment she thought, *How strange: it's gotten awfully hot in here.* Then she thought, *Winn.*

The space where Tredworth had been standing by the tables was already an inferno, and the flames were beginning to race up the red velvet curtains that lined the ballroom. Winn and Ainette were both lying a few steps away from Delly, dropped onto the floor by the blast like dolls discarded by a very unfeeling little girl. Delly rushed straight to Winn, using her magic to shove the heat away. Then she stopped. Winn was lying still and silent, one of her arms bent under her at an odd, sickening angle. Her lips were slightly parted. There was a glimmer of white showing between her eyelids. Ainette, beside her, was alive and awake and looking straight at Delly.

Ainette's voice was barely a whisper. "Will you leave me here?"

Delly looked back at her. The flames were growing closer. She said, "I can't get both of you out, Miss Wexin." She didn't think she would be able to get either of them out, not really. She was already working hard to hold back the flames.

"I understand," Ainette said. She sounded very calm. The light of the fire reflected off of her wet cheeks. "Tell Mayelle that I'm sorry. For everything." She reached out her hand then and took hold of Winn's pistol.

Delly gave a strangled shout. Ainette closed her eyes. "Go," she said. "Please. Quickly."

For a moment, Delly couldn't move. The smoke was growing thicker. Soon she wouldn't be able to breathe.

She turned away from Miss Wexin. She turned toward Winn. She shored up her walls against the flames, looped her hands under Winn's armpits, and started to drag her toward the stairs. She spoke to her. She begged.

"Please, Winn. Please, don't be dead. Th'art too brave for it. And what will your mother and father do without thee? Wake up, Winn. Wake up. Come down the stairs with me."

Winn didn't wake up. Delly started dragging her down the grand staircase, step by step. She was shaking. She nearly dropped her. Her arms were screaming. Her head was screaming. Halfway down the stairs she heard the shot.

Delly kept talking. Maybe it was a prayer, of sorts. It had been her
whole lifetime since Delly had prayed. *"Please, Winn. Please, God.
Please. Please."*

She got her to the front hall. There was a dreadful crash from the
direction of the laboratory: maybe the ceiling collapsing. She hoped
that it had. She hoped that all of those spiders in the attic would be
turned back to harmless metal by the flames.

A few more steps. Through the door. Down the front steps, past the
button Winn had dropped there, out into the street. Delly laid Winn
down in the mud, then went down on her knees in the mud beside her.
She pressed her ear to her chest. She couldn't hear her heartbeat. She
couldn't hear her breathe.

"Please, Winn," she whispered. It was hard to speak. "Please don't
go. Not when I—not when I've been so mean to thee. I'd give thee a
different answer now, Winn. I'd be a better woman for thee. Only
don't go away from me. Don't go away from us who love you. Not yet,
Winn. Please."

There was movement from the corner of her eye then. Buttons.
Buttons clambering out from her pocket. He pointed his paw toward
Winn's still body. Then he gave an imperious *"Bong."*

Delly swallowed. Then she scooped him up and placed him gently
onto Winn's chest. He made a little cooing sound, as if to thank her.
Then he began to hum.

It was a strange hum. A terrible hum. A hum with a familiar
thread. The rising terror and the clinging smell of death.

Then there was a man standing beside them. A plain man, sour-
faced and balding, dressed in shabby old-fashioned clothes. His edges
wavered when she looked at him. He looked back. Then he smiled,
crouched down, and placed his transparent hand on Winn's forehead.

On Winn's chest, Buttons began to fall apart. First his tail, then his
front paws, then all of him, all of him crumbling until there was nothing left, nothing but a tiny heap of bones. Winn gave a loud, gasping
breath.

Delly looked back at the man. He raised one hand at her to wave.

Delly's face was wet. Her throat was aching. "Good-bye, Buttons," she whispered. "You've been—a *wonderfully* good friend."

Buttons' smile grew wider. Then he disappeared.

Delly put her head down onto Winn's chest and sobbed.

In the distance, she could hear the hooves of horses clattering on the cobblestones, and Abstentia shouting her name, and the shrill wail of the fire engine. But around them, just beside Delly's ear, there was birdsong, and a brook ringing over the rocks, and the slow, gentle drumming of rain.

20

Wherein Dellaria Begins to Believe That Possibly,
One Day, Some Little Sprouty Green Things Might
Grow Up from the Ashes

Delly spent the next two days sitting by Winn's hospital bed.

It was a fine place to be. Convenient. The same nurse who had treated her mam came by, and Delly handed her half of the money that she'd been given by Miss Cat the day before. Fifty tocats. "Don't let her pop pay for any more of my mam's care," she said. "Please. I'll get you more as soon as I can."

The nurse, for her part, looked as though she'd be very glad to see the backs of all of them.

Delly stayed in her chair by Winn's bed. She ate in it, when a nurse had pity on her and dropped off a sandwich. She slept in it. She talked to Winn. Winn woke up, sometimes, for a few minutes. The doctors said that she'd broken her arm and cracked the back of her skull. They also brought a wizard in, who said that Winn seemed as if she'd been through some sort of unusual magical event and gave Delly a very suspicious look. Delly didn't care too much about the details. Winn was alive. She was resting. She would be better soon.

The third time Winn woke up, she looked over at Delly and smiled like she was seeing something really wonderful. *"Dell."*

Delly's heart gave a fairly humiliating flutter. "Hello, Winn," she said, and held out a cup of water and slid her hand behind Winn's neck so she could drink.

Winn drank. Then she sat back. "My head hurts like the absolute rilift and all of its blinkin' elderly relations," she said. "How long have you been sitting there, Dell?"

Delly's face went hot. "Uh," she said. "Not—so long."

"That's funny," Winn said. "Considering that you were there the last time I woke up, too, what?"

Delly blushed harder, then mumbled, "Funny coincidence, I suppose."

Winn's smile widened. Then she said, "Do me a favor and reach into my coat pocket for me?"

Delly blinked, then did as directed. Her back creaked out a loud protestation. She ignored it, fished around in Winn's pockets, then blanched. The only thing in any of them was the gold chain.

"Put it back on, Dell?" Winn asked. Her voice was very quiet.

"Winn," Delly said. Her mouth had gone dry. "I *told* you—"

"Bit puzzling, what?" Winn said. "Gull telling you that she doesn't want you to household her because she's interested in finding a householder who can blinkin' well tend to her daily needs for food and shelter and all of the additional frivolous whatsits a gull might blinkin' well enjoy. Bit ginny of you. I mean, that's what all of the balls and coming-outs and visits to Lord Wotsisname's country estates are about, eh? The gulls I met there weren't on the hunt for impoverished chaps who they could canoodle with in a drafty garret, either. The question is, *besides* the money—" She stopped and cleared her throat. "You know that I don't like to make a fuss. I don't want to go and demand that you write me reams of romantic verse. But I—" Her voice wavered a bit. "Oh, dash it all. I *love* you, Delly, and I'm not ashamed of it. All that I need to give me a bit of hope is to hear that you're the smallest bit fond of me, too."

Delly stared back at her. "Of course I do," she said. "I lo—" She cleared her throat, too self-conscious to finish getting it out. "I'm *dead* fuckin' fond of you, Winn." Winn would know what she meant.

Winn beamed, then scrubbed hurriedly at her eyes for a moment. "Well, that's all right," she said. "I'm dead fond of *you*, too. And looking *forward* to providing the food and shelter and frivolous feminine whatsits for the rest of the old earthly span, if you'll have me. So—put it back on, Dell? And we'll make a go of it?"

"All right," Delly said, and put the gold chain back on and tucked it safely under the collar of her dress. Then they smiled at each other like a pair of tipsy milkmaids on bonfire night until Winn fell asleep again. Delly dozed off in her chair not long after.

When she woke up again it was to the sound of the deepest voice Delly had ever heard.

"Think this is her girl?"

Delly opened her eyes. About a foot away from her face were seven-odd feet of muscle-bound, blue-skinned, yellow-eyed troll, stooping over her chair and staring at her.

Delly said, "*Ngah!*"

The troll stepped back and grinned. "Sorry."

"For God's sake, Tsira, you'll give the girl apoplexy," said another voice. A man's voice: soft, drawling, and distinctively clanny. Delly glanced over. There was a man sitting in the chair on the other side of Winn's bed. He was tall and lean and very expensively dressed, with silver-streaked dark hair and a face that was handsome in a way that Delly found immediately suspicious. Men should never be too good-looking. It gave them ideas. For a moment Delly glared at him, wondering what sort of ideas he might have in his revoltingly good-looking head. Then a few of the pieces of Delly's hopelessly scrambled-up mental jigsaw snapped into place.

Delly said, "*Ngah!*"

Lord Cynallum raised his eyebrows. "I *beg* your pardon?"

"You're *Winn's pop*," Delly said, and then groaned. "I mean, m'lord, begging *your* pardon, m'lord, but I wasn't expecting to meet you here,

m'lord." She reached to pat feebly at her dress, and then at her hair.
Her dress was the same smoke-stinking thing she'd worn to pull Winn
out of the burning house, and she hadn't washed her hair in—well. It
didn't bear thinking about, really.

Lord Cynallum's mouth twitched. "I apologize," he said, "for having put you out." Then he said, "You must be Miss Wells? In that case,
it seems that I find myself very deeply in your debt."

"Huh?" Delly said, intelligently.

"From what I've been able to make out from the staff here, you
single-handedly dragged her out of a burning building," Lord Cynallum said. Then he paused. "Though it *has* occurred to me to wonder
what exactly you were *doing* in a building that Lady Tredworth recently and inexplicably purchased in one of Leiscourt's less savory
neighborhoods as it was actively in the process of burning down, in the
first instance."

Delly licked her lips. "It's, ah. Bit of a boring story, really, m'lord."
Then, cravenly: "I'm sure that Wi—Miss Cynallum will tell you all about
it later, m'lord."

The troll—Winn's *mam*, goodness fuckin' *releft*, was there ever a
lot of her—spoke up then. She sounded amused. "Probably best not to
ask, knowing our kid."

Lord Cynallum raised his eyebrows at her. Then he said, "I suppose
that you would know best, dear, considering where she *gets* it from."

Winn's mother—*Lady Cynallum*? Surely not—only laughed at
him. Then Winn stirred and opened her eyes. "*Pop?*"

He was out of his chair and on his knees beside the bed in an instant, pushing her hair back from her forehead and smiling at her as if
she was a thousand-tocat prize. "*There* are those pretty eyes," he said.
His voice was even softer when he spoke to Winn. "You gave us a terrible fright, pigeon."

Winn's voice went all wobbly. "*Pop*," she said. "I'm—*awfully* sorry—"

Winn's mother leaned over the bed to murmur to her, too, as her
father stroked her hair and pressed her hand. Delly got up from her chair

and slipped off. She could leave her post for a minute, she thought, now that Winn had people with her who could help keep watch instead.

Delly went to Mrs. Medlow's then, to pick up her one remaining clean and not fire-damaged dress. Then she went to the bathhouse. She went to the bathhouse and got into the water and made it too hot for a regular person, and then she soaked. She soaked until her fingers crinkled up, and her back loosened, and a few stray tears of terror and worry slipped out of her and into the water. Then she bought some soap, and scrubbed herself clean, and dressed in the respectable frock that her respectable betrothed had bought for her, and left to go to the police station.

She waited for almost an hour in the dim, cramped front room of the station before a square-jawed, irritated-looking fellow with an enormous mustache emerged from the back offices and consented to hear her story. She stammered her way through her explanation of Miss Tredworth's involvement in the red-drip trade, trying to get out all of it without implicating herself or Winn too badly, trying to make him believe. The nerves made her West Leiscourt come out, which only made her stammer harder. She'd barely gotten the name *Tredworth* out of her mouth when the cop started shaking his head.

"I don't know what your angle is, miss, but around here we don't take too kindly to being told tall tales."

Delly's mouth tasted sour. She'd known, she'd *told* Abstentia how the police would treat her, but somehow it surprised her, anyway. "I have proof," she said. "I have—documents. I can show you."

The cop stood and shoved his chair back. "And with Lord and Lady Tredworth mourning over poor Miss Tredworth," he said, his voice full of the sort of emotion Delly would expect from a fellow who wept over the well-being of clanners as if that could make him one of them. "Ought to be ashamed of yourself. And I'd suggest you get out of here before I arrest you for making libelous statements and wasting the time of the police." He was looking at her like he was disgusted just by the sight of her filthy gutterwitch face.

Delly knew what was good for her, even if she could hardly ever manage to do it. She left. Then she walked. She needed to get the shakes out of her legs. She walked far, far out of the way of her neighborhood, into a part of town where the streets were full of well-dressed men hurrying to crowded offices. Then she stopped to stare at the words carved into the elegant marble edifice of the building across the street. She stared for so long that she was almost run over by a messenger boy, and she had to duck into the shelter of the entryway of a closed restaurant to chew over what she was looking at.

The *Leiscourt Crier*.

There was a coffeehouse down the street. She ducked into it and begged a pencil and some paper off of a sensitive-looking fellow who was sketching passersby from a window seat. Then she huddled up in a corner to write.

It took a long time to get everything down without leaving anything out, except for the bits that would be particularly encriminating to one Dellaria Wells. She invented a "person of her acquaintance" who was in service and had been employed for a few weeks by the late Miss Tredworth before quitting on account of her moral qualms over working for such a thoroughly wicked young lady, moral qualms that apparently did nothing to prevent this young person from reading other people's letters and listening at keyholes. Not very convincing, maybe, but Delly didn't know if that mattered too much. She still had Miss Tredworth's ledger in her pocket, to say nothing of the passionate letters. Even those were beginning to have the smell of evidence, to Delly. She was thinking about Winn, and everything she had said about the balls and country houses, and about what Jok Fairnbrook had said about the Crossicks' needing Mayelle for her money. The Tredworths were out of money, Abstentia had said, and doing their damnedest not to show it. Maybe the passionate young man who'd written her those filthy letters was just another thing that Miss Tredworth had been afraid she'd lose without the cash to pay for him.

Delly wrote and rewrote her account until she was satisfied with it.

Then she thrust it into her already-bulging pockets and headed across the street to the newspaper's offices.

She lurked outside the building for a while in what was probably a distinctly suspicious fashion, waiting for someone to walk out. Eventually, someone did. He wasn't a particularly promising-looking creature. A scrawny fellow with a shabby suit, a bald head, and a very loud yellow-and-green-checked cravat, smoking a cigar that looked thicker than his neck. As if Rat and Mr. Trell had engaged in horrible congress and the fruit of their union was blessed with the worst qualities of each. But there was no one else standing about, so she advanced upon him and hoped for the best.

"Begging your pardon, sir," she said, trying to convince her accent to, if not quite approach Cynallumesque heights of cream-filled gold-platedness, at least achieve a Tothamary degree of respectability. "But do you work for the *Crier*?"

He eyed her. He didn't look particularly impressed with what he saw. "If I did, then I didn't write whatever it is you're here to complain about."

Delly, to be perfectly honest, found herself quite bolstered by the idea that she sounded respectable enough to be the sort of woman who complained to newspapers about their articles. "No complaints," she said. "I'm here to give you a story."

If she had hoped that this statement would cause a great sensation, these hopes were dashed. "I'm on my break," he said. "Come back in twenty minutes."

Delly narrowed her eyes at him, then attempted to denarrow them. She didn't want to *fight* with the man. She wasn't *Abstentia*. "I'll wait here with you," she said. "If you don't mind."

He looked like he minded, but he didn't say so aloud, just stood there and smoked his cigar in resentful silence. Eventually he huffed out an irritated sigh and put his cigar out. "Fine, then," he said. "Come with me."

She followed him into the building, up the stairs, and into a big, crowded room full of sweaty, disgruntled-looking gentlemen working away furiously at enormous paper-shrouded desks. He sat down at his, gestured for her to take a seat across from him, then gave her a short nod. "Go ahead."

She handed over her narrative on its now somewhat crumpled sheets of paper. He put on a pair of narrow spectacles to read it, a process that felt as if it took about five years longer than Dellaria Wells had herself crept upon the face of the earth. After thirty years or so had finally passed, he looked at her over the tops of his spectacles. "Your writing's bad," he said. "But the story's good. Got a scrap of proof for any of it?" Then he said, "My name's Greyland."

"Wells," Delly said. They shook hands. "And I'd expect my writing to be bad, Mr. Greyland, when I was raised in an empty dustbin behind a house of ill-repute, Mr. Greyland, where I lacked any access to proper schooling, Mr. Greyland." Then she passed him the ledger and one of the passionate letters.

"A childhood almost as trying as my own," said Mr. Greyland, and his accent suddenly slipped into something that sounded an awful lot like what Delly was used to hearing around her own neighborhood. "I was raised in a *full* dustbin, behind a butcher's shop, and taught myself to read from the scraps of newspaper the butcher used to wrap up the discarded pigs' snouts, so." He paged through the ledger. He looked mildly interested. Then he read the letter. He looked *very* interested. "How much do you want for these?"

"How much are you offering?" Delly shot back.

He paused. "Ten for the ledger," he said. "Five for that letter."

Delly scoffed and reached as if to take them both back. "I'll take them both to the *Post*," she said. "Along with the rest of the letters."

His eyebrows shot up. "There are *more*?"

She counted them out onto his desk. There were sixteen, it turned out. He licked his lips. Then he said, "Let me speak to my editor," picked up the letter, and left.

Delly slipped all of her valuables back into her pockets the second he stepped away: she might have been nearly killed in a fire twice so far this week, but the Wellsian brain hadn't been broiled to the extent that she'd give Greyland a chance to copy anything down before she'd gotten what she was owed. She was already cursing herself for having let him walk off with the first letter.

Greyland came back after a few minutes. He looked pleased. There were blotches of color high on his formerly mushroom-complected cheeks. "Three hundred for the lot, and no more dickering," he said.

"Done," she said, and then sat back to look at him.

He sighed. "I'll go down to the fuckin' countinghouse, then," he said, and left again.

Delly hummed to herself, pleased. After a while he came back and handed her a slim envelope. Bank notes. Look at that. Dellaria Wells coming up in the world. She handed all of the stuff over. She felt lighter without all of that in her pockets. "Tell the world about it," she said. "I figure it ain't good for clanners to let 'em get away with too much, so."

He grinned. "Do my best to ruin their digestions every morning over breakfast." Then he handed her a card. "If you happen to dig up any more thousand-tocat stories about our badly behaved betters, come find me."

"All right," Delly said, and tucked the card into her pocket. "Though I don't intend on doing any digging. I'm a respectable betrothed lady, Mr. Greyland." Then she winked at him and trotted off.

She headed back to the hospital. It was a much more crowded scene than the one Delly had left. Abstentia Dok always managed to create an atmosphere of extreme crowdedness in any room that she entered.

Abstentia stood up from her chair by Winn's bedside when she saw Delly, and walked toward her so that they met in the middle of the room, far from Winn and her parents. "Hello, Wells," Dok said.

"Hello, Dok," Wells said.

They eyed each other.

"She's dead," Delly said. "Ainette."

Abstentia nodded. "I had assumed," she said. She licked her lips. "She must have—in the fire?"

"No," Delly said quickly. "No." She paused. "Shot herself."

Abstentia flinched. Delly reached out to press her hand. Didn't even think twice about it. "She told me to tell her sister that she was sorry," she said. "I reckon it won't be of much comfort. But I figured I ought to pass it on. Since she asked me to." She cleared her throat. "The Tredworths are about to be in every rag in Leiscourt, but I left the Wexins' names out of it. You ought to tell Mayelle what happened before she sees it in the papers. You might also want to tell Mayelle she should invent a sudden fever for Ainette. Just in case there's questions. I'll take charge of writing to the Tothams, if you'll take care of that."

Abstentia squeezed Delly's hand back, very briefly, before she released it. "I imagine that you're right about how little comfort it will be," she said. "But at this point I'm happy to convey any scrap of comfort you might dig up." She cleared her throat. "Thank you."

Delly shrugged. "Had a hard promise on me."

Abstentia regarded her for a moment. "I'll do my best to convince her that you've earned your pay," she said. "I don't know if you'll ever see it, though, considering the fact that she won't even receive a box of her sister's bones."

Delly shrugged again. "I'll do all right either way, I guess," she said. "I just sold Clairelle Tredworth's love letters to the *Leiscourt Crier* for a decent bit of clink." She was planning on sending all of that money to Mrs. Totham, but she didn't need to tell Abstentia that.

Abstentia barked out a laugh. "How thoroughly in character of you, Wells," she said. Then she *looked* at her again. It was starting to be positively unnerving. "Are you, Wells? All right, I mean? After— everything?"

Delly shrugged. Then she said, "You?"

Abstentia was still for a moment. Then, very deliberately, she shrugged, too. "I have my spring oral examinations in two weeks," she said. "I'm afraid that I'm not very well prepared for anything but the practical chemicastry." She paused. "You ought to come back to Weltsir."

Delly's frowned. "To *Weltsir?*" she repeated, assuming that she'd misheard. Maybe she'd gotten ash from the fire stuck up her ears.

Dok nodded. She looked faintly pained. "You only had a year there, and you're—quite frankly, one of the more accomplished young wizards I've ever met. Imagine what they'd make of you in five."

Delly blinked. Then she put out her hand. "I'll think about it."

They shook hands. Abstentia turned to leave. "Abstentia," Delly called after her.

Abstentia turned, her pretty eyebrows arched. "Yes?"

"They could have ten years with me," Delly said, "and they'd never make me half the wizard that you already are."

Abstentia smiled, very slightly. "Well, Delly," she said, "I should think that *that* was obvious." Then she walked out.

Delly went to sit down with Winn again, trying not to feel too out of place with her parents there. Winn's mother was telling her some sort of story about a factory girl and two clanners whom she'd found on the run from the law in her mountain village a few days earlier. Delly tried to keep her ears from pricking up too much. *Clanners behaving badly.*

Not the sort of thing she should go digging into. She wasn't going to go digging into it, even if it sounded particulariously interesting. She was a respectable betrothed woman now, after all.

Eventually, Winn's parents left, and the two of them held hands very daringly over Winn's coverlet, ignoring the barbed glances cast at them by the chaste religious nursing staff. "Feeling better, Winn?" Delly asked eventually.

"Oh, strong as an oak tree and sharp as cheese," Winn said. "Or I will be, in a few more days. And where did *you* go off to?"

Delly told her. Winn beamed as if Delly was relating the tale of how she'd slain a wolf man and rescued a wailing damsel, instead of gotten paid for posthumously revealing the secrets of a murderous drip-dealing clanner who'd spent weeks milking a woman of her very life essence in a poorly ventilated garret. "Demmed clever of you, Delly, really. If the police won't take the case, then the scandal papers jolly well will. Ermintrude deserves at *least* that, I'd say." She paused. "I think—we did all right, didn't we? Righting wrongs and foiling plots and mostly sticking to the right side of the broader moral whatsit." She paused again. "You especially, Dell."

Delly waved that off, embarrassed. She wasn't sure that any of that was true herself. If there'd ever been a line dividing good from wicked, she was pretty sure she'd spent most of the past few weeks weaving back and forth across it like she was about six gins deep.

She'd been *trying*, though, to do the right thing. She'd been trying *recently*, at least.

Maybe she was improving.

Winn cleared her throat. "And that reporter fellow wants to work with you more, he said?"

"Well, he said to find him if I dug anything up," Delly said. "But we're betrothed now, ain't we? So I'm bound to Hexos to be householded and—lounge under the pleasantly scented orange trees, and all that. Like we said, before." She paused. "Though—what your mam was saying about those runaway clanner girls up near her summer village. *That* sounded interesting."

"I *do* think that we ought to take a holiday," Winn said after a moment. "With the blazing sun, and the sea breezes, and the orange trees and other associated bits of blinkin' warm-weather scenery, what?" She paused. "Though—tracking down those girls does seem like a bit of a wheeze. Think their families might be worrying about them?"

"Oh, I think that's pretty likely, so," Delly said. "But that's no concern of *ours*, seeing as that we're off to Hexos. For the warm breezes. And the orange trees."

They looked at each other. Then Winn gave her coverlet a slap, as if she'd just remembered something. "Oh, dash it all. Memory's like a demmed sieve, after that bump on the head. You *know*, Dell, our going to Hexos for the orange trees and all of that wasn't our *original* plan. Before you said you'd like to go somewhere warm I'd been babbling on about bringing you to my mother's summer village, remember? I was quite blinkin' keen on the idea, as I recall it."

"I *do* remember," Delly said, because, in truth, she did. "With the babbling brooks, and the wildflowers, and the being interested in the wind blowing through the grass."

"And the chirpicating crickets," Winn said, and smiled at her. "I'm sure that Mother would be happy to bring us with her when she goes back. To—rest and recuperate, and be interested in the highborn winds dashing about inexplicably with the disreputable local grasses. We've got all of our lives for householdry in Hexos, what? But the interesting grasses won't just riliftin' well sit about waiting for us to come and make a story out of them."

They were grinning at each other. Delly squeezed her hand. "You're right," she said. "We shouldn't miss an opportunity to find interest in the beauties of nature, when we're both *so* fond of feeling interested."

ACKNOWLEDGMENTS

——

I'm incredibly lucky to have had so many wonderful people helping me and supporting me through getting this story into print. First, major thanks go to Jen Udden, my ever-patient and panic-soothing agent, and my editor, Jess Wade, the woman who always knows where I need to add and where I need to cut. Thanks also to Miranda Hill, Katie Anderson, Alexis Nixon, Jessica Plummer, Lindsey Tulloch, and all of the other folks at Penguin who helped to shepherd this book and *Unnatural Magic* into being. Tons of gratitude to Jessica Cruickshank, the artist who made the perfect cover.

Thanks as always to my husband, Xia Nan, and to my dad and two amazing sisters. Also to He-Kellen and She-Kellen, who are both always down to talk creative projects, and to Emily and Chloe, the other two wheels on our shared mental health tricycle.

Finally, all of the thanks in the world to my amazing mom, the wisest person I know. Every bird in this book was for you.

C. M. Waggoner grew up in rural upstate New York, where she spent a lot of time reading fantasy novels in a swamp. She studied creative writing at SUNY Purchase and lived in China for eight years before moving with her husband to Albany, NY. In her spare time, she volunteers, performs kitchen experiments, asks if she can pet your dog, and gardens badly. You can voice your complaints to the management (or sign up for her mailing list) on her website, or hunt her down on social media.

CONNECT ONLINE

CMWaggoner.com

C.M.Waggoner

CMWaggoner2

Ready to find
your next great read?

Let us help.

Visit prh.com/nextread

Penguin
Random
House